DATE DUE

OCT 1 6 2004	
OCT 1 8 2004	
OCT 2 7 2004	
JAN 2 8 2005	
APR 1 2005	
APR 1 5 2005	
SEP 1 7 2005	
MAR 2 2015	
JUL 0 9 2015	

MEG O'BRIEN

THE LAST CHEERLEADER

MIRA

ISBN 1-55166-723-1

THE LAST CHEERLEADER

Visit us at www.mirabooks.com

Printed in U.S.A.

ACKNOWLEDGMENTS

I would like to thank Sergeant Carlos A. Mendoza, Administrative Sergeant, El Segundo Police Department, El Segundo, California, for his unflagging assistance regarding police procedures in the El Segundo and Los Angeles area. Thanks for all the e-mails, and for being so quick to answer mine. If any errors remain, they are all mine.

Thanks again to my children and all my family for helping me in so many ways throughout the writing of my books. As I finish up number fifteen, it seems like just yesterday that I stood in that little health food store in Paradise, California, declaring, "I'm going to be a writer! I'll give it five years, and if it doesn't work out, I won't have lost anything but five years." I can't believe no one laughed. At least, not to my face!

It actually took eight years before my first book was published, but who's counting? From the birth in 1990 of Jessica (Jesse) James, my mystery series reporter, to *The Last Cheerleader* today, it's been a great ride, and I hope it goes on forever.

I would also like to thank my good friend Cathy Landrum for her invaluable research assistance, my son, Greg, for his sharp editorial eye, and another good friend, Nancy Baker Jacobs, for all the phone calls, support and helpful ideas along the way. No author should be without someone with whom to bat ideas around!

I am also grateful for the loyal friendship of Alice Austin in North Wildwood, New Jersey, who found me through my book *Crashing Down;* Michelle and John Jaceks, good neighbors even when they're off in their shiny new RV, and Bernice Cook, the smartest and dearest lady I know.

Last, but never least, I would like to thank Miranda Stecyk for being such a dream editor, and Dianne Moggy and Amy Moore-Benson for getting me started with MIRA—the best and brightest publishing house around.

"In Hollywood the woods are full of people that learned to write but evidently can't read; if they could read their stuff, they'd stop writing."
—Will Rogers

"The only 'ism' Hollywood believes in is plagiarism."
—Dorothy Parker

"I just want to tell y'all not to worry— them people in New York and Hollywood are not going to change me none."
—Elvis Presley

When a train comes bearing down on one, there's always a warning. The tracks shake and noise vibrates through them, like the sound of a thousand poor souls in hell. There's a heavy smell of oil in the air, and if anyone is on those tracks—if they can't get off, no matter how hard they try—there is also the dreadful, sickening scent of fear.

That's the way it was for me with Tony. I'd loved him far too long and should have left him long ago. For three years I was on those tracks, and I heard and smelled all the warnings. I just couldn't get off. I watched while he flirted with other women and didn't show up on time, drank my coffee and never even brought me a bean. Tony didn't spend much, and I always knew why. He held on to money as if it pained his palm to pull it out of his pocket. I tried to tell him that if you hold on to money like that it'll just stop coming, that it's like a cat, and if you pay too much attention it sticks its nose in the air and prances the other way. I told him he should be more generous, give some of it away, if only to a poor box at a church. I swore that it would always come back twofold, if not more.

Tony was horrified at that idea. He said he didn't

have "enough" to give away, and I always thought he felt the same way about love. He was terrified that if he gave that to someone, even himself, something terrible would happen. As if he'd wake one morning and find he wasn't there anymore, that so much had been given away, there would be nothing left.

And what about you? one might well ask. What was wrong with me, that for three years I hoped against hope that one day this fool would wake up in his Brentwood penthouse and find that he couldn't live another moment without me?

Well, this is what I tell myself, slipping out of my Gucci pumps and slinging my feet up onto my new antique desk: Tony wasn't someone I could all that easily leave. I'm a literary agent, known as one of the best, and Tony sold more books than all my other clients combined—books that turned, like little miracles, into movies and made millions of dollars. In these days of slow sales in New York, of literary agents dropping by the dozens back there and moving to places like Connecticut and Vermont, working out of their homes to squeeze a dime for all it's worth, Tony still came up with one blockbuster after another. And Tony was mine. To leave him might have been slaying the goose with the golden egg.

Slaying. An odd word to think of, under the circumstance. I've been dwelling more on Tony today because they found him dead last night. Worse— right next to him on the bedroom floor was Arnold

Wescott, who for the past ten years had been my ex-husband.

The police called at the crack of dawn to notify, as well as question, me. I drove from my home in Malibu to Tony's penthouse apartment in Brentwood to identify the bodies, my thoughts a jumbled mess all the way. Tony and Arnold, together? Murdered together? I couldn't wrap my mind around it.

It didn't get better with the terrible wrenching horror of seeing Tony on the floor with his forehead crushed in. As the police detective watched, I turned to Arnold, my heart thumping and questions like wasps still buzzing in my brain. Who could have done this? How did it happen?

I had questions but no answers. This was Tony's apartment, and in the first place, I couldn't understand what Arnold was doing here. So far as I knew, they'd never had any real connection to each other. Only once in a while did they cross paths in my office, and the two couldn't have been less alike. Even in death, while Tony's beautiful Italian face looked pained, Arnold's was placid, as if he'd finally found peace.

In fact, Arnold—a Woody Allen look-alike—didn't appear much different from any other day. All the time I'd been married to him, Arnold Wescott seemed largely comatose. The most energy I ever saw him put out was the time he asked me to wear a metal bra so he could see if it really would deflect bullets.

Arnold was sweet, if morose, and at the time I was still struggling to build my stable of authors from an old thirties-era storefront office in the wrong end of Hollywood. Nights, however, I was into any adventure that came. my way. So I stupidly let Arnold put the bra on me, his nervous little fingers shaking as he made sure my breasts were evenly cupped. Then, sweat pouring down his forehead, he stepped back six paces and let fly with the bullets.

Arnold was a toy designer, and how a man who spent thirty-two years in a clinical depression could possibly design a toy that a child would like is beyond me. Well, come to think of it, he never did manage that. After scaring half the world's children to death with GORP, a seven-headed beast that spewed forth murderous threats when his biceps were flexed, he'd turned to designing adult toys. The little rubber bullets were part of a mock-up for GOTCHA, his latest invention. Designed to be pointed at little models of ex-girlfriends wearing metal bras, he had a male doll, too, wearing a metal jockstrap.

That day, the bullets came zooming toward my chest, and I couldn't help it—I flinched, bent over, and one bullet went straight for my eye.

Arnold had to get me to the hospital, where an unbelieving intern was sure that my husband had deliberately popped me one. That only made me laugh so hard that tears stung the abrasion on my cornea. Arnold, violent? No way. Arnold was meek and mild, and he never once had deliberately lifted a finger in my direction—or any other appendage, for that matter.

So it was a bit of a shock when the cops called last night and said they'd found Arnold dead. Not only that, but he was found next to another man's body, in that man's bedroom. Further, the other man was Tony Price, my best-selling author and long-hungered-after love.

Even more of a shock was that both men lay side by side on the floor, and next to them was what the police were sure was the murder weapon—a rare ivory Chinese dildo, a favorite of the gay crowd in West Hollywood.

As I've said, the fact that Tony was dead, too, was something that stunned me for several moments. Once I managed to collect my thoughts, however, I realized that my opportunity to get off those train tracks had come at last. Oh, it might be a while before I got my whole body off, grief being what it is. I might leave behind a leg or a foot at first, but I wouldn't be trussed to the tracks any longer, and I'd have a chance to roll free.

If that sounds cold, it's only because I'd learned to restrain my feelings for Tony over a long period of time—a matter of self-preservation, having been given so little encouragement from that side. He loved going to dinner with me, taking walks with me, even traveling with me. He even said often that he loved me. "Just not that way," he would add. I'd begun to feel like one of those poor women who go on Montel Williams to reveal, at long last, their love for a male friend. Hoping, of course, that he'll bubble over with passion and cry, ''I've always loved you, too!'' Inevitably, the friend does end up saying that, but adding the same as Tony: ''Just not that way.''

Having lived through a brief and sexless marriage with Arnold, and then a ''relationship'' with Tony, whatever the hell kind that was, I'd begun to feel as if I had more heads than GORP, not to mention biceps in all the wrong places. Or maybe I was a Ms. Potato Head, with my eyes, ears and nose all screwed up, ugly as sin. The fact that my mirror didn't support any of that paranoia helped—well-cared-for masses of reddish-blond hair like mine being ''in'' now, as they are. But there were days...

Now, given the scene before me in Tony's apartment, I had to wonder—and not for the first time— *were* Tony and Arnold gay? I never was the kind of woman who immediately labeled a man gay if he wasn't interested in my womanly charms. But why else would the two of them be here in Tony's penthouse, and what else could the ornately carved Chinese sex toy be about?

The police, of course, wouldn't tell me a thing except that there would be autopsies, and that forensics could take a few days. A Detective Dan Rucker was in charge. He looked to be thirtysomething and I guessed that by some standards—not mine—he might be considered cute. He had bright blue eyes and sandy hair that curled below his ears, and he wore an Anaheim Angels baseball cap that he kept putting on and taking off. Every time he took it off, he ran his fingers through his hair as if to make sure it was straight, but it never was. He sported at least a two-day growth of beard, and overall the look was a bit too scruffy for me. He smelled nice, though. Like oranges warming under a noonday sun.

If this were a crime novel, of course, I would have been drawn to the good detective immediately, scruffy or not. We'd have fallen into each other's arms by sunset, and then we'd have gone off on a crime-busting romp together, to avenge the killing of my ex-husband and my...whatever.

This wasn't a crime novel, though, and Detective Rucker might have smelled like an orange, but he acted like a sour lemon.

''We'll need you to come down to the station in the morning to answer more questions,'' he had said abruptly, not even looking at me as he paced off the room. He didn't seem overly suspicious of me, even though I was so close to the deceased. The truth was, I got the distinct impression that the police were thinking of this as a ''gay murder.'' There had been several, beginning this past spring, and then two more since summer had arrived. Most were in West Hollywood, but one or two were in other areas. The sheriff's department in West Hollywood had waged a campaign to catch the killers, and while they'd found some of the murders to be gay-bashings by gangs, other cases were still open.

I had gone to the police station this morning, as ordered, for further questioning. But afterward I wondered: Would justice be done for Tony and Arnold? What if it wasn't a gay-oriented crime? What if it was something entirely different? And why had this happened to two men who were close to me?

I was staring out my office windows around ten-thirty and musing upon this when my phone rang, and a few seconds later my intercom buzzed. I'd asked Nia, my assistant, not to disturb me except for something important, so I knew I'd have to take the call, though it was the last thing in the world I wanted to do. I'd spent over an hour at the police station saying, "Yes, no, yes, no, I don't know," and "maybe." Detective Rucker still hadn't looked as if he'd had a shower or shaved, and I still wasn't impressed by his attitude. He was short-tempered with me and talked as if I was taking up his valuable time, whereas he'd been the one to tell me to be there. He seemed to find it hard to sit still, and was up and down, up and down, as we talked. I'd left there on edge, as if I'd taken his ragged energy in and brought it to the office with me. I definitely didn't feel like talking on the phone now, even though I knew I should, and why.

Paul Whitmore.

After a few minutes Nia stuck her head around the door. Her short black cut looked frazzled, and I knew she'd been running her pencil's eraser through it in irritation.

"That's Paul Whitmore on the phone," she said, confirming my every fear. "You want me to tell him you're tied up? He's called a half-dozen times since I came in this morning."

Nia came in at seven every morning because of the time difference between L.A. and New York. A lot of our business is done when editors are getting geared up back there, around ten o'clock or so. Nia fielded calls and returned ones that were important but didn't need my personal touch.

"Don't I wish I *were* tied up somewhere," I replied with a sigh. "Like on a warm desert island with a delightful man tickling my naked body with palm leaves. Anything but dealing with an editor right now."

Returning Nia's smile, I added, "But no. I'll talk to him."

Sliding my feet off the desk and setting them squarely in my shoes, I stiffened my spine, reached for the phone and held the receiver to my ear. At the same time my eyes scanned my beloved, newish office, with its floor-to-ceiling windows overlooking the high-rises of Century City. My desk was a Louis XV, and facing it were the antique chairs on which my authors sat. On a small cherry-wood desk sign were these simple words engraved in gold: *Mary Beth Conahan, Literary Agent*. In a corner, a white and gold floor-to-ceiling cage held two lovebirds that cooed loudly, as if sounding a warning bell at the mere mention of the name Paul Whitmore—the most important editor in New York City.

The lovebirds had been given to me one Christmas by Tony, and of course I foolishly saw them as a "sign" that he loved me after all. Until I found that he'd given the same gift to his assistant, his maid, his typist and several other people, as a thank-you for the good work they'd been doing.

I wondered how long my stylish digs would last, now that Tony, the golden goose, was gone. The rest of my stable of authors, though exemplary in many ways, wasn't in his best-selling category.

Putting a smile in my voice, I chirped, "Hello, Paul. What can I do for you?"

"For God's sake, Mary Beth, what do you mean, what can you do for me? We're in the middle of negotiations with Craig Dinsmore! I've been trying to reach you all morning!"

Paul Whitmore worked for Bronson & Bronson, one of the few publishing houses in New York City that, amazingly, still had deep pockets. As such, most agents bowed and kissed Paul's feet the minute he phoned.

Most. Not me.

"I'm sorry, Paul," I said softly with fake remorse. "Your last offer...it didn't really sit well with my author. And when you didn't call back yesterday afternoon, I assumed our negotiations were over."

Whitmore's voice, though still irritable, responded

to my tone. "Of course they weren't over," he said more reasonably. "My dear, you know I love Craig Dinsmore's book. Everyone in-house loves his writing. We just have to come to terms, Mary Beth."

"But I don't see how that's possible," I said, choosing not to take offense at the patronizing "my dear."

"What do you mean, not possible? Anything is possible!"

"Not if you don't come up with more money, Paul. Craig is firm on that."

I tapped lightly on my chin with my favorite gold pen, studied my luxuriously sheer stockings and six-hundred-dollar shoes and took a deep breath. The truth was, Craig Dinsmore was on the verge of bankruptcy, and Paul had offered a high six figures for *Lost Legacy,* Craig's true-crime book about a fallen mafia don. If the deal went through, it could save his neck. But the more desperate my authors became during negotiations, the more relaxed I had to be. And I wanted a solid seven figures. That was the one thing that would make Hollywood perk up its ears and clamor to make a movie out of Craig's book.

Because the truth is, it doesn't always matter how good or bad a book is. Once a seven-figure offer has been made and accepted, the news makes its way into *Publishers Weekly* and assorted media mags, and that's the kind of money that talks here in Hollywood.

"Dammit, Mary Beth, did you hang up on me?" Paul Whitmore roared through the phone.

I gathered my wits and tried to mimic my cooing lovebirds again. "Of course not, Paul. I was just thinking."

"I hope you're thinking that we've made a very good offer, and that Craig Dinsmore should be happy for what he can get. Rumors have it he's on the skids."

"Oh, *really?*" I said in my best "ridiculous!" tone. "Where on earth did you ever hear something like that? Craig is doing extremely well, Paul. He's just purchased a new home near Laguna Beach, you know. Not too far from the one Dean Koontz built a few years ago."

"I don't believe it."

"Oh, for heaven's sake, why would I lie?" I sure couldn't tell him that Craig was holed up in a cheap motel over by the airport, writing his brains out in a push to survive. Or that I hadn't yet told Craig about Paul's six-figure offer. I knew he'd want to grab it and not try for more.

"Listen, Paul, I have calls coming in by the dozens. I'll have to get back to you."

"Wait."

"I really have to—"

"Tell Craig Dinsmore we'll come up by ten thousand. That'll put him over the seven-figure mark, which I'm sure is what you're angling for. I'll also go from eight percent to ten percent on the paperback royalties. That's the best we can do, Mary Beth, and it's damn good.''

Screw you, I thought. If you're willing to go another ten, another twenty won't hurt a bit.

"I'll pass the word along, Paul," I said lightly. "That's if I can rouse Craig. You know, he's working round the clock to finish his next book, and he's not always answering his phone."

"Then send a messenger, Mary Beth! This is my final offer, and I need to know by five p.m. my time. The offer's only good till then."

"I'll see what I can do, Paul. Ta."

I hung up softly and sat thinking. Five his time meant two here, and since it was nearly eleven now, that gave me only three hours. Damn! My stomach was churning, and I realized I'd bitten off a nail during the call. I'd have to phone Craig and ask him if he wanted me to hold Paul Whitmore's feet to the fire or accept what he said was his final offer. I personally didn't believe it was final. Still, I couldn't play fast and loose with Craig's income without his consent, now that the offer was over seven figures.

I called out to Nia on the intercom and asked her to find Craig for me as quickly as possible.

"I'm already on it," she said. "He still isn't answering his phone, and his machine's turned off. I'm trying all the bars around that area now."

"You think he's started drinking again?" I asked worriedly.

"Not necessarily. I just don't know where else to

start. And you know how he likes to hang out in bars and talk.''

Craig became a near hermit last year when he began to attend AA meetings. Then, in the fall, he told me he wasn't going to the meetings anymore. He felt that saying ''I am an alcoholic'' only imprinted it on his mind—thus making it a fact that could never be erased, leaving no hope for a ''cure.''

''I'm going it alone now,'' he'd said. ''I'm doing yoga, meditation, vitamins and herbs. My yoga teacher says that while I may have a problem with alcohol right now, it's not right to label myself an alcoholic, or anything else, for life. That not doing so leaves the door wide-open for releasing the problem. Or, as he calls it, the challenge.''

That kind of approach made me a bit nervous. It was hanging out in bars and entertaining the other hangers-on with tales of past exploits and publishing successes that had started Craig on that downward slide. All too often talking becomes the highlight of the day, taking over an author's life and keeping him from applying his butt to a chair and his fingers to the keys.

Nia knocked softly and opened my door. ''No luck so far with the bars. You want me to go look for him?''

Her hair was even more disheveled now, and I knew she'd been tugging at it while on the phone. There were shadows under her eyes, too, as if she hadn't slept well.

"No, I'll go," I said. "You've done enough to-day, fielding all those calls."

She came over and sat tiredly in one of the chairs across from me. "Here are the messages." She handed a monument-size stack of them across the desk.

"There must be a hundred here," I said, groaning.

"Fifty or so, anyway."

"Anything urgent?"

She shook her head. "Mostly the usual, authors calling to see if you got their manuscripts and if you've got them a deal yet. Editors returning your calls from yesterday. Most of the editors called early, while you were at the police station this morning. How did that go?"

I stared out the window, questions starting to whirl through my brain again. "I don't think I was much help. They wanted me to tell them anything I knew about the private lives of Tony and Arnold. I haven't known much about Arnold's life, though, since we were divorced ten years ago. I told them I never asked for alimony, so there wasn't much reason for us to stay in touch. We ran into each other now and then in restaurants, and once in a while he came by here to talk about that toy-creations book I sold for him years ago. As for Tony..." I shrugged.

"How are you feeling about Tony?" she asked pointedly.

"Oh, I don't know. Confused, I suppose." I

looked at her. "Did you ever hear any rumors about either of them being gay?"

"Gay!" she said, her eyes widening. "Never!"

I remembered that she didn't know about the Chinese dildo or the police suspicions about the murders being a gay crime. The cops had asked me not to divulge any information at all about the crime scene. Detective Rucker, the scruffy one, had told me that they wanted to keep certain information out of the papers, the better to catch the killer.

Even so, I was tempted to tell Nia about it, as I knew how well she could keep a secret. It was only my word to the detective that held me back.

"Do *you* think they were gay?" Nia asked.

I shook my head. "Just wondering. Since they were together in Tony's apartment, you know? And other things."

"Other things like the fact that they were both basically unattainable?" she asked, raising a dark eyebrow. "Mary Beth, we've talked about that. As long as I've known you, which is now about three and three-quarter years, you've never even looked at men who were available. When you get interested in a man, they're always either married, engaged or gay. It's that Conahan Wall. In this case, though, just because Tony and Arnold were both more or less unattainable, that doesn't mean they were gay."

"I know that," I said a bit snappily, then took my tone back with a smile. A long time ago, I'd had to admit that Nia was right about me and the kind of men I chose to go for. I've even thanked her for pointing it out—not that I've changed any, just because I know about it.

"I wish you'd tell me what happened to you," she said. "What's that wall about, anyway?"

I opened the bottom drawer of my desk and took out my purse, then reapplied powder and lipstick. My hand shook from exhaustion, and despite the expensive black suit and Gucci heels I looked like hell. But since I wasn't going anywhere except to Craig's motel—which he'd told me was a run-down hole-in-the-wall—it didn't much matter.

"Let's talk another time," I said, closing my compact with a loud snap. "I just can't get into all of that now."

"It's not just now. You never want to get into it."

I ignored that and stood. "You'll hold down the fort till you go home at three?"

"Of course. And I'll keep calling around for Craig, in case you don't find him. Will you be back in time to talk to Paul Whitmore, one way or the other?"

"I'll have my cell phone with me, and if I know anything by two, I'll call him from wherever I am."

"What if you don't find Craig, and Whitmore calls here? What do you want me to tell him?"

I thought for a moment. "Tell him Craig flew to Maui yesterday to gather inspiration from his beach house there."

She grinned. "So he's supposed to be rich, confident and simply unreachable."

I grinned back. "Tell Paul I've tried and tried, but according to his housekeeper, he's incommunicado."

I held out the packet of messages. "Anyone else in this stack…if they call again, tell them I'm sorry I missed their calls and I'll be in touch tomorrow."

"Right," Nia said, smiling. "And would ye be wantin' me to stand on me head as well?"

"Gee, a black woman from Dublin with an Irish brogue," I said on my way out the door. "What a sight. Almost wipes away that scene at Tony's last night."

Traffic was heavy from Century City to El Segundo, which entailed going past LAX. I had time to think about Craig, Paul Whitmore, and what I was going to do to get Craig even more money—provided he wanted me to try.

Negotiating was a lesson I'd learned long ago, though more to survive in L.A. than anything. I'd worked in L.A. for a television station after finishing high school in San Francisco—just on the writing staff, but hoping to be on camera eventually. I'd even gone out to crime scenes on breaking news stories, both as an observer and to show that I had initiative and wanted to learn. I did learn, and as a result I knew more now about the law and crime than most people who aren't actually in the field. In fact, when

I decided to become a literary agent, it was largely because someone at work had shown me his book, a true-crime novel, and asked me to read it, to see if I thought it was any good. Arnold and I were on the edge of divorce and I had time on my hands, so I went for it.

The book was great, and after I'd fixed a few minor things for my co-worker, I encouraged him to send it to an agent. He asked me if I would act as his agent, and when I found out that all you really needed to represent a writer was a telephone and some letterhead, I went for it. I started making calls, telling editors I was "Mary Beth Conahan of the agency by the same name," and leaving my home phone and fax number. Within two months I'd sold the guy's book to a major publishing house, and negotiated a good contract for him, to boot.

I was twenty-two at the time, and it was the first I'd ever even thought of becoming an agent. I was also kind of naive, and had no idea what it took to set up my own business. So I just stumbled into it, willy-nilly, and set my sails toward becoming Mary Beth Conahan, Literary Agent, for real. The first few years were more difficult than I'd ever imagined they would be, and I have to admit I often drank too much at the end of the day. I even messed around with drugs a bit. But then something happened, and for the last seven years I've been clean of drugs and only drink wine now and then. I've also worked my ass off to succeed.

I started out with new, untried authors whose first books were exciting enough to interest publishers but needed editing before they were decent enough to go out. I edited their books free, feeling it was unethical to charge. Because of that, I've built a loyal clientele over the past seven years, and at the age of thirty-three I now have a stable of wonderful authors. I fly to New York and Europe at regular intervals, dine with editors, schmooze with them at all the important cocktail parties, and I've gained their loyalty by not sending them books I know are unacceptable—not even to please an anxious-to-get-going author.

One exception to that was Tony Price. I knew his first novel, which was dark and made a case for the death penalty, would be highly controversial, at a time when a sizable portion of the population was marching against the death penalty. I'd pushed it out there, though, and after nine publishers had turned the book down, one accepted it—and the rest is history. Since then, his work had grown increasingly lighter, which made it easier to sell, though it always did have an edge, a bite to it.

I know that in my thoughts I'd been hard on Tony this morning, but I think that's only a wall I'd put up at the sight of him, dead, so that I wouldn't be too gob-smacked by it. The good side of Tony Price was that he was intelligent, funny, supportive… about some things, anyway, like my work…and I loved hanging out with him. We had more fun together than I've ever had with anyone I've known.

The downside was that I kept wanting to jump his bones, and I could just see how that would turn out—with him pushing me away and assuming that "just friends" attitude that I never could seem to break through. So I'd never even dared to try.

Good thing, I supposed, now that it seems he was gay. Over the years of working in Hollywood, I'd adopted some pretty good radar for detecting whether a man was either married or gay. With Tony, however, I had to admit that I never suspected. If anything, I thought he was probably just nonsexual and put all his energies into his books.

It would have been so much easier if I'd just known up front. But like Rock Hudson, he looked, sounded, walked and behaved like the typical macho man. He was the first man, I do believe, to ever fool me that way.

The traffic finally moved and I came to Imperial Avenue, turning right and looking for the Lazy Sands Motel that Craig had told me about. He'd said it was one of the few still there from fifty years ago, and except for a rat, which he'd made into a companion, and the fact that it was filthy when he first moved into it last year, he liked his little hideout. He said it helped him to stay focused. And sober. In the early mornings, before most people were up and while there was little traffic along Imperial and Vista Del Mar, he would run down to the beach and do his yoga there.

He'd made his stay in El Segundo sound like an

adventure, and it didn't seem too bad a deal, I thought. Until I saw the Lazy Sands. It was several blocks up from the beach, on a lot that looked like a junkyard. Rusted-out, abandoned cars were everywhere, and there was even a junkyard dog—a mix that looked like part Lab and part wolf. I parked as close to the lobby as I could get, but Wolf still managed to get between me and the door, his fangs bared and a warning growl deep in his throat.

I use the word *lobby* loosely, because the windows were covered in graffiti and dirt that looked as if it hadn't been washed off since the seventies. The room had the shape of a lobby, and the usual kind of entrance to one, but I couldn't even see through those windows enough to tell if there was anyone in there.

I don't have a dog, but I love watching shows about them. So I smiled at Wolf and spoke in a high, soft voice, just like Uncle Mattie, the dog trainer to the stars, had said to do on PBS.

"Good boy, good boy!" I said cautiously, moving a foot forward. But Wolf came toward me and bared his fangs as if he really meant business this time.

It was then, fortunately, that the lobby door opened. An old man with gray stubble stood there, looking at me. "Tinkerbell!" he cried.

"Uh, no…it's not Tinkerbell," I said, bemused. "Just me. Mary Beth Conahan."

"Damn you, Tinkerbell!" he yelled. "Get away from the lady!"

Wolf—or Tinkerbell, as I now realized—backed off. She didn't go far, though, standing her ground about ten feet away. I calculated whether I'd be able to make a run for the inside before she could reach me.

"Don't worry, she's harmless," the old man said. "She just likes to let people know she's on the job. As long as you don't look her in the eye, she won't hurt you. If you look her in the eye she'll see it as a challenge."

"And then?"

"Well, then, God knows what she'll do," he said, shaking his head. "She's not mine, she's just been here forever. Some bum left her behind one day."

I carefully kept my gaze on the man. "I'm looking for a friend," I said. "Craig Dinsmore. Can you tell me what room he's in?"

"You mean that writer fella? Crazy as a loon, he is. In there all hours of the day and night, typing away. Have to charge him extra for lights if he stays here much longer." He peered at me. "You say he's a friend of yours?"

"Yes. I'm just checking up, making sure he's all right."

The old man didn't look impressed.

"He asked me to," I added.

"Well...it's no skin off my back. Paid his room through the next week, after all. Number twenty-six."

"Thanks," I said. "Can I get there without Tinkerbell here biting my leg off?"

"Like I said…" The man replied with a shrug.

"Yeah. Don't look her in the eye."

Relieved to get back in my car, I drove to Craig's room, parking in the space in front of it. Stepping out, I looked for Tinkerbell but didn't see her anywhere. As I stepped out of the car, though, I heard a growl. Startled, I looked around and saw that she was right behind my car, and had probably followed me from the office.

With more fear than I wanted to admit, I looked away and crossed over to Craig's room. I love dogs in general, but I don't like being around big dogs who take eye-to-eye contact as a challenge to ravage my neck.

I knocked several times on the green, peeling door of number twenty-six, and when Craig didn't answer I went to the window. It had six square-foot panes, and one of them was broken. It had been covered from inside with see-through plastic wrap, something I hadn't noticed when I'd parked. Curtains were closed across the entire window.

I wondered if the place had a repairman, then realized that repairs were probably done by the old man. He'd looked besieged by arthritis and possibly osteoporosis, as his back was badly stooped. Add to that the dirty lobby windows, and I doubted that he kept up with anything here. He probably got free rent for acting as "manager" for a slum landlord who never came around and didn't care. That would leave the tenants to make their own repairs. A sort of DIY motel.

Craig no longer owned a car, so the fact that his old BMW wasn't here didn't tell me anything. I finally decided that he must run to the beach in the afternoons as well as the mornings, since he wasn't hunkered down at his computer—as he'd sworn he was doing 24/7.

Unless he's hitting the bars again.

I took out my cell phone and called Nia. "He's not here," I said. "Have you had any luck?"

"No, I'm sorry. I gave his description to the bartenders at all the bars around there, from Playa del Rey to El Segundo, then to Manhattan Beach and LAX. Even the bars that are probably too expensive for his budget. No one's seen him for a couple of days."

"Does that mean he *has* been in some of those bars recently?" I asked.

"Two of them," Nia said. "I wondered if he'd been drinking, and I asked if they'd had any trouble with him. Both bartenders said that the times they'd seen him he was drinking only coffee. They said he drank a lot of that. Also—you'll like hearing this— he always had paper and pencil with him, and spent a lot of time there writing. That's when he wasn't talking to customers or the bartender *about* writing, of course. He did a lot of that, too."

I relaxed a bit. "I'll go down to the beach and

look for him,'' I said. Glancing at my watch, I saw
that it was one-fifteen. Less than an hour left now to
present him with Paul Whitmore's ''final'' offer.

"Tell you what, Nia. How about if you call Whitmore right now and tell him the story about Maui.
It'll sound better if we get back to him before his
so-called deadline, and that could give me more lee-
way. I'm willing to bet that if he thinks Craig is in
a beach house in Hawaii, pounding away at his computer, he'll give me more time.''

"He does seem to want Craig real bad. Funny,
don't you think?''

"Funny how?''

"Well, word gets around real fast in the writing
community, especially here in L.A., and especially
if it's news about a writer going downhill. Wouldn't
you think Whitmore and Bronson & Bronson Publishing would have heard about it by now?''

"As a matter of fact, I have thought of that,'' I
said, ''which is why I've been doing damage control
with Whitmore. But he really likes this book of
Craig's, and he doesn't seem too concerned about a
long-term contract. Which, in itself, makes me wonder. The book I sent him doesn't, in my opinion, call
for that kind of money or commitment. It's almost
as if something's going on that I don't know anything about.''

"You know,'' Nia said, ''I've been thinking the
same thing. Craig's always been a good writer, but

this mafia book isn't anything new, is it? Just the same old, same old?''

"I found it gripping when I read it," I said. "But I'll admit to being a bit stunned that Whitmore offered six figures for it, let alone seven. Listen, I've got to run. So call Whitmore and tell him the Maui story, but tread easy...oh, hell, you know what to do. You've got great diplomatic bones.''

"Thanks," Nia said, chuckling. "Are you still going down to the beach, then?''

"Yes. I'll let you know how it goes with Craig.''

I closed my cell phone and looked back at number twenty-six one more time. It was then I thought I saw a flicker of movement at the curtain inside Craig's window.

I was tired and hot and responded accordingly. *That bastard! Was he just not answering the door? How does he expect me to help him, for God's sake?*

Then, calming down, I realized that Craig couldn't know I had good news for him about *Lost Legacy*. He'd probably spotted me out here and thought I'd come to nag him about the three-thousand-dollar advance I'd loaned him against his next potential check from Bronson & Bronson.

Or he was just being typically hermit-like. Some writers develop agoraphobia while writing a book and never even go out to the store for food. They'd starve rather than leave the house and the book for even a moment. Many never answer their telephones or collect their mail for weeks, unless they think a check will be in the box.

Craig Dinsmore hadn't been like that in recent months, however. He was more the kind who needed to gab about his work, and as Nia had confirmed, he'd been out this week to the bars, doing just that. So if he was inside now, writing, and just didn't want to answer the door, I should feel relieved. That meant he was working hard on the next book, a follow-up to *Lost Legacy,* and if that was the case, his money troubles were over. And so, thankfully, were mine.

Still, where writers are concerned, I'd learned never to take anything for granted. No deal is a deal until it's signed.

I went back up onto the rickety little porch and banged on the window. "Craig, I know you're in there! Open up! I've had a new offer from Whitmore, and it's big. We need to talk!"

I listened intently and heard a sound like a bump inside.

"Craig, this is your life we're talking about!"

I shook the door handle, hoping it might be unlocked. It wasn't.

Resolutely, I trudged back to the lobby and pretended that Tinkerbell wasn't there, poised on her haunches to spring. The inside of the lobby was dusty and smelled of mold, making me sneeze.

"I need the key to number twenty-six," I said, dabbing at my nose with a Kleenex. "My friend isn't answering, and I'm afraid he's had another heart attack.''

"He's got a bad heart?" the old man said nervously.

"Yes," I lied. "And if he dies here, the cops will be milling about forever. They'll want to go through your room, too—your office, your books, everything.''

I had guessed right that this would not be a good thing. The old man's toughened hand quickly scrabbled along a board with hooks and came up with a key that had "26" on it.

Back at Craig's room, I slid the key into the lock and pushed in fast, before he could know what I was doing and push me right back out.

"Listen, Craig! I've been negotiating my ass off to get you a good deal—"

I stopped in my tracks. He wasn't here. There was only the one room, with a door to what must be a bathroom in back. Was he in the bathroom, then?

I walked closer to the door and called out, "Craig? It's Mary Beth. Are you in there?"

No answer.

Then who had moved that curtain? Was it just the wind, coming through that plastic-covered window?

But there hadn't been any wind that I had noticed. Not enough to have caused even a ripple.

On a round table in front of the window was a laptop computer that seemed fairly new. I wondered if Craig had bought it with money from the sale of his car. To the left were several used foam cups with dregs that must have been coffee, as well as the last crumbs of some sort of pastry. There was also an inexpensive, drugstore-variety answering machine that held nineteen unanswered calls, according to the blinking green light. A small portable printer was attached to the laptop and next to it were sheets of manuscript paper, about an inch high. An El Segundo library card was propped up against a lamp, and on the floor around the table were odd crumpled sheets that Craig had obviously tossed away as not right.

So he *had* been working. That was good. I started to turn back to the front door, but couldn't resist a peek first at the finished sheets of manuscript. They were upside down, so I turned the entire stack over and saw the title: *Under Covers*.

Odd. Did he mean *Undercover?* A spy novel? That didn't sound like Craig. He was more into investigative nonfiction like *Lost Legacy,* where real-life mafia slugs were found under upturned rocks.

A look at the next few pages revealed that the title was a play on words, and the book seemed to be a fictional account of the Hollywood scene ''between the sheets.'' He'd written about old Hollywood in the 1940s, accounts of wild exploits of high-level directors with young female stars, sexual harassment, and the fact that actors were forced to cover up their homosexuality to make them more of a heartthrob to female viewers. Names of stars, though, had been changed to protect the noninnocent.

I'd had no idea Craig was writing a book like this, and I couldn't see Paul Whitmore paying the same thing for this book as he was offering for *Lost Legacy*. While its mafia-don story had been told before, Craig had added a psychological edge to it that had made Whitmore take notice. This book, though it seemed well written, was as stale as yesterday's news. The casting-couch angle had been done before, over and over. In fact, some of it seemed familiar, as if I'd read it somewhere before.

What the hell was going on?

I'd taken a speed-reading course years before, so it didn't take me long to read the first few chapters. Confused and concerned, though, I stopped reading at page thirty-four. Setting the page down, I did something I'd never done before. Pushing the ''on'' button on Craig's computer, I sat on his chair and tried to bring up the *Under Covers* document. I was pretty good with computers, but there was something odd about this one: there were no documents on the hard drive. None at all. No letters, no memos, no books. If anything had ever been on the hard drive, it had obviously been wiped clean. Puzzled, I opened the CD-Rom drive and the floppy disk drive, but both were empty.

Before I had time to think it through, I heard a slight noise that seemed to be coming from behind the motel. A thud? Someone hitting the wall back there? Images of O.J. and Kato Kaelin came to mind—someone running into an air conditioner with blood on his hands.

Then I realized the sound must have come from the bathroom. Without thinking, I strode over there and threw the bathroom door open, determined to confront Craig about why he hadn't been answering his calls and why the hell he was hiding from me. It was his own fault, I thought, if I caught him on the john.

But Craig wasn't hiding at all. He was right there on the floor, blood all over his forehead that was slowly seeping onto the old, grubby tiles.

In shock, I could barely move. I looked at the window, which was open. Cheap plastic curtains in a gaudy flower pattern were blowing in a light salty breeze that came off the ocean from this side of the motel. There were marks on the sill that seemed to be blood, marks that might have come from a killer, possibly escaping that way.

I knelt down beside Craig, feeling for a pulse. I couldn't find one anywhere. I touched his cheek. Still warm. He hadn't been dead long.

Stroking his forehead, I couldn't hold back tears. The poor guy never got the chance to get out of the hole he'd dug himself into. And we were so close to getting what he wanted.

Then, as if in a nightmare, I saw that the blood had originated at a large gash on Craig's forehead, and that lying by his side was a bloody Chinese dildo—made of ivory, and intricately carved to please, I supposed, in all the right places. It looked very much like the one in Tony's apartment the night before.

I knelt there for a long moment, so staggered I wasn't able to stand. I guess I noticed the draft, finally, that slammed the front door shut. Grasping the bathroom sink, I pulled myself up slowly and realized there was blood on my skirt and my knees.

I was still standing over Craig's body, blood all over me, when the police banged on the front door and piled in. "Don't move!" they ordered, guns pointed directly at me.

I didn't even breathe.

El Segundo is a smallish town along the coast, south of Santa Monica and north of Redondo Beach. It's a nice town, growing perhaps too quickly, but the cops, I'd heard, were generally pretty friendly.

My experience, however, was a bit strained because I'd been found at a crime scene, with blood all over me.

Inside the El Segundo police station, I'd been allowed to wash most of the blood off me. A female officer stood outside the bathroom door, "just in case I needed help."

Yeah, right.

After I'd done the best I could, I was escorted to an interview room where a Lieutenant Davies sat across from me at a table. He didn't tell me much, but I knew by now that he was wondering if I'd also killed Tony and Arnold. Although the ESPD and the LAPD were entirely separate entities, surely they shared information when something as important as murder was involved.

The one thing that probably kept me out of jail, at least for the moment, was the open bathroom window and the blood on the sill. I could have set that up, they thought at first, to make it look as if someone else had killed Craig Dinsmore and then escaped out that window. But when my prints didn't turn up on the murder weapon and there was a third, unidentified person's blood type on that sill, they couldn't charge me.

Which did not, however, exonerate me entirely. I could have been an accomplice, the lieutenant said, and just didn't make it to the window before the police broke in.

"I've been wondering about that," I said. "How did you know to show up when you did?"

He hesitated again, but shrugged. "We had an anonymous phone call saying a murder had been committed in that room."

"Do you mind telling me when that call came in?"

He hesitated, but said, "One-forty or thereabouts."

"So, whoever it was, they called you while I was in Craig's room."

He didn't answer that, and for good reason, I

thought. If I were an accomplice to the crime, why would the other killer call the cops at a time when I'd be caught there?

I spent the next couple of hours in the interview room dealing with questions I had no answers to. In between questions I had time to think, and I figured that whoever had killed Craig did it while I was pounding on the door the first time. When I came back with a key, the killer was just getting ready to go out the window, but he hesitated when he heard me come in. The noise I'd heard while I was looking at Craig's manuscript must have been the killer climbing, finally, through that window. I'd been so quiet, he probably thought I'd gone.

Or maybe he was afraid that I might decide I needed to pee.

"Ms. Conahan," the lieutenant said at last in a hard voice, "I don't believe in coincidence. There were two murders last night in Brentwood, and the LAPD says that both men were closely connected to you. Now there's this third murder. I would think you might be getting nervous about that."

"Well, I'm not nervous," I said calmly. "I'm sad. I've lost two very good authors and an ex-husband who didn't deserve to die. But I didn't do anything, so there's nothing for me to be nervous about."

Lieutenant Davies fell silent, and I suspected he was using that psychological technique of not speaking, which usually forces the other person to break the silence by saying something.

He'd probably never had an agent as a suspect, and didn't know that we were well-versed in those kinds of tricks, from constant negotiations. Though, come to think of it, the odds that no agent had ever committed murder upon an author were probably worse than an old, broken-down nag winning at the Hollywood Park racetrack.

I reached for my purse on the table and stood. "Unless you intend to arrest me," I said firmly, "I'm leaving. I have work to do."

It was a bluff, but a safe one. If he'd had enough evidence to hold me, I'd be booked and behind bars by now.

The lieutenant smiled, but it was a tight smile, not quite making it to his eyes. I noticed that his teeth were very white against his tanned skin, and that there was an odd little scar on his left cheek. Overall he might be considered quite handsome, but the eyes took away from that. They were all business, not giving anything up.

"I have to ask you not to leave town," he said.

"I wasn't planning to," I answered.

He nodded and stood. "I'll walk you out."

I stopped by the office before heading home, and found Nia still there. She hadn't left at three after all, but was in my workout room, which connected to the office. She was sweating away on the exercise bike, a cordless phone from the office on the floor. The door from the workout room to the reception room was open, which meant that she'd been listening for anyone who might walk in.

"Hi," I said, dropping my purse on a chair and stepping behind the Chinese screen that served as a changing room. Pulling off my suit and tugging on workout clothes, I did my usual stretching exercises, then climbed on the treadmill next to Nia and started it up.

"Anything new?" I asked.

"I talked to Paul Whitmore after your last call about Craig, and it was weird. After how hot he seemed for Craig's new book, he didn't sound all that upset to hear he was dead."

"Really? How did he sound?"

"Quiet. Didn't say much, just to tell you he was sorry to hear it. Hung up rather quickly."

"Hmm. He was probably signing another author already. Whatever it takes to keep the coffers filled."

Not that I was anyone to talk. I'd been worrying a bit about my own coffers.

"And a Detective Rucker came by," Nia said. "Yum!"

"Yum?"

She rolled her eyes. "Oh, God, don't tell me you didn't notice. That curly hair, and those gorgeous white teeth."

I studied my teeth in the wall of mirrors in front of us. "You know something? Everybody has white teeth these days. Ever since all those actors started having their teeth whitened, everybody you meet has super-white teeth. If they all got together in a room and smiled, they'd blind each other.''

"Yeah. Well, don't laugh, okay? I'm thinking of getting mine done, too.''

"You're kidding. Your teeth are already white enough. You're beautiful, Nia. Don't you know that?''

"Not in the teeth,'' she said. "They're more a sort of off-white. How can I ever compete in the date market with off-white teeth?''

"True,'' I said in a hopeless tone. "I can see it all now. You as an old maid, living a joyless, loveless life with only your cat and your off-white teeth.''

She groaned. "That so possible, it isn't even funny.''

I slowed down my pace. "So you think Dan Rucker's hot?''

"Well, I didn't say he's *hot*. I just think he looks like he could be, under that untidy disguise. What do you think?''

I shrugged. "I didn't like his attitude.''

"Figures. He wasn't wearing a wedding ring, and I doubt he's gay. Why would you like him?''

"Oh, shut up.''

We worked out silently for a while, until Nia said, "Why do I feel like I'm riding a horse? This seat hurts like hell.''

"You want me to get a recumbent?''

"Really? You'd do that?''

"Anything for you, my treasure trove."

Nia was so good at her work, I had been thinking of making her a partner. I thought that I'd better wait though, to see how things went with Craig's book and my income from it. Would Whitmore withdraw his offer now, or still publish it?

My guess was that since the book was finished, he'd go ahead and publish it. But could I still legally represent Craig in the sale? I'd never had a situation like this before, but I knew my contract with Craig gave me the right to sign for him if for some reason he wasn't able to. For instance, if he'd just been impossible to reach and I had a great offer like the one from Whitmore, I could have signed for Craig rather than risk his losing the contract.

But what about when he was dead?

Damn. I wished now that I'd accepted the seven-figure offer from Whitmore that morning.

"By the way," Nia said, breaking into my thoughts, "he's coming back."

"Who?"

"Detective Rucker. He called a little while ago and said he'd be coming back."

"To see me?"

"What else? He's already seen me, and I don't recall any rings or bended knees."

"What does he want?" I asked, frowning.

"I don't know. He just said he had a few questions."

"But how did he know I'd be here, when I didn't know it myself until I left El Segundo?"

She grinned. "Maybe you're star-crossed lovers, meant to be together from the beginning of time. Like, he just *knew*."

"Oh, right. More likely he was following me. Or having me followed. I'll bet he called you from the cell phone in his car, not twenty feet behind me."

"Wow. He must really want to see you again, if that's the case," Nia said, laughing.

I couldn't help laughing, too. "Hardly. The El Segundo police are ready to arrest me, now that I've got bodies falling on the ground all around me. Detective Rucker probably wants to be the first to arrive with handcuffs."

"Handcuffs, eh? Now there's a picture worth taking."

"Oh, stop it!" I took the towel off my shoulder and wiped my face and neck with it. Bending over, I reached for my water bottle on the floor. I was standing with my back to the door, my butt in the air, when I heard from behind me, "No cuffs this time. If that's what you like, though, I'll make a note of it."

I whirled around and saw Detective Dan Rucker with his arms folded and the first smile I'd seen on his face. He hadn't shaved, but he was dressed in clean jeans and a black leather jacket over a white T-shirt. I almost thought I saw what Nia meant when she'd said *yum*.

"Whoa, Nelly!" she said now, slipping off the exercise bike. Looking at me pointedly, she said, "I'll betcha I have some work to do in the other room."

She disappeared into the outer office, pulling the door shut behind her and leaving me red-faced and with no sharp dialogue as backup.

"Have a seat, Detective," I said, taking refuge behind the Chinese screen. "I need to change."

Nia's teasing rang in my ears, along with the idea she'd put in my head—that Dan Rucker might be interested in me as something other than a suspect. I felt awkward, and my hands shook as I pulled off my workout clothes and wriggled back into my suit. Getting stockings on wasn't even an issue. I left them on the chair, rolled into a small bundle. Slipping into my heels, I was aware that Rucker could hear every movement I was making, and I felt like a little girl in fourth grade. That little boy behind her? He'd just sent her a note saying, *I like you—do you like me?* Was he looking at her braids, and were they straight or messed up? Was her dress buttoned at the neck in back? What did he really think of her?

The fact that I cared surprised me, and I wanted to disappear. *What on earth was I thinking?* There was nothing for it but to go out there with my chin up and confidence streaming from my pores.

"Now, then. What can I do for you?" I asked briskly, leading Rucker into my office. I took a seat at my desk and put my best negotiating face on. De-

tective Rucker didn't sit in the chair across from me
as expected, however. Instead, he came around beside me and plunked his butt onto the edge of my
brand-new-to-me antique desk. He was so close I
could smell the oranges again, and I gritted my teeth
and resisted the impulse to grab my letter opener and
stick him in the thigh with it.

"Nice office," he said, folding his arms and looking around, taking in the view. "You must be doing
well."

"I do okay. And I worked for it. No one handed
it to me."

He nodded. "You don't have to be defensive
about it. I know."

"You know?"

"Sure. I've been checking up on you. I know how
you started out and that you just moved here to the
high-rent district a couple of years ago. I know you
bought a home in Malibu, too, at about the same
time. Pretty nice digs."

I tried not to show how flustered I was. Standing,
I moved away from him and crossed to the other
side of the room, where I had a sofa and coffee table.
I sat on the sofa, crossing my legs and folding my
arms—an automatic defensive posture, I realized
suddenly. I never would have done this in front of
an editor, as it would have weakened my position.

Carefully, I unfolded my assorted limbs, leaning
back against the cushions and forcing my spine to
relax.

"I do all right," I said coolly. "Is there some purpose to this, Detective? Is it going somewhere?"

"I'm just kind of curious about your relationship with Tony Price. It seems you and he went out a lot. You even went on trips together."

"And?"

"And Price's murder looks as if it might have been a crime of passion."

I laughed. "You think I killed Tony in a moment of passion?"

"Stranger things have happened."

"Well, you're wrong. If anything, Tony's death will hurt me, especially in terms of financial loss. The best thing for me would have been if he'd lived to be a hundred."

"And kept writing till then, of course."

"All right, what are you getting at?" I snapped. Reaching for the cordless phone on the coffee table, I said calmly, "And is this supposed to be a formal interview? Do I need my lawyer here?"

"Nah, relax. This is off the record. I'll let you know when you need a lawyer."

He came over and stood above me, hands in his pockets. "The thing is, if Tony Price wasn't writing well, if he hit a wall and couldn't get going again, or if he'd decided to drop you as his agent—"

"Sorry to burst your bubble," I said, putting the phone down. "None of that is true."

I stood again and walked over to the windows, giving him my back while studying the traffic below.

It was a negotiating technique, one I often used to gain time and balance. I noted that the freeways were jammed with commuters winding their way from one end of the city to the other. It was late June, and I knew it was hot out there. I could picture the drivers without air-conditioning loosening their ties and belts, or the buttons on their blouses. Almost everyone would be swilling down bottled water so they wouldn't dehydrate on their three-hour commutes home to where the rents were reasonable.

I'd probably end up as one of them, now that Craig was gone, too. Even if *Lost Legacy* got published and I received my fifteen percent commission on it, that wouldn't last long after taxes and my current expenses. And Craig wouldn't be around to finish *Under Covers*.

"I don't want to talk about this anymore," I said finally, turning back to Rucker. "I've lost two valuable authors and an ex-husband I actually still liked. This hasn't been a red-letter day for me. If you're arresting me, just say so. I'll call my lawyer. If you're not arresting me, this is over. Now."

His eyes narrowed. "You're a pretty tough cookie, aren't you?"

"I can handle myself," I said.

I went back into the workout room, picked up my purse and took out my keys. "Especially with men like you."

Damn, Mary Beth. I bit my lip. Had that sounded

like the tough message I'd meant to send—or a challenge?

When I turned back he was standing only a few feet behind me. "I have no doubt of that," he said.

I thought a minute, then made a rapid decision.

"Look," I said, glancing at my watch, "I have to eat dinner. Would you like to join me?"

The eyes widened. "Are you asking me out on a date?"

"Absolutely not." I gave my laugh the tiniest bit of a scornful edge. "Get hold of yourself. I just thought that if you insist on pummeling me with questions, it might be better if we do it where I don't feel like I'm going to be thrown in a cell at a moment's notice. Tony and Arnold were important to me. So was Craig. I'd like to help find their killer."

"Uh...okay," he said, his tone sounding suspicious. "Where would you like to go?"

"My house," I said, handing him my personal card with the address and cell-phone number on it. Which, come to think of it, he probably already had, since he knew so much about me.

"Wow," he said, "gold-plated lettering for a gold-plated address. Malibu, California...home of the stars."

I sighed irritably. "Are you going to hold that against me?"

"Not at all. The view should be great."

"Eight o'clock, then," I said, sailing out the door. "Don't be late."

Better to be on your own turf and in power, I'd decided. The last thing I needed was to be summoned by the police again, just to sit and repeat, "I don't know, I don't know."

Besides, I had plans for the good detective. Before this night was over, Detective Dan Rucker was going to tell me everything he knew about all three murders.

At home I changed into jeans and a T-shirt and took a cup of coffee down to the beach. Gulls came and settled near me, hoping I had food. They soon left, though, and went back to dipping up and down over the waves.

It was seven o'clock and the sun had begun its downward slide toward the sea. The sky was blood-red from all the smog that had been blown west from what had, over the past few hours, become an unseasonable Santa Ana wind—hot, heavy and dangerous, blowing trees into houses and causing all kinds of havoc, according to the drive-time news.

Here at the beach, though, it made the evening air balmy and gave us some of our best sunsets. The smog blows westward from inland when pushed by the Santa Anas—Devil Winds, as they've been called for years—and the setting sun filtered through the smog is incredibly beautiful.

Too much of the Santa Anas, however, can make a person crazy in the head. When they go on for days I become irritable and off my feed. Some days I want to kill everything in sight—even my authors.

Fortunately, that's only a temporary aberration. I'd never really wished for any of my authors, including those three men, to be murdered. And now that they had been, where did that leave me? Grieving aside, that is.

And I did grieve. Now that I had time to be alone, I grieved for Arnold and Tony, both of whom I had loved so unsuccessfully, and for Craig, who deserved better and almost got it. He had worked hard to sober up and stay that way, and from the manuscript I'd seen on his desk in the motel, he was doing good work. Unexpectedly good work, even though the topic had been done before.

Why on earth would anyone want to kill him? Craig had been divorced for several years, and his ex, Julia, owned a successful antiques shop in New York City. Craig had told me Julia had never needed or asked for alimony.

Was it the new book, then? If I'd had time to do more than scan the pages, would I have found that he had tremendously damaging information against someone important? Information that was only lightly fictionalized?

But then the killer would surely have taken the manuscript with him.

Unless Craig had been clever enough to put a floppy disk or CD-Rom in a safe-deposit box, or some other secret place.

I sighed, drawing my knees up and leaning my chin on them, watching the neighbors walk by with their dogs or make their last run of the night. I usually made time each evening to run, but I hadn't been able to lately. I did work out three times a week, and sometimes more. Working out gave me an endorphin high, and I felt afterward as if I could take on the world.

Today, though, was different. Today I wanted to just sit in a funk and think about the state of my life.

As Rucker had said, I'd been living here at Malibu for about two years—the same amount of time I'd been at my office in Century City. My house was tiny and a fixer-upper, but it still took more money to get into it than my father had made in his lifetime. My pop had been a streetcar conductor in San Francisco, and a good man. He supported my mom and me the best he could, and even though times were often tough, we never really went without. When I graduated from high school I left home, like most kids, for freedom from parental control—but also because I wanted to get a good job and give the poor guy a break. He died a year later, almost as if it was a relief to leave, once I was out of the house and settled on my own. Sometimes I feel guilty about taking away his motivation to go on. Other times, I must admit I'm proud to have done so much for myself, as young as I was.

Not that I've always been thrilled with my career choice. The life of an agent, a manager, or any kind of broker, is unlike any other life I've known or even heard of. We spend our days walking a tightrope between editors and authors, trying to keep both of them happy with each other. Not always an easy task. A good agent, some believe, is the kind that's feared by New York editors. Most editors, on the other hand, will tell you that they prefer agents who are "easy to work with." Which sometimes means that those agents don't get the best deals, because they haven't got it in them to act like a shark with a friend.

Those of us who are "sometime sharks" believe that the only way to win is to make a difficult editor so intimidated that she or he will give the author a good deal, with either money or extra perks. We do whatever it takes to come to an agreeable conclusion. And though bullying is not a good habit to get into, it becomes one sometimes, before we even know it. As natural as breathing.

So yes, I've learned to negotiate, and I've been successful at it. When threatened, I always look at whatever skills I have to defend myself, and that's what I did this afternoon. Detective Rucker had accepted my invitation even more quickly than I'd expected him to. He would come here for dinner thinking he could get something out of me, because surely I was the main suspect in all three deaths so far. He'd play his game. But more importantly, I'd play mine.

If I didn't want to end up arrested, I needed something to go on—information of some kind that would help me find out who the real killer was.

"Nice place," Dan Rucker said, whistling softly. The sun had gone below the horizon, but the sky was still streaked with bright red, and my white sofa, carpet and walls were all tinted pink. The gulls were now wheeling over the beach in droves, probably scoping out dead fish.

"Look at that sunset," Rucker said.

"Beautiful, isn't it?"

He nodded, standing at the window with his back to me. "Mind if I go out on the deck?"

"Be my guest, Detective. I'll bring the wine out there."

I watched as he went onto the deck and sat at a patio table with four chairs. Putting his feet up on one chair, he seemed comfortable about making himself at home.

Well, good. A couple of glasses of wine and he'd be even more ready to tell me what he knew.

I took a cold bottle of Chardonnay out, along with appetizers I'd defrosted and nuked.

"Any trouble getting here, with the traffic?" I asked.

It seems like that's the first question people ask when a guest walks in and they don't know what else to say.

"A little," my guest answered, "but it's thinned out pretty well by now." He took a bite of a small cheese-and-ham tart and sighed. "Delicious. You're a good cook."

"Thanks," I said. "I've always been pretty handy with piecrust."

He looked at me intently and I had to look away.

"Okay," I said, flushing. "I got them at the store. You think I really had time to cook?"

He smiled. "But you heated them up so well."

"I did, didn't I? It's a talent I have...heating things up."

"I'll try to remember that," he said, grinning.

"Why, Detective, are you flirting with me?"

"You're the one who made the comment," he countered. "What else did you have in mind?"

"I, uh...nothing, really. And by the way, you're moving awfully fast."

"I don't mean to. I'd just like to get the sex stuff out of the way so we can get down to business."

I felt my face grow hot. "Sex stuff? Detective Rucker, wherever is your mind? And what do you mean by business?"

"I mean the real reason you invited me here," he said.

"You suspect me of having a secret agenda?"

"I suspect you of just about everything right now, Mary Beth Conahan."

He said it easily, as if he were merely commenting on the weather.

"The key word is *suspect*," I replied. "You have absolutely no evidence that I had anything to do with any of those murders. You can't possibly have, because I didn't commit them.''

He shrugged and took a long swallow of the wine. ''Maybe I do, maybe I don't. I just figured if I came here tonight you might feel more comfortable about telling the truth.''

''Then you've wasted your time,'' I said, ''because I already have.'' I took a sip of the Chardonnay. ''I honestly don't know who killed Tony and Arnold. Or Craig.''

''But you know something you aren't saying. I'd bet my badge on it.''

''Then I hope your badge doesn't mean too much to you.''

''It means everything. I wouldn't bet it if I weren't sure.''

''I think dinner's just about ready,'' I said, looking at my watch and changing the subject. ''I don't cook much, so I hope you like Poor Man's Lasagna.''

He smiled. ''Poor Man's Lasagna? What's that?''

''You cook some pasta, then layer it in a casserole dish with tomato sauce, garlic, sour cream, cream cheese and Monterey Jack. Takes about twenty minutes to pull it all together.''

''Sounds absolutely wonderful. A sure way to harden the arteries.''

''Is that a complaint?''

''Not at all. It's my favorite kind of food.''

A man after my own heart—if only he weren't

here to tear it out and roast it on a spit. I'd have to tread carefully with Detective Dan Rucker.

We were having after-dinner coffee, on the deck with Bailey's Irish Cream, my excuse for an easy dessert. It had grown dark, and I'd plugged in the little fairy lights around the railing. The night air was warm, even balmy, and the ocean waves were soft and muted. Thanks to the Santa Ana winds, the sky was clear now, and the moon illuminated the shoreline all the way down to Palos Verdes.

''There was a small piece on the evening news about Craig Dinsmore,'' Dan said, leaning back lazily in his chair, his feet on the middle railing. ''They said he'd once been on the track to stardom, but he'd fallen off track along the way. A 'friend' they interviewed said it was alcoholism, but that Dinsmore had recently cleaned up and was fighting his way back. The anchor ended up by saying in somber tones, '...only to end up dead in a seedy motel room.'''

''They'd make the most of that, of course. It's a great story for the media.''

''Is any of it true?'' he asked.

''Most of it, more or less. He did clean up and I've been negotiating a good contract for his current book. I'm not so sure about the next one. I saw a manuscript at Craig's motel room, just before the El Segundo police came crashing in. It wasn't the kind of book he told me he was writing.''

"What kind was it?"

"One of those Hollywood tell-alls," I said. "Nothing especially new or original." I remembered that the manuscript had seemed familiar to me, and suddenly I thought I knew why. Not for certain, but I had my suspicions. I'd have to go online and see if I was right.

"What about Tony Price?" Dan asked. "He was a best-seller, right?"

"Not if you want to be grammatical. A best-seller is a book. An author is a 'best-selling author.' Or to be even more grammatical, a 'writer of best-selling books.'"

"I stand corrected," he said, smiling. "Does it make a real difference?"

"Not unless you've got a tiny little editor sitting on your shoulder and you get bugged by those things."

He shook his head. "Living with you must be a challenge."

"Well, no one's ever had to come up to that challenge," I said, smiling sweetly, "so no problem." Then, sobering, I added, "Except, of course, poor Arnold."

Rucker was silent a moment. Then he said, "To get back to Tony Price, I would imagine that losing him will put a dent in your income."

"Eventually," I said casually, with more bravado than honesty. "There are still royalties to come in on his last book, and option money if a movie is made from it.'' I took a sip of my coffee and shrugged.

''And Craig Dinsmore?'' he asked. ''He wasn't making any money for you at all?''

I shook my head. ''Not much lately. A few royalties from his older best-selling books. Some from foreign sales. The book that's at the publisher's should do quite well, though. Why do you ask?''

''Just wondering.''

''Okay. But while you're wondering about that, enlighten me, please, about the Chinese dildos.''

He seemed surprised. ''You recognized them as that?''

''Sure. I have a couple of gay authors and they're a hot item in West Hollywood right now. Word goes around at parties, so yes, I've heard about them. Ancient Chinese sex artifacts, quite expensive. They were the murder weapons, right?''

''I'm not at liberty to say,'' he answered, looking away.

''I'll take that as a yes.''

''You may take it as that, but like I said—''

''You're not at liberty to say. But you know, I've been thinking. It'd take a lot of strength to bash someone in the forehead with one of those. Hard enough to kill them, anyway. And here we've got three someones. It would almost have to be a man.''

''Or a very strong woman,'' he said, looking at me. ''Someone who works out a lot, for instance.''

"Ah…so you *are* here on a fishing expedition. You think I killed them."

"I didn't say that."

"You're not saying much of anything. So what *can* you tell me? This little tête-à-tête has to be mutual, or I'm clamming up."

"You've already clammed up," he said. "You haven't told me a thing I can use to find the killer."

"Well, that shouldn't bother you too much, since you half suspect that I'm it."

"You think it's only half?" he asked, looking me intently in the eye. It was hard to break away because my breath caught and my hands were beginning to shake.

"Are you married?" I asked, setting my coffee cup down carefully.

"Nope. Never have been."

"Engaged?"

"Nope."

"Gay?"

"Not so far as I can tell." He grinned.

"Wait a minute. Are you saying you're *attainable?*"

He laughed softly. "I'd like to think I am."

"Hmm. So then, about that sex stuff. Can we get down to it now?"

The grin widened. "I thought you'd never ask."

For my part, I'd ventured into this with one thing in mind—well, almost one thing—to get information out of Dan Rucker. But we didn't talk at all, aside from some rather wild and passionate utterances that would have embarrassed me if I'd had neighbors on the other side of the wall.

He was a pretty good lover, quite skilled in the ways of pleasing a woman. But he still wasn't my type. And his beard scratched. He turned out to be cleaner, though, than I'd expected—and he still smelled like oranges warming in a noonday sun.

I never did get any information out of him, but never in my life had I felt anything like the way I'd felt with him. It seemed we matched in all ways physical, as if we'd rehearsed a thousand years ago for this moment—corny as that sounds.

When it was over, we both leaned back on the pillows and stared at the ceiling. He was the first to speak. "That was really...different," he said.

I was lying in a pool of sweat, and only half of it was from the hot Santa Ana winds. I cringed. "Different good? Or different bad?"

He leaned on an elbow and kissed my lips, rubbing his lightly back and forth over mine, and ending at the tip of my nose. "Different like...well, like your Poor Man's Lasagna."

I struggled to remember what he'd said about that. Thick? Fatty? Greasy?

No. *Absolutely wonderful* was what he'd said. I smiled.

"Do you have any orange juice?" he asked.

"Second shelf. Fridge." I turned on my side and snuggled under the down comforter.

"Well, don't get up," he said pointedly. "Let me get it."

"You're a prince," I murmured, yawning.

He swatted me on the ass.

While he rummaged in the kitchen, I thought about what had just happened. Truthfully, waking up in my bed beside Dan Rucker at five after midnight made me feel like the Whore of Babylon. I hadn't had sex in four years, and the lack of it hadn't bothered me much. Most of the men I'd been with didn't know an orgasm from a mild spasm, so the minute I'd get excited they'd let go and then quit on me. Eventually I found my work more thrilling, and it lasted longer, so I focused on that.

Except, of course, for my fixation on Tony. I don't know what I'd have done if we'd ever made love and it hadn't turned out well. With no more fantasies in that department, I might have had to settle down in a rocking chair and knit afghans.

The good detective came back with juice for both of us, so I sat up, pulled the sheets up to my neck with one hand and took the drink with the other. He stretched out beside me, leaning back against the headboard. For a few minutes we sipped our juice without talking. It felt really weird, this man in my bed, a man I hardly knew and yet had shared something rather spectacular with.

Staring out at the now-dark ocean—anywhere but into those dreamy liquid eyes that were so much like Paul Newman's—I sipped my juice and said, "It's cooling off out there."

"The Santa Anas are still blowing, though," he said. "They make me crazy. Always have."

"Me, too. In fact, I wonder if that's what happened with Tony, Arnold and Craig. Some random killer crazed by the winds."

"Who just happens to hit people you're close to?" he said skeptically.

I sighed. "No, I guess not. But, look, you don't really think I killed them, do you?"

"You mean, have I changed my mind because we had sex?"

"No, I mean because you wouldn't have slept with me if you thought I was a killer."

"What makes you think that?"

"Oh, how the hell do I know!" I said irritably, grabbing my robe and getting out of bed. I crossed over to the bathroom and stared at myself in the mirror over the sink.

God, I looked awful. Between circles under my eyes from lack of sleep and the matted hair, I looked like an escapee from a Colombian prison.

I started to brush my teeth. "Let's forget about you for a minute," I said, spitting. "Does anyone in the LAPD think they could be gay crimes?"

"I'm not sure. Were all three of them gay?"

"Actually, none were, that I knew of. But those dildos..."

"I'm no expert," he said, coming up behind me and pulling the collar of my robe aside to plant a kiss on my bare shoulder, "but I've been told that women use 'help' of that sort as much as men. In fact, more."

I knew that, but hadn't thought about it in this case. "I just wondered...I guess because I've heard that the gay crowd in West Hollywood is into those and Tony used to hang out a lot in West Hollywood. But Arnold? And Craig?" I shook my head. "You must have talked to a few people by now. Neighbors in Tony's building, friends, maybe even enemies. Are there any you suspect?"

He looked at me in the mirror and raised his eyebrows.

"Other than me," I said.

He stood beside me and studied his beard, combing it with his fingers. "As for Craig Dinsmore, the LAPD doesn't have jurisdiction in El Segundo. We may know more about a connection between them when we get the DNA tests and evidence back from Price's apartment. If there is a connection, we may also be asked to assist with the El Segundo PD's investigation."

"There is evidence, then? Something you may be able to arrest someone with?"

He grinned and went back into the bedroom, pulling on his pants and shirt. "I think I've said enough. And with very little payoff."

"Sex with me wasn't a good payoff?" I called out.

He laughed. "I was actually hoping for more information from you about the three murder victims. But since you ask..." He turned at the door. "I didn't see sex with you as a payoff. I thought it was more like fun."

I smiled and pondered that after he left, slipping into a pair of flannel pajama trousers and a sleeveless tee. Then I lay on my bed and listened to the waves crash for a while, until I fell asleep.

It was not to be an easy night, however, and there was more than sweetness and light to come.

I was dreaming about Craig and Arnold and crushed foreheads, Tony and my lost income, when my doorbell rang. I woke with a start and looked at my bedside clock: 1:25 a.m. Not very many people knew where I lived, and none of them would come here at this hour without calling first.

Had the scruffy detective come back for more? Or had he come to arrest me this time?

I drew my silk Chinese robe around me and walked to the front door, turning on a couple of lights along the way. Looking through the peephole I saw a woman blinking in the bright glare of the motion-sensitive light above my front door.

She seemed disheveled and badly dressed, like

women I've seen on the streets, sleeping in cardboard boxes. I shivered in the cold dampness that blew in from the ocean through a crack I'd left open in a window. I couldn't imagine what this woman wanted with me, but was doubly cautious because I'd heard from a neighbor that someone had broken into her house recently, and she thought it was "one of the homeless."

The way she'd said the word *homeless* was so disparaging, though, I had tended to discount her story and wondered if she'd simply heard a dog in her trash that night. In her circle, a homeless person probably just made for a better story.

"What do you want?" I asked through the closed door.

"I just really need a place to sleep," the woman said. "Can I come in?"

There was something oddly familiar about her voice, but I couldn't place it.

"I'm sorry, I don't have any extra room," I said. It was all I could think of. "Have you tried the missions?"

"Please, Mary Beth. Let me at least talk to you."

It startled me that she'd called me by name. "Who is it?" I called out. "Who are you?"

The woman started to cry. "Mary Beth, it's me, Lindy. Lindy Lou."

Lindy Lou? Lindy Lou Trent, from high school? Was it possible?

I opened the door a crack but didn't take off the chain. "Stand over here where I can see you," I said.

She did, and I had to admit there was a slight resemblance, maybe in the nose and eyes, but that's where it ended. Lindy Louise Trent had been my best friend in high school—and at the same time my arch-rival. Lindy had the looks, the money, the personality, and all the boys. While I slaved away on the school paper, she became the most popular cheerleader, the homecoming queen, and the one who got the homecoming king—someone I'd had eyes for but was too shy to go after. Lindy just had to toss her long blond hair, stick out her chest, and boys would follow her anywhere.

"Is that really you?" I asked now, though I could see with every passing moment that it was indeed her. I just couldn't believe the change that had taken place. Several inches of the roots of her hair were dark, and the blond that was still left was dry and frizzled. Her eyes were wide and staring.

My look must have spoken volumes.

"Please let me come in and sit down, Mary Beth. I'll tell you everything, but I really just need to sit down."

She started to sway back and forth alarmingly. I opened the door the rest of the way and reached for her. Putting an arm around her waist, I drew her into the living room and helped her to sit on the couch. She was light as a feather, and shaking so much I had to hold on tight for fear of dropping her.

"Oh, God, that feels so good," she said, groaning. "Just to sit. You can't know, Mary Beth. I've been walking for miles."

She wore low-heeled, pointed-toe shoes from a good designer, but when she slipped them off I could see that she wore no stockings, and two of her toes were bleeding.

"For God's sake, Lindy, let me clean that up for you," I said. I went to the kitchen and spoke to her from across the breakfast bar as I ran water to get it warm. "Where did you walk from?"

"Downtown L.A.," she said, her voice shaking. "I mean, I started out there, but then I got a ride to Hollywood. I walked down Sunset Boulevard till I got to the ocean, and then I turned on Pacific Coast Highway and came here."

I added soap to the bowl of warm water, and a soft dishcloth. "I don't understand. How did you know where I live?"

"I read a piece about you in the Sunday *Los Angeles Times*. They said you lived in Malibu, and then I ran into someone who knew you. He gave me your address."

Warning bells went off. Lindy shows up after all these years—fifteen, to be exact, since high school—and tells me that someone who knows me gave her my address? Who would do that?

For that matter, what were the odds of her "running into someone" who even knew my address? I protect my personal information from almost everyone, as I don't want agitated authors showing up at my door in the middle of the night. That had happened frequently when I had my office in front of the little adobe house in Hollywood. I didn't want it to happen here.

"Who was this person?" I asked.

Lindy shook her head. "I can't remember. I met him at a bar in Hollywood and we got to talking. I told him I'd been wanting to get in touch with you, especially after I read that piece in the paper. Just to tell you how happy I am for your success, you know."

I'll bet, I thought suspiciously. Lindy had obviously met with bad times. How much was she here to hit me up for?

I knelt down and began to wash her feet with the soapy water, then dried them carefully. "Leave the shoes off," I said. "I'll get a Band-Aid, and I've got a pair of socks and some tennies you can have."

"Thank you, Mary Beth." Lindy looked around and added with an edge in her voice, "You're doing very well now, aren't you?"

I looked up at her and she flushed. "I didn't mean it to sound that way. It's just that everything's turned around for both of us. You were poor and now you're not. I was...well, I guess you heard that I married Roger Van Court."

I looked back at her feet and then stood, taking the bowl back to the kitchen. "Yes, I think I must have heard that," I said vaguely. "It's been a while. Ten years or so, right? Since you were married?"

"Since right after college," she said, nodding. "I can't believe I was that stupid."

I didn't know what to say to that. The last thing I wanted to talk about was Roger Van Court. In fact, my pulse was racing and my hands had begun to shake at the sound of his name. I took a Band-Aid out of a drawer and tried to bring my focus back to Lindy and her plight.

"What's happened, Lindy Lou?" I asked softly. I applied the Band-Aid, then sat beside her on the couch, my legs crossed in tailor-fashion. It was the way we used to sit when we were teenagers, chatting till all hours of the night. A familiar scene—yet not familiar at all. Now that I could see Lindy more closely, I realized that though we were the same age, thirty-three, she looked closer to fifty. Her face was lined, and I could see now the gray in her dark roots.

My heart broke a little. In high school, Lindy's long blond hair had always looked sexy and a bit out of control, as if she'd just stepped out of a beauty salon into a warm spring breeze. With her high cheekbones and perfectly proportioned body, she could have been a high-fashion model. I'm sure she would have been hugely successful.

Instead, she'd married Roger Van Court.

There was a time when I might have jealously wished Lindy would end up down and out, but that was only because I never believed, in my wildest dreams, that she would. Though I hadn't seen her in many years, in my mind she had always been the same Lindy Lou—vivacious, laughing, flirting easily yet harmlessly with the boys—someone I longed to be like but never was.

Suddenly, a part of me evaporated as the real Lindy Lou sat beside me. I had wanted to be like her, but even Lindy wasn't Lindy anymore. A strange thought flew through my mind. *Where did that leave me?*

Lindy covered her eyes and began to sob. "Roger threw me out," she said between loud hiccupping sounds. "Three weeks ago. He changed...he changed the locks...and I couldn't get back in. To get my things, you know? He closed my bank accounts, too, Mary Beth, and cut off all my credit cards. I didn't have a thing, and I couldn't bear to tell any of our friends or ask to borrow money. We live in Pacific Heights now, and people there can be so damn hoity-toity."

I almost smiled at her use of the old-fashioned phrase. Instead, I just shook my head and said, "I'm sorry. I didn't know."

"Well, it's one of the priciest areas in San Francisco, and none of our neighbors would understand in a million years. They'd have it all over town that I was out on the street."

"Lindy, I don't get it. What on earth possessed Roger? I thought the two of you must be happy."

Which wasn't at all the truth, but I couldn't bring myself to tell her that now.

"I thought we were happy at first," she said, rubbing her eyes. I reached over to an end table for Kleenex and handed her a couple. She dabbed at her eyes and cheeks, then turned her gaze on me. "Mary Beth, I'm *so...damn...tired.*" She broke down then, gulping back huge, loud sobs.

I took her in my arms and patted her on the back. *There but for the grace of God go I?* That was something my mother had always said when reminding herself of how blessed she was, just to have food on the table and a light to read by. My mother had worked long hours as a waitress to support herself after my father died, and there wasn't much to go around. When she died shortly after Pop, her loss left a hole in my heart that no one else has ever been able to fill.

Taking the Kleenex, I dabbed at Lindy's eyes and held her back from me a foot or so. "Why don't you take a nice relaxing bath while I put some food on," I said.

"You don't have to go to that trouble."

"Don't be silly. I haven't been shopping this week, but I'll make us some grilled-cheese sandwiches. How's that? Just like old times."

Her eyes said it all: *This is not like old times.*

She came with me to my bedroom, though, and took off her clothes while I drew a warm bath, putting a scented bubble gel in it. When the water was ready, I went back into the bedroom, where I'd left a terry-cloth robe for her to change into.

Lindy was sound asleep sideways on my bed, the turquoise satin spread wrapped around her like a cocoon. The robe I'd left for her was on the floor. A light breeze lifted the sheer white curtains at the French doors leading out to the deck.

I sighed and drained the bathwater, then got a sheet and blanket from the hall closet and stretched out on the couch in the living room.

I didn't sleep well. Scenes that I'd long ago stuffed back into the far recesses of my mind, hoping never to see them again, kept flitting across my closed eyes.

Roger Van Court.

The bastard.

But how much could I—or should I—tell Lindy?

Lindy had knocked on my door at about one-thirty, and it was just after three, according to the clock over my mantel, when I woke, thinking I'd heard a sound on the deck. I sat up carefully and walked to the double French doors, which were similar to the ones in the bedroom. There was no moon, and it was hard to see if anyone was out there. Even harder to hear, over the ocean's roar.

I cussed myself out for having left everything but the front door unlocked. I'd turned off the lights in the living room, though, and I figured that was good. A long time ago, I'd learned in a self-defense class that it's better to be in the dark in your house when an intruder is there. The intruder doesn't know your house, but you do, which means you can navigate around it better than he.

On the other hand, flashlights can be useful.

Crouching close to the floor, I made it to the kitchen and was just reaching for my one flashlight in the utility drawer when I heard the doors leading from the deck to the bedroom slam open against the inside wall. Lindy screamed.

I grabbed the flashlight and ran to the bedroom, shouting, "Get out! Get out of my house!"—also a technique I'd learned in a class. Take the intruder by surprise and get him off balance. Stupidly, however, I hadn't remembered to stand to the side of the doorway, in case whoever was in there had a gun.

That thought blew through my mind only an instant before bullets whistled by my ear. There was no loud pop, but more of a quiet thud, which told me the intruder must have a silencer on his gun. I dropped to the floor and set the flashlight as far away as my arm could reach. Then I flicked it on and pointed it in the direction of a large, dark figure by the bed. The figure was big enough to be a man, but he wore a ski mask and was dressed all in black. In the perimeter of the light, I saw that Lindy was leaning back against the headboard with my sheets pulled up to her neck, her eyes wide open and horrified.

As another bullet zinged into the floor next to my flashlight, I wiggled around about eighty degrees and reached for the baseball bat I kept by my closet. The intruder's eyes must have adjusted to the dark by now, however, because he was on me before I had a chance to grab it. An arm came around my neck, cutting off my breath, while a knee in my back kept my lower body from moving. I couldn't kick, couldn't fight back in any way. I started to see pinpoints in my eyes, little flashes of light that told me I'd soon be left in eternal darkness.

Just when I thought I was checking out for good, though, the crushing weight of my attacker slumped on top of me. A few seconds later he hoisted himself to his feet. Cursing in guttural tones, he ran past me into the living room, kicking the flashlight aside.

"Mary Beth!" Lindy yelled. "Are you all right?"

I rose quickly and saw that she was holding the bat, and that was what had made the intruder fall. Little Lindy Lou had smacked the bastard with it.

I held two fingers to my mouth. "Shh. I think he's still out there."

"Oh my God," she whispered. "Do you know who it is? Is it Roger?"

I gave her a sharp glance in the dim light. "I didn't see his face. Why do you think it was Roger?"

She didn't answer. At the sound of a loud crash in the living room, I said, "Never mind!"

I grabbed her hand and the robe she'd never put on and pulled her, naked, out onto the deck and down the wooden steps to the beach.

"Mary Beth, wait! Where are we going? I need my clothes!"

I ignored her cries and pulled her along the sand—away from the usual floodlights that people who live here shine on the waves—and into the shadows.

"Put this on," I said. "Hurry!"

While she shrugged into the dark blue robe, I kept tugging at her, wanting only to get as far away from the house as I could. I'll admit I was panicked. Never in my life had I been shot at, nor had I ever had a break-in. I didn't know where I was going, and was running on instinct, just trying to put distance between us and my house.

Then it hit me—*Patrick*. Patrick Llewellen, who used to be one of my authors, lived only five houses down from mine. I dragged the half-clothed Lindy up along the sand toward the modern three-story house. She kept stumbling, and I just hoped she could make it up the stairs.

Still pulling her, I raced up the stairs to Patrick's deck, with its potted palms that were set off by colorful Malibu lights.

Damn. I'd forgotten that he kept these lights on all night, every night, without fail. We should have gone around to the front.

But I hadn't had time to think clearly, and this would have to do. I began to pound on one of Patrick's three sliding glass doors, then the other and the other, hoping I could rouse him from his sleep. He didn't answer, though.

God, what if he'd stayed overnight somewhere? What if we couldn't get in?

"Mary Beth, look!"

I looked back to where Lindy pointed, and saw a dark figure running toward us on the beach. It was less than three houses away. I ran over to another door and pounded on it. "Patrick!" I yelled. "If you're there, let me in! It's Mary Beth!"

The wait seemed endless, but finally a light came on inside. A drape was pulled back. "For God's sake, Mary Beth, what are you doing here!" Patrick said as he slid open the door.

"Just let us in. Hurry!"

I didn't waste time on the niceties, pushing by him with Lindy in tow. Once inside, I pulled the door closed and locked it, yanking the drapes shut.

"Someone broke into my house," I said, struggling to catch my breath. "They shot at us. He's right out there, Patrick! I need to call the sheriff."

Patrick wasn't in pajamas, and didn't look as if he'd been sleeping. He wore a forest-green silk robe over his trousers and an open-collared white shirt, looking for all the world like a screen idol—except for his nose, which was a bit on the large side. I liked that about him; it kept him from looking too pretty.

His jaw, however, had dropped in shock. "I can't believe it! Who on earth would do that?"

He glanced at Lindy.

"She's a friend," I said, still gasping. "Could

you—look, it's too bright in here.'' The light was coming from a Tiffany lamp next to a leather armchair. I leaned over and turned it off. There was only a dim glow left from the kitchen, on the other side of his dining room.

"Patrick, I'm truly sorry. I know this is an imposition. But I need to call the sheriff. While I'm doing that, could you fix Lindy some tea? Anything, really. I think she's in shock.''

"I'll put a shot of bourbon in it,'' he said, nodding. "And the phone's over here. Next to the light you just turned off.'' He shook his head. "You always were the type to take over.''

"Sorry. But before you go, are your doors all locked?''

"Yes. And, Mary Beth, I'm sorry it took me so long to get to the door. I was downstairs in the cave, working.''

Patrick's "cave,'' I'd learned years ago, was a dark enclosed room in the basement—the only place he could write in this house, as the magnificent views from every other room distracted him.

I picked up the phone and punched in 911. My breath had slowed a bit, but my side hurt, and Lindy sat huddled in a chair, her head down, twisting her hands. She was breathing heavily, and I remembered that she'd had a long walk earlier to get to my place. The poor thing must be totaled.

When the dispatcher answered, I told her what had happened, and asked that a car come around and check the house out before my friend and I went back there. She said they'd send someone right away, and we should wait where we were until the sheriff's deputy came to tell us it was safe to go back.

Hanging up, I walked to the sliding glass door and pulled back the heavy brocade drapes a crack, to see if anyone was out there. The outside lights would have revealed anyone on the deck, and a quick glance showed that it was empty. I couldn't tell about the beach.

I carefully put the drape back in place and turned on the lamp again, looking now at Lindy. I'd just heard a teakettle whistle, and knew Patrick would be back with tea soon. Before he returned, I wanted to find out a few things from my old friend Lindy Lou.

"Why did you think that might be Roger?" I demanded, standing over her with my arms crossed, in no mood to be gentle about this.

"I don't know," she said, shivering, her teeth chattering. "I guess I've been so afraid of him for so long, that's the first thing that came to my mind."

"Why have you been afraid of Roger?" I asked.

"Mary Beth, I told you what he did! He threw me out on the street with absolutely nothing. Why wouldn't I be afraid of what he might do next?"

I didn't say anything, but when she'd used the words *afraid for so long*, I'd gotten the distinct impression she might have been abused by Roger over the course of their marriage. I had good cause to wonder about that.

I reached for a faux-fur throw cover on Patrick's sofa and put it over Lindy. "Here, this should warm you up."

Patrick came in with our tea then, and there was no more time to talk confidentially. Besides the tea tray, he carried a cashmere sweater, and after setting the tray down he placed it around my shoulders, tying the sleeves under my neck.

"Thanks," I said, smiling a bit awkwardly. It seemed so strange to be taken care of.

I watched as he took a cup of tea over to Lindy. She smiled, said, "Thank you," in a small voice like a little girl's, and sipped the tea. There was a large stone fireplace on one wall, and Patrick went over to it and clicked a switch. The gas fire blazed up around fake logs. I imagined I could already feel the heat from it.

Patrick brushed both hands together as if he'd just stirred the logs with a poker. Coming back, he sat in a chair across from me and sighed. "There, that's better, isn't it?"

He put his feet up on an ottoman, and I saw that he wasn't wearing shoes, just argyle socks, which made me smile. I'd forgotten about Patrick's love for argyle socks.

Glancing over at Lindy, I saw that she'd set her teacup on the table beside her and seemed fast asleep. Good. She must really need to rest.

Leaning back in the chair with my cup, I said, ''I can't thank you enough for letting us in, Patrick. You know, I haven't been sure you'd still want to talk to me.''

One essential facet of being a literary agent—at least, for me—is cheering on my authors, helping them to believe they can succeed. A lot of good writers go down the drain after one or two rejection letters, and never write again. They need to learn to let the rejections roll off their backs and just keep going.

In Patrick's case, however, it was I who had rejected his latest book several months ago, not an editor. It was a dark book with serial rapes in it—too dark for me. I'd reached a financial point where I could turn down manuscripts that bothered me personally, and though I hated to let Patrick go, he had insisted on writing *In Peril*. We had clearly reached an impasse, and I finally had to let him go.

Patrick had been bitter at first, but then I'd heard that he was with another agent and his book was being picked up for almost seven figures. He'd been seen around town, dining in all the best restaurants with a smile on his face.

Now that I'd lost Tony and Craig, I almost wished I had gotten Patrick that deal. But oh well. Water under the bridge.

''Don't be silly, Mary Beth,'' he said now. ''Of course I still want to talk to you. I'll admit I was pretty upset at first, but that's just because I felt set adrift without a canoe. And now things are going really great. Did you hear that I'm with Nolan-Frey?''

''As a matter of fact, I did. They're quite a big agency, on a level now with CAA. And I heard that they got you a great deal.''

''Yes, well, it's... Maybe I shouldn't tell you this, but it's still in the negotiation phase, nothing certain. It's going well, though.''

Agencies like Nolan-Frey took on someone on the basis of liking their work, then helped them to polish and even rewrite it if they thought that was necessary. Like a book doctor, except that they didn't charge until after the book was sold, hopefully with a movie option. Usually they got significant options, with big money and stars attached, while the ordinary writer going through an agent who wasn't as top-flight might get only two thousand five hundred for the option, and the movie would never be made. The paybacks are often better, then, with the big agencies like CAA and Nolan-Frey, but they're harder for an author to get into. I was guessing they had taken on Patrick partly for his talent, and partly because I was his former agent.

Not that Patrick's books didn't pull in good numbers. But at the time he left me, he was more or less starting out fresh again after three years with no book out, which meant that in his genre, which was mysteries, Nolan-Frey might have had a hard time selling him again to a publisher.

''I heard they got you a high six figures,'' I said.

"I'm so happy for you, Patrick. I really am. And I'm sorry things turned out for us the way they did."

He made a doleful face. "Me, too. I miss you, Mary Beth. But I understood about the book. When you liked my work, you were the best agent in the world for me, and if you just couldn't handle that last one, well…" He shrugged. "I guess it was for the best that we both moved on."

"I'm sure you're right. And as I said, I'm happy that you're with someone who's doing well for you."

"So if my book is made into a billion-dollar movie, you won't be sorry for missing out?" he asked with a grin.

"Sorry as all get out!" I laughed. "But I'll be here with bells on at your celebration party." Raising an eyebrow, I added, "You will invite me, won't you?"

"Mary Beth, you will be first on my list. I'll never forget what you've done for me. In fact—I've been wondering. Would you like to go to dinner sometime?"

At my obvious surprise, he grinned. "It could be like old times. Old, *old* times. Before business got in the way. And then there was Tony…I mean, you and he seemed to have something going."

"Not really," I said. "Tony and I were friends. You've heard what happened?"

"It was on the evening news yesterday. About Arnold, too. What a shock."

"I didn't get a chance to catch the news. Was there anything about Craig?"

"Craig Dinsmore? No." His eyes widened. "Has something happened to him?"

"I found him dead in his motel room today. Well, yesterday, now. In the afternoon."

"My God, Mary Beth! It sounds like *Who's Killing the Great Chefs of*—except in this case it's your, well, you know...authors." He frowned. "Do I need to hire a bodyguard?"

"I doubt it," I said dryly. "Since you're no longer with me, I'd say you're safe. You might want to hear what the sheriff thinks, though."

He was silent and seemed to be pondering the possible threat to his own life. The truth was, until he said it, I hadn't really looked at it that way yet—that someone was killing off my authors. After all, Arnold had been murdered as well, and he was just my ex.

Then I remembered that I'd negotiated a deal for Arnold years ago, for one of his toy-creations books. That qualified me as his agent, as well.

But the idea was preposterous. Who would be out to get my authors? Or me? No, there was something else going on. I was sure of it.

Lindy, who had been dozing in her chair, the tea and bourbon growing cold on the table beside her, stirred. Sitting up like a shot, she gazed wildly around her. "What? Where—where am I?"

The faux-mink throw slipped to the floor, and I

went over to her and put it back in her lap. "Here, cover up. We're at the house of a friend of mine, remember? Patrick Llewellen. He used to be one of my authors, and we're waiting for the sheriff to come and tell us it's safe to go back to my house."

Lindy looked toward the sliding glass door we'd come through. "What if—what if whoever chased us down the beach is out there right now? What if he's just waiting for us to come out?"

"I saw a reflection of flashing red lights going by in front," I said. "I'm sure the sheriff's deputies are already there, and they'll check out the beach, too. In fact, I'll ask one of the officers to escort us back to my house."

When she didn't seem at all mollified, I said, "Would you like me to warm your tea? There's bourbon in it. It'll take off the edge."

"I noticed," she said, rolling her eyes. "Thank you, Mary Beth. I don't know what I've had done without you tonight."

Again, her words seemed fraught with another meaning, but I let it pass for the moment.

I left her with Patrick and went to the kitchen, while he sat on an ottoman in front of her, talking in low, soothing tones. I'd almost forgotten that about Patrick—how comforting he could be in a pinch. It was one of the things I'd lost when we split. That, and the sex—which, come to think of it, hadn't been nearly as bad as I'd tried to remember it.

* * *

The deputies came finally and spoke to us in Patrick's living room. First, they wanted to know who he was and how we'd come to end up here. I explained, and they moved on to the search of my house.

"We didn't find the intruder," one of the deputies said. "Your front door was wide-open, though. Did you leave it that way?"

I shook my head. "He went from the bedroom into the living room, and we ran out on the deck through the bedroom door, then along the beach. When we first got here we saw someone following us, though, about three houses away."

"And you say he shot at you?"

"Yes, in the bedroom. I ran in there when I heard my friend scream."

The cop who was asking questions looked at the other one. "Fits what we found at the scene," he said. Turning to me, he added, "You were lucky."

I felt a chill, remembering the displaced air as the bullets whizzed by my ear.

"We've checked the road and the beach," he continued, "and we couldn't find anyone. At least, anyone who shouldn't be here. We'll walk you back to your house, though, and look inside once more before we go."

"Thanks," I said, turning to Lindy. "Ready?"

She stood and came close to me, as if afraid to get too far away. I turned to Patrick and handed him the throw cover. Half smiling, I said, "Well, good night, then…not that it hasn't been lovely."

"I'll call you," he said, walking us to the door with an arm around my shoulders.

It took me a moment. "Oh, you mean dinner. Sure. Call me. It'll be fun."

The deputies left my house and I got Lindy settled in bed just in time to see the sky lighten up over the ocean. I checked to be sure the front door and windows were locked, then took a shower. After that I made some dark Sumatran coffee and took a cup out onto the deck, along with an old newspaper. My Adirondack chair was dripping with sweat, as usual, from a light mist, and I put the newspaper on it to keep my jeans dry. Over my clean tee, I'd pulled on a sweatshirt with a hood because the air was chilly. It was June, though, and by the time ten o'clock arrived the sun would be high and warm.

Living at the beach was something I'd always dreamed of. I didn't kid myself, though. With Tony gone, and with Craig's new contract a question mark, I might not be able to afford a house in Malibu and an office in a Century City high-rise. Oh, I'd do okay, because I'd made investments and saved, getting out of the worst stocks before they crashed. And there would still be commissions from Tony's royalties. Maybe more than ever, now that he'd been murdered.

Funny how dead writers and artists sell better after

they've passed on. It's as if the readers want to get into their heads, to figure out who they were and why they died. In the case of fiction writers, though, that's a misconception. Fiction usually contains bits and pieces of the writer, the writer's mother and father, the writer's neighbor, some guy the writer met while walking his dog, and umpteen characters he or she may have seen on television and in the movies. It would be difficult for an author to write about him or herself every time, as it's said that there are only thirty-six plots that exist in the entire world. The trick is to tell them differently and more originally each time. For that, you need a lot of people in your head.

Sometimes I wonder how they do it. Especially the ones who write about serial killers. How do they keep all that horror in their minds for the length of a manuscript, and not become affected by it?

As for Tony and my commissions on his royalties, I figured that those, along with my other authors commissions, would hold me for a while. Real estate around L.A., however, especially here at the beach, was out of sight. The mortgage payments on this house and the office in Century City would quickly eat up whatever monies the near future would bring in.

Well, that was the life of an agent, as well as just about everyone else in the entertainment and literary business in L.A. Up, down. Up, down. It was like riding a pogo stick.

That, or wearing a little pendant with cocaine in it. I know several who do that, and inevitably, they end up cheating their clients and keeping their money. They cash authors' royalty checks from overseas without telling their clients that they've come, and with this they pay for their drugs and their high-flying lives. Until someone catches them out and sues. Then they lose all their clients, several of whom have come to me with stories of having been betrayed that way. It takes a while for them to trust anyone after that, but some of the best authors around have come from that kind of situation and have stuck with me now for years.

There must be someone in that group, I thought. Someone with a potential best-seller sitting on his or her desk right now. I'd have to go over my list of authors and their books in progress, see what I could turn up, and what project might be worth putting my own personal energy into. It might not be so bad, working with an author again to pull a book into shape...page by inept page.

Oh, God. Save me.

I sighed and drank the fast-cooling coffee, turning my thoughts to Lindy and the night before. Had the intruder been Roger? The main reason I'd taken Lindy in was because I knew something about Roger that she didn't, and I'd felt sorry for her. But now what did I do with her?

Lindy answered that question herself, standing at the door with a coffee cup in her hand. "I'll be leaving soon," she said. "I just wanted to talk to you first."

"Come, sit down," I said, patting the seat of the chair next to me. "Here, it's wet. Let me put some of this newspaper on it."

I spread out a few dry pages, and Lindy plunked down on the chair with a tired sigh. Leaning her head back, she closed her eyes. "I feel so helpless. I don't know why I came here, Mary Beth. I just didn't know where else to go, and I felt like I was losing it. For good, I mean. I guess I've really been losing it for years."

"Do you want to tell me why Roger threw you out?" I asked.

She looked at me briefly, then glanced away. "It's not a pretty story."

"Something you did that angered him?" I asked. "Another man?"

"Oh, God, no. I've got enough to handle at home without another man in my life."

She appeared to be thinking over whether to tell me about it. Finally she said, "I found out something about Roger. Something really bad." She gave a bitter laugh. "Some marriage, huh? The homecoming queen and king, the perfect match. Most likely to succeed."

I didn't respond, but wondered how much I should say. I thought I knew what Lindy had found out about Roger. Not the details, of course, but in general. If I turned out to be wrong, though, I'd only be opening a hornet's nest.

Roger Van Court was someone I had loved from afar in high school. He was the rich kid in class—not that I was impressed by that, or the fact that he was captain of the football team. If anything, I saw those aspects of Roger as a cliché. His good looks were something else, though. He had the cutest dimple in his left cheek, and when he smiled it seemed like the sun came out. Who wouldn't want him, at the age of sixteen when flaws are never seen or even believed in?

I was horribly shy, however, and I always had my nose in a book. As for Roger, even before Lindy there was usually some gorgeous girl with him. When Lindy started going steady with him, I felt envious, of course. But I also lived vicariously through her. She would tell me all about their dates, and how wonderful he was, and how well he treated her. I could only hope that someday I'd have someone like that.

Be careful what you ask for, they say. Seven years ago, Roger had turned up at my storefront office in Hollywood. It was late at night and raining hard. I was finishing up some work but the office was closed, the blinds down. That didn't stop Roger. He knocked insistently on the door until I couldn't ignore the knock any longer. I peeked out cautiously through the blinds, as it wasn't the greatest of neighborhoods there. When I saw it was Roger, I was so surprised, I opened the door without thinking. He stepped in, shaking the rain off his coat and stamping his feet on my rug. After a few of the usual greetings—"It's been so long…! But you still look good…" and "Thanks, so do you"—he told me he wanted to talk about Lindy, that things weren't going well. The fact that he'd come to me about this was a shock, as I hadn't heard from either him or Lindy since high-school graduation.

It didn't take me long to figure out that Roger had been drinking. No sooner was he inside than he spotted the small bar I'd made out of an old, distressed buffet against one wall. I always kept a few bottles of wine and champagne there to celebrate with authors I'd gotten a good deal for.

Well, they say a drunk can smell liquor a state away. There was a bottle of Cabernet on the bar, which I'd opened a couple of days before when Mary Nance's latest cookbook was picked up for a high five figures. Roger spotted the wine immediately and uncorked it, pouring himself a large water-glass full. He held the bottle up and looked at me. "Would you like some?"

That was Roger, all right. The boy I'd had the hots for in high school, until eventually—through Lindy's increasingly eye-opening stories about him—I'd come to see how arrogant he could be. Offering me my own wine, no less.

I shook my head and reached into my bottom drawer where I kept a half dozen or so bottles of mineral water handy. I put a bottle on my desk and opened it, but didn't drink right away. Roger gulped the wine down as if he were dying of thirst, and then poured another glass. When that was gone, he opened another bottle without asking, bringing it and the tumbler over to the chair across from my desk.

As he drank, he talked on and on. I said nothing, just sat and listened, trying to figure out how I was going to get him to leave. I was getting nervous, wondering what on earth he was really doing here. Something—an odd shift of energy in the room now—didn't feel right. I thought about calling someone, a friend, and saying I'd be "late for our date, because Roger Van Court, an old acquaintance from San Francisco, had dropped in unexpectedly." That would let Roger know that someone else was aware he was here—in case anything happened.

But I discarded that idea as being silly and paranoid. I'd forgotten how important it is to listen to one's instincts, the little voice that screams, "Run!" when logic argues, "Don't be silly, there isn't anything to run from."

Roger set the wine bottle beside him on the floor. He sighed, and kept on talking—about living on a trust from his father's business empire, Courtland Pharmaceuticals; about Lindy having changed; about how happy they used to be, and how awful it was now. After the third glass of wine he began to slide down a bit in the leather chair. It was a small office, all I could afford back then, and the chair wasn't my taste. I'd picked it up at the Salvation Army store, and it was so old it was shiny and slick. I decided suddenly that if I was ever going to get him out of there, I'd better do it soon before he slid right off and passed out on my floor.

I remember all this now because I still sometimes try to convince myself that since Roger was so drunk, it made sense for me to think he was harmless.

"Why are you here?" I asked finally. "Roger, what do you want?"

He looked at me with that old twinkle in his eye that every girl in school had been prey to. The dimple moved and the teeth flashed. He was tall and had basically the same good looks. I'd noted that his face was a bit puffy, though, and he looked heavier, as if his football muscles had gone slack since high school.

I blinked as he said, "The truth, Mary Beth, is that I just can't get you out of my mind." He leaned forward earnestly. "I've been in L.A. for three days, and all I can think of is you. Knowing you were here, not all that far away…" He sighed.

I was so shocked, I didn't know how to answer that, so I picked up my bottle of water, took a deep swallow from it and just listened. Not that I had any choice in the matter. Roger was bent on delivering a monologue, his words slurring and that once-charming smile sagging from the alcohol like the skin of a sharpei dog.

"I always had an eye for you, you know," he went on, his voice a parody of seduction. "Even when I was dating Lindy. It could have been you, Mary Beth. You could have been my homecoming queen."

"Wow," I said.

The sarcasm in my tone wasn't lost on him. The gray eyes turned cold, and his voice took on a chill.

"Don't pretend you wouldn't have loved that." His arms were resting on the arm of the chair, and now one of his hands closed into a fist.

"Oh, hey," I said, "don't misunderstand me. It would've been the answer to a prayer back then."

I should have stopped with that, but couldn't help adding, "And just think—we could have been married. I could have had Lindy's life right now, with you out of town, drunk, and flirting with her old best friend. Like I said—wow."

If looks could kill, I'd have been dead in an instant.

"It's not my fault Lindy turned out the way she did!" he said angrily. "She's so damn empty-headed. Hell, she thinks she's still a cheerleader. Not that she looks like one, she's let herself go so much."

He looked at me through eyes that were already glazed. "You, on the other hand, Mary Beth—you're still a knockout."

When I couldn't hide my surprise, he said, "You always were, you know. Quiet as a mouse, but so pretty the guys were afraid to ask you out. That gorgeous red hair down to your waist, and those sexy green eyes…'' He shook his head. ''You always had a good mind, too. You were open to things you didn't understand. You didn't criticize people just because they had new ideas. Not like Lindy.''

If he was trying to impress me, he'd sure taken the wrong tack. Lindy and I might not have seen each other in eight years, but in high school we had always stuck together, no matter what. It was an unspoken vow we'd made, probably because I was able to keep her on balance, while she provided my life with the excitement I wasn't able to generate for myself.

I wasn't about to join her husband now in trashing her.

Not only that, but I was truly stunned about this declaration of interest in me. I'd long ago gotten over Roger Van Court, and to me he seemed now like every other Peter Pan man without a life—no real job, living on a trust fund, never growing up. Like so many actor-, entertainer- and screenwriter-wannabes in L.A. Except that they seldom had trusts, but worked at Johnny Rocket's hamburger joint as singing waiters.

I truly considered myself lucky for having escaped Roger Van Court.

''Look,'' I said. ''It's been years since high school. I've gotten over those kinds of crushes, and I've moved on. Surely if you and Lindy are having problems, you could have your pick of women. Why on earth would you want me?''

I could think of only one reason—that I had rejected him once, when he'd flirted with me behind Lindy's back. It was at a Valentine's Day dance in our senior year, and at first I thought he was playing a joke on me. But we were dancing, and when his hand slid over my breast I realized he meant to kiss me—right there, where Lindy might see.

I was inexperienced, and horrified that he was being disloyal. I yanked away and ran outside, to the shadow of trees beyond the floodlights of the parking lot. Sitting on the ground shaking, I didn't even realize that grass stains were seeping into my second-hand gown. Finally I left the dance and went home, scrubbing those stains off in the bathroom sink as if they were blood.

All I could think was, *What if Lindy had seen what he'd done? How could he hurt her that way?*

Roger was distant to me from that day on. He was always civil enough when we were around Lindy, but his eyes were cold when they were turned on me.

Boys like Roger, I thought, sitting in my office some eight years later, never get over a rejection like that. Or they brush it off and forget about it entirely. Denying it happened.

Which had it been with Roger?

It didn't take long to find out. Roger stood and came around my desk, walking unsteadily. The wine in his glass splashed out and fell to the floor, staining my worn gray carpet. Lazily, he set the glass on my desk. I tried to move my chair back and away before he reached me, but quick as a flash his hands were on the arms of the chair, blocking me in.

I tried to laugh to defuse the situation. "Stop! Stop this, Roger! This is crazy!"

His answer was to lean down toward my lips and brush them lightly with his. How many times in high school would that have been my dream come true? Now, however, I was revolted by the smell of alcohol on his breath, and the arrogant way he reached for my breast. With one of his hands off the chair arm I pushed past him with all my strength and made it off the chair and around my desk, putting it between us.

Roger laughed as if I were simply being coy, or a skittish colt that needed breaking. I ran for the door, but before I could open it he was on me, his breath hot and reeking at the back of my neck.

"C'mon, Mary Beth, you know you want it."

I whirled around to face him, smiled deliberately and stomped one of my sharp heels on his foot, as hard as I could.

"You bitch!" he yelled, his face turning a deep red. He began to double over from the pain, and I brought both hands up, punching him with my fists under the chin. When he whipped up and backward from the pain, I kneed him in the groin.

I was tired from the late hour and the day's work,

though, and my movements lacked strength. He ignored the hit to the groin as if it were a mere feather, and when I raised my leg for another try he grabbed it. Toppling me to the floor, he came down fast on me. His heavy weight was brutal and smothering. I tried with everything in me to fight him off, but he had me pinned, and I couldn't move. I felt his knee forcing my legs apart, and one hand held both my wrists above my head while the other ripped my blouse and yanked my skirt up. I tried to scream, but his mouth covered mine and I could barely breathe. It was not a kiss, but a bruising assertion of power. His hands were all over my body, and everywhere he touched there was pain.

When it was over, I lay on the floor, numb. I sensed when he got off me but it was something far away, not having to do with me at all. Like one of those near-death experiences they talk about, where the patient, in her mind, is floating above the operating table, looking down on herself—a self who is completely detached emotionally and physically from what's going on.

I heard Roger stumble out the door—in fact, felt the door as he yanked it open and it hit me on the hip. I started to come back, then, and curled into a fetal position, sobbing. It wasn't until the sun came up that I was able to get up, go into the bathroom and shower.

Part of me knew I should have gone to a rape crisis center and the police. I should have made a report. The other part of me—the one that won out—didn't want to remember it, think about it, or have to relive it ever again.

Life is not that kind, however. I spent four months that year supposedly "in New York City, making contacts." That was the official release. In reality, I'd closed my agency in L.A. temporarily while my body grew and I delivered, in Sacramento, a beautiful baby girl.

I had always dreamed of having a baby, but the timing was never right and the right man was never there. In this case I was terrified that if I kept my baby girl, Roger would hear of it somehow. He would do the math, figure she was his, and in all likelihood try to take her away—if only out of a need to assert power. I had gathered from his conversation that night that he had more money than he'd ever need or could use. I also knew that there would always be the Van Court family and its lawyers behind him, getting him out of scrapes as they had in high school.

As for me, I had very few assets. I couldn't live with the thought that Roger might use that to gain custody, and that my baby might end up with a man like that for a father. At the very least, if he fought for joint custody, I would have to share her with him. I could never do that to my child. Have her spending weekends and holidays at the home of an alcoholic rapist? Just the thought of it gave me chills.

Six weeks after the rape, a private detective came

to my house with an offer from Roger: He would pay me one million dollars not to ever tell anyone what had happened.

I was stunned. And tempted. A million dollars would be nothing to Roger, but my house was old, in a bad neighborhood, and my office wasn't much more than a storefront. I had dreams I wanted to put into effect, and a million dollars would help me do just that.

When it came down to it, though, I couldn't pay the price for taking money from Roger. He would want some kind of control over me besides the money. And he'd find out I was pregnant.

At first, I tried to think of ways to make the pregnancy work—like a marriage of convenience to someone else, then pretending to the world that my baby was his. There was no one in my life, though, no one responsible and settled. No one I could trust to do that for me.

Briefly, I'd thought of Patrick Llewellen. The little adobe house in Hollywood was a duplex, and Patrick lived next to me then, which is how we met. He and I had become friends—and more. Eventually I'd ended up representing him. The problem with asking Patrick to front for me, as my baby's father, was that I just never felt I knew the *real* Patrick, or that I could trust him with the fact that I was pregnant. He seemed too much of a flirt, a playboy. There was also something about Patrick that always seemed hidden; something that lent him a mysterious air.

So I'd gone away to have my baby, and then, though it broke my heart, I gave her up for adoption. The social worker assured me she was going to a good home, with loving parents who would treat her as if they'd given birth to her themselves. I got to hold her only once, minutes after she was born. She had a mark the size of a dime on her neck that I worried about. The nurse said it was a birthmark called a "port-wine stain" and reassured me that it would fade away in time. I began to cry then and asked her if my baby had gotten that because I'd done something wrong. I'll never forget what she did. She put my baby in her little nursery bed and held me in her arms, patting my back. She didn't tell me not to feel bad that I was giving up my child, for which I was grateful. Of course I'd feel bad, she said—there was no way out of that. Instead, she kept murmuring, "It'll get easier with time. Just like your baby's birthmark, it'll fade away in time." I thought she was an angel, and that surely I didn't deserve her, but I thanked God for putting her there by my side.

When I left the hospital I cried for two days straight before I had the strength to leave the motel in Sacramento and drive back to L.A. There was a lot of time to think on that drive home, and the one thing uppermost in my mind was that I'd never survive the loss of my child if I couldn't somehow put her out of my mind. Finally, I made the decision to throw myself even more into my work. I swore I would do whatever it took to build *Mary Beth Conahan* into a world-class literary agency.

The thought didn't escape me, though, on that long, lonely stretch near Bakersfield, that I'd made my agency "my baby."

My attention jumped back to Lindy when she asked, "Mary Beth, where did you go?"

"Hmm? Oh, sorry. I was just thinking of things," I improvised. "Trying to figure out what's going on with my authors and now us. You don't really think Roger tried to kill us last night, do you? I mean, why would he?"

Lindy got up slowly, as if every muscle in her body hurt, and walked over to the railing. She looked frail, even old. It was as if she'd lived many more years than I, by some strange warp in time. Staring out at the ocean, she said. "You know, don't you, that Roger's family owns a pharmaceutical company?"

"Of course. Courtland Pharmaceuticals, isn't it? I used to sort of poke fun at that when we were in school. Court-*Land*. Surrounded by sky-high fences with guards at the gate. Like it was a country unto itself."

"That's exactly what they had in mind," Lindy said bitterly. "Roger's father has always felt he had some…I don't know, Divine right to do whatever he wanted, whether with business or family. The man is a tyrant. He's dying now, though."

"Really? He must be rather young still. In his early sixties? What's wrong with him?"

She turned to me, her mouth curving in a cold smile. "A brain tumor. He had surgery years ago, and they thought it went away. Fortunately, it came back."

"Fortunately?"

"I hate that man. I hope he dies, Mary Beth. I really hope he dies."

"Lindy! You can't mean that!" But I wondered. Did the apple not fall far from the tree, in terms of violence? "Has he done something to you? Something personal, I mean, since you married Roger?

"Not to…" She paused. "No."

I hesitated, but somehow I knew that if I didn't push, she'd never get it out. "Lindy, you've got to tell me what's going on. Maybe I can help."

She sighed and sat in the chair next to me again, drawing her knees up and encircling them with her arms, as if to warm herself. "It's ugly, Mary Beth. I found out something he was doing. Him and Roger. Something so awful…" Tears filled her eyes.

"Having to do with pharmaceuticals?" I asked.

"I…yes."

She still wasn't coming out with it. "Tell me," I said firmly.

Tears slipped onto her cheeks and she wiped them away with the back of her hand. "If I do, you can't tell a soul. Promise?"

"I…okay, yes, I promise."

"The thing is, I confronted Roger and threatened to go to the police. He said if I ever told anyone, he'd take Jade away somewhere and I'd never see her again."

"Jade?"

"My baby." Lindy's voice shook. "She's the most beautiful child in the world, Mary Beth. She deserves—" Lindy shook her head, burying her face in her hands. "She deserves a better mother than me."

"Oh, Lindy, you have a baby? But I don't understand. Have you done something—"

"Not me, no. It's Roger. But dammit, Mary Beth, I should stop him, and I don't know how. I can't risk him taking my baby away."

For the first time, I was genuinely frightened for her. This was just the kind of threat I would have expected from Roger if I'd let him know I'd had his child and then he'd fought me for custody.

"Look, start at the beginning. What exactly is Roger doing? And why do you hate his father so much?"

She took a deep breath, and sat straight, as if stiffening her spine. "I'm not sure I know when it really all started, Mary Beth. But for the past year or so, Jade hasn't been well. She has chronic infections, and last year her pediatrician said her immune system was compromised. She didn't know why, but she was set to do more tests. Before Jade could have them, though, Roger canceled the appointment and insisted on changing to another doctor. One recommended by his father.''

''Do you know why?''

''I didn't at first. So when Roger insisted on using a new drug on Jade—something the research scientists at Courtland came up with—and the new doctor agreed, I thought it must be all right. In fact, I was relieved when I learned that Roger and his father thought they'd found the so-called 'magic bullet' everyone's been looking for. Do you know what that is?''

''I have some vague knowledge of it. Apparently, medical research scientists have spent years looking for a drug or vaccine that will cure or prevent all diseases, and with no side effects. Something that'll rid the world of cancer, heart disease, everything down to the common cold.''

Lindy nodded. ''The one Courtland's calling a magic bullet is a drug that supposedly strengthens the immune system to a point where disease and viruses can't take hold. Especially the ones antibiotics don't work on anymore. They say it can even protect people from chemical weapons and biowarfare.''

''But that sounds fantastic,'' I said. ''If Roger and his father have discovered that, surely it must be good for your baby? Not to mention for the world?''

She shook her head. ''I found out that the only human testing Roger and his father ever did was in secret, and only on homeless people they paid to be guinea pigs. I confronted Roger with this and asked him why they hadn't done the usual type of clinical testing, the kind they always do before they send a drug to the FDA for approval. After all, Roger is president of Courtland now. He's the one who should be making sure this new drug was tested properly.''

"And?"

"And he said the FDA takes too long, and it could be years before they approve the drug. He said Jade could be really sick by then, if not worse, and that a really bad infection could kill her at any time. He said we couldn't afford to wait that long."

I thought back to information I'd read in a book by one of my authors, about the way drugs are approved—or not approved—by the FDA. A lot of it was about the agency's sluggishness in approving drugs, and the people who die while waiting for them.

"I hate to play devil's advocate," I said, "but I think I can almost understand what Roger is talking about. There's just one hitch. Courtland won't be able to sell the drug on the open market until the FDA approves it. Is Roger planning to use it only on Jade until then?"

"God, no! That's the other thing. He's already selling it to countries that don't have such stringent rules about pharmaceuticals. And you'll never guess who's paying the most for it."

"Who?"

"Some Middle Eastern countries. I'm not sure

which, but Roger sells the drug to pharmaceutical companies, and they sell it to their military. It's supposed to make them immune to smallpox, anthrax, and all those biological and chemical weapons you hear about. That way they think they can use those weapons on us in a war, but they won't be hurt by them.''

''My God. Lindy, you're not seriously telling me that Roger has his hands on something that could keep our armed forces and our entire population safe from bioterrorism, and he isn't rushing to get it through the FDA? So that *we* can be protected? Instead, he's raking in bucks by selling it to countries who've declared themselves our enemy?''

''It gets worse,'' Lindy said. ''Apparently, the first batches of BZT-21—the ones Roger tested on the homeless—were defective. The drug worked the way it should on some people, but on most of them it worked in reverse, weakening their immune systems instead of strengthening them. You know those stories in the news about that latest mystery illness that's been killing Middle Eastern troops? So far, they haven't linked that illness to the first batch of BZT-21. But Roger and his father are worried that it's only a matter of time.''

''Why would they think there's a link?'' I asked.

''Like I said, it gets worse.'' Her voice began to shake more, and I could barely hear her. ''Three-quarters of those homeless people died, Mary Beth. The rest ended up with illnesses they hadn't had before the trials, and they're either very ill now, or have already died, too.''

I was speechless, I was so shocked.

''But nobody will ever know,'' Lindy said, her voice filling with tears, ''because none of their families knew where they were, anyway. And you know what Roger did to cover up what had happened to them? He paid a fortune to have them all cremated, without any records being kept.''

''My God! And this is the drug he's using on Jade?''

''He said it wasn't, and that he's using something new on her now. BZT-22, they're calling it, and it's supposed to be safe. But a few weeks ago there was blood in Jade's urine. Roger claims that it's a normal side effect. But Mary Beth, there aren't supposed to be *any* side effects, let alone blood in the urine. I'm really worried.''

''What does her doctor say?''

''That's the other thing. I don't trust the one Roger's father recommended, and he wouldn't let me take Jade to her old pediatrician. The thing is, Mary Beth, I think he's making her sicker than she was, and he can't afford to have anyone find out.''

''And you've known this how long?'' I said. ''A few weeks? Lindy, I can't believe you haven't done anything about it! You haven't gone to the police and had Roger locked up?''

She turned on me angrily. ''Of course not! He'd get right back out on bail, and I told you, he's threat-

ened to take Jade away. Or have someone else take
her away, if he's locked up. She's my *baby,* Mary
Beth! I don't think even you would risk something
like that.''

I chose to ignore the ''even you'' part. Lindy had
always accused me of being emotionally cold. She'd
have no way of knowing that I could understand
what losing a baby was like.

''Besides,'' she said, ''if I had Roger arrested, the
pharmaceutical company would go down with him.
Their experiments would be dropped, and they'd
never find a cure for Jade. Don't you see, Mary
Beth? The very people who are making her ill are
the only hope she's got.''

''Lindy, that's just not true. What if Jade could be
placed in a good hospital and her records, along with
Roger's notes, were put into the hands of one of the
top scientists in the world? Surely if this story about
a magic bullet that turned out to be dangerously defective came out, that's what would happen. There
would be scientists and doctors clamoring to find out
what went wrong and if they could improve upon
the drug. Jade could be treated, and you and she
would both be free of Roger.''

''No,'' she said, shaking her head. The tears began
to flow again. ''I can't risk it, Mary Beth. I just
can't.''

I studied her—the bent shoulders, the helpless-
ness—and knew she never would go against Roger,
even for her own child. Had he beaten her down so

much, she didn't believe in her own ability to make a decision anymore?

I sat and thought for a few moments. Finally I said, "You know, it's hard to believe even Roger would put his own child in danger this way."

"I don't think he sees it that way. He's been strange lately. Angry all the time, and I think he's so anxious to prove that BZT-22 is safe, he's in denial. He swears he's actually trying to heal Jade, and I'm not sure anymore if he's lying or he really believes that."

"What do you think is making him so desperate?"

"Money," Lindy said, her lips curling in derision. "The business hasn't been doing well, and if it turns out BZT-21 is what caused the deaths of those soldiers in the Middle East, he'll never be able to sell BZT-22. He stands to lose everything."

"Including his life, Lindy. He could be charged with mass murder."

"I don't think he even cares about that. That's what I mean, Mary Beth. He's obsessed with this drug, and he'll do anything to prove it works."

"Even so, to experiment on his own daughter? Lindy, if you're correct and he believes he's doing the right thing, he'll never stop. You've got to fight him on this, while there's still time."

"God, Mary Beth! Don't you think I know that? Have you been single so long you can't even imagine what it's like to fear for your child? If I fight Roger, he'll hide Jade away and I'll lose her com-

pletely. If I don't fight him, she...she could die.''
Lindy covered her face with her hands and sobbed.

I wanted to ignore the tears and snap back at her
for her accusation. But I held my tongue and
watched a little girl below, on the beach. She was
skipping over the waves with her mother, her shoes
and socks in one hand and her dress hiked above her
knees with the other. She reminded me of a picture
in a book of poems by Robert Louis Stevenson.
Something about, ''little Louis, on the shores of
Monterey.''

Finally, I was calm enough to realize I'd only
filled Lindy's mind with more fear, and she'd responded by sniping at me—just as she had when we
were teenagers.

You think you're so much smarter than me, she'd
say when I'd try to lead her away from one disaster
or another. *And you're not! You're a sissy, Mary
Beth, you know that? You don't even know how to
have fun!*

She was probably right; I *was* too serious in high
school. But Lindy's idea of fun usually landed her
in a heap of trouble. I was the one with the cool
head, the one who thought things through first. Not
that she always listened. Sometimes she'd go off
half-cocked into a risky situation, and then come to
me to help her clean things up.

Which, I thought, is why she's sitting here with
me now. The only question being, how involved did
I want to get—even for someone who'd been my

best friend for years, the one I'd shared childhood secrets with, practiced putting on makeup with, and even bought my first bra with? So many memories...and a large part of them laced with giggling and laughter, tears and fears, and vows of always being there for each other.

That vow had gotten lost over the years, for both of us. Still, maybe it was time to renew it, if only on my part.

"You know," I said as Lindy's tears subsided, "maybe what Roger is doing really isn't hurting Jade. I remember something in one of my author's books, about years ago when scientists couldn't afford clinical trials. They experimented on themselves and their own families instead. Most of them were well-meaning, I guess. They honestly thought they had a cure. And if they did have one, they could somehow get the drug out there."

"Sounds like Saint Roger, all right," Lindy said sarcastically. "Sure, it's all about curing Jade. Even the blood in her urine."

"Well, of course you're right, if he's continuing to use something on her that's giving her a bad side effect. And if he is—"

"Then he's more wicked than you or I ever thought!" Lindy broke in. "Not that I blame you for sticking up for him. You always did have a bit of a crush on Roger in school, didn't you? Why wouldn't you think the best of him?"

If only she knew.

"That was long ago, Lindy. I've moved on. And it sounds like you should, too. Not just for Jade, but if Roger is selling defective drugs to the Middle East, have you any idea how that might reflect on our country? We could be accused of doing it on purpose, of hiring pharmaceutical companies to poison people. You don't want to be in the middle of that if Roger is caught."

Something about all this puzzled me, though. I'd apparently been wrong about Lindy being an airhead, considering what she'd been telling me.

"How did you find out about this defective drug and the sales to the Middle East?" I asked.

Her voice was full of scorn. "By being a jealous woman. Way before I knew what Roger was doing to Jade, I started listening in on his phone conversations. I was sure he had a mistress, and I even followed him sometimes to see where he went when he was supposed to be going to Courtland."

She flushed and said, "Please don't judge me. We weren't having an easy time of it, even then. I did find out about the girlfriends—not one, but two. I never dreamed, though, that I'd overhear a meeting Roger was having with one of the Middle East buyers. When I heard the things I just told you, I flipped. I wanted to confront Roger right then and there. Either that, or go straight to the FBI, because by that time I'd heard him on the phone with his father, and I knew Roger was using BZT-22 on Jade. I thought if I turned him in, I could get her away from him.

Then I thought, no, why not wait a few days more? After all, the deals with the Mideast would be his word against mine. I needed hard proof—like a tape, or a deal on paper. I figured with that, I could prove he was...well, I don't know. A traitor, or something. You know what that would mean, Mary Beth?"

"A firing squad?" I said dryly. One could only hope.

"I don't know about that. But it would mean I'd have Roger Van Court locked up and out of my life forever. I'd be free."

That was something I could give my wholehearted support to.

The sun was high and moving over my house to the west. Lindy and I were in my room, dressing. I had to go into the office, and I had plans for her.

"May I use your hairbrush?" Lindy asked, standing in front of my mirror and trying to comb her matted hair with her fingers.

"Sure," I said, applying lipstick and blush.

She ran my comb through the brush to clean out the hair.

"I used to get after you about cleaning *your* brush," I said, smiling. "Since when have you become Mrs. Clean?"

"Since no when. I guess I'm jittery. My hands have to keep moving."

"Great. You can start on the kitchen next."

"Ha." She bent over from the waist and used

long, slow strokes to get the tangles and God knew
what else from her hair. I'd have to put a new brush
on my shopping list.

"So you've never had any children, Mary Beth?"
she asked.

"No," I said shortly.

"Well, I'm sorry. I mean, for that comment earlier. But you could adopt, you know. I mean, if you
don't want to get married. In that article I read in
the paper, they mentioned that adoption book you
just sold for one of your authors. Have you ever
considered that for yourself?"

"No," I said again. "For heaven's sake, Lindy,
don't count me out yet. I'm only thirty-three, and
my biological clock has barely started ticking. Besides, I could probably drag some poor man into
marrying me if I really wanted to."

"No, but that's what I meant. If for some reason
you *didn't* want to." She shrugged and said awkwardly, "It's just that since you haven't married yet,
I thought maybe...I mean, if you were thinking
about having a baby you could, you know, raise it
by yourself. A lot of women do that these days, don't
they?"

"I suppose."

"I guess I'm just wondering what it'll be like if I
do get custody of Jade someday. Raising her alone
and all."

"You'll probably do fine," I said, getting up to

take our cups out to the kitchen. Adoption wasn't a topic I wanted to continue with.

But Lindy was in a mood to talk. She followed me into the kitchen.

"You know why I never realized until recently what was going on with Jade, Mary Beth? Because Roger would take her out with him at first, like to work. He said the staff loved her and they entertained her when he was busy. But then I got an anonymous phone call from a woman, telling me that he was testing some sort of experimental drug on Jade."

Lindy paused, tears streaming from her eyes. "Mary Beth, when he had her at work, he'd inject her with something and he wouldn't tell me. All I knew was that she kept getting sicker. But I just thought it was some illness she'd come by naturally. That's why I didn't do anything at first."

I didn't know how to respond to that, and when I didn't, Lindy said, "Roger's changed so much. When his reign as prom king ended, he tried to go to college. But he flunked out and had to work for his father. Ever since then, he's been treated like a little boy again. Oh, he's got the title of president of Courtland Pharmaceuticals, but his father still rules the family and the business with an iron hand, even from his hospital bed. Roger has to toe the line or things will go bad for him at Courtland."

"It sounds like you're making excuses for him," I said irritably. God help her if she went back to him and let all this blow over.

"No, not at all," she said quickly. "I just meant that Roger becomes more like his father as he gets older, and his weaknesses grow instead of his strengths. In his mind he's still a playboy, and that's the only escape he thinks he has anymore. That's why he has girlfriends, I'm sure. They make him feel like a man again."

Some man. I wondered how many of those girlfriends had actually been rape victims.

"Ready?" I said.

"Uh-huh." She went to the mirror in the foyer and fluffed her hair.

"Ready for Freddy!" she said with a giggle, her face still wet with tears. "Remember our mothers saying that all the time? Ready for Freddy! It was supposed to be cool, but today it'd sound pretty gruesome."

I tried not to sigh, but since Lindy arrived it was becoming a habit.

Picking up my cell phone and keys, I hustled her off to the car, carrying a cup of coffee and a slice of wheat toast. Lindy had eaten two yogurts out of my fridge earlier, and said she didn't need anything else. She kept eyeing my coffee longingly, though, so I finally told her to take it.

While she sipped it, I nudged my little fifties-era MG into the traffic on Pacific Coast Highway and said, "Okay, look. The way I see it, you've got to get Jade some good, objective medical care. You need to know what's really wrong with her, and you need to know for sure what Roger's been giving her, and if it is actually harming her.''

''That's exactly what I *want* to do,'' Lindy said plaintively. ''But how?''

''Well, can you get into the house at all? I know you said Roger changed the locks, but you must know other ways to get in. A window that's left open all the time, a door that's left unlocked during certain times for delivery people?''

''No, but...'' She hesitated and gave me a quick glance.

''What?'' I said.

''If I tell you, you can't breathe a word.''

''Oh, for God's sake, Lindy, just tell me!'' I was so irritated, I wrenched the wheel to the left too quickly and had to brake to keep from hitting oncoming traffic.

''Yikes, Mary Beth! Watch out!''

I gritted my teeth, and Lindy swore under her breath.

''You still drive as crazy as you did in San Francisco when we were in high school,'' she said. ''Remember when we got stuck on a hill behind a cop car and you started beeping your horn at him to get going? I thought I'd die.''

''I was just trying to break out and act as crazy as you,'' I said, smiling.

She didn't take it as the joke I'd meant it to be, however. Her face paled. ''I'm not crazy, Mary Beth!''

I turned briefly to look at her. "Sorry. I was kidding, Lindy. Geez, lighten up."

"It's just that…well, my mother. Do you remember her?"

"Sure."

"After my father died, my mother went all funny in the head. She had to go into a mental hospital. Two years later, she died there."

"Lindy, I'm so sorry. I didn't know."

She fell silent.

"So what's the big secret?" I asked, to change the subject. "You were going to tell me something about getting into the house, I think."

"Yes, but you've got to swear first."

I sighed. "I swear," I said, as I'd often done when we were kids, "on my mother's red hair."

Lindy laughed and punched me lightly on the forearm. The joke was that my mother *dyed* her hair red, unlike I, who came by it naturally from my father and his father and so on down the line to county Clare.

"Okay," Lindy said. "Here goes. It's Jade's nanny, Irene. She said she'd help me if she could. I called right after Roger threw me out, and Irene said she felt bad about it and that Jade missed me horribly. She told me she had orders never to let me in, but if I came by once a week or so when Roger wasn't there, she'd let me in. Just for a little bit, to see Jade."

"Well, that's something. Have you done that?"

"No," she admitted. "I've been afraid. I knew I'd have to be careful, because Irene could lose her job if Roger found me there. And God knows what he'd do to me. Jade could end up with none of the people she loves. Nobody who'd take care of her right, anyway."

"Hmm. How much could you count on Irene to help you get Jade out of there?"

"You mean just take her? I couldn't do that!"

"But if you could—would Irene help?"

"I wouldn't even ask her. I don't think she knows anything about what Roger is doing. He's always acted like he's just trying to make Jade well, and I'm pretty sure she's always accepted that."

"If she knew, then. Would she help?"

Lindy shook her head, and I could feel her mentally digging in her heels. "I don't think I could ever count on Irene for much more than letting me in to see Jade. Roger pays her salary, after all. Irene's been kind to me because she knows how much I love Jade and Jade loves me, but beyond that..."

She folded her hands in her lap and bent her head, saying helplessly, "Even if I could get Jade out of the house, I wouldn't have any money to take care of her."

For a brief moment it occurred to me that this might be some kind of scam after all. Was Lindy here to "borrow" from me and then disappear? God help me if I'd fallen for the oldest sob story in the world: *My child is desperately ill, and I need money to take care of her.*

No. Lindy wouldn't do that to me, would she? And there was no way I could turn my back on her now. It might have been me, six years ago, with no money and a baby to feed.

"There must be someplace safe," I said, "where you could leave Jade until you get back on your feet."

She shook her head. "Not since my mother died. You remember how close they were? My mom and dad?"

I nodded as I shifted and passed a lumbering truck going fifteen miles an hour.

"Well, I always thought she couldn't live without him," Lindy said bitterly. "And of course she had to go bonkers and prove me right."

"I'm so sorry, Lindy." I remembered that Lindy had always felt like an outsider in her own family. Her parents were so involved with each other, they barely noticed her. Now that I thought about it, that might have been why Lindy had always looked for attention and affection to a greater degree than most of us.

"Aren't there any other friends you can ask to take care of Jade?" I asked.

"Not really," she said, her tone one of misery. "That's why I came to you, Mary Beth. My other friends from school? They gave up on me after I married Roger. He has a way, you know, of cutting people off. Like he really wants me all to himself? But he doesn't, so I don't know why he bothers.''

"Lindy," I said in as firm a voice as I could muster, "the way I see it, Jade is your first priority. You've got to get her out of there and to a good doctor.''

"I told you, I don't have any money for a lawyer, Mary Beth. Criminy, haven't you been listening? Stupid me, I even left my checking account in just his name. You know how it is when you're young and in love. You think the other person would never do a thing to hurt you, so you don't take steps to protect yourself.''

I was about to reverse my opinion about Lindy's lack of airheadedness. Any woman these days who doesn't protect herself financially is a fool.

To be fair, though, Lindy wasn't entirely at fault. She'd followed a Trent family recipe, handed down through generations: Lasso a rich man, let him take care of you, and you'll never be without.

Unfortunately for my old friend, times had changed since that recipe worked. Women who counted on men to take care of them these days were often in for a big surprise, and not a pleasant one.

I felt angry, suddenly, that Lindy hadn't been smarter about her life. "Why on earth didn't you leave Roger long ago? How could you go on so long with a man like that, a man who could—"

She interrupted, and I supposed that was good. In

my anger, I'd been about to pour out the whole miserable story about the rape.

"You don't know him, Mary Beth!" she cried. "God only knows what he'd have done if I'd left him, instead of him forcing me out. He had to have an heir, see? It's all about money now. That's even what Jade is about. Roger's father wanted a boy as an heir to the Courtland business, but that's one thing, at least, that Roger fought him on. He insisted that Jade could do just as good a job as a boy."

"Really?" I couldn't keep the sarcasm out of my voice. "How liberated of him."

"Well, he knows we're never going to have another child, so that's the only way he could placate his father. He had to convince him Jade was enough. Otherwise, Roger wouldn't inherit a thing. That's the way his father's will is set up."

I was so grateful I'd never married into that family.

"It sounds like you've been doing the best you could in a bad situation," I admitted.

"Well, I'm not as dense as everyone thinks I am. Oh, I know I seemed that way in high school, but that was just part of a plan to convince the boys I was just a little blond airhead. That way they weren't so intimidated by me and I got lots of dates."

"Intimidated?"

"Like they were by you, Mary Beth. You with your library books and your glasses and cool air that put up a wall between you and them. I tried to tell you, remember? I even wanted to do a makeover on you. You wouldn't go for it.''

It had been a long while since I'd thought of myself as I was in high school. Carrying a baby for nine months and then giving it away—along with a large chunk of my heart—had made me feel like an entirely different person. It was if I'd had a certain life before my baby, and then someone new had come in, taken over my body, and was living this one. ''Walk-ins,'' my paranormal-book authors call it. Some say that's what happens in a near-death experience. When a person's life force is nearly gone, someone new and better can come in and take over. That's why, they say, so many who've had near-death experiences come back renewed and full of faith, ready to do good deeds.

Or, if the paranormal book is a thriller, they come back as vampires.

I was getting fanciful. I shook myself mentally and got back to Lindy.

''Is all this part of a plan, too?'' I asked, aware for the first time of what a good little actress Lindy had become over the years. ''And is dragging me into your troubles part of it?''

''No! No, at least I didn't mean it to hurt you. I never would have come to you if I'd thought Roger would find me here. I was just trying to hide from him, Mary Beth. I heard he was looking for me, and that he wanted to hurt me. I came to you because I was desperate, that's all.''

"Well, what a lucky stroke, then, that you met someone in a bar who just happened to know where I lived."

She looked away, not meeting my eyes.

I pulled over into a parking lot, and turned to her. "What the hell are you really up to, Lindy? I'm not buying this whole 'on the streets' business. I can't even begin to see Lindy Lou Trent living in a cardboard box."

"Well, I have been!" she said angrily. "Almost, anyway. Like I said, I'm not stupid, Mary Beth. I always knew it wasn't going to last with Roger, so I was salting money away until this happened. I took some from the grocery bills and the dry-cleaning bills and stuff, and over the past few weeks it added up. I kept the money in a secret compartment in my purse, so I had it with me the day Roger locked me out."

"So you *do* have money for a lawyer."

"No! Dammit, Mary Beth, I don't know how long I have to make this money last, so I don't dare spend the little bit I have left. I've been staying in the worst dives—dirty, flea-ridden motels I used to just drive by and not even look at, they were so grimy and old. And if I don't figure out something soon, I *will* be living in a box! That's if I'm lucky enough to find one." She folded her arms and gave me a mutinous look, like a child. "And I did really walk down Sunset to your house. I…I hitched a ride partway, that's all."

I couldn't help it. I sighed. "Okay, then. So just how long do you think you'll need, to figure things out?"

"I don't know. Like I said, I have to get some sort of hard proof of what Roger is doing with that drug, and once I get that, I can go to the police. Then I can get a lawyer and sue the bastard for all he's worth."

"And you're willing to leave Jade there in the meantime, even is she's in jeopardy? Who knows how long that will take? Lindy, *think*. Forget nailing Roger for the sales to the Middle East. The first thing you've got to do is get your baby out of that house. She needs to be with you."

Lindy shook her head. "You mean fight for custody? I told you, Mary Beth. Roger would disappear with Jade before we ever got to court."

I studied her and noted, in the bright sunlight, the deep lines around her eyes and mouth. The strain of living with her problems was written all over her face.

"Lindy," I said finally, "pardon my French, but screw the courts. We're not doing it that way."

"We?" she said, her eyes widening.

"We. I have to do a bit of planning, but trust me— we'll get your baby out of that house."

I had pulled into the parking lot of the Malibu Beach Inn. Sliding into a parking space, I turned to Lindy. "Let's go."

"Go? Where? Mary Beth, I have to get back to

San Francisco. If you've convinced me of anything, it's that it's time I tried to see Jade.''

"You're absolutely right, it is time. But let me figure out how to help you first. Okay?''

The misery evaporated and she looked at me like a lost puppy who'd finally found its way home. "Thank you,'' she said in a small voice. "I'll never forget this, Mary Beth.''

I'd decided to trust Lindy's story, come hell or high water. I just hoped I wouldn't end up in the deep end. Meanwhile, I wanted her where she'd be reasonably safe while I was at work. After hearing Lindy's whole story, I didn't really think it was Roger who'd broken in the night before. After all, he'd gotten rid of her, and he'd also effectively tied her hands. As long as he had her convinced that he'd hide Jade away where Lindy would never find her, she couldn't make a move against him.

Whether or not he would actually do that, or if it was a bluff, she couldn't know. Nor could I.

And, since I couldn't be absolutely sure that it wasn't Roger the night before, I wanted Lindy where I wouldn't have to worry about her too much. That, to me, meant the older and highly respectable Malibu Beach Inn, easily the classiest small hotel in town.

When Lindy saw her room and the ocean view, she looked as if she'd just fallen into paradise. "You have no idea...'' she said with tears in her eyes.

"And, oh, look, Mary Beth! A fireplace! And a balcony!"

I guessed that it didn't take too long in motel dives to make one appreciate the finer things in life. As for the cost of all this, I figured I owed my old friend. If I'd told her years ago that her husband had raped me—if I'd pressed charges—she wouldn't be in this situation now.

Whether it would help to press charges now, I didn't know. But I'd been thinking about it. It would mean having everyone know about the baby I'd given away, a secret I'd made untold sacrifices to keep. But if it would help Lindy and *her* baby—and if the statute of limitations wasn't up—it might be one way to free her, and to set her on a path to a better life.

Pressing charges would take time, though. It would have to go through the courts. And as I'd told Lindy, screw the courts—at least for now. What I had in mind would take far less time.

I gave Lindy strict orders to stay in the room, not open the door to anyone, and call me on my cell if she had any problems. When I left her, I felt as if I were leaving a child behind.

Home alone. What trouble might my little charge get herself into?

At the office, I skipped my usual workout. Nia and I went through my remaining client list, looking for that one author who might save the financial day.

"There's Audrey Birkoff," Nia said. "Her English mysteries are a bit on the dull side for me, I'm afraid.''

"But she does have a large readership," I pointed out. "And she brings in steady money."

"True. Then there's Bea Lorman," she said. "Bea hasn't been producing lately. And her writing's gone downhill."

"She's been sick," I said.

Nia rolled her eyes. "She's always sick."

"Meaning?"

Nia sighed. "We've talked about this before and I thought we decided she must be bipolar. She goes through these periods—up and down. When she's up she can write like crazy. When she's down she always finds a way to sabotage herself."

Nia was right. Bea had been doing that for years, and I'd only kept her on because I knew there was real talent there. If she ever got her emotions straightened out, she'd be a wildly successful author.

"Maybe we could get her on Paxil," I said, only half kidding.

Nia grinned. "Can you imagine that? A completely well Bea Lorman?" Sobering, she added, "No kidding. She could replace Tony as your number-one best-selling author."

"She might," I agreed. "Right now, though, I need to see who's bringing in the most bucks today."

She smiled. "Will you wine and dine that person?

Hold his or her hand? Smile pretty and speak softly?''

''You betcha,'' I said, grinning.

''Well, there's Lucy Watson.''

''Our own Jackie Collins?''

''As far as her vocabulary is concerned, that's the same Lucy Watson.''

I'd been building Lucy up to be as big a seller as Jackie Collins, if that were at all possible, given Jackie's long lead. Lucy wrote books about Hollywood and she had all the four-letter words and sex down pat. There was something missing, however.

I said as much to Nia.

She nodded. ''You know what I think? She's a nun in disguise.''

I laughed. ''Now, that would be good for a ton of PR, wouldn't it? But no, I think it's just that she doesn't have a strong enough will to succeed. I still have to teach her how to dress when she goes to New York.''

Nia agreed. ''You should get her to burn those jeans, then take her shopping on Rodeo Drive.''

''We already did Rodeo Drive, right after she got lipo and the breast implants. She's got everything she needs in her closet—two-piece suits, cocktail dresses, dozens of great shoes and purses. She just keeps showing up looking like a cowgirl.''

''Maybe that's because she is one,'' Nia said.

''No, Lucy comes from Long Island.''

''I mean at heart,'' Nia replied pointedly. ''There

are all those wild stallions following in her wake
every time she goes out. They must like the way she
squeezes herself into the jeans and low-cut tops. I'd
say she gets a bit of riding in before the night's
over.''

I tried not to smile too much. ''She has gained
weight again,'' I agreed. ''She's looking a bit—''

''Bosomy?'' Nia finished for me. ''Buxomy?''

''To be kind, let's say she's starting to look like
a lusty seventeenth-century barmaid.''

Nia chuckled. ''That's *kind?*''

''I just mean she's not yet the slick Jackie Collins
image we've been trying to turn her into.''

I didn't care what most of my authors looked like
when they went to New York, as long as they
dressed professionally, as if they were winners. Lucy
Watson was another matter. It was taking a derrick
to move her up the ladder. So much potential, but so
little, socially, between the ears.

I changed the subject, not wanting to get into the
habit of tearing my authors down. I'd been in some
agents' outer offices when they didn't know I was
listening, and I'd heard them say the most awful
things about their clients. I've always wondered how
an agent could successfully represent someone they
didn't like, or whose writing they despised.

The worst of them tore other agents down, as well.
One had started a rumor about a top New York agent
from France, saying he wasn't really French, that he
came from Alabama and that even his French accent

was false. That rumor had sped around literary circles like wildfire, and it had all started with one mean-spirited agent in Los Angeles who was jealous of the French agent's success.

At least, I'd always assumed it was a mean-spirited rumor. But what if it was true? I wondered. The thing is, once an agent's reputation has been sullied, it's hard to get it back. The thought's been placed in the minds of people, and there's no Paul Revere to ride around shouting, ''The Frank is real, the Frank is real!''

I stretched and leaned back into my chair.

''You look tired,'' Nia said.

''Well, I haven't told you about my night yet, have I?''

''Out carousing?''

''Sure, that's me, all right,'' I grumbled. ''No, I had an old friend show up, and in the middle of the night someone broke in and tried to kill us.''

Nia's indrawn breath and shocked eyes reminded me of just how unsettling last night had been. I'd tried to push the incident to the back of my mind, telling myself that the intruder wasn't Roger—it was a simple break-in, like the one my neighbor'd had recently. There was a bad guy in the neighborhood, and all I had to do from now on was get new locks and a mean lean dog.

The dog part I liked, but it wasn't feasible at the moment. Changing the locks was something else.

''Would you do me a personal favor?'' I asked

Nia. "When we're finished here, would you call someone to change the locks on my front door and the two French doors? I'd also like some kind of extra security for the windows. See if you can get them over there right away. Tell them I'll pay extra."

"Thinking mighty positive today, aren't we? Paying extra?"

Nia knew just about everything about me—how I'd gone out on a limb to open this office and buy the house in Malibu, and how hard it could be now to pay for it all.

But she jotted down the instructions. "I do require some pay for this. You've got to tell me what happened last night."

"If you insist." I told her from the beginning, with Lindy showing up and on through to the way we'd raced to Patrick's house and he'd taken us in till the sheriff arrived.

"Patrick Llewellen? He lives near you?"

"Just a few houses down," I said.

"That's pretty handy. What about the sheriff's department? Did they find anything?"

"Not a thing. They combed the area and asked if we had any ideas about who might have broken in, but we couldn't tell them much."

"What about your friend?"

"Lindy? I hadn't seen her in years."

"So, all of a sudden she shows up and you nearly

get shot in your own home? C'mon. This person must have been after her.''

"Possible. She thought it might be her husband. He threw her out of their house a few weeks ago, and she's been living on the streets, more or less. I just don't know why he'd want to kill her.''

"Well, maybe what happened last night didn't have anything to do with her. Maybe it had to do with the three murders.''

"I thought of that, too.''

"Even so, what reason did she give for showing up at your door in the middle of the night?''

"She needed a place to stay. I put her up for the night.''

"Yikes. You took a chance, didn't you? If you hadn't seen her since high school? And who knows what she's been doing on the streets?''

"I know. But at the time it seemed the thing to do.''

She shook her head. "What a softie.''

"Not really. She was a friend, Nia. You wouldn't turn away a friend who'd fallen on bad times.''

"Ha. Just try me.''

But her smile told me she would have done the same thing.

"Speaking of the murders,'' she said. "Do the police know yet who committed them?''

"Not that they've told me. I only know they believe the three men are tied together in some way.''

"It just seems so odd,'' she said. "Two of your

authors, your ex-husband, and now that break-in at your house. It really looks like..."

"Someone's out to get me, not Lindy," I finished for her.

"But why? And aren't you afraid? Even a little bit?"

"I think I'm too tired today to be afraid. And yesterday there was too much else happening. Once I catch up on my sleep I'll probably be a raving maniac."

Nia smiled. "Let me know when that's about to happen, will you? I'm due for a vacation."

"Nia! Oh my God, I forgot. You're *over*due! You were supposed to take it the minute summer started. So get going, girl. Hie ye off to Peru or one of those other metaphysical places you love, with all the vortexes and stuff."

"Oh, please. Like I'd really leave, with all that's going on here now." Nia sipped her coffee.

"No, really, you don't have to stay here just because of that. I'm sure it'll all blow over soon."

"You aren't getting rid of me," she said firmly. "This is the most exciting thing that's happened around here since Charlie Dunkle drowned in Clyde Rivera's swimming pool last year."

I groaned. "Don't remind me of that." *Dunk, Dunk, Dunkle,* were the headlines emblazoned across the gossip rags. One fun night in his boyfriend's pool in West Hollywood and poor Charlie—along with his romance novels, which had been selling so well under the pseudonym Charlene Dark—was gone forever.

"So how was it when you found Craig?" Nia wondered. "You didn't say much on the phone."

"I didn't have much time. There was a high-pressure El Segundo police detective waiting to hear my pearls of wisdom. *Why was I there? What time did I get there? How did I get in? How long had I known Craig? Did he have any enemies?*"

"Geez. All that, a shooting, and a shopping bag lady at your door."

I gave her a look and she said, "Sorry. Your *close friend* at your door. What a night."

I didn't see a need to tell her that even before Lindy arrived, the "yummy" Detective Rucker and I had become close friends, too.

Or whatever one might call it.

Nia went back to her desk, but left the connecting door open so we could talk back and forth if necessary. I continued to go through my author files, calculating who to push for the big money next—who was already in place to get there, and whose numbers were where they should be.

Now and then my mind wandered back to the previous night and Dan Rucker. I was busy wondering if I'd ever hear from him again, when my outer-office door opened and Himself walked in. He was accompanied by another man, dressed in a gray pin-striped suit and wearing an out-of-date bowler hat. He had a severe expression on his face that might have been permanent or might have had to do with me. I couldn't be sure.

Nia started to get up and shoo the uninvited out, but I stood and motioned to her to stay where she was.

"Nia, you've already met Detective Dan Rucker," I said. I turned to the other man. "And you would be…?"

Dan introduced us. "This is Mr. Gerard Burton. Mr. Burton is an attorney from San Francisco, and he would like to talk to you about the incident at your house last night."

Dan was poker-faced, giving nothing away, so I was left to wonder how Mr. Gerard Burton, all the way up in San Francisco, had heard about the break-in. And why was he here with Dan, an LAPD officer, when the break-in had been in the sheriff's jurisdiction?

I held out my hand and said, "Nice to meet you, Mr. Burton. Please, sit down. Would you like coffee?" I looked at both men.

Dan shook his head, but Gerard Burton, Esquire, said in a rather mannered voice, "That would be quite nice. I've just now come off the plane, and I could do with a bit of caffeine."

"I'll make some fresh, then."

"I'll do it," Nia said. "I have a few phone calls to return, and I can do that while I wait for the coffee."

I nodded and sat, glancing at Dan, then turning to

Gerard Burton. "You wanted to talk to me about the intruder at my house? And you're from San Francisco? I'm amazed you heard about that so quickly— or that the break-in could possibly interest you."

"News travels fast...in some circles," Burton said delicately. "I've been sent here at the behest of a client who was not able to come personally."

"A client in San Francisco?" Let me guess, I thought. Couldn't be anyone but Roger. Still, I think I managed to look baffled.

"I see," I said. "What can I do for you then, Mr. Burton?"

I gave Dan another quick glance, and he made a small sideways movement of his head. It was so minimal, I knew it must have been meant only for me.

Now, I thought, if only I knew *what* it meant.

"I understand," Gerard Burton said, "that there was another woman with you last night when the...the incident occurred."

"That's right," I said, knowing it had to be on the police report. "A friend."

"According to the police, your friend's name is Lindy Louise Van Court?"

"Are you asking or telling me?" I countered.

"Simply confirming. Tell me, where may I find Mrs. Van Court? I'd like very much to talk with her."

"Oh, I'm sorry. I'm afraid you're too late," I said. "She left my house early this morning, and I haven't seen her since."

In a way, it was the truth. Dan gave me a look, though, that said he knew it wasn't quite the whole story. I wondered how he could know, but was grateful when he said nothing.

"I have a few questions of my own," I said. "Did Mr. Van Court—Roger, that is—send you here?"

"My dear young lady, no one *sends* me *anywhere*," Burton replied in a huff.

"Except for your client," I said quietly.

"I beg your pardon?".

"You said you were here at—I think the phrase was—the behest of a client."

He went silent.

"Mind telling me if your client is Roger Van Court?"

He stared at me a few moments and finally said, "That information would be confidential."

I stood. "Well, the incident at my house last night was not confidential. I told the sheriff's deputies everything I knew, and their report is a matter of public record. You could have saved yourself a trip all the way down here, Mr. Burton, just by asking them to fax you that report."

I walked over to the door between my office and the outer one. Nia was at the coffee machine, pouring hot brew into cups. "Nia? Sorry, but we won't be needing the coffee after all. Could you please show the gentlemen out?"

"Mary Beth—" Dan began.

"In case you've forgotten, Detective Rucker," I

said stiffly, "I've suffered a few losses in the past two days. I really don't have time for this, and I would appreciate it if you would call before you bring anyone else by to interrogate me."

"I would hardly call this an interrogation," Mr. Burton said just as stiffly. "I merely thought it might help you to remember a few important details if we talked in person."

"Sorry," I said. "I have no more details. Check the report."

Turning to Dan, I said, "Just what is your connection here?"

"Professional courtesy," he answered. "Mr. Burton called the captain and asked if someone from the LAPD would escort him from the airport to your office. He and the captain are old friends, so he asked for a volunteer. That's me."

"Well, isn't it a nice coincidence that you happened to be around and available. For escort service, that is. They must give that duty to their finest."

I ignored Dan's exasperated look and went back to my desk, sorting through papers. When he didn't follow the San Francisco attorney out the door I raised my head. "Something else I can do for you?"

"You are audacious," he said.

"Really? You didn't mention that last night."

"I had other things on my mind last night."

I couldn't help blushing as his gaze undressed me from head to toe. "Look, I really do have a lot to do this morning," I said, staring down at the papers.

"What about tonight?"

"Tonight?" I looked up.

"I thought I might take you and your friend to dinner."

"My friend? Oh, you mean Lindy? I told you, she's gone."

"Not to worry. I'll bet I can find her."

I studied him. "You know where she is."

"You betcha," he said, closing the door softly behind him.

As soon as Dan and Gerard Burton left, I called the Malibu Beach Inn and asked for Rhonda Parks, the name I'd registered Lindy under. She answered after a few rings.

"Mary Beth? Oh, God, this place is wonderful! I've been out on the deck just soaking up the sun! You know how often you see sun in San Francisco in the summer? Almost never! And I ordered lunch up here, I hope you don't mind. I ate it out on the deck and the gulls came by and tried to scoop the lettuce off my plate—it was such fun, Mary Beth! Really, it's heaven here."

"You ordered lunch in?" I said. "I told you not to open the door to anyone."

"Well, I had to eat, Mary Beth! And room service isn't just anyone. I didn't think you meant *that*."

Since I hadn't even thought to provide her with a lunch, I let it pass. "Have you talked to Roger?" I asked.

"Roger! No, of course not."

"How about anyone else? Anyone who might have told him you were here."

"I haven't talked to anyone but you, Mary Beth. You told me not to." Her tone became wary. "Why? What are you saying? Does Roger know I'm here?"

"I don't think so. I'm not really sure. Lindy, you said you've decided to try to see Jade."

"Yes."

"And you're not afraid of running into Roger at the house?"

"Well, of course I have been, but now I think it'll be okay, if I call and talk to Irene first. She can tell me what hours he'll be at work for sure, and I can go during that time." Her voice softened. "I think you've given me the confidence to do that, Mary Beth."

"Well, if I have, I'm glad. Now, does Irene live in? Is she at the house all the time?"

"Yes. I could call her now—"

"No, don't do that yet. Just listen. I'm going with you, and I think we should leave tomorrow morning. I have some things to finish up here today, but I'll try to leave early. Just stay there and don't talk to anyone. Don't even answer the door. No room service, no nothing. Promise me, okay?"

"Okay, sure, Mary Beth. That won't be hard. My soaps are coming on soon, so I'll just lie in bed and watch them. That should be all right, shouldn't it?"

"Yes, Lindy. That should be fine."

I felt uneasy, hanging up and just leaving her there. If Dan Rucker knew she was there, how had he found that out? Had someone been following us since last night? And if so, for what purpose?

I couldn't get the vision of Craig Dinsmore out of my mind, lying dead on that bathroom floor. God help me if someone got to Lindy.

"You're a world away, Mary Beth," Nia said, coming in with coffee cups in each hand.

"Not that far, I'm afraid. Just at a deadbeat motel on Imperial Avenue."

"Speaking of which, what about Craig's wife? Do you think she knows about Craig?"

"Julia? They were divorced long ago. I don't even know how to reach her."

"Come to think of it, I seem to recall that she moved to New York City."

"Right. She owns an antiques store."

"I don't have an address for her, though."

I tapped on my desk with my nails, thinking. Finally I said, "Try to find her, will you? If you can't, well...somebody has to bury him, Nia. And the others."

"Yes." She sat there sipping her coffee till the lightbulb went on. "Good God, Mary Beth, not you! You need to stay as far away from that mess as you can now."

"Nia, I cannot let my authors get buried by the county in some bare, ugly plot. Besides, Craig was with me for a long time."

"*With* you, maybe, but he wasn't producing lately. You haven't even made enough in royalty commissions from him the past couple of years to pay for a funeral."

I was surprised at Nia's reaction, but then I realized she was only trying to give the situation some balance and keep me from overreacting—something I tend to do now and then, when emotions run high.

"You haven't even cried yet, have you?" Nia asked.

"You mean for Craig? No, of course not. It's not as if we were personally close."

"Not for Craig, silly. For Tony. And maybe even a little bit for Arnold. That dear, sweet man—"

"Nia, Arnold was a nutcase," I said, though not without fondness. "He actually tried to get me back a few months ago. Remember the Memorial Day party at Tony's? He kept putting on CDs with all my old favorite songs. Then, as we were both going out to our cars, he tried to kiss me."

"Geez, I didn't know that. What did you do?"

"I reminded him that he never really liked kissing me. Or any woman."

Nia smiled. "You know what? If he wasn't gay, maybe he was a monk in another life, and he just doesn't like sex at all in this one. You know, a carryover from his other life."

"You think monks don't like sex?"

"Hmm. You may be right. Anyway, about Arnold, it must have taken courage for him to try to get you back. He was probably really hurt after you left him.''

''But that was ten years ago. He should have gotten over it by now, don't you think?''

She shook her head. ''Arnold was a Virgo. Some Virgo men tend never to forget their first loves. They also tend never to forget how those women hurt them, and they like to believe their sorry lives are all the woman's fault. Which makes for a rather difficult and bitter blend.''

''Well, it's not as if I left him without reason,'' I said defensively. ''For God's sake, Nia, you'd have thought I was wearing a chastity belt! A couple of years of that was about all I could take.''

''And I'm guessing you're making up for lost time now?'' She said it with a smile, so I couldn't take offense.

''I have no idea what you're talking about,'' I said.

''Oh, no? The attractive Detective Rucker? I saw the way you were looking at him.''

''You did not,'' I argued. ''You're just guessing.''

''Hardly. He was looking at you the same way.''

Heat rose in my face. ''Well, I never saw any of that.''

''Uh-huh,'' she said, sashaying out into the front office.

''Swing your hips any more,'' I called after her, ''and you won't fit them through the door.''

* * *

While Nia was in the other office returning the last few calls, I spent some time thinking. The calls had slowed down today, she'd told me, which was to be expected now that we were well into June. In summer, just about all of New York takes flight to the beaches, and very little work gets done. Most agents and authors know that, so we try to get important proposals in before the end of May. Otherwise, we might as well twiddle our thumbs till September.

Right now, I was grateful to have a slower schedule than usual. I would have to make appointments today to work out burial plans for Tony, Arnold and Craig. Tony and Arnold had both lost track of family after moving to L.A. years ago, though not by design or by a mutual choice of any kind. It's just what happens, sometimes, when people—especially young men who are sowing their oats and think they have no need of family—end up in La-La-Land.

As for friends, Tony had always boasted about having a huge number of them, but the truth was, he never really was close to anyone. He spread himself too thin, going for quantity rather than quality. And when he referred to someone in the "arts," as he rather proudly put it, he would say, "My friend the dancer," "My friend the screenwriter," "My friend the author." So he never actually dropped the names—only the jobs they did. I often wondered if he even knew what their names were. Even when he'd introduce me to someone, he'd say, "My friend the agent."

I know what you're thinking. *Three years. Three years you lusted after this schmuck.* I'm beginning to believe that what Nia has always said is right: I did it because he was safe. If he'd ever come near me with anything fatter than a pencil, I'd have probably run a mile.

Which I know is contradictory to my fall from grace with the good detective. But there it is.

Gulping the last of my coffee, I reached for a phone book on the shelves along a wall next to my desk. The five shelves were piled high with manuscripts and published books, while the runover was stacked on the floor. In an ordinary week I might get hundreds of manuscripts, some at my request, but most not. Every night Nia took home a bunch of the ones I'd requested, where she would read them and write up her thoughts about each book. I paid her extra for this, as I would any reader, since they're the angels in an agent's life. Being an agent entails long hours on the phone making deals, and there isn't time to read much when one is trying to sell books. Even the ones we do read are accepted or rejected on the first ten or twenty pages. That's usually all it takes to know whether the book is written well and if it's right for us.

"There aren't any calls to return," Nia said, sitting in the chair across from me. "Or, I should say, nothing important. There have been all kinds of calls from the media, wanting information on Tony. How he died, what's going to happen with his books now, does he have any family, etcetera. I started telling them 'no comment,' but they kept on and on, so I've decided to let the answering machine pick up and weed them out.''

''Good idea. I'm not expecting any urgent calls today. Are you? About book business, I mean.''

She shook her head. ''I took care of the ones who called yesterday. As for editors and so on, it seems that word's spread around NYC about Tony and Craig, so there's probably no one you need to inform.''

''That's good. You know, this is all starting to catch up with me.'' I rubbed my eyes. ''I think I'll go home and take a short nap, then make an appointment with an undertaker. I also have to find out when the bodies are going to be released.''

Nia crossed her arms and gave me a stern look. ''So you won't listen to reason and forget all that?''

''I just don't think I can.''

She shook her head. ''Well, then, how can I help?''

''I'm glad you asked. I have to go away for a couple of days, maybe longer. Could you hold off on that vacation till I get back?''

''Like I said, I'm not going anywhere.''

''Great. I'll call in on my cell, but I don't want anyone to know where I am.''

"Ooh, a mystery." She rolled her eyes, then sobered. "Are you gonna be all right, girl?"

"I'll be fine. As for you, you go home now, too. Take a nap, whatever. You stayed here late last night, didn't you?" I hadn't missed the small mountain of foam coffee cups in the wastebasket next to her desk.

"Well, I didn't do much. Just stuck around reading manuscripts, in case you called and needed me. Oh, one other thing. I did some research on Chinese dildos."

"Oh? Where did you hear about them?" I asked sharply. The police had specifically told me not to mention that aspect of the case, and I was certain I hadn't told Nia.

She blinked. "I, uh…I don't think I remember. Maybe someone who called yesterday mentioned it. *ET* or one of those magazine shows. Does it matter?"

"No…no, I guess not." *ET* and *Access* seemed to get info out of nowhere.

"Anyway, I looked them up on the Net yesterday when I didn't have anything else to do. Specifically, I checked out ancient Chinese dildos."

"Really? What did you find out?"

"First of all, archeologists recently found seven ancient bronze dildos in a Han dynasty tomb. Apparently this is the first time they've found so many from that era, around 25 A.D., but it seems they've found dildos in China that date back twelve thousand years. In fact, the Chinese were the first known people to make and use them. The ones they found recently were cast from a mold, which means they might have been made by an artisan who specialized in them. It might have been someone whose lifework it was.''

''Fascinating,'' I said, meaning it. ''But how does this relate to the murders?''

''Well, they were apparently widely used by homosexuals.''

I nodded. ''I did know that. But I still don't quite believe Arnold or Tony were gay. I think this was meant to look like a gay crime, which would have made sense to the police because there have been several in the past few months.''

''You could be right, of course. Archeologists also think the dildos uncovered in Xian could have been administered, shall we say, by eunuchs—to satisfy sexually deprived concubines.''

''Concubines? Hmm. If I'm remembering my history right, the concubines in Imperial China were second wives, who usually had few legal rights—and a very low social status.''

''Right. So they were often neglected,'' Nia said, ''except for the 'help' of the eunuchs and the dildos.'' She grinned. ''I wonder if the wives were okay with that? Maybe they even preferred it. Or did they have to do the laundry, cook the meals, clean house and go out and get a job besides?''

I smiled. ''Now, *that* I would complain about.''

We sat there for long moments in silence. Finally I stretched, yawned and took up a pen.

"I appreciate all this, Nia. Now go home. And don't forget to bill last night as overtime."

"Okay. You really want me to close up?" she asked, looking at the delicate little French watch she always wore. "It's only one o'clock."

"I doubt anyone but the press will come beating down the doors this afternoon. Unless you want to hang out and play no-comment games?"

"Say no more. I'm outta here."

Once alone, I sat there drinking coffee and pondering my fate for another hour or so. Truth is, I catnapped through the whole process, so no conclusions were reached. The only good result was that I didn't miss the messenger who brought the new keys to my house.

Finally, I gave it all up and went home.

Stepping cautiously into my living room, I looked around. Not a soul, good or bad, in sight, and the locksmith and alarm people had both left their cards and bills on my breakfast bar, signifying that they'd done their jobs. Even so, I walked cautiously into the bedroom, throwing open the closet doors to see if anyone was lurking there. But the new locks had apparently done their job of keeping out burglars and/or murderous husbands.

For a few minutes I just sat on the side of the bed, staring at nothing. My mind and my body were so tired, they were numb. *A bath,* I thought. That would do the trick—if it didn't just knock me out.

Ordinarily, I would have opened my living-room and bedroom doors to the deck, letting in a cool ocean breeze. When the sun came around to the west, it was stifling in here without that. Now, though, it seemed better to keep the doors closed and locked when I was in the tub. Funny how vulnerable a break-in can make you feel.

While the bathtub filled, I sat on the edge and called the cell-phone number Dan had given me. When he came on the line I turned away from the running water and said, "I need to know where Tony's, Arnold's and Craig's bodies are, and when they'll be available for burial. I know Craig's murder wasn't your jurisdiction, but can you help me with that?"

"Sure. But why?"

"There's no one else to bury them. I'm going to talk to an undertaker and see what I can do."

"That's awfully nice of you," he said. But there was a question in his voice.

"You want to know if I'm feeling guilty or something," I guessed.

"I don't know if I was thinking about guilt, so much as—"

"Sure you were. And yes, I feel guilty. If I hadn't been so preoccupied with my new wonderful life, I might have known what was going on in theirs."

"From what I hear, you actually did pay a bit of attention to Tony Price," he said.

"And where would you be hearing that from?" I said sharply.

"Oh, gossip. Here and there."

"Yeah, well, you should know better than to believe everything you hear in this town. Tony and I were friends, and I was his agent. That's it. No more."

"I wasn't suggesting there was anything more," he said.

"Maybe not, but there was something in your voice. I told you everything there was to tell about Tony and me the other night in Brentwood. So don't waste your time picking at it."

There was a small silence before he said, "Mary Beth, it's not me. It's higher up."

"Oh?"

"There are questions being asked, especially since Craig Dinsmore's murder yesterday. Two of your authors, an ex-husband—"

"They don't really think I killed them!" I blurted out.

I could almost see him shrug, as if to let me know he didn't put much stock in the talk. But that didn't stop me from feeling a genuine tug of fear.

"Why don't we talk about it at dinner?" he suggested.

"No, I want to talk about it now."

"And I can't. Look, there are people around. Meet me at seven at the Captain's Dinghy. You know it?"

"I know it."

"And your old school friend is coming, too. Right?"

"Lindy? I haven't spoken to her about it yet. Why do you want her there?"

"Just make sure you're both there," he said.

I tried to ignore his tone and what it meant, but it wasn't easy. Did someone at the LAPD really think I might have killed my authors and my ex? And could they possibly think Lindy was involved as well?

That seemed crazy, and it was all I could do to remember why I'd called in the first place. As he was hanging up I said, "Wait, what about the bodies? Where are they?"

"Someone from the L.A. County Coroner's Office would have been called to the scene when the El Segundo police were first notified," he said. "I know the two bodies from Brentwood are still being autopsied there, and I would imagine that's the same with the one from El Segundo. I'll give the coroner's office a call."

"I can do it," I said.

"You could, but officially, I can get more information and get it quicker. I'll have something for you by dinner tonight. Okay?"

"You know, I was looking forward to a nice charbroiled steak for dinner. Now it sounds like Lindy and I are the ones getting grilled.''

''Just be there,'' he said, hanging up.

I soaked in the bathtub and thought about Dan's words, and the fact that there were questions being asked about me and the three murders. Finally, since I knew I was innocent, I decided not to worry too much about it at the moment. Better to think about real problems, like money.

The only other author I could think of who might have filled Tony's shoes—at least as far as being best-selling and bringing in major bucks—was Patrick. I wondered if he'd agree to come back. I couldn't ethically approach him with the idea, but if we did go to dinner as he'd suggested, he might bring up the idea himself—that is, if he was unhappy with his current agent. I hadn't seen any sign of that from him, but sometimes authors are too embarrassed to admit they've made a mistake. Also, he'd acknowledged last night that the ''big deal'' that was being touted around Hollywood had not actually come together yet.

Was there a problem? I made a mental note to look for any potential openings in the conversation.

Other than that, I had four authors who were making everything from the mid-to-high five figures writing cookbooks, how-to texts and true-crime novels. With my fifteen percent commission on those, I wouldn't starve. But I'd have to make a lot of changes.

Building an author up to bestsellerdom is a catch-22. Publishers are reluctant to pay for publicity until the authors are selling tons of books. But without publicity, there's no way to sell tons of books. It's true, of course, that now and then a publisher will tap an unproven author on the shoulder—usually a new author without bad sales figures in his or her past—and "make" that author's book a best-seller with massive amounts of publicity. Most authors, however, slug along as "midlist"—meaning that they don't have a prayer of making it to the *New York Times* top ten best-seller list, at least not in their lifetime.

I yawned and pulled the plug on the bathwater. It was getting cold, and I hadn't yet addressed my personal feelings regarding the three murders. I would probably miss Tony most, because he was such fun to be around. A world without Tony Price in it seemed dimmer somehow, not as bright as the one that existed three days ago.

As I dried myself, my thoughts turned to Lindy. I'd better call her about dinner, I thought. It was growing late, and I'd almost forgotten my little charge.

She answered immediately and sounded excited about going out.

"We're meeting a friend of mine," I said. "Okay?"

"Sure! The more the merrier. You know me."

Not so much anymore, I thought, hanging up after a quick goodbye.

Looking through my closet, I wondered what I should wear for dinner with Detective Rucker. I took out a red dress, then a blue one, holding them up to me. *Hey, not bad. Sexy, even.*

"Too sexy for tonight," I muttered. No sense giving Dan Rucker the wrong idea at dinner, since I wasn't so sure how much I trusted him anymore. Finally, I dumped both dresses back into the closet and slid into jeans and a T-shirt. My worn leather jacket, which I slung over my shoulder in case the night was cool once the sun went down, completed this deliberately drab little outfit. On my feet I wore running shoes for getting a head start on my male dinner companion.

Not that I planned on having to actually run anywhere, but when one is dining with cops, one never knows.

At the Malibu Beach Inn, I took the elevator up to the third and top floor, walked down the hall and knocked on Lindy's door. I held my breath, thinking for some reason that she might be gone. But the door was thrown open almost immediately by a Lindy Lou who looked a hundred percent better than the one who'd blown in from the streets last night.

"I thought you'd never get here!" she cried, grabbing my arm and tugging me inside. "I can't wait to get out of here! And to a real restaurant! My God, have you any idea how long it's been?''

I stared at the glass coffee table in front of the sofa. There was a closed pizza box on it and two bottles of wine, one of which was empty. Looking back at Lindy I saw that her face was flushed and her eyes glazed.

"Lindy, you're drunk! And you ordered from room service again, when I told you not to!''

She laughed and spun around like a child. "No, silly! I wouldn't do that. Now, don't you be mad at me, Mary Beth, but I was getting bored here alone all day, and I finally just walked over to the deli across the street and down a ways, and got some food! Then I took a walk on the beach, and—''

"Lindy! I told you not to let anyone see you. You were supposed to stay right here and not even open the door! What the hell were you thinking?''

She looked immediately contrite, but that didn't stop her from babbling on. "I was careful, Mary Beth. I made sure no one was around watching, and I put a towel around my head and wore the terry-cloth robe they give you in the bathroom, like I'd just gotten out of the shower! Here at the beach everyone dresses real casual, so I didn't think anyone would notice a woman going to the deli with a towel on her head. And I didn't wear any makeup. Of course, I don't have any, but the point is, if anybody was looking for me, they never would have recognized me! I thought you'd be proud of me, Mary Beth.'' Her blue eyes brimmed over with tears.

I sat on the sofa and ran my hands over my face. I was enervated rather than energized from my bath, and couldn't think how to handle this.

"It's okay," I said finally. And when that wasn't enough I said, "Really, I'm proud of you, Lindy. You did good."

She looked somewhat mollified, and I said, "I hope you haven't ruined your appetite with that pizza."

"Believe me, I could eat three more of those and dinner, too. Where are we going?"

"It's a steak house called the Captain's Dinghy. Like I said, we're meeting a friend of mine there, and it'll be fun. It's dark there, like an old English pub, dark wood, red booths and all that. No one will recognize us."

She gave me a sharp look and her voice rose to an almost hysterical pitch. "Recognize us? Like who? You mean Roger? Is he here in L.A.? Is that why you didn't want me to leave the room?"

"Hell, I don't know, Lindy! I just think we should be careful after last night. Keep a low profile. Not that you're helping things much."

She sat next to me on the couch and began to cry. "I know you're mad at me, but I only did what I did this afternoon because I miss my baby so much. It's tearing me up, being away from her, and I couldn't just sit here thinking about her. That's all I do, think of her. All the time. And sometimes I feel like I can't stand it anymore.''

I patted her back and did my best to soothe her. The truth was, I could understand how Lindy felt. Six years after giving up my child, I still thought of her, missed her, and worried about where she lived and whether she was being treated well. At one point I even thought of looking for her, but I never could justify interfering between her and the only mother and father she'd known all these years.

Not that getting her back would be possible, anyway, but it was a fantasy I had now and then. Taking her for walks on the beach, buying her pretty clothes, watching her grow and learn new things every day...

I forced myself to block out the sweet baby face that filled my mind, afraid that Lindy and I would drown in our own puddles.

''Let's get cleaned up and go to dinner,'' I said. ''The food should be great, and we both need a change of scene.''

Lindy nodded, but then looked down at herself, still in the terry-cloth robe. ''I don't have anything to wear, though.''

I handed her a dress-shop bag I'd brought along with me. ''Try this.''

She peeked inside. ''Oh, Mary Beth! Are you sure?''

''Of course I am. Now, hurry up.''

She almost skipped into the bathroom, carrying the little blue and silver bag. I could hear her moving about in there as she changed into my favorite dress. *Let Lindy be the sexpot tonight,* I'd thought at the last minute, tossing into the bag the deep pink dress that showed off my tanned arms and legs. Lindy's were more like porcelain, white and creamy. The kind of skin that lets you know she's been pampered all her life, and that she's never had much physical to do.

When I didn't hear any sounds from the bathroom for a couple of minutes, I walked to the door and called out.

"Lindy? Aren't you dressed yet? We have to go."

She didn't answer, and I tightened up. "Lindy?" I called out more loudly.

"Bruthing my teeth," she lisped. "Be there in a min."

Thank God. There weren't any stairs from here to the beach three stories below, but the more I saw of Lindy Lou, the nuttier she seemed. Part of me wouldn't have put it past her to shinny down a drain-pipe and run off to some place like Grauman's Chinese Theatre. I could just see her there, hopscotching over the stars' handprints in her toweled head and terry-cloth robe.

The Captain's Dinghy was on a quiet side street in Santa Monica, not far from Pacific Coast Highway. I kept the MG's convertible top up, all the way to the restaurant. In addition, I kept a sharp lookout to see if anyone was following us. Gerard Burton,

Esquire, for instance. I hadn't told Lindy about him, and I was very curious about what he'd been doing here and why he was looking for Lindy.

If he was tailing us—though I couldn't really imagine that prim little man doing so—he was good. The cars behind us on PCH kept changing, and once we neared the restaurant there was no one behind us at all.

I'd made no special effort to disguise myself, as it seemed a silly and unnecessary idea. I gave Lindy a scarf from my back seat, though, one I keep handy for windy days with the top down. She took great care to wind it around her head turban-style, and with sunglasses and no makeup, I never would have known her.

But that didn't mean Roger wouldn't. *If* he was looking for her. And if that was the case, I could only hope he was like one of those husbands on shows like *The Dating Game,* who can't even remember the color of his wife's eyes.

When we arrived, Dan was already seated at a booth, and the maître d' took us there, setting the menus down quietly and with none of the irritating fuss that attends dinners in the more upper-crust L.A. restaurants. A white-coated waiter filled our water glasses immediately and asked if we wanted before-dinner drinks. Lindy's face lit up and she started to nod, but I said, "No, we're fine."

She glared at me, but when the waiter was gone she seemed more interested in checking Dan out.

"Lindy, this is Dan," I said, leaving out the title "detective." "And Dan, this is Lindy, an old friend of mine."

"Nice to meet you," Dan said, turning on more charm than I'd seen from him before. He reached for her hand as if to shake it, but then kissed her fingers lightly. "*Very* nice to meet you."

Here we go again, I thought, with Lindy getting all the guys. Why on earth had I let her wear my killer pink dress?

And what did she think of that scruffy beard scratching her knuckles?

I watched her relax and smile coquettishly from beneath her lashes. If the whole scene hadn't been so fascinating, I might have thrown up. Fortunately, before that could happen the waiter was there again. He told us the specials—including the prices, which was nice. *See, you're already thinking of cutting down, starting with ordering from the right side of the menu. So Tony or no Tony, you'll do fine. You won't end up living in a park. You can sell the MG and get a Dodge Dart, sell the house and find a run-down shack in Death Valley.*

Silently, I groaned, wondering how hot it really does get in Death Valley.

"Your turn, Mary Beth," Dan said, jarring me back to the moment at hand.

I focused and realized the waiter was looking at me, pencil poised and ready to take my order.

"Filet mignon, please," I said. I didn't know if

Dan was paying or I'd have to, but I figured what the hell. This might be my last good meal.

"I'd like it with no sign of blood on the plate," I added. "Baked potato. Salad with blue cheese. Coffee."

"Would you folks like to order a bottle of wine?" the waiter asked.

Lindy opened her mouth to jump right in, but I beat her to it again. She'd already indulged too much this afternoon, and the last thing I wanted was a comatose Lindy sliding under the table into a crumpled pink mess on the restaurant floor. I flicked a glance at Dan and saw by his expression that he agreed.

"I don't know about you ladies," he said, "but I prefer after-dinner drinks, so my appetite isn't spoiled. Of course, Lindy, if you would really like wine now…"

I thought she might die trying not to blurt out, "Yes, hook me up to an IV!" But Lindy always had been a geisha type, doing whatever pleased the boy she was with—right on down to copying him as closely as possible, so that he'd think she was his "type." She also had a reputation for giving boys anything they wanted, so afraid was she to say no and lose the heartthrob of the moment.

I don't mean that to be as critical as it sounds. The truth is, I always wished I could be a bit more like Lindy. Playing the game, gathering the flies in with honey.

"You're absolutely right, Dan," Lindy said quickly. "Drinking with a meal just spoils it. Besides, it makes me hungry and then I eat more, and I really have to watch my waistline." She smoothed her hands over her tiny waist, which served to accentuate her breasts.

I took my jacket off and tried to stick out my chest while laying the jacket along the back of the booth.

Nobody noticed.

"All right, then!" Dan smiled, leaning his elbows on the table and looking for all the world relaxed in a brown leather jacket, white shirt and no tie. "So, Lindy. How long are you here for?"

"I...I'm leaving tomorrow," she said, looking at me as if she wasn't sure if she'd said too much.

I just smiled.

"That's too bad," Dan said. "Don't you like our little town?"

"Little town? Los Angeles?" she said, smiling playfully.

"I guess it tends to seem small now that I've been here a while," he answered. "Are you on vacation or business?"

Lindy looked at me again, and I gave a small shrug. How much she told him was up to her.

"I'm on vacation," she said. "I need to get back to San Francisco soon, though."

"Well, like I said, too bad. I'd have enjoyed showing you around. Do you have a husband waiting, then? Kids?"

She didn't answer immediately, and I thought he'd gone too far.

"I don't—" she began.

"Dan," I broke in, laughing, "you are the most curious man I've ever met. Quit with the questions, okay?"

"Sorry. You're right." He smiled and leaned back, resting his arms along the back of the booth so that the tips of his fingers lightly touched Lindy's back. My jacket fell on the floor. A cute young waiter picked it up and I batted my eyelashes at him, saying, "Thanks." He looked at me as if I had a Tourette's tic, and backed off.

"I really am sorry, Lindy," Dan was saying. "If you don't want to tell me about your family, that's perfectly understandable."

"No, it's all right! I don't mind," she said quickly. "I just…well, my husband and I are separated."

"Oh, I'm sorry to hear that," Dan said. Then he grinned. "Well, sort of. Since that's the case, maybe you'll let me show you around town after all? How about after dinner?"

Lindy blushed—actually blushed—which made her eyes bright, her face pink, and her overall look beautiful. Even her lines had disappeared, and the difference between us was monumental.

Well, didn't you plan it that way? my inner Jiminy Cricket whispered. Listen, he's nothing to you. A one-night stand, that's all. And look at him, falling all over little Lindy Lou, like any other hungry male in the world.

Lindy excused herself then to go to the rest room. She asked me if I wanted to go with her, but I was more interested in talking to Dan alone.

"Okay, what is all this about?" I said when she'd gone. "She hasn't told you a thing about herself that I couldn't have told you as well."

"I'm sure you're right," he said. "And that's what it was all about."

"Huh?"

"I wanted to see if she'd be open, or act like she was covering up something. Now I know."

"Know what?"

"That she's covering up something. In fact, I think she's hiding a pretty big secret," he said, buttering a huge, flaky roll. "And you know what it is, don't you?"

I didn't answer. There was no way I was going to break Lindy's confidence, even with Dan.

"Okay, forget that," he said. "The point is, she wants something from you."

"Oh? Why do you say that?"

"You don't think she showed up at your place after all these years by coincidence, do you?"

"No. But she was on the streets and getting desperate."

"Mary Beth, that woman has not been on the streets. I'd stake my badge on it."

"Okay. In a way, you're right. She admitted she's been staying in old, run-down motels."

He shook his head. "Maybe. But she doesn't have that beaten-down attitude, the hopelessness people get when they're on the skids."

"You didn't see her when she first came to my house. She's better now because she's had food and a decent place to stay."

"The Malibu Beach Inn? Yes, and wasn't that a bit of a stretch, even for an old friend?"

"I wanted her safe," I argued. "Just for today, while I was at work. Besides, how did you know she was at the Malibu Beach Inn?"

"I told you I knew where she was," he said.

"I haven't forgotten. My question was, *how* did you know? Have you been having us followed?"

He didn't answer.

"Why?" I asked. "Why on earth would you—" I shook my head, understanding coming on like a hard slam. "Is that why you slept with me, too? To see how much I know about those murders? It is, isn't it?"

"Would you believe me if I said the murders had nothing to do with it and liking you had everything to do with it?" he asked, reaching for my hand.

I pulled away. "Save the fake charm. It might have worked on Lindy, but that's only because she wants to believe you really care."

"And you don't? Want to believe it, I mean?"

"I'm only here because you promised to tell me about the status of the, uh…bodies. So?"

"So, they won't be available for a couple more days. I'll let you know."

"Why the holdup? I thought it didn't take that long anymore."

"Well, they're running tox screens, and that takes a while."

"Tox screens? For poisons?"

He shrugged.

"I thought their deaths were caused by blows to their foreheads."

"That may have just been a final touch, so to speak. A decoy of sorts."

"Meaning?"

"It could have been a way to make it look as if they were gay murders, when they were really about something else entirely."

"And that's why your buddies in blue are looking at me now? Because of my connection to each of the victims? They're not really buying the gay-murder angle, and none of the three men had family who might have done them in, which is usually the first place you look. In fact, I was the closest to each of them."

I sat thinking a moment. "Listen, I didn't do it, whether you or anyone else believes me or not. That means someone else did."

"So," Dan asked, "why do people murder authors?"

"Could be anything. But how about because they're writing something the murderer doesn't want made public? An exposé of some kind? Something horribly embarrassing that might even ruin their lives."

I remembered, suddenly, Craig's manuscript on the desk in his motel room. Not the one I'd thought he was writing, but some kind of Hollywood tell-all. The manuscript had fled my mind after finding Craig dead, but now I wanted another look at it. Maybe it held a clue.

"What are you thinking?" Dan asked.

"I'm not sure," I said. "Ask me again later."

"Okay. Tell me about Lindy's husband, then."

"Roger? I guess it depends on whose side of the story you want—his or mine."

"I'll take yours—for now," he said.

"Gee, thanks. Well, the short version is this. I had a crush on Roger in high school. I thought he was wonderful. Now I know better."

"What changed your opinion?"

"Let's just say Roger is a violent man who drinks too much and doesn't really like women, though he pretends to be a playboy."

"Hmm." Dan went silent a few moments. "Did he hurt you?"

I looked away. "He hurt Lindy."

"Yeah, but he hurt you, too, right?"

I almost denied it. But then I thought, who better to ask the question that was bothering me. "If I ask you something, will you keep it confidential? It's not anything to do with this case. It's personal.''

He hesitated only a moment. ''Okay,'' he said, though his eyes were wary. ''But if it turns out it's connected to these murders—''

''It's not. Trust me. Just tell me what the statute of limitations is on rape.''

''In California? Ten years now. It was raised from six to ten a few years ago, when—'' His eyes narrowed. ''Why? Is that what Roger Van Court did to you?''

''It was a long time ago,'' I said, glancing toward the rest rooms. ''And Lindy doesn't know a thing about it, so please don't ask me anything more. Just take my word for it, Roger Van Court is bad news.''

''All right,'' Dan said. ''I won't ask you about it now. But I want to know about it. *Soon.*''

''There's really not that much to tell,'' I said. ''It happened, it's over, and it doesn't matter anymore.''

''Like hell it doesn't.''

His eyes were so angry, I had to look away. ''Listen, all I meant to say was that it *might* have been Roger who broke into my house and took a shot at Lindy and me. Or maybe just at Lindy. I wouldn't have put it past him.''

''You don't really believe it was a burglar, then?''

''I honestly don't know what to believe. I've been trying to convince myself it was a burglar for Lindy's sake. But my deepest instinct tells me it was Roger—or at least, someone he hired to do it. I just don't know why he'd want either of us dead. He's already thrown Lindy out of their house. And if I'd wanted to hurt him, I could've done it years ago.''

Lindy came back to the table then, and I changed the subject quickly. As she slid into the booth I smiled and said, ''I didn't think to tell you this, but Dan is a detective on the LAPD. We've been trying to figure out who murdered my ex-husband and my authors. Right now the El Segundo PD is pointing its finger of fate at me. At least for Craig's murder.''

''But if you didn't do anything, they can't have anything on you,'' Lindy argued.

''Tell that,'' I said, ''to all the people who've been executed for murder and then exonerated by DNA that proved they were innocent.''

Dan cleared his throat. ''I didn't plan to mention this tonight, Mary Beth,'' he said, looking down at his hands and avoiding my eyes. ''But we need you to come in and give us a DNA sample.''

''Oh?'' I hadn't missed the ''we'' rather than ''they.'' So Detective Rucker was now putting himself and the LAPD on one side of the fence, and me on the other, eh?

That cast a pall over the table, at least for me. While I sat staring at my cold steak, wondering if there was some way I could choke to death on it without some buttinsky Samaritan jumping up and saving me with the Heimlich maneuver, Lindy made the best of my pink dress and her renewed golden-haired beauty by flirting with Dan.

It certainly wasn't my night.

* * *

After dinner, I checked Lindy out of the Malibu Beach Inn and brought her home with me. I'd expected some sulking about that, but she surprised me by being willing. I didn't think there would be another break-in and I figured that for the night, at least, we'd be safe at my house. As for tomorrow, I'd made reservations on a flight to San Francisco for both of us, leaving at eight in the morning. Now I needed to inform Lindy of this and tell her about my plan.

After getting into comfortable sweats, we sat on the couch drinking hot chocolate, and I told her what I thought we should do about her situation and getting Jade out of the house. Lindy nodded now and then, but she was half-asleep from two warm after-dinner Amarettos at the restaurant. I had to work to keep her on track.

"You aren't going to mess this up, are you?" I asked. "You don't seem entirely committed."

Lindy looked down at her hands and picked at her cuticles, as if that was an important job she had to do. Finally she gave a shrug and let her hands lie in her lap.

"I guess I'm worried about what will happen if something goes wrong," she said. "I'm not as brave as people who are homeless all the time, Mary Beth. There were some nights when I had to stay in shelters instead of hotels, to save money, and it was scary there. Especially at night. If I have to go through that again…"

I covered her hands with one of my own. "You won't. I promise. No matter what happens with Roger, you and your baby will be all right. I'll make sure of that."

How I would manage it, I didn't know, but Lindy seemed reassured. "You really think we can make this work?"

"Yes. I'm sure of it."

She started to cry, huge tears rolling down her cheeks that she mopped at with her sleeve. "This is so kind of you, Mary Beth. You don't owe me anything, after all these years of us not even talking to each other. I just—" She hiccupped.

"Let's not even think about that. The most important thing is Jade. Right?"

She nodded and said tearfully, "Right."

To stop her from crying, I said, "Tell me about her."

"Jade?" Lindy brightened immediately. "Oh, Mary Beth! She's the most beautiful baby in the whole world! I've loved every minute with her, watching her do funny things and play with toys I've bought her. And you know what? She's really, really smart. Not at all like me."

I began to say something reassuring, but she shook her head. "No, you don't have to say anything. I know I'm not really stupid. But I played my way through school and didn't retain a thing, even in college. Now Jade, she's already showing signs of being different. She's going to be real smart, Mary Beth. Oh, God, I miss her so much.''

I pictured Lindy with her baby and felt an over-powering rush of sadness for the loss of mine. I should never have asked her what her child was like, but I'd opened the floodgates now.

''I bought her one of those pretty little stardust dresses,'' Lindy went on. ''The kind with a full pink skirt and bits of glitter on it. You should have seen it. She really was a little princess. And you know what? I found a really beautiful dress for a dollar in a thrift store, and it's hardly worn. It reminds me of that other one, and I can't wait to see her in it.''

Her voice was rushed and jerky, something I remembered from years ago when she was holding something back.

''Lindy? I have to ask you a question. Don't be upset, okay?''

She glanced at me quickly, on her face a look of apprehension.

''Have you really been on the streets?'' I asked. ''Or even in motels and shelters?''

''I told you—''

''I know. I just thought you might have been somewhere else.''

Her blue eyes widened. ''Like where?''

''I don't know. Maybe like hiding out somewhere in San Francisco?''

Her face paled. "God, no, Mary Beth! Why ever would you say that?"

"It's just hard to imagine you on the streets, even for three weeks. And now that I know about your baby, I thought that you might have found someone after all, a friend, maybe, to stay with up there. So you'd be closer to Jade, I mean. It really doesn't seem to make sense that you came all the way down here just to ask for my help."

Lindy's eyes grew hard. "I can't believe you think I've been lying! It's that cop, isn't it? Dan. He said I was hiding something, didn't he? And you believed him!"

I tried to remain calm, hoping it would calm her, too. These emotional ups and downs when she had too much alcohol in her system were something else I remembered about Lindy.

"It wasn't just Dan," I said quietly. "Lindy, I've known you for so long, and it doesn't seem as if you'd let this happen to you."

She jumped up and began to pace. "Listen, Mary Beth, I don't think you know me as well as you think you do. Roger, either. You have no idea what he's capable of, and you don't have a clue how strong I am. I can take care of myself when I have to! And believe me, I've had to!"

"Okay," I said softly. "I'm sorry. I shouldn't have assumed—"

She stopped pacing and faced me with her hands on her hips. "See, that's the trouble with you, Mary

Beth. You assume a lot of things about people that aren't even true. You always did.''

"I'm really sorry," I said again. "You're right. I shouldn't have thought I knew you that well anymore.''

"Having a baby changes a woman," she said, her voice shaking. "It makes her do anything to take care of that baby, to save her from harm. I did what I had to, leaving her at home, Mary Beth. And I did what I had to do coming down here. You would probably never understand the things a mother has to do for her child!''

Her words stung even more than the sound of the slammed door as she disappeared into the bedroom. I sat quietly thinking, wondering if I should go in there. But a few minutes later, she came out fully dressed, the ratty tote bag she'd arrived with over her shoulder.

"I really thought you'd understand," she said. "I thought we could be friends again. Silly me.''

"I *do* understand," I said, getting up and walking over to her. "Lindy, please don't leave like this. I told you, we've got reservations to fly up to San Francisco in the morning. We've got a plan, remember? I know it can work.''

When she shook her head, I grabbed her by the shoulders. "Lindy, this isn't all about you. Or me. It's about Jade.''

She wrenched away. "You know what? You're

cold, Mary Beth. You always were, and I guess you haven't changed a bit.''

With that, she left. Just walked out the door. No goodbye, no ''Thanks for everything.'' Just a hasty retreat, blowing out as quickly as she'd blown in, like a fallen leaf in a storm.

Which didn't fool me at all, even though she'd slung her worst at me while departing, and had appeared to leave because she was angry with me.

It was my questions—questions that had been getting much too hot for Lindy Lou.

I wondered what she was hiding.

I tossed and turned all night, and when the sun came up I still had no fix on what was really going on with Lindy, or why she'd come here. The only thing I still knew for certain was that I'd help her, whether she liked it or not. And I was clear about my reasons: not just loyalty to an old friend, but as a way to pay back Roger for what he'd done to me.

Something had been stirred up in me, and throughout the night it had reached a boiling point. How dare Roger Van Court do the things he did to women? How dare he play God in women's lives, making them move this way and that like so many chess pieces? I dreaded to think what Lindy's baby would grow up to be like under her father's tutelage.

While showering, I decided to use my reservation to fly up to San Francisco this morning. The eight o'clock had already taken off, but there were flights out every hour, and I was pretty sure I could get on one for ten or eleven.

Over coffee, however, I had second thoughts. What if Lindy hadn't gone back to San Francisco at all? What if she was still in L.A., or still on the road, hitchhiking north? And how would I ever find her, even if I went to San Francisco?

I supposed I could get the address of her and Roger's house from Dan, who would probably have that information. Or, once in San Francisco, I could go to Gerard Burton's office and ask him to give me Roger's address.

I doubted that he would, though, and to show up on Roger's doorstep after seven years might tip him off that I'd been in contact with Lindy.

I'd have to think about that one. Besides, Lindy herself might have had second thoughts about going home. What if she came back here tonight, only to find me gone.

It seemed best to stay put until later. If I hadn't seen nor heard from Lindy by tonight, I'd ask Dan for her address in San Francisco and take it from there.

What I would do once I got there, I really didn't know, as my plan wouldn't work without her cooperation. The only thing I did know for certain—if anything could be called certain where Lindy was concerned—was that she'd wind up in San Francisco eventually to see her baby.

I finished my coffee, read the L.A. *Times* and

checked in with Nia, who said everything was running smoothly at the office. She offered to pass the time answering phone calls and mail, while I called undertakers and took care of some other business at home.

The first undertaker I called sounded as if he were talking from a sepulchre, like an old bit-player in *The Addams Family*. He was helpful, however, and not the money-grubbing kind I'd heard about. Once I'd explained the situation, he advised me that it would be less expensive if all three bodies were picked up at the coroner's office together. He also told me I could save money on the caskets if I got them directly from the manufacturer rather than him, which I thought was nice and more than ethical. He gave me a number to call and told me what models to ask for, saying I could have them delivered to his mortuary. They were all coffins that were simple and relatively inexpensive, he said, but decent.

I made a note to call the coroner's office and ask when the remains would be released, then thanked the man with the otherworldly tones. ''I'll get back to you after I know that they're finished with the autopsies,'' I said, my stomach doing a flip-flop. Never had I started my day off with such gruesome tasks.

''Feel free to drop in, meanwhile, to choose the service, the flowers—''

''No,'' I interrupted with a shudder. ''I'm not sure

there will be a service. We can talk about that later, okay? Thanks very much for your help.''

Relieved to be hanging up, I placed my next call to the El Segundo PD, Detective Division. After a few questions I was connected to Lieutenant Davies, my nemesis from the day Craig was murdered.

''How can I help you?'' he asked.

''Well, I've been thinking. When I was at that motel, the day I discovered the…uh, body, I saw a manuscript next to Craig Dinsmore's computer. Do you know what happened to it?''

''Any special reason you're asking?'' he responded.

''I feel an obligation, as his agent,'' I said, making up a reason quickly. ''Craig was working on a book that I was trying to sell on a proposal. If I can get another writer to do something with it, a sale could help satisfy any creditors he left behind.''

The truth was, Craig's estate would have something to say about that, so finding him a postmortem sale—while a valid enough idea in the world of publishing—wasn't the only reason I wanted his manuscript.

Still, my answer seemed to work for Lieutenant Davies.

''The forensics team probably bagged the manuscript to check for DNA, prints, and so on,'' he said. ''I don't remember it, but I'll see what I can find out.''

''You don't think the book could have been

thrown away, do you?'' I asked, horrified at the sudden thought. ''Would they do that?''

''Not likely.''

''Well, just so you know, they'll find my prints on the manuscript. I was curious about how much work Craig had done, and when I first walked into his room I thought he'd just gone out for a run. So I...I sort of flipped through it.''

When Lieutenant Davies didn't respond right away, I panicked. ''I mean,'' I added lamely, ''I didn't know Craig was lying dead in the bathroom all that time. I just wanted to see the manuscript so I could ask him about it when he came in.''

''If there's a clear set of your prints on the manuscript,'' the lieutenant said, ''I'm sure forensics already knows. We took your prints that day, remember.''

''Oh. Right. I guess I didn't realize...''

I hadn't yet thought through what my prints being on record might mean. If they didn't find any others on the scene, would that make me their *prime* suspect?

''Does that mean you'll be keeping the manuscript for evidence?'' I asked. ''Because my prints are on it?''

''Can't say. Why don't you call tomorrow around this time. I might have more information for you by then.''

I wasn't ready to give up. ''Lieutenant, all I really

want to do is read the manuscript. Couldn't I do that down there? I don't need to bring it home."

"Sorry. Can't let you at it until we know for sure if there's other evidence on it, and what that evidence means. You'll have to give us some time."

I was pretty much out of words, and couldn't think of anything else to say.

"You will be available, of course," the lieutenant said coolly, "if we need to talk to you further."

I was pretty sure that wasn't a question. "Of course," I answered. "No problem."

So. The plot was thickening, and it looked as if the author of this little mystery might be turning me into the surprise villain.

The worst of it was that my tough, sharklike skills seemed to make little or no impression on the authorities, who were nothing like New York City editors. All they could do was turn down a book. Brother Law could send me to jail.

I fixed myself a turkey sandwich and worked for a while on my computer at home, going through my finances and figuring out my assets versus debts. I barely knew what time it was until the late-afternoon sun started burning my arm through the open window. I closed up the computer and went into the kitchen, pouring and drinking two glasses of water.

By seven o'clock I still hadn't seen nor heard from Lindy. It was too late to fly to San Francisco, and belatedly I remembered that Patrick had left a message on my voice mail about dinner. Talking about old times with an ex-lover/ex-author sounded more like stress than relaxation to me, so I'd been dragging my heels about whether to go or cancel.

The outcome of my financial report decided it. I could and would do almost anything to have Patrick back in my stable of authors. He not only had a book finished and ready to go, but Patrick was as dependable as Tony had been, and would come up with one year after year.

If he came to me from his other agent, of course, he would have to split his royalties three ways. I was certain she'd never give her share up, and he would still have to pay my fifteen percent.

I called Patrick on his cell phone and told him I'd meet him at the restaurant, as he was visiting someone in West Hollywood and it would have been out of the way for him to come to Malibu. He'd suggested a new "in" restaurant in Beverly Hills that had been given five stars by every critic in town. It was also very pricey, and it felt good to be taken out for once without having to foot the bill.

When I got there he was already at a table, looking handsome as ever. His dark hair was ruffled and damp, as if he'd just stepped out of the shower. Further, he managed to pull out my chair before the waiter could get to it, even going so far as placing my napkin on my lap. I had to smile at his show of chivalry, but it felt good not to be the one in charge for a change.

By the time I'd finished an excellent salad, prime rib and Yukon Gold potatoes buried in garlic butter, I was ready to talk about anything—even old times. It didn't hurt that Patrick had ordered a perfect Cabernet, one of my favorites.

Over coffee we sat and talked about bygone times, carefully skirting the old arguments and the breakup. The wine helped, casting a rosy glow around the good memories.

"Remember how we started out?" Patrick said, smiling reminiscently. "You were living in that ugly little place in Hollywood—"

"Hey, hold on there. It wasn't ugly, it was just old."

"You can say that again." He grinned. "One of my first jobs as your neighbor was to fix the plumbing the night you almost drowned in your own—"

"Water," I said quickly, blushing at the memory. How embarrassing, having a man you've only dated for two months plunging your toilet and mucking out your bathroom. "It was your own fault for living right next door," I added.

The grin widened. "But what other neighbor would do that for you? Only a man in love. Besides, if we hadn't lived next door to each other, we might never have met."

I sipped my wine and smiled. "It *was* fun back then, wasn't it? Not the cranky plumbing, of course. But looking back, even the hard times seem like laughs. I guess being…you know…made them bearable.''

There must have been a wistful tone in my voice, because he reached across the table for my free hand. ''Being in love, you mean?'' he asked softly. ''Isn't life as much fun now, Mary Beth? Is it less bearable than back then?''

I laughed. ''No. Not really. Just more… conventional? Less interesting?''

''Hmm. I can see we've been apart far too long. And you know, I don't even remember how that began. Why did we break up, Mary Beth? Not last year, over the rape book, but before that. As a couple.''

''You don't remember?''

''Not really.''

''Well, I'm pretty sure it had something to do with one of your books. Didn't we argue over the negotiations for it? You wanted more than their final offer, and I thought you should take it, rather than go a whole year, or possibly more, with no book coming out.''

''You thought the publishers would drop me if I didn't accept that offer.''

''Not drop you. But the reality is that if one author doesn't want a deal, there's always another one who does—someone who's ready and eager to step into that author's shoes. We talked about that, Patrick. I was trying to do what was best for you.''

''Oh, I know,'' he said, squeezing my hand. ''I

never doubted that for a minute, Mary Beth. But why the hell did we break up?''

"Darned if I can remember," I said. "Lord knows we had enough arguments and always made up."

"And did we ever!" he said, good memories making his dark eyes shine. "Remember that night on the beach? That was long before you got your house in Malibu, and I think we went down to Redondo after a fabulous dinner at that little Armenian restaurant in Hermosa Beach." He frowned. "Come to think of it, what were we doing in Hermosa?"

"We went there to see Jay Leno at the Comedy and Magic Club. That's where he always went to try out his *Tonight Show* jokes, remember?"

"Yeah, that's right. You think he still does that?"

"I don't know." I sighed. "I've been too busy to go to comedy clubs lately."

"Me, too."

"There were several couples walking along the beach that night," I recalled. "The air was soft and warm, and there was no cloud cover, so you could actually see the stars for a change. An absolutely brilliant night."

"And when we couldn't keep our hands off each other any longer, we hid underneath a lifeguard station," he reminded me.

"Well, *barely* hid. It's a wonder someone didn't turn a hose on us and call the cops."

Patrick was silent a moment, stroking the back of my hand with one of those long, tanned, slim fingers

I remembered doing so many magic things to my body in the past. Looking up at me then, he said, "We could have that again, Mary Beth. I'm not with anyone now, and you're—I guess I should ask, are you?"

"No. Not really." Unless my newish "relationship" with Dan Rucker qualified me as being "with" someone.

He lifted my hand and drew his lips softly over my palm. "Why don't we ditch this place and go to mine."

I felt a moment of shock as his mouth touched my skin. It was still there, the old tingle, the chemistry thing. Without even thinking, I was ready to leave with Patrick in a hot second.

Which probably makes me somewhat of a slut, having so recently been in bed with Dan Rucker. Still, when the chemistry's there, it's hard to ignore it.

That hot second got a dash of cold water, however, as our waiter arrived with a dessert list. I wanted to say "No, thank you," but Patrick insisted that the lemon custard with Cointreau was out of this world, ordering for both of us. When the presentation came, it was so beautiful I really had to try it. The one thing that could seduce me more than a man— any day—was a great dessert.

After that we had coffee. Patrick seemed to want to linger, and to have forgotten how desirous he was of bedding me only minutes ago. My hot second had passed, and I found I was okay with that. We ate and talked, ate and talked, mostly about everyday things. It wasn't until we'd finished our after-dinner coffee that Patrick brought up the subject of his current representation—the reason, it turned out, that he'd been lingering all along.

"It pains me to admit it, Mary Beth, but I'm not completely happy with the way Nolan-Frey is handling things. In the first place, just about everyone at the agency is doing drugs. It's not all that shocking, since almost everyone in L.A.—at least, in the business—does drugs these days, it seems. But the thing is, I think they're making bad decisions about my career because of it."

"Really? It's that bad?"

He made a grimace of distaste. "I was there one day when the agent I was talking to sent his assistant—not an agent, but a gofer—downstairs to pick up his 'mail.' The kid came back with a manila envelope and the agent pulled out a baggie half-full of cocaine right in front of me. He was using the kid as a runner, Mary Beth. A mule."

I wasn't entirely surprised by this story, as I'd heard similar ones over the years. Even so, I said, "You're sure it was cocaine?"

"Oh, I'm sure. He used it right there in front of me. Even asked me if I wanted some. It's all out in the open, Mary Beth. Nobody turns anyone in because so many are doing it, and I guess the kid couldn't tell anyone what was going on because he'd lose his job. You know how hard it is for kids to break into those places and do well there.''

''Uh-huh. It's a real coup when they do.'' I sipped the last of my wine.

''And that's not all. There's one agent there whose girlfriend likes someone to watch while they have sex. So he calls his assistant in and they do it, right there on the agent's desk—while the assistant, who's so embarrassed he can't do anything but gulp, stands there watching. I'm telling you, Mary Beth, it's dirty as hell out there.''

''I'm sorry to hear that,'' I said, trying to be patient until he got to the point. Was he ever going to ask me to take him back?

''Look, it's not that I'm a moralist,'' he said. ''You know that. But with all this going on, when can they get any work done? I've been waiting four months for the negotiations on my next book to wind up, and they never seem to get anywhere.''

''Who's your agent inside Nolan-Frey? They've got thirty of them by now, don't they?''

''Closer to forty. It's a zoo, and if an author hasn't been tagged for greatness, he can get lost there. My agent is Eustice Lamb, and she's up pretty high on the ladder, but she's not doing a damn thing. In fact, she's just as bad as the men. The stories I could tell you—''

I cut him off, not wanting to talk with a potential client about other specific literary agents and what they were doing. "What are you saying, Patrick? Do you want to leave Nolan-Frey?"

"I want to, but…" He leaned across the table and took my hand again. "Would you take me back, Mary Beth?"

I let him wait a second or two. "I don't know, Patrick. I guess I'll have to think about it. Is that why we're having dinner tonight? Are you wooing me, hoping I'll take you back?"

He dropped my hand. "Lord, no! Tonight has nothing to do with that. Mary Beth, when I saw you at my house the other night I realized how much I'd missed you. We had such a great connection. Didn't we?"

"Yes, we did," I agreed. "But Patrick, if I were to take you back as a client, you'd have to accept my decisions this time. I can't believe you'd like that any more than you did before."

"No, that's where you're wrong," he said. "These past few months with another agent have been an eye-opener. Before this, I'd never had an agent besides you, and I didn't have anything to compare you with. I realize now how ethical you are, and how unusual that is in this town. I don't know, maybe New York agents are different, but here in L.A. it's a damn sewer."

I didn't entirely agree with him, but I knew what he meant. A lot of eager young writers got discouraged here by the politics, the ethics, and sometimes the just plain meanness of people in the biz. Dog eat dog was the motto of the day in La-La-Land.

But it was that way in a lot of businesses, and it wasn't fair to blame the entertainment industry alone.

"You'll have to let your other agent go," I said, "before I can officially represent you. You need to write a letter, and I'd suggest talking to her in person as well. I don't care what you say, but she needs to know it's your choice, and that I didn't approach you first."

"Sure, I can do that," Patrick said. "I'll fax her a letter first thing in the morning. If she writes back or calls and sounds upset, I'll talk to her."

I nodded. "That should do. But first, just as friends—between you and me—what are you working on now? Is it the same book you showed me, with all those rapes?"

"Actually—" his face turned slightly pink "—I decided you were right about that. There was too much violence, and I really wanted to write something different."

"Really? Tell me about it."

His book, he said, was about Hollywood and drugs, the things he had learned while with his management agency. It wasn't an exposé, he said, but a novel with a central character who starts out good but gets caught up in drugs and commits a crime that he never would have if he'd been straight. He wanted to develop the fact that there is a serious problem with drugs in the industry, more than anyone realizes, and he wanted to delve deep into the main character.

"Remember that auto accident I had a few years ago?" he said. "The lawyer I had was maybe twenty-eight, and he kept finding reasons to leave the deposition and go shoot up or sniff, whatever. Oh, he didn't let on he was doing that, but he'd act like I'd said something wrong or was saying too much, and he'd ask the other lawyer to excuse us, like he had to counsel me. Then once we got into the hall he'd leave me standing there and go to the men's room. When he came back, his eyes would be all glazed over. After the first couple of times this happened, I knew what he was doing. So did the other lawyer, the one for the defendant. Hell, it was pretty obvious. And you might remember, I never got what I should have in the settlement."

He ran a hand over his dark hair and frowned. "Like I said, Mary Beth, I'm not a moralist. I've got plenty of faults, and far be it from me to call the kettle black. But we're paying these people to do jobs for us, and they aren't getting them done. That's what rankles."

I had to agree with him. In the years after coming to Los Angeles, and before I became pregnant, I'd done a few drugs, including alcohol. In fact, I'd been kind of a wild child. I finally realized that if I had to be drunk or high to be wild, it just wasn't worth it. Too many dry mouths in the morning, and too many headaches at work.

When I was pregnant, of course, I never touched alcohol or drugs. Then, after I gave my baby up, my business became my life, and it suddenly seemed too serious to mess around that way. As Patrick had said, when you're paying people to do a job, they should do it and not be out on cloud nine all day. I know now beyond a doubt that if I hadn't cleaned up, I never would have been able to build my agency into the success it's finally become.

As for other agents, especially here in L.A., sooner or later the ones on drugs get caught stealing their client's royalties—or authors begin to see that they aren't being represented properly. Word gets around, and after a while you don't hear those agents' names being mentioned anymore. At least, not in a complimentary way.

"Why aren't you writing a nonfiction book instead of a novel," I asked Patrick, "if you feel so strongly about this issue?"

"Are you kidding?" He laughed softly. "You ever hear of that book *You'll Never Work in This Town Again?* Or was it *lunch* in this town again?'"

"I think it was *You'll Never Eat Lunch in This Town Again,*" I said. "Julia Phillips wrote it, and it's a pretty bitter diatribe against Hollywood. Supposedly it led to her downfall, although I think that really began when she was a producer. She was supposedly fired from *Close Encounters* and I guess she never made it back to the top before she died."

"Well, I don't see much sense in alienating people

in the industry by outing them in a nonfiction book as criminals or even jerks. If I write it as fiction, everyone who reads the book will think I'm writing about some other person they know.''

I had to smile. ''Just be careful to *name* the person you're really writing about and say she or he is pure as the driven snow. Make it clear that your evil character is *not* that person or anything like him or her.''

''Oh, sure, that goes without saying. So, Mary Beth, what do you think?'' He seemed to be holding his breath, waiting for my answer.

''I'd have to read the manuscript, Patrick, before I can say. I'll be curious to see what you've done with the premise. Send it over to my office in the morning, okay?''

He nodded.

''But not until you've faxed or talked to your current agent. Right? She and I would have to work something out.''

''Right.''

He stood and gave me a hug, saying, ''Thanks for everything, Mary Beth. This is really great.''

It wasn't until he'd gone, leaving me there with an empty glass of wine, that I realized he hadn't paid the check.

I was still upset with Patrick for sticking me with that dinner check, and with myself for letting it happen, when I walked through my front door. The first thing I noticed through the open curtain of the doors onto the deck was that someone was out there. A small, ornamental deck light was on, and I clearly saw a silhouette moving on the steps that led up from the beach.

I left the inside light off and slipped into my bedroom, grabbing my baseball bat. Tiptoeing back into the living room, I saw that the person who'd been on the stairs was coming toward me across the deck. His face was in shadow, but he looked much like the intruder from the other night, in dark clothes and a knitted cap.

"Hold it right there!" I yelled through the glass door. "Don't come any closer!"

"I'm not promising anything," a male voice said.

My heart jumped into my throat. "Who is it?" I called out, lifting the bat. "I'm calling the police!"

"It's me," Dan said, laughing. "I'm already here."

"Oh, God." I felt my strength leave me and my knees shake. "What the hell are you doing out there?"

"Nothing sinister," he said. "Just waiting for you to get home."

I unlocked the French doors and stepped out, not realizing that I still held the bat.

"Are you going to bash me with that?" he asked.

At my irritated look, he said, "Just checking."

I rested the bat against the wall, next to the door, and folded my arms.

"What do you want?"

"I have some questions for you, and I thought I'd just drop by. You weren't here, though. Where have you been?"

"I don't think that's any of your business. I do have a social life, you know. And it's personal."

He held his hands up, palm out. "Okay, okay. Don't bite my head off."

"I suppose you want to come in," I said.

"It would be better than standing out here in the damp and dark."

I turned and led the way into the living room. "Have a seat," I said, motioning to a chair.

"How about some hot coffee?" he asked, crossing his arms and slapping them as if to warm himself.

"Sure. Help yourself."

"You have some made?"

"Hardly. I just came in," I pointed out. "You make the coffee while I change."

"Like I said, a hard-hearted woman."

"You don't know the half of it."

I left him on his own while I went into the bedroom to take my black silk dress off. Pulling some comfortable navy-blue sweats from a drawer, I put them on and tied back my hair in a ponytail. If Dan had come here tonight for anything more than talk, this look should sufficiently daunt him. I was far too tired after Lindy, Patrick, *et al,* to mess around.

The coffee was dripping and smelled wonderful when I went back into the living room. Dan sat at the breakfast bar and I went over and sat in a chair across from him, folding my legs under me.

"You look...comfortable," he said. "Sort of sexy."

"That wasn't the plan." I looked away.

He grinned. "Actually, I like your hair up like that. It makes you look seventeen."

"In which case, you'd be committing a crime to lay a hand on me," I pointed out.

He sighed. "That's okay. I don't have the stamina for that tonight."

I was surprised to find that I felt almost disappointed.

"So what did you come here to ask me about?" I said, sliding off my stool to get the coffeepot and cups. Putting the cups on the breakfast bar, I filled them to the brim.

"I've been wondering about Nia," Dan said. "She's very unusual, isn't she?"

"You mean because she's a black woman with an Irish accent?"

"An Irish accent that comes and goes," he observed.

I smiled. "And naturally, you find that suspicious. It couldn't be that she's lost some of her accent since she came to live here? No, more likely she bashed three men with a Chinese dildo and then came into work as if nothing had happened. Right?"

"The first two men, anyway. Could be. Tell me about her."

"Okay, but you're barking up the wrong villain."

He blew on his coffee, then slurped an inch off the top. "Maybe so. Tell me about her anyway."

I held my hands around my cup to warm them. "Nia was raised in Dublin. Her father was a respected doctor there, and he now has a successful practice in London. When Nia was fifteen, though, her mother was caught in IRA crossfire. She didn't survive. Nia lived in Dublin with her father until she was eighteen. Then she came to the States."

"By herself?"

I nodded. "I take it she knew someone in New York who helped her get started there. She's reluctant to talk about it, so it may have been a man she was having an affair with. I think Nia's the type who would be embarrassed to tell anyone if that was the case."

"How did she end up with you?" Dan asked.

"Around four years ago she came here looking for a job. I'd advertised for an office assistant, and Nia couldn't type or file worth a darn. I saw right away, though, that she had a way with people. Since that's one of the most important things I need from an assistant, I took her on."

"And the arrangement's worked out well?"

"It's the best thing I ever did. My last assistant was too shy and couldn't cut it, but Nia—well, she does just about everything right. It's a huge burden off my shoulders, having her here."

"You said she didn't have much secretarial experience. What did she do in New York?"

"That's the other reason I took her on. Nia worked as a freelance editor for hopeful writers. A book doctor, it's sometimes called. If a book has potential but needs work, the book doctor helps the writer to pull it into good shape before the writer sends it to an agent."

"And they charge for this?"

"Of course. It's a valid service, and most unpublished writers need it. Also, finding someone with really good editing skills is difficult. Nia is an excellent editor, and someone with her smarts working on a book is a blessing—for the writer, the agent and the editors who will eventually read the book."

"She worked for a publishing house?"

"No, on her own, from her apartment. She advertised, and in a city like New York, word gets around."

"Does she do this kind of editing for you?"

"Absolutely not. I don't like the idea of book doctors working for agents. All too often the writer gets the idea—whether it's from the agent or just wishful thinking—that the agent will sell the book once the book doctor's done. That's not necessarily true and, more times than not, a first book doesn't sell. Getting a freelance editor to vet the book often ends up being more of a beneficial kind of schooling, a way to learn how to write better. I believe both agents and editors should be up-front with their writers about that."

"Are they?"

I shrugged. "Many are. Some aren't. It's a tough business, and people need to eat. As my father used to say, ethics sometimes go out the window when hunger walks through the door."

"Sounds about right. What about you?"

"What about me?"

"Is hunger walking through your door? You've just taken quite a kick in the butt, with your most popular author being murdered. If things get too tight, will you toss ethics to the wind?"

"First of all," I said with an edge, "I've never said things are going to get tight. And even if they did, I started at the bottom and I never cared where I lived or how much money I had. That hasn't changed."

He lifted an eyebrow. "Malibu? The top-drawer office?"

"Sure, Malibu is fun. So is Century City. I'll admit I've got a lot of toys, and I'll also admit I enjoy them. I don't really want to lose any of them, and I'll fight to keep them. But if I have to move on, I'll build my playground elsewhere. And I'll still have fun."

He raised his cup in a toast. "Attagirl. If anyone can do it, I'm sure you can. In fact, I think you could do just about anything to make your life what you want it to be."

There seemed an undercurrent of something other than praise in his tone.

"What exactly does that mean?" I asked.

"Just that you seem strong, independent...a woman who can get things done. When they need to be done."

I wasn't sure what to say to that, and I didn't like the personal direction the conversation was going in.

"We were talking about Nia," I said. "You don't have to worry about her. I'm sure she has nothing to do with those murders. In fact, I'd bet my life on it."

"You're that certain, are you?"

"It's a sure thing. You can bet against me if you like."

"Okay. What shall we go for?"

"How about a dinner at Spago in Beverly Hills?"

"Ouch. I live on a cop's salary, don't forget."

"Yes, but you seem to think you're right about Nia. Why worry? I'll be paying—unless you're wrong."

He groaned. "You really are a tough cookie, Mary Beth Conahan."

"You betcha," I said.

He finished off his wine. "Okay, then. You're on. But where was Nia when Craig Dinsmore was murdered?"

"Oh, please. I've won already."

"How so?"

"Nia was in my office. I reached her on the office phone right after I found Craig. Which also happens to be right after the killer fled out the bathroom window. Oh, wait, I know—Nia transported herself to the motel, à la *Star Trek*.''

"Not quite. Look at it this way. Since we don't have the exact time of death, we don't really know that the person who went out that window was the killer.''

I was startled, but realized immediately that he was right. "I never even considered that. You think someone else was there at the same time I was? Someone perfectly innocent?''

"And afraid of getting caught with a body, so he or she skipped. It's possible.''

"If that's the case, Craig might have been killed anytime and by anyone,'' I said.

"Not quite anytime. Sometime between about eight and eleven, when you found him. Plenty of time for Nia to get to the motel, kill Dinsmore, and then make it to the office before you got there.''

"No! I can't believe Nia would do something like that. I'm telling you, Nia is one of the best people I know. Besides, what would be her motive?''

"Well, think about it. She might have had something going on with the victims. After all, she's one other person who was connected to all of them.''

"And that means she killed them? That's ridiculous. The only connection Nia had with any of them, as far as I know, was that she worked for me. She talked to Tony on the phone frequently about business, but much less often to Arnold. As for Craig, we had contact with him when he had a proposal to sell, but when he was actually writing the book, we hardly ever heard from him.''

''You're using the word *we* as if you and Nia are one person and you know everything about her. Yet you said, 'as far as I know.' Obviously, you're not really all that sure about her.''

I felt exasperated. ''I don't understand why you're so down on Nia all of a sudden.''

''And I don't understand why you're so defensive about her. Do you want to find this killer, or not?''

''Of course I do! But you're talking about someone I've known for almost four years and trust implicitly. I'm even hoping to take her on as a partner. Frankly, I think it's crazy to try to implicate her.''

''I'm not implicating her, Mary Beth. I'm just covering all bases. We have to do that.''

''Maybe you and your fellow cops do, but I don't,'' I said, picking up my cup and putting it in the sink. ''Look, I'm really tired tonight. Can't we talk about this tomorrow?''

''Sure. I've got someplace to go anyway.''

He shoved the knitted cap back on, shrugged into his leather jacket, and headed for the front door.

''Really?'' I said. ''At this hour? It's almost midnight.''

''Yes, at this hour. I've got a social life too, you know. And it's personal.''

I gave him a look that would have shriveled anyone else. Unfortunately, it didn't seem to have shriveled anything on Detective Dan Rucker. He was smiling.

In the morning, there was still no Lindy, nor any word from her. I lay awake a while thinking about what I should do, and finally I called Dan, reaching him on his cell phone.

"I didn't think to tell you last night," I said, "but Lindy left the night before last."

"I know."

"Of course you do," I said. "So tell me, where did she go? I'll bet you know that, too."

"Took a red-eye to San Francisco. Not long after we had dinner at the Dinghy. You think I scared her off?"

"I'm not sure. It might have been me who asked too many questions. Anyway, I'm worried about her. Where did she go in San Francisco?"

"Can't help you there, I'm afraid. The San Francisco police have too much on their plate to follow someone who hasn't been charged with a crime."

"Great. Well, can you at least give me her address in San Francisco? The one where she lived with Roger?"

"Why? You planning to go there?"

"I might be. Why not?"

"Because I heard the El Segundo police asked you not to leave town."

"Yeah, well, it's not like I took an oath not to. If they don't want me to leave town, they should arrest me. But they haven't, have they, because they don't have any evidence against me."

Dan sighed. "I can't say about the evidence. But you're certainly right that you haven't been arrested."

"So I can go anywhere I damn well please."

"Uh-huh."

"What does that mean?"

"Uh-huh?"

"No, the tone you said it in. Like I don't know what I'm doing."

"I was just thinking of Lindy's husband. If he's the one who broke into your house the other night, what's he going to do if you show up at his?"

"I don't plan to be there when he's at home."

"Plans don't always work out the way we think they will," he said.

"Look, I didn't call you up so you could grouse at me!"

"Okay. Well, good luck. Call me on my cell if you need anything."

"Wait, don't hang up! I need the address of Roger and Lindy's house."

He sighed. "Give me five minutes. I'll call you back."

I hung up and began to pack my overnight bag, wondering if Dan was looking up the address in these five minutes or doing something else—something I wouldn't like.

When he called back, though, he just gave me the address and wished me luck again.

I don't know why I felt he was leaving something out.

It's less than two hours in the air from L.A. to San Francisco, but if you factor in the shuttle to the airport, then the check-in and security lines, the trip can take five or six hours. In the same time, you can drive there. I considered that option, but just didn't have the energy for it.

Not that flying helped much. I was exhausted by the time I arrived in San Francisco, and wanted to just flop on a bed and sleep. I knew I was far too tense to relax, though, so I checked in at a hotel I'd been to before, and changed into sweats. Then I went up to the gym on the top floor and worked out for a while. There's a track in a circle around the workout area, and windows all the way around overlook the city—or the "City," as locals call it, capital C. The view, night or day, is awesome. A lot of people hit the bars in this hotel for that view. But at eight to ten dollars for a glass of wine, free access to a gym is a hell of a lot cheaper.

Besides, I could think in relative peace and quiet here. There was only one other person at the gym, a man on an elliptical trainer, several rows behind me. He was probably in his thirties, and took no interest in me whatsoever. Which was fine, as all I wanted to do was plan my next step in my head.

I could call Roger and Lindy's house, and ask if she was there. But that would alert whoever answered that I thought she might be on her way home. And that person—a maid or butler, most likely—might tell Roger and mess up Lindy's visit with her baby.

I finally decided just to go over there, look for Roger's car, and if it wasn't anywhere around, I'd knock on the door. I'd tell whoever answered that I was an old friend from out of town and just thought I'd say hi to Lindy while I was there. The plan seemed relatively foolproof, I thought, stepping off the treadmill and wiping my face and neck with a towel.

So how come I didn't remember that nothing is ever foolproof, and that chaos was now the rule of the day?

Lindy and Roger's house was actually a mansion. Even in Pacific Heights, flanked by other mansions, it stood out among the rest. It had tall white columns and fifteen or twenty broad steps that led up to the porch from a well-groomed green lawn. I parked my rental car in front and went up to the door. Knocking, I waited. Finally I heard a rustling inside, and the sound of muffled footsteps.

A maid, dressed in traditional black with a white apron, answered the door.

"Hi," I said. "I'm a friend of Lindy's, and I'm sorry I didn't call first, but I guess her number's unlisted. I'm just in town for a few days and thought I'd stop by and say hello.''

The maid didn't smile, nor did she budge an inch. She was young, with curves in all the right places and platinum hair.

I remembered maids like this from old 1930s Hollywood movies. Usually those films were about a woman with a lecher for a boss. I wondered if Roger sat in a nearby chair, watching every time she bent over, hoping for a peek. Or more.

But she was talking, telling me that Lindy Van Court didn't live there.

''She doesn't?'' I said with false surprise.

I stepped back and looked at the address number over the door. ''This is 245,'' I said, feigning bewilderment. ''I was sure I wrote the number down right. But of course, I took it from an old address book.''

The maid gave a slight shrug. ''I'm new here. There might have been someone here by that name once, but she isn't here now.''

''Oh. Is there a Roger Van Court living here, then?''

''Uh…yes,'' the maid said cautiously. ''I'm not sure he's available right now.''

''He's home, though?'' My heart sank.

''Yes, but like I said—''

''That's okay.'' I backed away. ''I really just wanted to say hi to Lindy. But if she doesn't live here anymore…''

I turned and had one foot on the top step and a hand on the porch railing when an all-too-familiar voice came from behind me.

"Well, now, if it isn't Mary Beth Conahan," Roger said. "What on earth are you doing here?"

I looked back to see that the maid had withdrawn into the house and Roger had taken her place. He was heavier than when I'd last seen him, filling up half the open doorway. His hair had thinned and I was reminded of how lucky I'd been not to marry this man. Aside from being essentially evil, he hadn't even had the sense to maintain his good looks. Evil people, I thought, can get away with a lot if they're good-looking. Take Bundy. Ugly evil people, though? They don't stand a chance.

In a voice as steady as I could summon, I said, "Hello, Roger. I'm in town on business, and I was hoping to see Lindy. Your maid tells me she doesn't live here anymore, though. I don't get it. Did you two get a divorce?"

Roger folded his arms, and his eyes took on the beady look of a desert snake. "Oh, I think you do get it, Mary Beth. You get it all too well."

"What's that supposed to mean?" I asked. "Just say it, Roger. I'm in a hurry."

"What it means," he answered coldly, "is that you know very well that Lindy doesn't live here anymore, and why. I'm sure she's told you—*her good friend*—all about it."

"Oh, for heaven's sake! I haven't seen Lindy

since high school. When would she have told me anything?''

He smiled, and it was that same blank, icy smile I remembered from when he was raping me, his face over mine and his body crushing me so hard I thought I might stop breathing and die. My stomach heaved, and I tried not to show it.

''I know she's in L.A.,'' Roger said. ''And I know she was at your house.''

''What makes you think that?'' I countered. ''Come to think of it, someone broke into my house the other night. Was that you, Roger?''

His laughter was harsh. ''Me? I hope you know I have a bit more class than to burgle houses.''

''I know all about your class,'' I said. ''No, you wouldn't burgle. Rape is more your style.''

I heard an indrawn breath from inside the doorway, and wondered if the maid had been there all along, listening. Roger started to look behind him, but then stepped outside and pulled the door shut.

''You bitch,'' he said in a soft tone. ''You don't know what you're talking about.''

''Getting senile, Roger? Or have you raped so many women, you can't remember that one of them was me?''

''I never raped you,'' he said in a low voice, his face flushing. ''I never came near you, and if you tell anyone that I did, I'll sue you for slander.''

''Sue ahead, then, because I'll tell whoever the

hell I want. In fact, I'll countersue. Or I may just have you hauled away to prison.''

''Impossible.'' But he began to look uncertain. ''You have no proof. You'd lose.''

''Ah, but Roger, you have no proof that you *didn't* do it. I wonder who they'll believe.''

I longed to say that I'd had a baby nine months after the rape, and that her DNA would match that of the rapist who stood before me. But I no longer had my baby, and even if I did still have her, Roger could just say that I'd ''asked for it.'' Or worse, that getting together was my idea, and he was drunk and didn't know what he was doing. He'd wiggle out of it somehow.

''I refuse to talk about this idiocy any longer,'' Roger said angrily, reaching for the doorknob. ''I don't know why you came here, when you know very well that Lindy is in Los Angeles. My detectives tell me she's been staying with you.''

''Really? And did they tell you she's left my house and I don't know where she is? Did they tell you she's been living on the streets ever since you threw her out?''

''Don't tell me you actually bought that story. It's a good one, lots of the kind of high drama Lindy enjoys. Except that it's not true.''

I hesitated, because I myself had wondered if she'd really been on the streets, just as Dan had.

Roger smiled. ''I see you've had your doubts. Well, good for you. Lindy's crazy, Mary Beth. She just recently got out of a mental hospital. Following in the footsteps of her nutcase mother.''

"I don't believe you.''

He smiled again. "Well, it's true.''

"You almost sound as if you'd be glad if it were,'' I said.

"Not glad, not sad,'' Roger said. "Whatever Lindy does, and wherever she is, doesn't concern me anymore. It's over.'' He began to open the door, to go back in.

"So that's why you have someone following her?'' I said. "Because she doesn't concern you anymore?''

It was a shot in the dark, but a look crossed his face that I couldn't read, though I thought it might be a touch of fear. "You are even more annoying now than when you were playing Lois Lane on the school paper,'' Roger said. "You'd do well to watch your back, Mary Beth. You know what they say about curiosity killing the cat.''

I felt a chill at the threat, but held my own. "I also know what they say about shining light into dark corners. That's what journalists are supposed to do.''

"But you didn't become a journalist, did you?'' he said contemptuously. "You're someone who makes a living off the skills of other people.''

"And you, Roger? How do you make your money? Off the blood of homeless people?''

His face turned dark red, and his right hand raised

slightly, as if he was going to strike out and hit me. I was glad to be standing outside, rather than inside his house.

''You don't know what you're talking about, you fool. Did you hear that from Lindy? I told you, Mary Beth, the woman is certifiably crazy. She should be back in the hospital, and if I ever get my hands on her, that's where I'll put her. Tell her that, when you see her again. If she keeps ranting on and on about things that aren't true, I'll see she's committed. And for good, this time.''

I left Pacific Heights with my head so full of thoughts, I hardly knew where I was going. I walked downhill for a while, then onto Lombard. Finally, near Fisherman's Wharf, I jumped on a trolley that I knew would take me somewhere near my hotel at Union Square. The trolley rocked back and forth, and I hoped it would unjumble my brain, so I could figure all this out.

Was it true, what Roger had said? Had Lindy been committed to a mental institution at some time? And why? Was she really ill, while I had assumed she was just distraught and exhausted from having been through all the things she'd told me about with Roger and Jade?

Or had all of that been a fabrication, a web comprising truths, half-truths and lies, spun from a crazy mind?

Another possibility existed, of course. Roger could

have had her put away to shut her up about his sales of defective drugs, and to keep her from interfering with Jade's treatment. Surely he wouldn't want anyone to find her credible if she did talk about those things.

I thought back about the way Lindy had behaved since she'd shown up at my house. A little bit flighty and airheaded, even at the restaurant when we met Dan. But she'd always been that way, with the exception of the booze. Lindy seemed to drink a lot now, whereas in the past she'd been airheaded all on her own.

And she'd done things at the Malibu Beach Inn that were stupid and dangerous, like going out for food and walking on the beach instead of staying inside. No wonder Roger had been able to find out where she was. Little Lindy Lou didn't seem to be covering her tracks very well.

Could that, for some reason, have been deliberate? Did she want him to find her?

At this point, I tended to believe Lindy, though to be honest, I wasn't exactly sure *which* story of hers to trust.

Back in the hotel gym, I worked out, trying to clear my head. To begin with, Lindy was living through some kind of hell now. I wondered if she could be in a postpartum depression since having her baby. Maybe that was why Roger had institutionalized her. Not that it was the right kind of help for her, but it might have helped him—a lot.

Marie Osmond had written in her book about getting into her car and driving off into the blue during her postpartum depression. Fortunately, she snapped out of it enough to call someone for help. But Lindy? Who would she have had to help her if her personality had begun to change because of the baby blues? Certainly not Roger, who wouldn't have had the sensitivity of a brick.

And it wouldn't be the first time a woman was locked up and called nuts when all she had was a medical problem. Postpartum depression might also explain why Lindy had been so careless at the Malibu Beach Inn. At a time when she should be afraid that Roger might find her, she had cast all caution to the winds.

Well, not all. She had made an attempt to disguise herself, but more like a female villain in a black-and-white Veronica Lake movie—towel around her head, sunglasses, and all. She must have stuck out like an old Hollywood ghost, crossing Pacific Coast Highway that day.

I sighed. Nothing Lindy did had made much sense in the two days she was with me, and why I still cared, I didn't know. Maybe I just didn't want Roger to win—to get away with anything anymore.

Even after a half hour of working out, I was strung as tight and tangled as last year's Christmas lights. Back in my room, I dragged out the tote bag I'd brought with me and went through my assorted goody bag for something to help me sleep. Tension

Tamer tea with passion flower, hops and chamomile? Too much trouble to heat the water. *Ah*...kava kava. That would do it. I slugged down a nice horse-pill-size capsule and was asleep within the hour.

It didn't stop my dreams, though. They were of Lindy holding out her arms, pleading for her baby, tears streaming down her cheeks. When I awoke, I remembered something I'd pushed out of my mind in the past six years—myself, sitting in a hospital bed and holding my arms out that same way, my eyes filled with tears. "Please, let me just see her once. Once, that's all. Let me hold her before you take her away."

At least Lindy could still see her baby, if only with the help of the nanny. And if she got a good lawyer she might be able to use whatever evidence she gathered against Roger and his father to get her child back.

By the time I'd had my morning workout, then breakfast in the downstairs coffee shop, I had decided to come down on the side of Lindy, unless I found out that Roger was telling the truth about her. If nothing else, I might be able to help her baby—who seemed the one true innocent in all this.

It was a little after ten in the morning when I began to watch the house in Pacific Heights from across the street, well hidden by full-branching trees. The homes on this side were nearly all Victorians, strung together in colorful rows and with several steps up to the front door. I sat on the steps of one of them that looked unoccupied and waited there, hoping Lindy would appear. If she was ever going to see her child, I hoped it might be today. But even if she didn't show, I'd be here tomorrow and the next day, if it took all week.

Around one o'clock, I pulled out the fried-egg sandwich I'd brought from breakfast and wolfed it down like there was no tomorrow. Afterward, my stomach growled, and I longed for a bathroom. I might be getting kind of good as a private investigator, but I'd honestly never thought how a female P.I. took care of her bodily needs while on a stakeout. Men, they've got bottles, but a woman would need a Costco-size mayonnaise jar, and even at that, she might end up impaling herself on the steering wheel.

I didn't have to wait much longer, however. A cab pulled up beside the house, on a street that ran at a forty-five-degree angle to the one in front. It stopped halfway down that street, and Lindy stepped out. At least, I thought it was Lindy. This time she wore a black suit and a hat with a black veil, à la Joan Crawford or Bette Davis. Geez. I'd have to have a talk with this woman. Clearly, she'd been watching too many black-and-white forties' movies.

She didn't come around the corner to the front door, but went through a side gate in a brick fence that I assumed led into a garden behind the house. I couldn't see her after that, but the cab had driven off, so I knew she'd be longer than just a few minutes. I waited another five, then went through the same side gate. It did lead into a garden, one that was immaculate and beautifully laid out. There were several wind chimes and fountains, and one corner was decorated with a sort of pageant of garden gnomes. I could just see Lindy setting them out there in a whimsical moment during better days.

In the center of the lawn was the largest fountain, with a statue of an angel holding a baby. I wondered if Lindy had put it there in the months before she had her child. There was no water running through it and now I noticed that weeds were growing up against its foundation. It looked sad and neglected, unlike the rest of the garden.

I went up to the back door and knocked softly. No answer, so I knocked a bit louder. After a few moments I heard footsteps approaching the door. Someone pulled the lace curtain aside and peered out. She had short, curly brown hair that was graying, and her cheeks were rosy. She studied me through Ben Franklin-type glasses that perched on the end of her nose, and I couldn't help thinking that she looked for all the world like Mrs. Santa Claus.

Just in case she wasn't, though, I decided to be firm and tell her I was here to see Lindy and she'd have to let me in, or I'd get the police.

This wasn't necessary, however. The woman surprised me by opening the door quickly and pulling me in. She wore a conservative but nicely tailored green uniform, with the name Irene embroidered on the lapel. This was the nanny, then. Irene. The one who had told Lindy she would let her in once a week to see Jade, when Roger was gone.

I wondered where the sexy blond maid was, the one who'd been at the front door the day before.

"Mrs. Van Court saw you come into the garden," Irene said. "She's asked that you wait in the parlor until she comes down."

"Is Roger here?" I asked as I trotted behind her along a hallway.

"No. Mr. Van Court is running late today."

"What time does he usually get home?" I asked, looking at my watch.

"It varies."

She didn't meet my eyes, and despite her appearance, she didn't seem particularly friendly. Clearly, Nanny Irene didn't like the position she was being placed in. Not that I blamed her, if she could wind up being fired for letting Lindy see her baby.

But could Lindy really trust her? I wasn't so sure.

Irene motioned for me to follow her into a huge foyer that had stairs curving up on both sides to the second floor, meeting a balcony that spanned the entire width of the upstairs hall.

The usual family portraits, one of which I recognized as Roger's father, graced the walls. By their clothes, it looked as if the others were ancestors going back at least five centuries. Oddly, there were no women. No mothers, no grandmothers, no sisters or aunts. Women didn't seem terribly revered in this house.

The nanny was waiting for me by a door that led into a formal parlor. I entered the room after her and took a seat on a stiff Victorian chair. The rest of the furniture was just as staid, and the marble fireplace was ornately covered with gold lion heads.

I couldn't for the world see the old Lindy Lou Trent decorating her home this way. In fact, it didn't seem as if her personality had made a dent on this place. I wondered how long she had actually lived here, and asked the nanny as much.

"Since about the time I came here," she said.

"And how long ago was that?" I asked.

"I came to help Miss Lindy when—" She broke off then, as if she'd said too much for an employee who wasn't supposed to talk about family matters.

I sat in an awkward silence for another five minutes or so while the nanny stood by the door, fidgeting and twisting her hands nervously. Finally I heard the faint tip-tapping of a woman's heels on the stairs in the hallway.

"That'll be Miss Lindy," Irene said. "I'll go now."

I smiled and thanked her for her trouble.

If Lindy's personality hadn't made a dent on this house, it had certainly had its effect on her. She swished in, looking for all the world like the mistress of this overdone house. Dressed like a society matron in a dove-gray designer suit, she wore matching stockings and shoes. Her hair was pinned up in a smooth twist, and between this Lindy and the one I'd seen in L.A., there was little resemblance.

"You shouldn't be here, Mary Beth," were the first words out of her mouth. She sounded angry.

"It looks like you shouldn't be, either," I said, gesturing to our surroundings. "What the hell is going on, Lindy? And why are you dressed like Mrs. de Winter coming back to Manderley again?"

"I had to change into something clean," she said defensively, "and I took this opportunity to get some clothes from my closet. These are the only kinds of clothes I have here."

"Well, I hope you're not planning to go back on the streets dressed like that. You'll get mugged."

"That's none of your business! And you had no right to come here. You have to go."

"Not until I find out why you skipped out on me the other night," I said. "I want to know what you're up to. And by the way, so do the cops."

"I was coming back," she said angrily. "I had every intention of coming back. I just had to see my baby." Tears welled in her eyes, and her mouth shook.

"Have you seen her?" I asked. "Is that what you were doing upstairs?"

"Dammit, Mary Beth! This is all I have, these few minutes once a week. I don't want to spend them defending myself to you!"

"Lindy," I said quietly, "I just asked if you had seen your baby."

"Of course I have!" she snapped. "What is it that you don't understand, Mary Beth?"

"I guess I don't understand why you're so upset to see me here."

"I just told you. I need all the time I can get with my child. When I want to see *you,* for God's sake, I can see you in L.A.!"

"Sure you can," I said. "Just knock on my door, any hour, any night."

She flushed. "I'm sorry. I know I asked a lot of you. But, Mary Beth, Roger could come home any minute. I have to finish my visit and get out. So I'm begging you. Will you please leave? I promise I'll come back to L.A. I'll be there tomorrow."

"Lindy," I said softly, in case anyone was listening outside the door, "what about our plan? We were going to get Jade out of here. I'm here now. Let's do it."

"No! No, I can't do it right now. Look, it's got to wait."

"For how long?"

"I'm not sure. A few days, maybe."

"Lindy…what's changed? Why are you backing out of this?"

"I—I'm not backing out, not really. I just need a few more days." Her gaze flicked over to the front windows. "Please, Mary Beth, you've got to go."

There wasn't anything I could do to force her to

come with me, or to force her to bring Jade with us. To me, it seemed like the perfect opportunity. We could be out of here in five minutes at the most. How difficult could it be?

Instinctively, I wanted to race upstairs, grab Lindy's baby and run with her—even if Lindy refused to come, too. Some gut instinct told me there was something terribly wrong here, something Lindy hadn't told me about.

I could just see jolly old Roger bringing charges against me for kidnapping, though. And if Lindy for some reason refused to testify against him, I wouldn't stand a chance.

There had to be some other way to help Jade.

I wrote the number of my hotel on the back of a business card and handed it to her. "I'll be staying in San Francisco tonight. Call me if you need me, okay? I'll be flying home in the morning, so you can reach me down there, either at my house or the office. Just *call* me. I'm worried about you, Lindy."

She grabbed the card and quickly shoved it into a pocket in her dress. "I will, I promise. Now go, Mary Beth. Go out the back, just like you came in. I'll have Irene show you out."

As we crossed the hall, she called up the stairs, "Irene? Can you come down here, please, and show my visitor out?"

"It's okay, I can find my way," I said.

"No, let Irene walk with you."

"Lindy, don't be silly. I can remember my way to the back door."

But Irene was hurrying down the stairs, and Lindy almost pushed me at her. The nanny took my arm and issued me out the back door. In old-time detective novels, when someone was being got rid of so obviously, it was called the bum's rush.

Hmm. Lindy was giving me the bum's rush. And I hadn't a clue as to why.

I drove along the Embarcadero and stopped at the Fog City Diner on my way back to the hotel. The garlic potatoes and pot roast called to me like a siren song, just as tempting as when I'd had them a couple of years ago up here. Still, I planned to work out before calling it a night, and I didn't want to feel heavy. I ordered a chicken salad with avocado, pepitas and lime, and a cup of coffee. While I waited for the meal, I took a pad and pen from my purse and started to make notes.

First of all, what did I know about Lindy, and why she had come to L.A.?

She had told me that Roger had thrown her out. She'd been on the streets for three weeks, she said. Then, she ran into someone in an L.A. bar who gave her my address.

I still found it hard to believe that she "just happened" to meet someone in a bar, who "just happened" to know where I lived.

But if that *were* true, who could it have been? I

had been spooked the day I moved out of the little adobe duplex in Hollywood, and I had insisted no one know where I was moving. My mail went to my office, and I'd told Nia never to give out my address or phone number at Malibu. She'd sensed that something bad had happened, so I finally told her the whole miserable story about how the woman I'd hired to clean my house in Hollywood, after I moved out, had found a camera in the heater vent of my bathroom ceiling.

I had just seen a show on television about landlords spying on tenants, and I was horrified and embarrassed to think that my landlord—an unmitigated scuzz-ball—must have seen every single thing I'd done in that bathroom. I even worried that he'd put pictures of me on the Internet, the way men like that sometimes do.

I called the police immediately and they came out and dismantled the camera, saying that it looked as if it had been there for years. I felt violated, as if everyone could see through me. Especially the cops, who I overheard snickering in the bathroom.

They did their job, though. They talked to my landlord, and the next thing I knew he'd been arrested. He kicked and screamed and swore he was innocent, while the D.A. said she was just as sure he wasn't. He was a registered sex offender, she told me, but unfortunately, she didn't have proof that he'd put the camera in my bathroom. They'd found no tapes in his house, or any fingerprints on the camera, which, even though it was dusty, had at some time been wiped clean.

I was almost relieved that the case wouldn't go to trial, as I didn't want to end up as a story on *20/20,* where everyone I knew could learn about my humiliation. And since I was moving out anyway, it no longer mattered.

For weeks after, though, I'd wake up in the middle of the night in a cold sweat, afraid, even in my new home, to go into the bathroom. I got up on a step stool several times a week and took the vent cover down to see if there was a camera behind it—though who would have done that, I can't say, since I no longer had a landlord. It was out-and-out paranoia, yet it took me a year or so to get over it.

So who could have given Lindy my address in Malibu? My oldest friends were Martina and Deb, who still lived in Hollywood where I'd met them in the old days. We hadn't been in touch for a while, however. We made it a priority to meet once a year at a restaurant for lunch, but as my business grew it seemed we had less and less in common. Martina was a waitress at a place where I'd worked years ago, and Deb had gotten married, given birth to four kids, and was now a single mom. I found their conversation about hairdos, men and dating to be much more interesting than my own contributions, but not interesting enough to make me want to pursue more frequent get-togethers.

Had I given either one of them my new address at the beach house? I was sure I hadn't.

Besides, what kind of freaking coincidence would it be for either of them to have run into Lindy—another old friend I hadn't seen in ages in a city of ten million?

No, it was too much of a stretch. I should have pressed Lindy for more information the night she showed up at my door. I would have, too, if she hadn't fallen asleep on my bed.

Now I wondered if that had been deliberate—a way to get out of talking to me further, of being nagged into telling the truth.

I barely noticed when my coffee arrived. Certain things had been bothering me since seeing Lindy at her house. Her anger, most of all. I knew she was surprised to see me there, but why the anger? And why had the nanny kept so close an eye on me while I was there? Even escorting me, her hand firmly on my arm, out the door?

My salad came and I wolfed it down with a few bites of a buttery garlic, leek and basil loaf that was so tempting I had to ask the waitress to take it away. When I finished eating, she wanted to know if I'd like dessert. "The bread pudding with rum caramel is especially good tonight," she said.

I groaned, paid my check and got myself out the door in a matter of seconds, before whatever willpower I had left, left me.

My list had ended with a row of question marks.

I just didn't have enough information to figure everything out, though I was beginning to have certain suspicions. In the hotel, I dropped off my purse and coat in my room and took the elevator to the gym. At the locker that had been assigned to me for as long as I stayed, I changed into sweats and pulled my hair back with an elastic band. Looking at myself in a full-length mirror, I sucked my stomach in. Despite my decision to eat light, there was a little bit of a pouf I didn't like. Well, they say that after thirty it gets harder and harder to keep it off. Thank God my muscles were still strong.

I frowned into the mirror and was just shutting my locker, when the lights went out. Stumbling against a bench between the row of lockers, I stopped, waiting for the emergency generator to come on. Every hotel, I told myself nervously, has one.

As I waited, I became aware that I was no longer alone in the room. I heard a foot scrape on the tiled floor, then something banged softly against metal. A janitor? An electrician? The manager?

''Hello?'' I called out. ''Who is it?''

I heard an indrawn breath not more than a few feet away. My heart jumped. I put out a hand, but couldn't see it in the dark, nor did I touch anything. I took a step backward, and that's when the arm came around me from behind.

I managed one scream, just before a hand clothed in a thick glove covered my mouth and nose. I couldn't breathe, and I kicked backward, trying to strike a knee, a foot, a leg. But I was getting weak, and there were stars in my eyes...the kind that only come before blacking out.

I didn't know the man who knelt beside me, holding a cool cloth on my forehead. I'd seen him, though. He was the other person in here this morning, the one working on the elliptical trainer.

It finally dawned on me that the reason I could see him was that the lights had come back on. Up close, he looked like one of those millionaire yuppies who'd made it big in their twenties. His dark hair was cut short and his muscles nicely tanned. In fact, this guy probably had muscles in places no one could see them. At the same time, he didn't look like the many young, dumb and useless types in Hollywood. He was sweaty, and breathing hard.

"Don't try to move," he said. "You've got a huge lump on the back of your head."

Oh, great. I finally meet a good-looking, non-Hollywood-type guy and here I am with a lump on my head. And not just a lump. A huge lump.

"What happened?" I asked, my lips barely moving.

"I'm not sure," he said. "I was out on the track. All of a sudden the lights when out and I heard you scream. I made my way over here and ran into something big—some*one,* actually. I felt him raise his arm, and I could see from the outside lights that he had something in his hand—a pipe, maybe. I tried to get it away from him, but before I could he'd hit you with it. Then he ran.''

I sat up, despite my rescuer's protests. "He wanted me, then,'' I said. "Not you."

"Maybe. Do you know anyone who wants to hurt you?"

I thought of some of my ex-authors and tried to laugh. "Probably plenty of people have wanted to bash me on the head at some time or other.'' The wet cloth had fallen into my lap, and I picked it up and held it to my aching head, remembering Tony, Arnold and Craig, and how they'd ended up. I'd been pretty damn lucky.

"You probably saved my life,'' I said, looking up into gorgeous, soft brown eyes.

He grinned. "Does that mean you're my responsibility for all time now?"

"Well, now, that's a fascinating idea. I guess we could send Christmas cards back and forth each year.''

The grin became wider, and on him I didn't mind the white teeth so much. "I was thinking of something more like dinner,'' he said.

"Oh. You mean tonight?"

"You name it."

I shook my head, trying to clear my mind. "I...I still have to work out."

"You're kidding. I meant that I'd take you to dinner after the hospital."

"What hospital?"

"The one I'm taking you to, to be checked out. And while you're getting checked out, I'll call the police."

"No way. No hospital, no police. I'm fine. The last thing I need right now is to sit around an emergency room all night answering endless questions about why I was attacked, who did I know who might have done it, and what am I doing in San Francisco in the first place."

He was silent a moment. "All right, then, but I'm calling the house doctor. You could have a concussion. Or worse."

I thought about that, and it didn't seem such an awful thing to lie in my bed with the house doc attending and Mr. Wonderful by my side.

But I couldn't actually call him that. "What's your name?" I asked.

"Greg Levine," he said. "I'm here for a medical convention, but I live in L.A."

Oh, thank you, God. He's geographically datable. "You really live in L.A.?"

He smiled. "Yes. Why?"

"Where?"

"Actually, I have a little place in Beverly Hills."

"A *little* place, huh?"

"Yeah, well, I'm single. I don't need much."

"Okay, let me get this right. You're a doctor."

He nodded.

"Then why can't *you* just check me out?"

"I already have," he said. "But it's an insurance

thing. And a legal one. You need to have it on record that you were attacked here, in case you have complications later on.''

''But you think I'm okay?''

''That's not a good legal question to ask me,'' he said.

''You mean, since you were here when it happened and you're a doc, you might have to testify that you thought I was okay? And that could—what?''

''Hurt your case, if you decide to sue,'' he said. ''The fact is, there should have been some sort of security up here.'' He looked at his watch. ''But it's been a good twenty minutes or more, and no one's even come to see if anything's wrong.''

I didn't think I'd want to sue, and I didn't think there would be complications. But Doc Wonderful's eyes were dark and dreamy, and before I risked falling into them, I just went all feminine and let him call the house physician.

The next morning, having been given a clean bill of health, I flew back to L.A. and went straight to my office. I'd left my cell number with Doc Wonderful, but didn't expect to hear from him. After a very nice dinner the night before, I'd gone to my room and then to bed. Alone. And in my experience, men you meet out of town never call unless you've given them the best sex in the world.

Unfortunately, men's opinions on what constitutes

the best sex diverge wildly. Some who've heard of Tantric sex have been panting like sled dogs for water to try it with someone. Tantric sex, I'm told—though I can't say from personal experience, I swear—is lovely and warm, touchy and feely. Some say Tantric sex is a spiritual experience, and the lovers become so close they feel they've touched God.

It can take hours, though—and a lot of work—to achieve nirvana with Tantra.

So that was out from the get-go. And I really wasn't up to discovering what else Doc Wonderful liked. It might have meant standing on my head, as in the *Kama Sutra,* with my legs bent in positions it would take me weeks and an orthopedic surgeon to undo. I certainly wasn't up to that.

In the end, it was a wise decision. When I got to the office I was glad I'd taken the house doc's pain pill and had a good night's sleep.

The office door was closed and locked, and Nia wasn't there. She must have had a change of heart and gone on vacation, but I wondered why she hadn't called me before she left, to tell me where she was going and how to reach her. I didn't have time to call her at home, though, because the minute I walked into my inner office, everything changed. Someone had been here, and they hadn't left a calling card.

My files were strewn all over the room, and most of my stacks of manuscripts had been gone through as well. Pages of one book were mixed in with pages of another, as if someone had been looking for something specific and hadn't bothered to put things back in order.

My desk drawers had been rifled through, too, and all the contents had been dumped on the floor.

One thing I noticed immediately were the cards from my Rolodex file, on which I kept each author's name and the titles of their books. It was an old-fashioned way to keep track of things, rather than putting that information on the computer. But the cards also had the current status of each book—sold, not sold, being read by such and such editors, etcetera. I liked the easy accessibility to that information when an author called.

After I got over the shock, I called Dan on his cell phone. When he answered, I told him I was just back from San Francisco and needed him to come over.

"Right this minute?"

"If you can. Someone's broken into my office."

"You mean it's been vandalized?"

"Not randomly. I think they were looking for something in particular. My file cabinets have been broken into, and the files are all over the floor. The petty cash, though, hasn't been touched."

"You haven't called 911?"

"No. I'd rather you came, because I have some ideas about why this might have been done. But if you don't have time—"

"No, I'll be there. Give me twenty minutes."

I didn't know where he was, but one thing I did

know was that to locals, everything in L.A. is twenty minutes from everywhere else. It would probably take Dan a half hour to get here if he wasn't in the vicinity. An hour, if he was out in the Valley.

Meanwhile, I couldn't just sit around twiddling my thumbs. I tried to reach Nia, to see if she'd been in the office at all since I'd last talked to her. I knew she couldn't have seen this mess, because she surely would have called me, not to mention the police.

But she didn't answer at home, and I was starting to get worried. Dan arrived sooner than I'd expected him, though, and I didn't have a chance to think about Nia again till later.

"What a mess," he said, coming through the door and shaking his head. He studied the room a few moments. "It looks like a couple of piles didn't get touched."

He walked over to two neat stacks of manuscripts and nudged one with his toe.

"Those are manuscripts I've been saving to read," I said, "or eventually to send back to who-ever sent them to me."

"All these?" Each pile was over three feet high.

"All these and more. People often mail them to me without asking first, and I don't usually accept those. Plus, I figure if they came from professional writers, they'd have a SASE attached."

He sent me a questioning look.

"A self-addressed, stamped envelope," I said. "Or box. Agents can't be expected to absorb the expense of mailing back hundreds of manuscripts a week.''

''That makes sense. But the first thing that comes to my mind is whether the writers of these manuscripts ever get resentful about not hearing back from you?''

''Absolutely. That's why I've been going through them. I've been writing down the author's name from each one, and then I'll look at my files for letters or phone messages, to see if anyone sounds angry enough to do this.''

''So, basically, you've been messing with the crime scene,'' Dan said.

''Not to worry. I haven't touched anything else yet. These stacks were off to the side, not all over the floor. I doubt whoever did this looked through them.''

''I'll call the crime scene investigators,'' he said. ''They can take prints and so on.''

''You know, I'd really rather not make a big thing of this. I just wanted to talk to you about some ideas I have.''

''You don't want to report the break-in?''

''No. I'm afraid word would get out and it would only make my authors nervous. They'd wonder if someone had broken in to steal their work.''

''You're kidding.''

''Not at all. Writers are a paranoid lot. Especially mystery writers. If they weren't, they wouldn't be able to write a decent book.''

He shook his head again. "What a business."

"Besides, I think I know—in a way—who did this."

"In a way?"

"Well, I don't think it was a disgruntled writer."

"And how exactly did you come to that conclusion, Ms. Marple?"

My knees were shaking, and I suddenly realized how tired I still was. I sat behind my desk and leaned my elbows on it. "Well, look at it this way. Tony and Craig were both authors of mine, and I once sold a book for Arnold. Since I know I didn't kill any of them, I wondered at first if someone was trying to set me up. But then someone broke into my house, and now into my office. So it looks like the real killer is after me, too."

I told him about being attacked in the gym of the hotel in San Francisco.

"Dammit, I warned you not to go there! Are you all right? Did you see who it was?"

"Yes, I'm all right, and no, I didn't see who it was. The lights were turned off. I thought it must have been Roger, though, because I'd seen him that day at his house. He didn't exactly extend a warm welcome."

"Which is precisely what I tried to tell you would happen."

"Yeah, yeah, yeah." I waved that off with a hand. "But why would Roger break into my office? The house, I can see, because Lindy was there. But this?''

I waved my hand around the scattered heaps of papers on the floor.

''Okay, so what do you think happened?'' Dan asked.

''I'm not ready to say yet, because I could be all wrong. I just wanted to tell you that I think there could be two murderers on the loose, not one.''

''Two.'' He looked disbelieving.

''Yes, and if I'm right, the El Segundo PD and the LAPD are barking up all the wrong trees.''

''But you're not going to tell me anything more,'' he said irritably. ''I drove all the way over here, and you're not going to give me a name. Or names.''

''I just need to do some research first. And if I'm right, you'll be the first to hear.''

Glaring at me, he said, ''If you know something, if you're withholding evidence—''

''I'm not. It's all in my head so far.''

He sighed, but came around the desk and put a hand behind my head, drawing me to him and planting a kiss on my lips. ''It's such a pretty little head, too. Except for the bump, anyway.''

By the next day, the coroner had released the bodies, and the only thing he told me was that his final report would hinge on toxicology and other lab tests. I had all three bodies removed to the ''Addams Family'' funeral home, where they were prepared for burial and laid in the caskets I'd ordered. There was no service, but those who cared gathered at the grave site to pay their respects.

I was surprised at how many people—and who—showed up. There was the usual cast of cops lurking around the outer edges of the plot, hoping the murderer would be there. But how could they tell? They were all watching me.

Amazingly, Paul Whitmore had flown in from New York. Craig had written four books for Bronson & Bronson, so I guess he felt he had to come. We had a brief talk before the service, during which he told me he was definitely still interested in Craig's book. I told him we could talk, and that I'd call him in a few days. He seemed jittery, looking around as if to see if anyone had overheard us. So far as I could tell, no one else was within fifty feet.

When we finished talking, I felt as if a weight had been lifted. It looked as though I might still get my fifteen percent on that seven-figure book. Still, I just couldn't figure out why Paul was so anxious to pay that much for a book I considered good but definitely midlist. This called for some looking-into.

There was one person at the funeral whose presence surprised me: Julia Dinsmore, Craig's ex-wife. I thought I had heard that there was no love lost between them. Julia stood beside Patrick, his arm around her shoulders, and I remembered that Craig, Julia and Patrick had been old friends before Julia moved to New York. I wondered what their relationship was now.

A few people had brought flowers, and although there wasn't a full service, I had asked a local minister to say a few prayers for the deceased. He did a nice job, and then talked with the "mourners" to make them feel better. Truthfully, though, it didn't look as if anyone really mourned Craig except Julia. And me.

When it came right down to it, I had three people here to mourn, and I still hadn't been able to really cry. Other than the tears I'd shed over Craig's body, it seemed as if my emotions had been locked up since the night Tony and Arnold were murdered. For the time being, I preferred to keep it that way, rather than break down in a bawling mess the way Julia was doing now.

I wondered if the divorce hadn't been her decision. Maybe Craig had left her, instead of the other way around, and she'd never stopped loving him. Who knew what really went on between married couples?

The only other people at the grave site were two acquaintances of Tony's, whom I had met at a party at Tony's house. They were a gay couple, and of course that brought to mind again the question of whether Tony and Arnold had been gay. I still found that hard to believe. But given that Tony had been so nonsexual around me and even other women, it was always possible. Then, too, there were the ornamental dildos to consider, and the fact that they'd been widely used by homosexuals since thousands of years ago in China.

It would be interesting to know if the one in Tony's apartment just happened to be there, or if the killer had intentionally brought it with him.

When the burial was over, I said goodbye to everyone and went over to Julia. She was in such bad shape, she could hardly walk, and Patrick had disappeared. I felt sorry for her, and asked if she'd like to come back to my office with me. "I have some wine there," I said. "And something stronger, if you need it."

She clung to my arm as I led her to my car. "Did you drive here?" I asked, wondering what time the cemetery closed, and if we'd have to come back for her car.

"No, I've been taking taxis," she said. "I've just been in my hotel since I got here. I was hoping someone would give me a ride wherever I had to go."

"Your business must be going well," I said conversationally on the way to Century City. "Taking cabs around L.A. costs a fortune."

"Well, I got used to taxis in New York, and I think I've even lost the knack, a little, for driving since I've been there. These freeways, for instance. They scare me to death."

"I know what you mean. Every time I go on a trip and come back, I feel like a country kid just getting her first taste of the big city."

"The pace gets faster and faster every time I come here," Julia agreed. "And the way they tailgate—" She shuddered.

"I wonder where Patrick went," I said.

"He told me he had to talk to some people."

The gay couple, I thought. He must know them from parties at Tony's, too.

She laughed slightly. "I thought I could count on Patrick to look after me. But then, he's a man. One minute here, the next not."

"He's usually quite gallant, though," I said, smiling. "A bit old-fashioned that way, but nice to have around."

Except when he sticks you with a hundred-and-forty-dollar restaurant bill.

Julia smiled, too. "Doesn't he remind you a bit of Errol Flynn in his good days?"

"Errol Flynn? Hmm. I don't know, I've always seen Patrick more as a young Clark Gable. Except for the nose."

"Maybe," she agreed. "Certainly not Cary Grant, though. Cary Grant was dapper and handsome as all get out, but I never saw him as being an action hero."

I laughed. "Don't tell me you see Patrick as an action hero."

"Oh, I don't know. He does seem to have hidden depths, don't you think?"

"I guess I've never even considered Patrick Llewellen that way, before, so I'll have to give the idea some thought.''

The cleaning crew I'd hired had straightened up the office, and as I walked in and glanced around, it looked as if nothing had happened. I still hadn't heard from Nia, and I was so worried, I'd asked Dan if there was anything he could do to find her.

''It's not right that she didn't leave a note,'' I said. ''Nia would never have gone off without doing that. What if whoever trashed my office took her with him? What if she's been kidnapped?''

Dan had agreed to look into it, but lacking a ransom note, he seemed to think it was more likely that Nia had left on vacation after all. I hoped he was right, but couldn't help worrying about her.

Leading Julia over to the camel-colored chenille sofa, I told her I'd get the wine. My arm was around her waist, and she seemed thin and breakable. I could actually feel her shaking.

''Bring the bottle, will you?'' she asked. ''Better yet, have you got any vodka?''

''I think so. Would you like anything with it?''

She shook her head. ''Straight.''

The small mahogany bar and fridge had been built into the office before I moved in. Now and then it came in handy. I poured out a hefty couple of inches, and Julia lit a cigarette. I was about to ask her to put it out, but couldn't bring myself to do that to someone who was grieving. I turned up the air-conditioning instead and brought a saucer over to the coffee table as an ashtray. Handing her the vodka, I watched her gulp it down as if it were water.

"Oh, God. More," she said, leaning her head back against the sofa and holding out the glass.

I hesitated. I know that people can still feel a certain kind of love for their partners even when they've divorced, and I really did want to help Julia. Still, all I needed was yet another wounded bird to take care of. And if she passed out here…

"More, *please?*" she said plaintively, like a little kid asking for a third dip of ice cream.

I shrugged and poured her another glass. But when I went to hand it to her, I found her bent over, her face buried in her hands. When she looked up I saw that she'd been silently crying. I set the glass on the coffee table and sat down next to her. I didn't say anything, just offered a sympathetic presence, as I often do to a disappointed author. I knew she'd begin talking to me eventually.

After a few minutes she gulped the vodka down and set the glass on the coffee table with a *thunk*. "Do you have any idea, Mary Beth, what it's like to live with a writer?" She looked at me. "I know you have your own problems with authors, but you can at least go home at night. Imagine living with one. Especially a male writer. Most of them have wives who take care of them, you know. They do the shopping, the cooking, the cleaning, while His Holiness sits and writes all day. Or not." She made a grimace of distaste. "And we don't get much in return. When Craig and I were first married, he wrote his way through every holiday. Twenty hours a day, seven days a week. We never even had time to talk, and when he came to bed he was so tired we didn't do much else, either.''

She puffed on the cigarette, then stabbed it out angrily in the saucer. ''As he got older he would lock himself into his office and put out a Do Not Disturb sign, for God's sake. If I even tried to feed him lunch, he'd snap at me for daring to breach the barrier, for disturbing him while he was working on his 'next best-selling novel.' Most of which, as I'm sure you know, never lived up to that promise.''

''Craig did well for a while, though,'' I said, only partly in defense of myself as his agent. ''Eight books in six years, and two were best-sellers. Plus, all the others sold-through, which meant that his royalties paid back his advance and then some. That's not easy to do these days, Julia. As for his next book, Paul Whitmore was all over me about it today.''

''I wondered what he was saying to you.''

''You know Paul?''

''Not really well. We run into each other in New York at various functions. I've known of him, of course, for years, as Craig's editor. But it's not as if he visited the house.''

She took a sip of vodka. ''Did you know Craig was a gambler? That's where all his money went. *Our* money.'' Then, shrugging, she added, ''It wasn't the money that bothered me, really. I always had a hand in the antiques business, and after Craig and I divorced I did very well. I never needed or asked for alimony.''

She took a deep breath and dried her eyes with the tips of her fingers. ''The thing that hurt was the constant rejection, feeling that he was only living with me because I kept a nice house and took his clothes to the cleaners. As if our home was a hotel, and I was the chambermaid.'' Her eyes welled again. ''When he finally *did* want to have sex, I felt like a prostitute. Like I was still serving him, but on another level.''

''I'm so sorry, Julia. That must have been awful for you.''

Her smile was grim. ''It was. But I didn't take it for long. I finally got to the point where I pushed him away, rather than feel the way he made me feel.''

She reached for another cigarette, and I wanted to stop her so bad my teeth ached. Even more than that, though, I wanted to hear what else she had to say, and I didn't want to break the atmosphere of confidence.

''That's when he started going to Vegas,'' she said, her hands shaking as she took a silver, art deco–style lighter from her purse and held it to the cigarette. ''I knew even before we married that he went several times a year to gamble, but when I started to reject him, his trips became more frequent, like several times a month. I really think he bought women there, too. Women he could just use, I mean, and then toss them out so they wouldn't be a bother when he wanted to write. He always refused to take me along, of course. He'd say he was 'doing research' for a book, and he wouldn't be any fun.''

She looked at me. ''But he never did write that book, did he, Mary Beth? About gambling, I mean.''

I shook my head. ''Not that I know of. But you know, authors don't always show their books to their agents, especially if they aren't happy with them and don't think they're ready.''

''No, he never wrote it, I'm sure. You know how I'm sure? Because to tell a good story, Craig would have had to tell the truth about gambling. You know—the dark side. And Craig was so addicted, he never would have admitted that there *was* a dark side. So never in a million years would he have been able to write a decent book.''

''If his addiction was that bad, I'm sure you're right. I just never realized. I saw Craig only occasionally, and if I had thought there was something wrong, I probably would have assumed he was drinking again. So you think he went broke from the gambling, then? That's why he was living in that motel and trying so hard to come up with a best-selling book?''

''I don't know. But most addicted people just go from one addiction to another. They give up drinking and start gambling. Or they drink too much coffee, or build too many model boats. Hell, what do I know? I just think it might have been someone he met in Las Vegas that killed him. Maybe he owed a lot of money to somebody there.''

''I guess that's possible,'' I agreed.

''Do you know if the police are looking into that aspect?''

''No. I don't really know anything much. Except that they seem to suspect me.''

''What? You're kidding! Why on earth—oh, because you're the one who found his body, right? I forgot. But surely they don't suspect you of killing Tony and Arnold!''

I shrugged. ''Who knows? I guess they have to look at everyone connected to all three men.''

''Well, that's ridiculous,'' Julia said. ''Especially as far as Craig's concerned. It'd make a lot more sense if they just talked to his connections in Las Vegas.''

''Maybe they don't know about that,'' I said. ''Have they talked to you yet? Did you tell them about Craig's gambling?''

She shook her head. ''They called me in New York. I wasn't home, but they left a message saying they wanted to meet with me when I came out for the funeral. I called back and they said the day after the funeral would be okay, since I wasn't coming in till last night.''

She picked up her drink and took another hefty gulp. ''Mary Beth…there's something else. I was hoping you'd help move things along for me.''

"Things?"

"The book sale. The one Craig finished and that Paul Whitmore wants. This may sound mercenary under the circumstances, but I really need a fresh inflow of cash. I'd like to get some of the money back that Craig threw away all those years."

"But how? Legally, the advance and royalties will go to his estate now. And you and Craig were divorced, Julia. I'm not a lawyer, but as an ex-wife, you probably can't make a claim against his estate."

She gave a short laugh. "Oh, God, Craig didn't tell you? Well, I guess I shouldn't be surprised. Mary Beth, Craig and I *are* married. Or we were, before he died. We got married again, almost a year ago."

I was so stunned, it must have shown on my face.

She sighed. "I know, I know. Lends a whole new meaning, doesn't it, to the theory that people keep marrying the same people over and over again."

"But you and Craig? Once you knew all this about him, why on earth would you marry him again?"

She took out another cigarette and lit it, then puffed on it hard, as if doing so might save her life. "Because I was stupid, what else? I fell for the same old story. Craig swore to me that he'd be faithful this time, that he realized now that there was no one for him but me. Then I caught him with another woman, surprise, surprise. I wanted to divorce him again right away, but he had just about hit bottom financially, and somehow I didn't have the heart to do it. I went back to New York, though, and we've been living apart.''

"How long ago did you leave him?" I asked.

"A few weeks after we married," Julia said. "Just before he started writing *Lost Legacy*. I remember him calling me one night and saying that our reconciliation had given him the incentive he needed to write the book, and that it was going to be really good.''

"Had you remarried here in L.A.?"

Surprisingly, she smiled. "I flew out here one weekend to be with Craig. We'd been talking on the phone a lot, and it suddenly made sense to get together and see if we still worked at all. We met at the Beverly Hills Hotel, which I paid for. Craig said he wanted to wine and dine me, but I was pretty sure he couldn't afford that, so I offered to pick up the whole tab—meals, room, far too much liquor…''

She broke off and rubbed her eyes, leaving them covered for a few moments. Then she straightened her back and began again.

"At the end of the weekend I was certain I still loved him, and he swore he loved me, too. We got married in one of those quickie wedding chapels. You know the kind? A fake nineteenth-century heirloom certificate, fake flowers, canned music, thirty-minute ceremony…''

She smiled again, as if recalling a good memory. "We drove up to Big Sur for our second honeymoon, and stayed at the Post Ranch Inn. Do you know it?''

I nodded. ''Gorgeous view of the ocean from the cliffs.''

She laughed. ''There were yoga classes in the morning. You should have seen us, trying to stretch muscles that had never been stretched before. Then, at night, they had some guru from Esalen, that New Age place, giving talks.''

''Sounds romantic,'' I said wryly.

Julia had the most expressive dark eyes I'd ever seen, and now they were so misty they seemed luminous. ''Actually, it turned out to be a great four days. We could hardly keep from laughing during the ceremony, and afterward we laughed all the way back to Beverly Hills. Big Sur was just the icing on the cake. We giggled our way through the yoga, too.''

She gave a shrug, and the exquisite silk suit she wore moved over her shoulders in soft ripples. ''Somehow, it *was* romantic. Don't ask me why.''

Having loved someone who was easy to laugh with, I understood why. Ask women what they find sexy in a man, and the majority will tell you ''humor.'' Tony and I had gone to a college play once that was so boring we couldn't stop giggling, our hands over our mouths. The campus kids must have known how bad the play was ahead of time, because the auditorium was suspiciously empty of all but a few other people. We finally couldn't control ourselves and had to sneak out, laughing all the way home. It was one of the best times we ever had.

Except that I would have liked to make love afterward, having ended the evening on such a high note. Instead, Tony gave me a chaste kiss on the cheek at the door and I was left standing there alone, hating what I would have to do to get rid of all those feelings.

It was clear that Julia still had deep feelings for Craig, despite his flaws. I felt sorry for her loss, which in a minor way paralleled my own. I knew in that moment that a small part of me would always love Tony Price, no matter what direction my life took from now on.

I was tired from the funeral and Julia, and half-asleep on my bed, watching TV, when the doorbell rang. I wasted no time getting to it, hoping the visitor was Lindy. She had sworn she'd come back to L.A., but I hadn't seen or heard from her since leaving her house a couple of days ago.

It wasn't Lindy, though. Patrick Llewellen stood there, leaning against the door frame and looking tipsy. He had a bottle of wine in his hand.

"I thought you might like to join me in mourning the dead," he said. "A last farewell."

"It looks like you've been mourning all day," I said dryly, taking the bottle from him.

"No, just celebrating."

"Oh?" I put the bottle on my breakfast bar.

"Here, let me open that for you," Patrick said.

"It's already open." I held the bottle of Cabernet up and saw that there was only an inch or so left. "Where the heck have you been?"

"Oh, here and there. Gay bars all over West Hollywood. They aren't my type, of course, but when all you need is to get drunk, they suffice."

"Don't tell me you've been driving like this. And with an open bottle? For God's sake, Patrick."

"No, ma'am. I've been taking cabs. Julia insisted, and she paid for them."

"Julia Dinsmore? She went with you?"

"And Mark and Gary, from the funeral. They invited me, and Julia came because she thought I'd need somebody to keep me on the straight and narrow. Besides, I didn't want her sitting around her hotel room alone."

Letting Patrick get this drunk wasn't my idea of keeping him on the straight and narrow. Still, Julia's experience at dealing with someone under the influence may have kept him from getting worse. If nothing else, she'd paid for the cabs and kept him off the road.

"Go sit down," I said. "I'll make coffee so you don't get arrested for drunk walking on your way home."

He laughed. "Drunk walking! Hey, that's funny!"

I sighed.

Patrick sat on the couch, then, and talked about the old days when he and Tony hung together, while

I made the coffee. Some of his stories were funny, but then he'd well up and go quiet. Seemed to me I'd had a lot of broken-winged birds showing up lately. How did I get to be the neighborhood vet?

I put a large mug of black coffee on the coffee table and sat on the couch with him.

"You really do miss Tony, don't you?" I said.

He raised the coffee to his lips and took a sip, saying, "Ow! That's hot!" He put down the mug and faced me. "Oh, hell, Mary Beth. The truth is, I didn't even like Tony Price all that much."

"You didn't? But I saw you at all his parties, at least the ones that he gave for people in publishing."

"Yes, well, we all show up for the parties, don't we? Even the ones we don't want to be at. It's part of the game—the glad-handing, the networking."

"I didn't realize you felt that way."

I wondered if he'd been jealous of Tony's success, and the thought must have shown on my face.

"You think I was envious of him? Ha. If you only knew...."

His voice trailed off, and I said, "Knew what? Come on, Patrick, out with it. I've never known you to pussyfoot."

He picked up his mug, blew on the coffee and took a deep swallow. "Okay, but you have to promise not to tell anyone about this."

I didn't know what to say, and he pressed me on the point. "Swear, Mary Beth. I won't tell you, otherwise."

"I guess...if you think it's that important."

"It is. The thing is, Tony and I used to be good friends. But then he got burned out. Did you know that?"

"I knew he was getting tired of doing the same kinds of books, but he told me he was working on something new he was excited about."

"Something *new*," Patrick said sarcastically. "Yeah, it was new, all right. You know what he was working on, Mary Beth? *My book.* The bastard stole my book."

"What?" Patrick must be drunker than I thought. "I can't believe that!"

"Oh, you can believe it," Patrick said. "Tony didn't steal it physically—not the actual manuscript. But we went out for drinks one night and I stupidly talked about it. *In detail.* I was stuck on a point, and I thought it would be fun to work it out with another writer." He made an angry sound and set his mug down. "I forgot how easily that can end up in plagiarism."

"You're saying Tony stole your ideas?" I asked. "But ideas can't be copyrighted, Patrick."

"Not just my ideas. It was worse than that. A few weeks later I was at a party in his apartment—you remember the one he had to celebrate winning the Docher Award? You and Tony and a few other people were in the kitchen, and I was looking for a pen and paper to write down some thoughts. I opened up a drawer of that fancy desk he had in his living room and found a forty-page synopsis for a book. *My* book, Mary Beth. The one I'd been working on for months.''

"I don't understand. You mean he came up with a similar synopsis?"

"Dammit, Mary Beth, no! It was an almost exact duplicate of the synopsis I showed him that night we talked. A couple of paragraphs were switched around, and a few words changed, but that's all. I remembered then that Tony never did have any suggestions, anything that would help me with the point I was stuck on. All of the ideas in that synopsis were mine—and they were there in black and white, in absolute detail, with the words *by Tony Price* under the title. He must have been taping our conversation that night, Mary Beth.''

"My God," I said, stunned. "I never would have believed that Tony would do such a thing."

"Well, he did. And when I confronted him about it after the party, he said he didn't remember talking with me about my book that night at all. Said he remembered we went for drinks one night, but he thought we'd gone there to pick up girls.''

"Pick up girls? He liked to pick up girls in bars?" I wondered if I'd ever known Tony at all.

"It's one of the things he didn't talk much about, but a few of us knew it. We went out together sometimes, and Tony would flirt with any woman in sight."

"But the way he was murdered..."

I realized then that Patrick didn't know about the Chinese dildo found at the crime scene, as the police still hadn't given that information to the media. Or the fact that from the beginning, they had been thinking that Tony and Arnold were gay.

Of course, I knew that some gay men make a point of flirting with women, as a cover. And some just enjoy flirting with women, cover or no.

"What do you mean, the way he was murdered?" Patrick asked.

"Oh, nothing," I said, quickly changing the subject.

Patrick's eyes widened. "You mean, you thought they were gay?"

"Well…"

Patrick shook his head. "Tony would roll over in his grave if he knew you thought that. He liked to portray himself as quite the ladies' man."

I smiled. "Oh, Patrick, you're so quaint. It's *player* these days, not ladies' man."

"Scorn me if you like," he said with a smile. "There are some women who like the old-world type."

"Patrick, was it the rape book that Tony and you talked about? Was that the synopsis you found?"

"No. It was the newer one, the one I gave my other agent. I haven't heard back from her, by the way. I did tell her I wanted to return to you."

"Well, she's probably busy. Patrick, have you told the police that Tony plagiarized your book?"

"No."

"Why not?"

"Isn't it obvious? They'd probably think I killed him."

I studied him a moment, and then I said it. "Patrick, you didn't...did you?"

Anger filled his eyes. "You really think I'd do that? Over a damn book?"

"No...I mean, I don't know. If you were counting on the book selling, and Tony stole it out from under you..."

He glowered at me. "I never should have told you. If I even for a minute believed you would think that, I never would have. Thanks for your support, Mary Beth."

"I'm sorry," I said. "I do want to support you, and I don't really think you did it. But anyone would have asked that question, Patrick. And if the police find out what Tony did, they'll be asking it."

He stood, brushing his trousers off fastidiously, though there was nothing on them. The gesture was more like a nervous tic.

"Thanks for the coffee," he said. "I have to get home."

"You don't have to leave yet, Patrick. Don't you want to hear what I decided about representing you?"

"No. If it's a rejection, I don't need to hear it right now. Maybe some other time."

"But—"

I was going to tell him I'd like to represent him again, but before I could, he stalked out, his shoulders rigid, his walk stiff. I was astonished that he had become that angry over a mere question.

Pouring myself a glass of orange juice, I sat on my deck and thought that over for a while. Patrick had been his usual charming self, even to wearing a burgundy velvet smoking jacket over his trousers, à la Nick Charles in an old *Thin Man* movie. If Patrick hadn't been a writer, he could probably have pulled off a career in acting.

Had he been acting with me? Only appearing not to have anything to do with Tony's and Arnold's murders?

But why would he have killed Arnold? Just because he was there? And what about Craig?

Yes, I thought. Anyone would have asked the question—if only because making a connection between the three murders had turned out to be so complicated.

Or it could be complicated, if it weren't for the theory of Ockham's razor: *The simplest explanation is always the best.*

I believed that. But now, what did I do with it? How did I apply it to this situation?

The next morning I went to my office to check phone messages, mail, and return calls. I half believed Nia would be there, and I'd find she'd had a family emergency of some kind that kept her from

leaving me a note. I knew that Dan had put out un-
official feelers around town, but he hadn't gotten
back to me yet.

If Nia didn't turn up soon, I would have to report
her missing. My hesitation to do that was based on
one other occasion when she'd disappeared for a day
or two, and I'd later learned she'd been with a boyfriend and somehow lost track of all time. That was
her story, anyway, and though I didn't fully believe
it, I figured it must have been something important
to take her away like that. And since then, the incident hadn't been repeated.

At any rate I no longer seriously worried that the
person who broke into my office had taken Nia and
was holding her hostage. As Dan had said, it didn't
seem likely, since I hadn't received any threatening
calls, or an offer to exchange her for whatever the
burglar had been looking for. So in the end, raising
a ruckus at this point, and possibly embarrassing Nia
in the midst of a romantic rendezvous, didn't seem
the right thing to do. Yet.

After I took care of the phone messages and mail,
I sat at my desk, wondering what the person who'd
broken in had wanted. The piles of manuscripts had
been straightened up by the cleaning crew, and I'd
paid one of them extra to make a list of every single
manuscript and who had sent it. I pretty much knew,
therefore, what was in those piles, and nothing from
that gave me a clue.

Finally, I closed my eyes, picturing my drawers,

my files, everything that I'd ever put anywhere, or that Nia had at my request.

After I'd done that for five minutes or so, I had an idea: whoever had done this hadn't touched my exercise room.

At first look, there doesn't seem to be much in there but exercise equipment. But behind the screen where Nia and I change our clothes, there's a large wall safe inside a closet.

The safe had been installed by a previous tenant, but I'd never used it for money or valuables. Until I moved here, I didn't really have any valuables. As for money, I keep a small amount of petty cash in my desk drawer, but that's all. Purchases like furniture and business supplies are put on my business credit card.

The things I did use the safe for, and often with amusement, were odds and ends of material from writers I represent. As I've said, writers can be a paranoid lot, and sometimes the things they worry about don't make a lot of sense. A few of them, for instance, regularly send me the first drafts of their proposals for books, accompanied by copies on floppy disks or CDs. They're afraid of fire or computer crashes at their homes, and of losing a book that way. While that has certainly happened, they don't understand that anything in an agent's office is usually lost in a pile of manuscripts and all other kinds of chaos. They'd be much better off getting a safe-deposit box at their bank—or at least e-mailing their manuscripts to a friend.

As for the rest, my authors sometimes sent me family photos and recipes. One person had sent me a pile of research notes, written in longhand, that might or might not one day mean something to her book. The book had sold years ago, without her ever once asking for those notes.

The first time I saw the safe, though, I thought: Why not? There might never be anything of importance in it, but it would probably comfort a writer to hear that his or her materials had been locked up. So that's where I kept things I barely looked at, once I'd realized what they were.

Now I wondered if there was anything of value in that safe that I hadn't noticed. Anything at all that might lead to the killers of Tony, Arnold and Craig.

I made sure my front-office door was locked and went through the connecting door from my office to the exercise room. There wasn't much in the change area, but Nia and I each left a set of clean business clothes and shoes in there, in case of an emergency. We never explicitly said what kind of emergency we thought there might be, but we'd both seen the movie *Volcano,* where L.A. is devastated by molten lava. Maybe we thought we might need a change of clothes to keep appointments with survivors, if fiction ever became fact.

Other than the business suits, there were sweats and other workout clothes that, by coincidence, effectively hid the three-foot-high safe. I opened the lock and took out the brown carton of materials it held, taking them back into my office. There I spread them on my desk, going through each piece of paper one by one.

After a while I began to get discouraged. Most of the papers in the box were outdated and really did need to be thrown out or returned to their owners. *One more thing to do.* It was a shock, then, when I saw a small blue envelope with *Craig Dinsmore* scrawled across the front in Nia's handwriting.

I opened it with shaking hands, because suddenly I knew I'd hit gold. The envelope looked reasonably new, and I half remembered shoving it in the safe a while back. I had assumed it was full of the kinds of obscure ramblings I'd seen from him before, when he was drinking.

I didn't know at the time that Craig had quit drinking. If I had, I almost certainly would have opened the envelope. But when Nia put it on my desk without a note from her, I'm sure I just pushed it off to a corner of my desk until one day I filed it in the safe.

The single sheet of paper inside was written in longhand, and with a pencil that hadn't been too sharp. The writing was faint, so I smoothed the paper out on the desk to see it better.

It was a list of pharmaceutical companies, from Eli Lilly to GlaxoSmithKline and a host of others, some I'd never heard of. Each name had a line through it, as if Craig had eliminated them or they didn't meet his needs. But the second from the last was *Courtland Pharmaceuticals.* He'd underlined this one twice.

I felt a shock run through me. What kind of connection could Craig have possibly had with the company Roger Van Court and his father owned? And was this just some weird coincidence, or an answer to who murdered Craig Dinsmore?

I mulled this over on the way home, and by midafternoon I thought I was on the right track. I fixed a cup of coffee and put some crackers and cheese on a plate, for sustenance. Taking them into the living room, I sat at my computer and logged on to the Net, then went to Google.com, typing in the search line *nonfiction books lives of the stars*—the kind of manuscript I'd seen in Craig's motel room.

Those words didn't bring up what I was looking for, so I next tried *Hollywood stars expose.* With no way of putting an accent over the ''e,'' I came up with a lot of sites about Hollywood stars exposing their naked bodies in magazines and on calendars. I waded through that and finally found what I was looking for.

I wanted to shout, to pat myself on the back, and celebrate.

But there wasn't time for that. Instead I got in my car and drove to the closest library. There I looked for and found a book called *Timing's Everything,* circa 1940s. Taking it over to a table, I opened it up and looked at the first ten pages. My smile must have been similar to the Cheshire cat's.

Next I called Lieutenant Davies at the El Segundo PD, asking if I might see the contents of Craig's desk from the motel room. He pointed out in a not-too-friendly tone that since it was evidence, just as the manuscript was, I wouldn't be able to see it until after the trial.

"The trial?" I wondered if he meant mine, and if I'd made a mistake calling him. Maybe I shouldn't have reminded him of my existence.

"We'll catch whoever murdered Craig Dinsmore," Lieutenant Davies said. "And you can bet there will be a trial."

"Oh. Well, I hope you do," I said briskly. "Find the killer, I mean."

I hung up and shrugged off the feelings of impending doom that had settled in around me at the sound of Lieutenant Davies's voice. I had to keep my mind clear and not let anything get in the way of what I had to do now.

Which was to get my hands on that evidence.

I called Dan and left a message on his voice mail. When he called back, I said, "Is there some way I can get a list of what they took from Craig's motel room as evidence?"

"Have you tried asking the ESPD?"

"Yeah, and that helped a whole lot. Lieutenant Davies really loves me, you know. He practically asked me for a date."

"A date, huh?"

"You bet. The kind where he arrives with two big brutish officers to cart me off to jail."

Dan chuckled. But then he said seriously, "I wouldn't joke too much about that, if I were you. It could happen."

"Don't think I don't know that. Look, I've got to get to Craig's stuff somehow—anything he had in that motel room. I think I know something about Craig's murder, and if I can prove it, they'll be carting someone else off instead of me."

"And who might that be?"

"I don't want to say till I'm sure. But it's big, I promise you that."

There was a brief silence. "Okay," he said. "I'll see what I can do. But only if I'm the first to know."

"No problem. Any word on Nia yet?"

"No. I've checked with the hospitals and the various law enforcement agencies around here. No one's seen her. Which, in a way, is a good thing."

"You mean because she isn't dead."

"Well…not so far as we know."

"Gee, thanks for the positive input. Listen, I'll be waiting to hear back about that evidence."

"At your service, ma'am."

While I waited to hear back from Dan, I tried Nia's apartment again for the fifth or sixth time. This time, someone answered who said she was Nia's niece.

"She went away for a few days," the young girl said. "I'm just house-sitting."

"Do you know where she went?" I asked. "Nia works for me, and I'm just worried that I haven't heard from her."

"Oh, you must be the agent. Mary Beth Conahan, right?"

"Right."

"Nia talks about you a lot," the girl said. "I'm Anita. You can call me Neets, though. Everybody does."

I smiled. "Well, Neets, I'd really like to talk to Nia. Did she leave a phone number with you, or tell you where she was going?"

"Sure. She's at the Ritz-Carlton in London. She went to visit my uncle. Her father, I mean."

I think my jaw must have dropped. "Oh. Did she leave a message for me?"

"Not that I know of," Neets said.

"Do you have the number in London, then?" I asked.

"Sure." She gave it to me and I wrote it down.

"Thanks," I said.

"Anytime. Ms. Conahan, can I ask you something? Would you look at a book I've written?"

"You wrote a book?" I smiled. "How old are you?"

"I'm seventeen," Neets said, "but I've been writing all my life."

All my life. At seventeen, I remembered, it seems one has lived forever.

"Sure, I'll look at it," I said. "But give me some time to read it and get back to you. I've got a lot on my plate right now."

"Hey, that's okay!" she said excitedly. "I didn't really expect you to say yes. Nia always says not to bother you because you're so busy."

"Well, Nia's right—about most things. But this is different." Neets might be a budding *New York Times* best-selling author, after all. Who knew?

We hung up and I looked at the London number. If anything, I was more concerned than ever. Why would Nia go so far away and not leave me a note or talk to me first?

I'd forgotten about the time difference, but when I reached Nia at the Ritz, she was having a late dinner in her room.

"Hi. What's up?" she asked.

"You didn't tell me where you were going," I said. "I've been worried."

"I'm sorry. You didn't get my note?"

"What note?"

"I left it on my desk. I didn't know I was coming over here until the middle of the night, and I thought that was too late to call you."

I couldn't remember a thing on her desk. It was as pristine as she left it every night.

"There wasn't a note. Lots of stuff in my office, though."

"Oh?"

"Someone broke in and rummaged through all the files."

"My God! Are you all right?"

"Yeah. I was hoping you might have seen something before you left."

"Not a thing. Like I said, I left you a message. It was right on my desk. And when I left, everything was fine."

I heard a male voice in the background, and could tell that Nia had covered the mouthpiece of the phone with her hand. She was laughing, and sounded as if she was having way too much fun.

"Nia?"

"Yes. Sorry."

"Who's there?"

"Oh, nobody." She giggled. "I mean, nobody you'd know."

"What about your father? Have you seen a lot of him?"

"Not enough. I needed his expertise on an idea I've had."

"An idea?"

"Yeah, well, I'm…trying to write a book."

"Nia! Why didn't you tell me?"

"I thought you might laugh. Especially if you read it." She chuckled.

"Never!" I said. "Let me see it when you get back, okay?"

"We'll see. Anyway, that's why I thought I'd take

a couple of days, while business was slow, and fly over here. Dad's been really busy, though. He's working on something having to do with a new drug. Seems like he's more and more into biochemistry lately.''

''Oh.'' Curious, I said, ''Do you know what he's working on?''

Nia's laughter was muffled again. ''Stop!'' she said to whoever was in her room.

''I haven't a clue,'' she said to me, coming back. ''I've been…a little distracted, shall we say, since I got here.''

''When are you coming home?'' I asked.

''Why, do you need me?''

''Not really. I just wondered.''

''I've been thinking I might spend a couple more days here. Is that okay?''

''Sure. You've more than earned it.''

''Thanks, Mary Beth. You're the best. Have the police found the murderer yet?''

''I'm not sure how to answer that. They seem to think it's me.''

''You? That's crazy!''

''Tell it to the judge,'' I said.

''Don't worry, I will.'' She laughed. ''Wait a minute, that didn't sound right. I should have said, 'Let's hope I don't have to.'''

''Thanks.''

When we hung up, I felt as if Nia were a million miles away. I wished, now, that she'd waited to go on vacation. Nia was really the only friend I had who I could talk to about the kinds of things that were going on here.

Apparently, though, the police hadn't told her not to leave town. They had interviewed her shortly after the murders, and must have cleared her of any suspicion.

I wondered why I was left with questions lingering in my mind.

At 2:25 the next morning, I was in front of the El Segundo police department in the back of Dan's SUV. With us were flashlights, a box cutter, an evidence box and my notebook computer.

"I don't know about you," I said, "but I hate being all scrunched over like this. My back is killing me."

"That'll be the least of your troubles," Dan said, "if anybody discovers I sneaked this evidence box out for you. I could lose my badge. And so could the cop who looked the other way. Damn good thing he owed me a favor."

"Stop making me nervous," I said. "I work better when I'm calm."

"I don't give a duck's ass if you're calm. Just work fast. I've got to get this box back within the hour."

I cut through the tape carefully with the box cutter, so that the cut wouldn't show when I finished, and put my own tape over it. On the top of the box were pens, pencils and other desktop items in Baggies, which I didn't touch. Meanwhile, Dan watched every move I made, so that if he was asked one day, he could say I hadn't taken a thing. I lifted out the top Baggies carefully, and dug down through others filled with foam coffee cups and paper plates. There were some lined yellow pads and paper clips, carbon paper and postage stamps. The sort of thing people keep on or in a desk.

But the manuscript I'd seen on Craig's desk wasn't there.

"What do you think happened to it?" I asked Dan.

"They could have somebody reading through it to see if there are any clues in it. Same thing you wanted to do."

I sat back on my heels. "Not anymore. I'm looking for the real manuscript now."

"The real one?"

"I remembered the other night why the manuscript on Craig's desk looked so familiar, like it had been done before. That's because it *was* done before—years ago, by another author. The manuscript on Craig's desk, at least the first few pages of it, was something he'd typed, word for word, from another book."

"How do you know?"

"I wasn't sure until I found the other book on the Net. I put a few choice words in the search line, and the book I remembered popped up within minutes.

Then I went to the library and looked at an actual copy. Wanna know what I found?''

"More than banana cream pie," he said.

"You like banana cream pie?"

"I'm crazy for it. But go on."

"I found that the manuscript on Craig's desk was an exact duplicate of *Timing's Everything*. That's a book written by a member of the paparazzi who was well-known in the forties. He thought he could write an exposé of the stars based on his knowledge of them as a photographer. Unfortunately, he didn't write very well, and the book came out and sunk without a plop. Today, there's hardly anyone who even remembers it."

"And you're saying Craig Dinsmore plagiarized it? Why would he do that with a book that didn't even sell well?"

"I don't think he plagiarized it, at least not to sell it. I know this may sound crazy, but I think that book was a decoy. Something for people to look at if they ever broke into his motel room, so they wouldn't know what he was really writing. Why else would he spend so much time and energy retyping an old book and leaving it out on his desk like that?"

Dan whistled. "He retyped the whole book?"

"I didn't have time to read the whole thing, but the first few chapters, yes. The rest might have been blank pages."

As I was telling him this, I was still digging down through pads of notepaper to the bottom of the box.

And there it was: not a paper manuscript, but a CD. The handwritten label had the name of an album on it—''Come Away With Me.'' The vocal artist was Norah Jones, one of my favorites, but that wasn't why I suddenly felt so excited. As far as I could remember, Craig was a devotee of classical music. He was, in fact, a snob about anything new and popular. So unless I was mistaken, this music label was yet another decoy, and Craig had probably copied his real book onto this CD—rather than keep a hard copy of it around for anyone to see.

I reached for my notebook computer and put the CD in, then hit some keys till it came up on the screen.

''I was right,'' I said, restraining myself from shouting it out. ''It's his real book. And look at this. Craig was writing an exposé of pharmaceutical companies and their illegal and unethical practices.'' I fell silent, scanning through a list of names.

''My God. He's written that Courtland Pharmaceuticals was one of them. Not just one, but the main one, it seems.''

''Courtland? You mean the family business your friend Lindy married into?''

I eased my legs out of their cramped position. ''The very same.''

He was silent a few moments. Then he said, ''You know what this means, don't you?''

''That there's a connection between Roger Van

Court and Craig. And the connection could be murder.''

''Makes sense,'' he agreed. ''Either he or someone he sent here threatened Dinsmore if he didn't turn the manuscript over. But how could he know that Craig Dinsmore was writing a book like this about Courtland?''

''I'm not sure, but Craig talked a lot about his work,'' I said. ''He hung out in bars, even after he stopped drinking. He and Patrick had the same fault, in fact, if you want to call it that. They both liked to talk to people about their characters and plots.''

''So you think Roger Van Court, or someone who knows him, overheard Craig talking about his book in a bar? Isn't that a bit of a coincidence?''

''It is, yes. I just threw out the idea as a possibility. Maybe he found out some other way.''

''Look, I've got to get this box back to the evidence room,'' Dan said. ''Are you finished with it?''

''I am. Just let me copy this CD and put it back.''

I copied it onto my hard drive, put it back in the box and taped the box up. Just as I put the roll of tape down, though, a car pulled up behind us. Its headlights shone through the back window of the SUV.

I just had time to throw a blanket over the box before Lieutenant Davies climbed out and began to walk toward us.

Dan put an arm around my shoulders and pulled

me down so we were lying close together. Quickly, he arranged the rest of the cover over us.

Davies reached the SUV and pointed a flashlight through the tailgate window. He motioned for us to open the tailgate. Dan sat up, reached over and pushed it open.

"What the hell are you two doing out here?" Davies demanded.

"I…uh, came down to check out some files," Dan said, sounding somewhat embarrassed to be caught with a woman like this. "That domestic-murder case we've been working on together—Leon Green, remember?"

"I remember Leon Green. What I don't remember is anything on that case that's important enough for you to come down here in the middle of the night, Detective." He motioned to me. "What about her?"

"Mary Beth? We were having dinner earlier, and she came along afterward…you know, for the ride."

I wasn't sure Davies was buying it.

"I guess I should recommend you to the LAPD for a promotion, Rucker," he said. "Your devotion to duty is impressive. Must have been a long dinner, though." He looked at his watch.

"I was showing Mary Beth the city lights from Palos Verdes," Dan said.

"And you gave up a nice romantic night like that to come here and look through Leon Green's files? My, my."

"Right. We have to get going now, though. It's getting. late."

"It certainly looks that way. Were you going to sleep here tonight?"

My cycs followcd his to thc blankct.

"No, just taking a rest," Dan said. "Before we hit the road to Malibu. I didn't want to fall asleep at thc whccl."

"Now that you mention it," Davies said, "you really should have some caffeine before you go. Come inside. I'll put on a pot."

"Uh, thanks," Dan said. "But I'm really not that tired, and we can have coffee at Mary Beth's house—"

"Absolutely not," Davies said, interrupting. "I insist. It's a matter of public safety, after all."

He stood there at the open tailgate, waiting, and when we hesitated, he waved us out with a hand. "Come on."

I looked at Dan and he looked at me. I planted a kiss on his cheek. "Sounds good to me, honey," I said. "I'd love a nice strong cup of coffee right now."

We sat in Lieutenant Davies's office, with a big, redheaded cop standing just inside the door, arms folded. I figured he was Davies's muscle, in case we decided to run.

Not that the thought had entered my mind. It might have entered Dan's, though. I'd never seen him so jittery. All Davies had to do was go down to the basement, look in the evidence room and discover that Craig's effects were gone. He'd search Dan's car and find the box. Dan and I would both land in jail, and Dan would lose his badge.

I wished now that I hadn't gotten him into this. But I wondered if Davies would see reason if I told him what we'd found. Craig's tell-all book about Courtland Pharmaceuticals would point a finger directly at Roger Van Court, and Davies could be the one to solve a murder that had occurred in his own backyard. It could be a real plum in his promotional pie. Which might get Dan off the spot.

Or not. Especially if Roger had covered his ass in some way since Craig had written the book.

We drank the coffee Lieutenant Davies set before us, like two good children drinking their milk. For his part, Davies seemed as if he didn't suspect a thing. He rambled on and on about the Leon Green case, and Dan responded tiredly.

Then it got tricky.

Looking at me, Davies said, "I know you've been anxious to see Craig Dinsmore's effects. This might be as good a time as any."

Oh, God.

"I have wanted to see them," I said quickly, "but please don't go to any trouble tonight. It's late, and I really need to get home—"

"Nonsense. Kevin?" He looked at the cop standing by the door. "Go down and get the box of evidence from Craig Dinsmore's motel, will you?"

"Yes, sir," the cop said, turning smartly on his heel.

Dan sat there, silent and unmoving. Which couldn't be said for me. I had to force myself not to squirm, and beads of sweat broke out on my face. What was the punishment for lifting a box of evidence from a police station?

Lieutenant Davies sat back in his chair, his fingers linked over his stomach, and looked at me, then Dan. Clearly, he knew he had us, and he couldn't wait to lower the boom.

The silence in the room grew heavy, almost unbearable.

"I guess you've already been through Craig's effects," I blurted out. "For clues, I mean. Did you find anything?"

"As a matter of fact, no," he said. "Maybe you'll have more luck."

"Not me," I said, laughing slightly. "I'm not good at that sort of thing. I just wanted to read some of his manuscript, see if it's salable."

"Well, you should be able to do that...right about now." Davies smiled as we heard Kevin coming down the hall.

But the other cop entered holding the box from Dan's SUV, and that wiped the smile from Davies's face.

I didn't dare look at Dan. Kevin was his friend, it

seemed. The one who'd owed him a favor and let him take the box out.

He had just saved Dan's neck, mine, and his own.

We didn't talk much in the car on the way home. But once in my house, Dan rubbed his face and heaved a sigh of relief.

"That was much too close," he said. "If Kevin hadn't thought fast and gone out to my car, I'd hate to think what might have happened."

"He's a good friend," I said.

"And a smart one. He was on the LAPD long before Davies's time at the El Segundo PD. We worked a lot of cases together."

"Did you see Davies's face when Kevin walked in with that box? I wanted to laugh, but I didn't dare."

He smiled. "Good thing. Davies was sure he knew exactly what we were doing here tonight, but he never dreamed Kevin would go out to my car for the box."

"I wonder why he didn't just go through the SUV when we were out there."

"Because he didn't have sufficient cause to search," Dan said. "A cop can't just go around looking in people's vehicles. Not unless he's pretty certain there's something incriminating in it. With me being a cop and knowing that, Davies didn't want to take the chance he was wrong."

"Well, thank God for that. Would you like anything?'' I asked, going into the kitchen. ''Coffee? Wine?''

He followed me in. ''Not really. What about you?''

''No.''

He looked at his watch. ''It's almost five. Neither one of us is going to get much sleep now.''

''True.''

''We should go through that manuscript together.''

I shook my head. ''I have a better idea. I speed-read, and I do better at it when I'm not so tired. Why don't I make you a copy to take with you. We can compare notes later in the morning.''

''Sounds okay to me. But you know, Craig's murder isn't in my jurisdiction. If I find anything on this CD to nail his murderer, I'll have to tell Davies about it.''

''I know. But talk to me first, will you? There's more involved here than Craig's murder, and whether Roger killed him. I'd like to make sure Lindy is safe first.''

''Watch your back there,'' he warned. ''For all you know, her husband may have sent her down here on a treasure hunt for this manuscript. That may have been her main reason for showing up at your door with a sob story.''

I hadn't told him about Lindy's troubles with Roger yet, or about Jade. And I hated to think he might be right about her coming down here to look for Craig's book.

"Or, maybe she's completely innocent," I theorized, "and Roger—"

"Is not," he said. "If this book is a tell-all about Courtland, as you seem to think it is, then Roger Van Court certainly wouldn't want it published. It could be argued he'd do anything to prevent that, including murder." He shook his head. "Still, the book is just circumstantial evidence, unless we can prove Roger knew about it."

"Which is exactly what I'm hoping for—a name. Someone Craig might have talked to about this book. Someone who worked at Courtland, or for Roger, and might have told him what Roger was doing."

"Mary Beth, don't take this the wrong way. But I only stuck my neck out with Davies tonight because I'm trying to solve a murder."

"Meaning?"

"Meaning that I can only hold off on telling Davies about it for so long. And not just Davies, but my captain. This could still be tied into the other two murders, you know. And they *are* in my jurisdiction."

"You mean they're tied in because of the murder weapon."

"That, and other things."

"What other things?" I asked.

He took his ball cap off and rubbed a hand over his head. I smiled at the way his hair stuck up in tufts, no matter what he did. "That's not important now."

"All right, if you're not going to tell me, how about this? When you tell your captain about this new theory, how are you going to explain how you got the CD out of the evidence locker in El Segundo?"

"I'll figure out something." But he didn't look happy.

"So hold off telling anyone for a little while, okay? Just give me a chance to talk to Lindy. There's no love lost between her and Roger, and she could turn out to be a prime witness for the prosecution."

Dan folded his arms. "All right. I'll give you a little time. I just don't know why I ever got hooked up with you. You are the most stubborn, most irritating—"

"Partner in crime?" I finished for him.

He sighed. "If you let me down—"

"You'll do what?" I said, smiling.

"Never mind. You want to sit up and talk for a while? Have some breakfast?"

"No. I'm really revved up. That was pretty exciting tonight."

"You think so?"

"Yeah."

He nodded. "I can relate to that. You want to go for a drive?"

"No."

"A walk on the beach?"

"No."

"I give up. What *would* you like to do with all that energy?"

"Let's have sex," I said.

The sex turned out to be more comforting than carousing in nature. In fact, we were so exhausted we barely made it through before we fell asleep. Dan left around nine, and I struggled to keep my eyes open long enough to make coffee. I put yesterday's grounds in a drawer, and burned the egg I forgot to watch. Burned the toast, too, and finally gave up and drank a bottle of orange juice instead.

Finally I opened my notebook computer and the manuscript I'd copied from Craig's CD. Everything that Lindy had told me about was in there: the sales of defective drugs to the Middle East, and the testing on homeless people, most of whom had died after being injected with the first version of Roger's experimental drug.

According to what Craig's informant had told him, it was just as Lindy had said. No one ever learned about the deaths of the homeless. Roger had them cremated secretly, at his own expense and at an unethical crematorium. The families of these men, women and two children would never know what had happened to them. In Roger's files they were listed only as numbers.

I felt sick, but forced myself to read on. According to Craig's notes, Courtland Pharmaceuticals had kept two sets of books for years, and in one they had fudged their income for tax purposes. The other set of books was of their true assets, which had grown to immense proportions in the past few years.

Roger had given Lindy the impression that the business was failing, and that Courtland desperately needed the money from the Middle Eastern buyers. But if Craig's information was right, it sounded more like Roger and his father had developed a grand case of greed.

Craig had even written that Roger Van Court had used "family members" as experimental guinea pig for his drugs—and that the results had not been good.

How on earth had he found that out? And who were the other family members he'd experimented on?

His father? Was that why he was dying, too? It seemed there was no love lost between them, and maybe Roger wanted to be out from under his father's thumb.

Before I finished reading through the manuscript, I had to close my computer and take a shower, then get dressed. My hope was that the shower would clear my head and help me figure out what to do next. Once Dan read his copy, if he hadn't already, he'd want to set the wheels in motion to arrest Roger on any number of counts: tax fraud, the murders of the homeless and the Middle Eastern people who had died after being injected with his defective drug…

The possibilities were endless.

And then there was Craig's murder. The day Roger was hauled off to jail would be a red-letter day. I couldn't wait.

But if Dan didn't move fast enough—if he got caught up in red tape—Roger might have time to get away. With Jade. He could disappear into a country where the U.S. didn't have an extradition treaty. Once there, he might never be arrested, and Lindy might never see Jade again.

If only she would call was my mantra in the shower.

We must have been on the same wavelength, because the phone rang while I was still sending Lindy messages over the ether. When I got out and checked my machine, the message was from her.

"I'm real sorry, Mary Beth, for acting the way I did when you came up here. Could you call me? Please? I really need you."

She left me a cell-phone number, and sounded desperate. I called her back immediately.

"Oh, thank God," she said when she answered. "I've been sitting here with the phone in my hand, and I didn't dare hope you'd call me back, but I'm so glad you did."

"What's wrong?" I asked. "And where are you?"

"I'm still in San Francisco, at a budget motel on Lombard," she said. "It's costing me seventy-five bucks a night and I'm just about broke, but it was the cheapest thing I could find without a reservation.''

"I can help you with that when I get there," I said. "I have what I think is good news."

"Really? What is it?"

"I don't want to tell you over the phone."

"You're coming here, then?" she asked.

"Yes. And Lindy, I've learned some things about Roger and Courtland. You were absolutely right to want Jade out of that house, and I want you to be ready to carry out our plan this time."

"I'm ready now," she said. "That's why I called. I was afraid, at first, what would happen if we got caught. But when I saw Jade, she looked worse than ever. You were right, Mary Beth. I need to get her to a good doctor. And fast."

"Okay, then, listen. Hang up and go to a pay phone. Give me ten minutes, then call me at this number." I opened my address book and gave her the number of a pay phone at Gladstone's, one I'd often used on the way to work when I forgot my cell phone.

"Why do we have to do that?" she asked.

"Because I don't trust my cell phone right now. Too many people could be listening."

"Okay," she said. "I'm sure there's a pay phone downstairs in the lobby."

"No! Don't call me from there. Go to a restaurant, or some other public place. But don't go too far. I want to talk to you as soon as possible."

"Okay," she said again. "I'll go to Mel's Diner. Give me ten minutes, too."

It was more like fifteen when she called me back. I waited at the pay phone in Gladstone's, listening to the everyday, ordinary sounds of people dining: women laughing, glasses tinkling, the pungent scent of fish and steak broiling in the kitchen.

How many times had I been one of those diners, watching the sun set over the ocean, without a worry in the world? And now I was planning to kidnap a child.

I just hoped it wouldn't be called kidnapping if the child's mother was along.

The ringing phone jolted me out of my brief reverie. I grabbed it. "Lindy?"

"Yes."

"Okay, look. Get the nanny—Irene—to let you in again tomorrow. You can do that, can't you? Even though you've already been there this week?"

"I...I'll try. As long as Roger's not home, I think maybe she'll let me in again. I can tell her I won't be able to come next week."

"Okay. Say whatever you have to. Just get her to let you in. Now, I don't think we should be seen together, so call me on my cell phone tonight, to let me know for sure what time you'll be at the house." I gave her the number of my other cell—one I seldom used and that the police wouldn't be as likely to know about. "I'll be somewhere in San Francisco, waiting to hear from you. Tomorrow, I'll park near your motel, and when you drive to the house I'll be right behind you. Make sure to leave the back door unlocked. Once I'm in the house, you can distract Irene. Okay?''

"Okay."

She didn't sound too sure, and I could only hope she'd remember all of that.

"Distract her," I said, "and I'll go upstairs. Is there a room near Jade's that Irene doesn't go into?''

"Just the bathroom. She always uses the one off her own room, but there's one right across from Jade's, in the hall.''

"I'll wait in there, then. You come up as if you're having your usual visit with Jade. Get some clothes and toys together for her, but do it fast. As soon as you're ready, come out into the hall and I'll take Jade while you go back down and keep Irene out of the way. I'll carry Jade out the front and put her in my car. You get out there as soon as you can without alerting Irene.''

"Okay. Uh, Mary Beth?''

"Yes?''

"Hearing you say it that way, it feels sort of bad. Just grabbing Jade, I mean, and running off with her. I don't know if we should be doing this.''

I sighed. "Lindy, listen to me. Do you want your child to suffer her whole life because of what Roger's doing to her now? For God's sake, what if she dies?''

I could hear her starting to cry. "But what if he

really can make her well?'' she said. ''What if this is all wrong?''

''She's your *child,* Lindy. Do you really want to risk that?''

''No,'' she said softly, on a sob. ''You're right, of course. I can't.''

''We'll find her the best medical care possible,'' I said. ''We'll find out exactly what's wrong with her. And Lindy? We'll get Roger, his father and anyone else involved at Courtland arrested. That's what I wanted to tell you. We've got proof now, of what Roger's been doing. The police will make him tell the truth about what he's done to Jade, too. Then we can get good doctors, good research scientists, working on a real cure.''

She was sobbing quietly. ''I know we have to do this. Just please, Mary Beth, don't let anything happen to Jade.''

''I won't,'' I said.

''*Promise.*''

''On my mother's fake red hair,'' I said. ''Don't worry about it, Lindy. I'll take care of everything.''

Dan called at noon and said he needed to come over. He didn't say why, and I assumed it was to talk over the manuscript.

''I haven't had time to read it yet,'' he said. ''I've been kind of busy.''

''Okay. Bring coffee beans,'' I said.

''Coffee beans?''

"It's a sign," I said.

"Of what?"

"A giving heart," I said, thinking of Tony. "Never mind. What about Tony and Arnold? Anything new there?"

"The tox screens came back negative, and the official cause of death, in layman's terms, is severe blows to the head. Which brings up the question, can you imagine Roger Van Court doing that? With ancient Chinese artifacts, anyway?"

"Not personally. But if he sent someone to do the murders, and told them to make it look like gay crimes…"

"Why would he do that? Did he even know Tony and Arnold?" Dan asked. "And why would he have killed them, too?"

"You know, I've been thinking about that. What if the dildos had some other meaning to the killer?"

"Like what?"

"Well, Arnold was a toy designer. A failed one, but he kept trying."

"Go on."

"When we were married he came up with the idea of a seven-headed beast that he named GORP. The toy was too scary for kids, so it failed. He recently redesigned it and tried to sell it under the name Beast, but he had all kinds of problems. A Japanese toy company had already come out with a line of toys and a series of shows called Beast Wars 2. They fought his using the name Beast for his toy, and Arnold finally had to give up.''

"Okay,'' Dan said, sounding unimpressed. "I'm sure you're going to tell me sometime today what that means to the murders.''

"Well, it's just a thought. But I remember Arnold telling me that one of the characters in the series was named Majinzarak. I take it he was a kind of robot, or Transformer. It was said that he wasn't a controllable weapon, but a monster. And guess what Majinzarak's weak point was? The thing that got him killed?''

"His name?'' Dan said wryly.

"No, silly. It was his third eye.''

There was a small silence. Finally Dan said, "Third eye?''

"The seat of the soul. It's said to be an area in the middle of the brain linking the physical world to the spiritual world. People who are trying to develop their psychic and spiritual powers meditate on the third eye, focusing their attention on the center of their foreheads. That's how they cross over from this plane to a better one. At least, that's the way it's supposed to work.''

"Holy sh—'' Dan started to say. "I see what you mean. All three men were bashed with those dildos in the middle of their foreheads—right over the third eye.''

"Exactly,'' I said.

"The question is, why?''

"Well, let's take it step by step. Assuming the third eye is thought to be the doorway to the soul, whoever attacked them may have been attacking each person's soul. Or maybe he was making some sort of statement."

"Again, like what?"

"That Tony, Arnold and Craig didn't have souls."

"Or didn't deserve them," Dan said.

"That's possible."

Dan sighed. "This all may turn out to be helpful down the line, but right now I don't see the connection to Roger Van Court. I need to come out and talk to you. It's important."

"Okay, but don't you want to tell me what it's about now?"

"What I have to say won't take long," he said. "But I'd rather do it in person."

"And why doesn't that sound good?"

"I'll see you in twenty," he said, hanging up.

Dan arrived an hour later, and he was having trouble meeting my eyes.

"I've got good news and bad news," he said without preamble. "Which do you want?"

"Might as well hit me with the bad news first," I said lightly, though I had a feeling of dread.

"Okay." He leaned against the breakfast bar, facing me as I stood in the living room. "You might want to sit down."

"No, I'm fine. Just say it." He was dumping me. I knew it.

Dan rubbed his face and sighed. "When I got in this morning there was a message from Davies. The ESPD wants the cooperation of the LAPD on Dinsmore's murder case, since it and the other two murders seem to be linked."

"I see. That's the bad news?"

"Not quite. The bad news is that I met with Davies at the El Segundo PD right after the call. I thought it was a routine meeting, and all I was supposed to do was bring Davies up to speed on Craig Dinsmore's case."

"And?"

His expression was so miserable, he might have just been told that his dog had died.

"Mary Beth…look, I hate like hell to tell you this, but I can't not tell you. From what I heard there today, I'm afraid they're getting close to arresting you."

My mouth went dry. Until this minute, I hadn't really considered that seriously. I thought for sure they'd come up with the real murderer before that could happen, or that Dan and I might nail Roger for it. Especially with the new evidence from Craig's book.

"When?" I asked.

"In the morning. I just wanted to give you a heads up, but please don't tell anyone I told you, or—"

"You could lose your badge," I said shortly. "I *know*."

I sat on the couch, as my legs had gone weak. "They can't have any evidence. I didn't do it. Did you tell them about Craig's book and Courtland Pharmaceuticals?"

"Not yet. You asked me not to, and I said I wouldn't without talking to you first. Besides, I'm not even supposed to know they're arresting you."

"Then how—"

"My friend Kevin. He was going off his shift, and there was just enough time for him to tell me they were going to pick you up tomorrow morning. Then Davies stuck his head out of his office and called me in."

I felt dazed. "I don't understand," I said. "Why are you telling me this?"

"Why do you think?" he said, looking at me intently.

"I don't know," I answered, looking away. "Maybe you're just a good guy."

"And maybe I'd like to help you. If you'd let me."

"Well, thanks," I said. "I guess. But wait a minute. What's the *good* news?"

"It's only good if you see it that way, and I hope you will. I thought I'd pick you up in the morning before they get a chance to, and let you turn yourself in. I'd be right there with you when they book you."

My smile must have been cynical, because my

words were. "Are you *kidding?* You want me to turn myself in for something I didn't do? Or maybe you think I did, now. Just how many gold stars do the boys in blue get for bringing in a murderer?"

"Dammit, Mary Beth! I'm willing to drive you there, that's all. I thought you might want somebody to lean on."

"Lean on." I laughed. "And would you be using handcuffs in the car? I might put up a fight, you know. Jump out along the way."

He threw up his hands. "You are such an aggravating woman. I thought it would be easier for you that way. And no, you wouldn't be wearing cuffs if you turned yourself in." He glared at me. "You *will* be if somebody has to come and arrest you, though."

I was silent, and he shoved his hands into his pockets and walked out on the deck. I saw him take his ball cap off three times and put it back on, in what I'd learned was an angry gesture.

He came back inside a few moments later, and seemed to have cooled off. "Sorry. I guess I read you wrong. Maybe I should have just kept quiet about it and let them pick you up at your office in the morning."

I tried to picture that: sitting at my desk on the phone, and all of a sudden the cops bust in. The print and television media pour in after them like a tidal wave, shouting over and over, "Why did you kill them, Mary Beth? What have you got to say?" It'd be on *ET, Access Hollywood,* and in all the gossip rags. Hell, it'd almost surely be on Fox News.

But what about Craig's book? Once the police knew about it, they wouldn't want me, would they? Not only did it tell about Roger's sales of defective drugs, but it gave him a motive for killing Craig. With the author dead, the book would never be published. The witnesses could be bought off. At least, that's the way Roger would think.

I realized, then, that he must have been looking for the manuscript in my office that day. And at my house that night. Maybe he didn't know I was home, or even that Lindy was there. He was just looking for the manuscript.

Still, there was nothing in Craig's book to connect Roger to Tony and Arnold. No reason at all for him to have killed them the same way Craig had been killed.

Damn Ockham's razor. There was no "simple" answer.

"I guess you're right," I said to Dan. "I should turn myself in, and then do whatever I have to do to prove Roger is guilty. Sorry if I sounded ungrateful. I'm just a bit rattled."

"That's okay. This whole thing is rotten, but I thought knowing ahead might give you time to do whatever you need to do first. Contact a lawyer, make arrangements for Nia to cover the office... whatever."

"That's very nice of you," I said. "I do have some things to take care of."

"Do you have a good lawyer?" he asked.

"Yes."

"He can probably get you out on bail," Dan said. "You shouldn't have to spend more than a day or so there."

"Bail?" I looked at him skeptically. "For triple murders?"

He looked away, and I knew he'd only been trying to make me feel better. But I'd called it right. If the El Segundo PD and the LAPD combined forces, they would arrest me for all three murders. I'd be in jail till my bones turned dry.

I was visibly shaking, and Dan noticed it. "Are you all right?" he asked.

"Yes. Yes, I'm fine," I said.

"Can I get you something?"

"No."

I got up and began to pace, thinking that only a few days ago I was worried about whether or not I'd go broke and have to sell this place. Now I wondered if I'd ever see it again after tomorrow. I started to memorize the conch shell on the glass coffee table, the white, weathered woodwork, and the filmy turquoise curtains lifting in the ocean breeze. Every piece of furniture, every picture, every ornament, purchased so carefully weekend after weekend, at flea markets and garage sales. I hadn't had enough money after buying this house to furnish it with "good" stuff, but it had come to look good to me. I loved every inch of this house.

Dan startled me, saying, "I'm sorry, Mary Beth. I'm so sorry."

I folded my arms and stared out the window at the beach, the bright sun and the kids playing on the sand. *I'll never have another child, either.*

"Are we all right?" Dan asked from behind me.

"Yes. We're all right."

"I'll see you in the morning?"

I turned and he seemed to be looking into my eyes for any sign that I might back out. Change my mind.

"In the morning," I said. "What time?"

"Nine o'clock? I'll swing by your office?"

"Sure." I gave him a hug at the door and smiled at him. "Sorry about the handcuffs comment. I really thought we'd use them for something fun one of these days."

"We will," he said, hugging me back. "Don't worry. Everything's going to be fine."

You betcha, I thought. *Everything's going to be fine.*

After Dan left, I fiddled around for a while in the kitchen, cleaning out the fridge, wiping off the stove, scouring the sink. There were four chocolate chip cookies in a bag on the counter that were so hard I could have used them to knock off a gaggle of gulls. Or was it a flock? I didn't know, and since I wasn't inclined to knock off gulls anyway, I tossed the cookies into the trash.

When Dan had been gone a half hour, I figured the coast was clear. I threw some things into a canvas book bag I'd acquired at the last writers' conference I'd attended. Taking only that and my purse, I locked up, got into my car and took a route that could be leading to my office but didn't. Through some backtracking and U-turns, I was finally on my way to LAX, and I was pretty sure I hadn't been followed.

Parking in the short-term lot, I walked as fast as I could through the terminal, but not fast enough to attract attention. At the Alaska Air counter I grabbed a ticket on a flight out within the hour, and didn't stop to breathe till the plane was in the air.

It was late afternoon when I landed in San Francisco. I rented a car and chose a nondescript gray model that looked like every other car on the road. I knew the cops could find me through the credit card I'd used, but I hoped that by the time they caught up to where I'd been, I'd be gone.

Next I checked into a shoddy motel where no one would ever think to look for me. No gym here, no room service, not even a telephone in the room. There was a sixties-style nineteen-inch black-and-white TV on a rusty bracket nailed to the wall, and it had one of those old security devices that set off an alarm if anyone tried to heist it. The view out the window was the side of a brick building less than ten feet away.

Perfect.

There was nothing to do now but hole up here until I heard from Lindy that she'd arranged to be at the house tomorrow. If she hadn't been able to pull it off for tomorrow...well, I could be in for a long haul.

But where better for "Lorelei Lee" to hide from the cops? The clerk downstairs might have looked askance at the name, but he probably figured I was a hooker. Which was fine with me.

I turned on the TV to catch up on the evening news, but since there was no cable and half the screen was snow, it was hard to tell who was killing or crashing into who. I finally just turned it off and stretched out on the lumpy bed, staring at the ceiling and thinking.

The cops could trace cell-phone calls now. It took a while, but they could do it. I could use the pay phone in the hall to phone Lindy, but if they had put a trace on her cell, I was pretty sure they could find me here once she'd called me.

I'd just have to stay on the move. Dan would start looking for me after nine in the morning, and it would take him some time to find me. Especially if, when I left here in the morning to go to Lindy's house, I didn't come back.

The timing was close but not impossible. I just needed to get Lindy's baby out of the house and get her and Lindy to a safe place before they caught up with me.

I wasn't sure, yet, where that safe place might be. Certainly not my house in Malibu. The El Segundo cops would be all over it by noon, if not before. When they didn't find me there, they'd put out an APB, and every cop up and down the coast, if not the country, would be looking for me: Mary Beth Conahan, mass murderer.

I'll admit my plan wasn't perfect. A lot of it had been put together when I'd talked to Lindy. Now I had the added fun of dodging the law and keeping myself out of the pen until Lindy and Jade were okay.

To calm my nerves, I ate a Hershey bar that I'd grabbed at the airport so I wouldn't have to go out for dinner. Even before I opened it, I heard my mother say, *That'll keep you up all night, young lady. There's caffeine in it, you know.*

My mom was a wonderful woman, but she had a lot of fears. She died when I was twenty, and I suddenly inherited a lot of those fears. It was as if they'd been left behind in a box with a black mourning ribbon around it, and once I opened the box I couldn't stop hearing the warnings. *Watch out for this, watch out for that.* I think I drank and partied in my early years to stop those voices, or at least muffle them. Then, when I became pregnant and I gave up partying, I began to rationalize those voices away. The last thing I wanted was for my baby to grow up full of fears that she might catch, like a virus, in the womb.

They still popped up now and then, though, and at the most inconvenient times.

I'd brought my notebook computer, and I opened it and went into Craig's manuscript to finish reading it. Scanning the final pages, I knew I had enough here for the police to arrest Roger, his father and at least two of the research scientists at Courtland. Craig had included the names, addresses and phone numbers of people he'd interviewed, some of them ex-employees of Courtland. Long before they told him what was going on there, some had left voluntarily, unwilling to work for the company any longer. Others had been terminated for a variety of reasons that sounded as if they were mere excuses to get rid of "troublesome" employees. I wondered if they'd asked too many questions.

Craig had felt certain that most of the ones who'd quit weren't holding grudges and would make good witnesses. Personal notes to himself read, "This is going to be the biggest book of the year. *New York Times,* here I come."

I finished up and closed the document, turning off the notebook. My elation over finding the evidence the police would need to arrest Roger was dulled somewhat by the fact that Craig wouldn't be around to accept his accolades for this book. He could have been a millionaire, and this would have won him awards by the bucketful.

Unfortunately, Lindy and I would still have to get Jade out of that house first. Showing this evidence to the police and getting them to arrest Roger would take time. Roger's lawyer would get the trial delayed over and over, and Roger might be ninety before he ever landed in jail.

Meanwhile, if he thought Lindy had anything to do with his downfall, he would still carry out his threat to have Jade taken to some secret place and hidden from her. It was his ace in the hole, that threat to separate her from her child forever, the one thing he could still use to hurt Lindy now that he'd stripped her of everything else. And I had no doubt he'd use it.

I was overly tired from the night before and my little adventure in El Segundo. Before I knew it I'd drifted off for a while, despite the chocolate bar. When my cell phone rang an hour or so later, I jumped a mile. I grabbed it, pushing the Talk button but remembering at the last minute that the caller could be Dan. I waited until I heard Lindy say, "Mary Beth?"

"Here."

"It's set. We can go tomorrow."

"Good. What time?"

"Two o'clock."

"I think that instead of going to your motel, I'll be at the house at one forty-five, and I'll hang out in the car until I see you go in the back door. Five minutes later, I'll follow you in."

"Okay… Uh…Mary Beth?"

"Yes?"

"I'm really scared. I just keep thinking, what if Roger comes home and catches us?"

"We'll be in and out within minutes," I said. "Don't worry."

I had been hiding my own anxiety for Lindy's sake, but I was a bundle of jitters as I sat in the car the next day, waiting for her to arrive. What if she never came? Chickened out at the last minute? Maybe I should have told her I was about to be arrested and this was our last chance to go through with our plan.

Finally, she arrived. Ten minutes late, but better than never. How many times had she said that when we were in school? *Better than never, Mary Beth.*

After I saw her enter the gate into the garden as before, I waited five minutes and then went to the back door. As instructed, Lindy had left it unlocked. I paused in the hallway, hearing voices from somewhere. The kitchen, I remembered, was to the left, and the dining room was on the right side of the hall, at the rear end of the living room. That's where voices were coming from—Lindy's and Irene's. The door to the hall was closed and they were talking softly. I couldn't hear what they were saying.

I continued to the front of the house and up the left-hand stairs to the second floor. The bathroom, Lindy had said, was right across from Jade's room.

But which one was Jade's room? Damn! I hadn't even thought to ask. I didn't want to risk opening doors one right after the other because I might wake Jade. She might start crying, and if she did, the nanny might insist on checking on her.

No, I thought. I could trust Lindy to make sure the nanny was busy elsewhere.

I stood another few moments trying to figure out where a bathroom would be placed. Surely at the top of the stairs, where guests could easily find it during parties. But there were two doors, one at the top of the left-hand stairs, and one at the top of the right-hand ones. Between the stairs was the long balcony tying them together.

Good God. Why hadn't Lindy been more explicit? And why hadn't I made sure she was?

I held my ear to the door on the left-hand side, and didn't hear anything. Moving as quietly as possible, I then stood at the door across from it, listening. There was music playing softly in this room. Quiet, easy music, the kind that might lull a baby to sleep.

Just then I heard Irene's voice grow louder, as if she was heading toward the foyer below.

"Wait, Irene," Lindy said, loud enough for me to hear.

I ran softly to the other door, opened it, and heaved a sigh of relief when it turned out to be the bathroom.

Then I heard Lindy say from the foot of the stairs, "I'll go up, Irene. I want to spend every moment I can alone with her. Do you think you could make Jade some warm milk? Cookies, too. Could you warm them in the microwave?''

I couldn't hear Irene's response, but I thought the footsteps on the stairs must be Lindy's. They were. I opened the door a crack and she saw me and came over.

''That was close,'' she whispered nervously. ''I think she'll be busy long enough for us to get Jade out, though. Is everything okay? I forgot to tell you which door was the bathroom, and I was worried you wouldn't know where to hide.''

''Everything's fine,'' I said. ''Maybe I should come in the room and help you pack, though. We really need to hurry.''

''Okay. Just let me make sure first that Jade is all right, before she sees you. And don't get too close, okay? She's afraid of strangers sometimes, and of course, there's the problem with her immune system.''

I followed her over to Jade's room, and hung just inside the door as she crossed the room.

My first feeling was one of disorientation. The room was quite large, with a hardwood floor, and the bed at the far end wasn't a crib, as I'd expected, but a full-size bed with a canopy. The canopy was draped in pink lace, and what I could see of the covers looked like the kind that would make any little girl feel like a princess. The bed, though, was far too big for a baby.

The room was full of tall plants and potted flowers carefully arranged with stuffed animals and other toys. The thing that caught my eye, however, was a large photograph on a stand. The object of the photo was a little girl of about four or five, in an old-fashioned dress like the ones you see in photography studios for little kids to dress up in. It was dark green velvet with a high lace collar, and cuffs. The white of the collar made her hazel eyes stand out, and her dark chestnut hair was upswept. She was beautiful, but looked fragile, like a porcelain doll.

I grabbed Lindy's arm and pulled her back. "Who is that?"

"That's Jade, Mary Beth, a few years ago. When she was four."

I couldn't believe it. "Dammit, Lindy, I thought she was a baby! An infant."

"No, that's her," she said, laughing nervously again. "I just call her my baby because she's always needed taking care of, you know? She's way too young and innocent to have gone through so much in her short life."

"But my God, Lindy! You should have told me. I expected to be traveling with an infant. I didn't realize we'd have a child this age to hide, someone who might be afraid and who will want to know what's going on."

"I don't think that'll be a problem, Mary Beth. Despite her age and condition, Jade is a strong little girl. Besides, as long as I'm with her, she'll be all right. She won't cause any trouble.''

I relented. ''I wasn't worried about trouble, Lindy. I just don't want to scare her to death, running out of here with her.''

''We can bring some of her dolls,'' Lindy said. ''She'll be okay. Let's go, Mary Beth. I thought we had to hurry.''

She walked swiftly over to the bed and bent down, saying, ''Hi, honey. It's Mommy.''

''I thought you couldn't come today,'' a little voice said.

''Well, here I am,'' Lindy said. ''And I've brought a friend.''

I walked over and stood about five feet from the bed, looking down at Jade. She was lying on her side, curled up with a rag doll.

''Hi,'' I said. ''I'm Mary Beth. Your mom and I thought it might be nice to take a ride. Is that okay with you?''

She didn't answer immediately. Instead, she looked at Lindy. ''What if Daddy comes home?''

''That's why we have to hurry, honey. I'm going to pack a few things for you and then I'm going downstairs while Mary Beth looks after you a few minutes. She'll bring you down when it's time, okay?''

''I guess,'' Jade said. But she didn't look as if it was okay.

''I'm not here to hurt you, Jade,'' I said. ''I'm just

trying to help you and your mom. If you don't want to come, it's okay.''

"No," she said after a moment, "I guess it's okay. Daddy doesn't usually let me go out, but—"

She broke off. "That's Daddy."

"What, honey?" Lindy said.

"That's Daddy." She looked toward one of several windows that spanned a back wall. "He's here. Didn't you hear his car in the driveway?"

Lindy shook her head. "No. Are you sure?" She looked at me, fear in her eyes.

"What shall we do?" she whispered.

"Go down and meet him," I said. "Irene will tell him you're here, anyway. I'll get Jade ready, and the first chance we get, we'll go. You'll have to get rid of him and signal me somehow."

"I...I don't think I can do that," Lindy said, her voice shaking. "I don't know how to explain what I'm doing here."

"Lindy, for heaven's sake!"

"I think you should talk to Daddy," Jade said as if she were the mom and Lindy the child. "You should ask him if we can go for a ride."

For a moment, Lindy just stared at her. Then she turned to me. "Okay, I'll go. Maybe I can get him to leave."

I watched her slight form, her shoulders bowed as she went into the hall. Then I heard her footsteps heading slowly down the stairs.

God help us if she couldn't stand up to him. He would almost certainly call the police. Or worse.

Turning to Jade, I said in what I hoped was a reassuring voice, "Well, now. Let's just assume we'll be going for that ride. What would you like to take with you? Your rag doll? We can't take too much, because we have to hurry."

"Why do we have to hurry?" she asked, getting up and sitting on the edge of the bed.

"Because it'll be dark soon," I said reasonably. "We wouldn't be able to see anything in the dark."

"I think you're lying," Jade said.

Oh, great. Despite having Lindy for a mother, the kid was pretty smart.

She also had a fever, I thought. Hair curled over her face in damp wisps, and it looked wet where it trailed down her neck to her shoulders. Besides that, her cheeks were too pink.

I couldn't help touching her forehead lightly, confirming my suspicion.

"How are you feeling?" I asked.

"Hot," she said matter-of-factly. "I probably have a fever. But I have one most of the time, so I'm getting used to it."

Hearing her say that as if it were an everyday natural occurrence dissolved the last of my qualms about taking her out of here.

I looked through the closet quickly for an overnight bag, and settled for a worn but large Winnie the Pooh tote. Several shelves held clothes, neatly folded. I shoved some shirts, pants, underwear and socks into the tote. There was a stuffed rabbit on one shelf that looked like the Velveteen Rabbit, as if it had been loved so much its eyes had fallen out. I put that in the tote and went back into the room.

"Did you know my mommy doesn't live here anymore?" Jade asked.

"Yes, I did. We're going to fix that, though."

"You are?"

"We are." I stuck out my little finger and smiled. "Pinkie promise," I said, just as I had so many times with her mother years before.

She smiled shyly and hooked her finger with mine. "Pinkie promise."

Her finger was very hot, though. "I'm going to get your clothes together now," I said, "so we—"

Before I'd finished the sentence, I heard voices raised as if in argument downstairs. At the same time, I was certain someone was outside in the hall.

"Shh," I said to Jade, putting a finger to my lips.

Stepping back quickly, I went to the closet. Opening the door, I slipped inside.

And none too soon. The door from the hallway opened and closed, and I heard Irene say, "So we're awake now, are we, missy? Well, here, let Nanny fix your pillows. Would you like a snack? I could make you a nice bowl of fruit."

"Why are Mommy and Daddy fighting again?" Jade asked.

"Now, never you mind about that," Irene said.

"I'm going to get you that fruit, honey. And water, with a slice of lemon in it. You like that, don't you? I'll be right back."

"Nanny, wait!" Jade said. "Somebody—somebody's here."

I froze.

"What? What do you mean, honey?"

"Don't leave me. Somebody's here!"

"Of course she is, honey. Your mommy's here. You just asked me about her. Are you forgetting again?"

"I want my mommy to come home and live," Jade said petulantly.

"I know you do, dear. I know. And soon, maybe—"

"You always say that, and I don't believe you anymore," Jade said. "And you don't even believe me, either. I told you, somebody's here!"

I didn't know what I'd do if Irene took her seriously and started looking around. As it was, the cedar walls of the closet were threatening to make me sneeze. If the nanny didn't leave soon, we'd all be in one hell of a mess.

"Hush, now," I heard Irene say. "Nobody else is here, Jade. You must have been having one of your nightmares again."

"I wasn't!" Jade insisted.

"Maybe you just didn't know it," Irene said soothingly. "Lots of people have dreams that they think are real. And you know how you mix things up sometimes, sweetheart. It's the medicine, that's all. Your mommy is downstairs with your daddy, and there's no one else in the house. You just rest now, all right? Your daddy will be coming up soon, and he'll take care of you.''

I could hear the rustle of Irene's uniform as she turned away from the bed and walked toward the door.

''No! Don't go, Nanny!'' Jade cried. ''Tell him I don't need any more shots.''

''I can't do that, Jade,'' Irene said firmly. ''I know you hate the shots, but they're for your own good. We've talked about this.''

''But they make me sick,'' Jade pleaded.

''Nonsense. Now you be a good girl while Nanny gets you some juice.''

Irene left, and her footsteps faded as she went down the stairs. I hesitated a moment before stepping out of the closet. Why on earth had Jade told Irene about me?

Because she doesn't know you, a small voice said. *And she's known Irene all her life.* Besides, she's scared to death.

That made sense. But before I could push the closet door open and step out, I heard a couple of loud raps on the bedroom door.

''Jade?'' Roger called out.

I nearly fainted. Dammit all, anyway! Why hadn't Lindy gotten rid of him?

I kept as still as I could, trying not to breathe too

loud. My pulse was racing, though, and I'd begun to sweat. It was hot and musty-smelling in the closet, and all of a sudden my nose tickled. I forced back a sneeze, but that made it worse.

Through the crack in the door I could see that Roger had come in and was standing at the foot of Jade's bed, holding a tray with assorted metal and glass articles on it. Jade was back under the covers, and it seemed she was pretending to sleep. After a minute or two, Roger went around to the side of the bed and shook her shoulder. She stirred, then opened her eyes and rubbed them. Her chestnut hair was tousled and she reached up as if by habit and pulled it like a curtain over the sides of her face.

The poor kid, I thought. There's so little she can do to defend herself.

"Daddy?" Jade said in a small voice. "Why did you wake me up?"

"I have your medicine," Roger said, setting the tray on a night table and taking her arm.

"I don't want any more shots," Jade said, inching back against the pillows.

"I know, Jade. But we've talked about this. You need the medicine to make you well."

"No! I'm tired, Daddy! I'm tired of being in bed all the time, and I'm tired of getting medicine all the time!"

Memories of the force Roger had used on me came rushing back, and it was all I could do to stop myself from flying into the room and beating him till he was dead. I just kept thinking, *Lindy will be here any minute. Now that I'm here she'll feel strong. She'll get him out of the house, and everything will be all right.*

But Lindy didn't come. Roger murmured something to Jade that sounded like, "I know, I know," while at the same time reaching for her arm again and pushing up the sleeve of her nightgown. Taking a cotton ball, he soaked it in what I assumed to be alcohol and swabbed her arm. She seemed to have given in, but when he came at her with the syringe, she flailed about, crying, "No!"

I couldn't stand it any longer. I burst out of the closet and ran across the room, grabbing Roger's free arm. Spinning him around, I hit him with my fist, yelling, "Get your hands off her!"

His shock at seeing me there helped. I'd taken him off guard, and that gave me an advantage. But I knew it wouldn't last. I shoved him with as much force as possible against the wall. He dropped the syringe and half bent over. I yanked at his hair and pulled him down farther, knocking him to the floor. Grabbing the heavy lamp on the nightstand I raised it and yelled, "Don't get up! Stay right there!"

Always yell, I remembered. *Yell as loud as you can. It sets them off balance.*

On the table was a Barbie doll phone. I reached for it, but before I could dial 911, Roger was on his feet. I swung the lamp but he grabbed my arm and twisted it. Pain blazed from my wrist on up, and my shoulder felt as if it had been wrenched from its socket. My fingers went numb and I dropped the lamp.

Jade screamed. "Mommy, Mommy, help!"

I turned to her, an instinctive response to a child's cry, but Roger didn't let her cries stop him. He slapped me hard on the side of the head. I fell to the floor, my cheek searing against the roughness of a throw rug. His foot came down on my back, and it felt like déjà vu from seven years before.

But this wasn't seven years before. I was stronger now. And smarter. I wrenched my torso halfway around, grabbed for his ankle and pulled. As he fell, I twisted away so that he wouldn't fall on me. I saw him go down, and I saw his head crack against the nightstand. He didn't move, and I thought he was unconscious.

Jumping to my feet, I grabbed the phone again. But Jade was crying, and she was still screaming, "Mommy, help! *Mommy!*"

"It's okay," I said, reaching for her and dropping the phone. "Your mommy's downstairs. I'll take you to her."

I picked her up in my arms and was halfway to the door when her hair fell back and I saw something that shocked me to the core. For a long, fateful moment I didn't move. *Couldn't* move. My mind whirled. I felt as if I'd seen a ghost.

On Jade's neck was the same kind of port-wine stain that had been on my child's neck when she was born.

It'll fade eventually, the nurse had said. *It might take years, but it will go away.*

I was so confused, I could barely think. The birthmark was the same shape and in the same place as my baby's had been.

I looked into Jade's eyes, and now that she was out from under the canopy bed, they looked more green than hazel.

Green like my own.

The other thing like me was her hair, which, when the sunlight fell on it, as it did now, looked more like red than chestnut brown.

"*What?*" she said loudly, snapping me out of it.

I grabbed her close and ran with her to the door. Every step of the way I could feel her heart racing against mine.

My child's heart? Against mine?

Impossible. How could Roger—

But I knew, suddenly, that it was true. Roger and Lindy had adopted my child. My child and Roger's.

Tears filled my eyes and words started coming from my mouth, words laden with six years of heartbreak and love. "It's all right, baby, it's all right. I'm here, I've got you." I reached for the doorknob and twisted.

It didn't open. I twisted it harder then, remembering Lindy's words, "You have to push it at the same time." I did, and this time it worked.

"Too late," Roger said from behind me, kicking the door shut.

His arm came around my neck, squeezing. "Drop her!" he said. "Put her down. Now!"

He pulled me back against him, tightening the hold on my throat. I gagged and made an involuntarily choking sound.

"Don't, Daddy!" Jade pleaded, crying. "Don't hurt her! I'll take the medicine. I'll do anything you want."

She tried to wiggle out of my arms, but I couldn't let go. I deliberately held her so close there wasn't even a breath of air between us, as if I could make her disappear into my womb again, make her part of me again, a part Roger would never be able to touch.

"Lindy!" I screamed. "Lindy!"

"Save your breath. Lindy isn't coming." Roger squeezed harder and I began to black out.

"When I let go, run," I whispered in Jade's ear. "Run as fast as you can."

I let her slip from my arms and felt her energy, her heart, move away from me. She grabbed the doorknob, pushed, and threw the door open. I caught a glimpse of her little white nightgown with the yellow ducks on it disappearing down the hall toward the stairs.

In the next moment I reached back with my thumbs for Roger's eyes. They connected, and I pushed against his eyeballs as hard as I could, at the same time digging with my nails into his forehead to get a better grip. He screamed and released his hold on me.

I turned fast, and while he still covered his eyes I pushed as hard as I could. He fell back against Jade's photograph, losing his balance and falling against the easel and picture. I whirled back to the door and ran.

I was already racing down the stairs, but when I heard Roger stumble into the hallway I started to take them two and three at a time. I felt as if I were in a nightmare, flying, with only the banister to keep me upright.

When I reached the bottom step, I didn't know which way to turn.

Then I heard Jade crying. Soft little whimpers, like a cat nuzzling her kittens. I ran into the parlor and saw Lindy on the floor by the fireplace. Jade was kneeling beside her, her head on Lindy's chest, quietly crying.

I ran over to them. Kneeling down, I felt for a pulse in Lindy's wrist. There was one, but it was faint. Roger, I thought, must have hit her, knocking her down.

"Jade, honey, move just a little, so I can help her."

Jade gave no sign that she'd heard me, but the crying stopped.

"Jade? Please move a little so I can see what's wrong."

"I'm not leaving my mommy!"

"I know, honey, I know. We're not leaving her. Just let me see her."

Jade moved down a bit, closer to Lindy's legs. It wasn't much, but it gave me some room.

"Lindy," I said, touching her face. "Lindy, wake up. It's me."

Her eyes fluttered. "Mary Beth..." she said, so softly I could hardly hear her. "Promise..."

I shook my head, forgetting in the moment what she had asked me earlier to do. "Promise?" I said.

"Take care of my baby."

"I will," I said. "I told you I would. But you're going to be all right—"

"No," she said breathlessly. *"Yours. Jade is yours."*

Her eyes closed and I reached for a pulse at her throat. There was none. Then I saw it. A thin wire around Lindy's neck. Her flesh, swollen, pushed against it so hard, it was nearly invisible.

"Oh my God, Lindy, oh my God!" Tears welled in my eyes. I spotted a phone near the fireplace and ran for it, to call 911.

But before I could get to it, Roger was there. The double doors from the hallway, which I'd left open, slammed shut. I heard a click as the inside lock fell into place.

Roger leaned against the doors, swaying. Blood seeped from one of his eyes. He was still holding the syringe, and it looked full. He held it in front of him like a weapon.

Carefully, I picked up Jade and held her tight, inching away from Roger and toward a door I thought must lead into the dining room.

"Stop!" Roger said, coming toward us.

"I just—I just want to put Jade down where she'll—she'll be safe," I said, my voice shaking so much I could hardly speak.

"Jade will be fine. Put her down, Mary Beth. Right there, on that chair."

"But she's afraid. Lindy…"

"Jade will survive," he said harshly. "Children are resilient."

My anger gave me strength. "It's too much, Roger! To see her mother like this, and to know that her father—"

"Shut up!" he said. "Just shut up!"

His face was red, and his eyes were wide and staring.

"Don't make her see you like this, Roger," I pleaded. "She's just a little girl."

He began to sway more, and his free hand went to his head. His face contorted with pain.

"All right, all right! Jade, go in the dining room. Wait there. I'll come for you."

"No," Jade cried. "I want my mommy!" She looked over my shoulder at Lindy. "What's wrong with my mommy? Why can't she wake up?"

"Jade," Roger said in a voice that brooked no nonsense, "you'll see your mommy later! Now, dammit, go into the dining room!"

She stared at him a moment, and in her eyes was a look of bewilderment, fear, and not a little anger. Her lack of trust in her father was clear, and that gave me strength.

"Go ahead, honey," I said softly. "It'll be all right."

That seemed to be the watchword of the day suddenly. *It'll be all right.*

But would it?

I put Jade down and watched as she ran into the dining room, her tiny feet catching on a nightgown that was probably meant only to sleep in, as it was too long for her. I couldn't have expressed what I felt at that moment. Pain...anger...heartbreak. I wanted to just run and grab her up, take her out of this house and never let her out of my sight again.

"She's mine, isn't she?" I said, turning back to Roger. My voice was thick with tears. "How could you? How could you keep her from me all these years?"

"She's my child, too," he said angrily. "I had every right to—"

"You raped me, you son of a bitch! You had *no* right! And how did you even know I was pregnant? How could you know when she was born?"

"Oh, Mary Beth...hell, I gave you more credit. To think that all these years I've worried that you'd figure it out. Why the hell didn't you just take the million dollars."

"Million—"

Then, in one horrible, ugly moment, I knew. "The detective? The one you sent a few weeks after you raped me, to buy my silence? I turned him down, and then I had to excuse myself to throw up. He told you that, didn't he? And you worked out the timing and figured I was pregnant?"

"Let's just say I hoped."

"But how could you be sure? I might have had the flu. And how could you know when I was due, and where I went to give birth?"

"Easy," he said, shrugging. "My detective planted a camera in your bathroom. Clever idea, don't you think? What better place to find out if a woman is pregnant?"

My shock and disgust were so great I could hardly speak. I'd accused my landlord. I'd had him picked up. He'd sworn his innocence, and no one had believed him. If there had been even an inkling of evidence against him, he'd be in prison now.

I began to shake all over, and it felt as if my blood had turned to ice. Not once in all these years had I realized the evil that was winding its way, like a poisonous snake, through my life.

"Why?" I asked, the words choking on my rage.

He leaned back against the door, as if to prop himself up.

"Why? Simple. Lindy couldn't have children. Didn't she tell you that? No, I suppose not. And I needed an heir, or I'd be disinherited. Once I knew you were carrying my child, it was the perfect solution to all my problems. I never even had to force a custody issue."

The smug smile on his face made me want to kill him. "You gave the baby up," he said. "*Your own baby.* You gave her away without a second thought."

"You don't know a damn thing about my thoughts! You have no idea how tormented I've been since that day!" The shaking had been replaced by weakness, and that was all that kept me from launching myself at him and killing him with my bare hands.

"So anyway," he went on as if he hadn't heard me, "once I knew for sure you were pregnant, I had your phone tapped. I knew when you talked to the adoption agency in Sacramento and asked about giving your baby up. And when the time came, I was in the right place at the right time to take her."

"Impossible!" I argued. "You can't adopt a baby that quickly."

Roger smiled. "You'd be surprised how many bureaucrats are looking for ways to increase their income these days. Tax free, of course."

"My God. Lindy was right about you," I said, my voice cracking. "You are rotten through and through."

His gaze flicked to Lindy's body, lying a few feet from me on the floor. "Little Lindy Lou," he said sarcastically. "The last cheerleader. They don't make them like her anymore, you know. Women aren't that willing to support their men through thick and thin.''

"You loved her once," I said, feeling an acute sadness for Lindy. How terrible it must have been for someone like her to feel she had to support a monster like Roger, just because he was her husband.

"Lindy was a cute little thing in high school," he agreed. "But she's been a pain in the ass ever since."

"Did she know all along that Jade was mine?" I asked. "Was she in on stealing my child?"

"Stealing? Oh, cut the dramatics, Mary Beth. When I took possession of Jade, she was no longer your child. You gave her up, remember? All I did was give her a good home."

"*A good home?* Lindy told me about the drugs you've been pumping her full of. You've used my child. No, you've abused her. It's only by the grace of God that you haven't killed her."

"For God's sake, Mary Beth, settle down! You're starting to sound like Lindy, you know. The truth is, Jade hasn't suffered. If there have been side effects, I've always brought her back to good health."

"And what about while she was sick? You think that was being *good* to her?"

"Jade has an immune deficiency," he said coldly. "She's been sickly from the time she was three. All I've done is try to heal her, and she's lucky I adopted her. God only knows what would have happened if you'd kept her."

"I'm so very grateful," I said sarcastically. "But you still haven't answered me about Lindy. Did she know Jade was my baby?"

"You mean when I brought her home? Not at first. But as Jade grew, I'm sure she began to wonder. She has your red hair and green eyes, after all. Some might say she was the spitting image of you. And Lindy knew I was having affairs. She never said a thing, though, until a few weeks ago when she saw an article about you, with your picture in it. You were hyping one of your authors and her adoption book, telling everybody how great adoption can be. I guess Lindy began to put two and two together then, because that's when she started asking questions about whether I'd seen you since school."

"What did you tell her?" I asked.

"I didn't see any point in lying, since our marriage was all but over anyway. So I admitted it. I told her you and I had been together the same month Jade was conceived."

"Been together. That's what you're calling it?"

"That's what it was, Mary Beth. I don't know why you can't get beyond your literary fantasies about rape and see it that way."

I held in my anger and said, "So that's why Lindy came to see me. To find out for certain if I was Jade's mother."

I remembered her using my brush, and pulling my hair out of it. It had seemed so innocent a thing to do at the time, but now I wondered if she had kept that hair, hoping to use it for a DNA test.

"And that's why," I said, "she asked me so many questions about whether I'd ever had, or would want to have, a baby. She even mentioned adoption and I still didn't get it. Not when she kept calling Jade her 'baby.' I kept thinking Jade was an infant, not a six-year-old child."

I wondered now if that had been deliberate. Lindy must have been desperate for help, yet at the same time she would want to keep Jade's identity from me for as long as possible.

In fact, she might have hoped that I'd never figure it out. But then, when I started asking questions that night at my house, she got cold feet and left suddenly. Her fear that I might figure out who Jade really was might also be why she was so unwelcoming when I showed up here the other day uninvited. She was afraid I'd see Jade and guess that she was mine. That's why she had Irene escort me out.

For the first time, I wondered where Irene was. Had Roger sent her somewhere before killing Lindy? Or had she seen him kill Lindy and managed to slip away somehow? Would she have called the police? And if so, why weren't they here by now?

The only thing I could think to do was keep Roger talking and hope for the best.

"How much did you have to pay for my daughter?" I said angrily. "How much was my baby worth to you?"

He sighed. "A sizable sum, I'm afraid. But really, I think the caseworker felt sorry for me, too. I told her how much my wife and I wanted a baby, and how long we'd tried. Turned on the old charm. Remember that?"

"Sure," I said. "Like the way you were so charming the night you raped me."

His eyes flickered with anger. "You wanted it that night. You know you did."

I couldn't stand it anymore. I felt violated all over again, and I kept picturing Roger, and who knows who else, looking at videotapes of me undressing, getting into the shower, going to the toilet—

None of which was as bad as his stealing my child. Outright stealing her, no matter how much he'd paid the person at the adoption agency.

And now he was accusing me of "wanting it." The rapist's eternal defense: *You know you wanted it.*

I began to move back toward the fireplace and the stand I'd seen there that held a poker and broom. But then quickly Roger was in motion. He seemed unsteady, yet he began to come toward me, extending the hand that held the syringe.

"Before I came down here," he said, "I took the time to put something a little more deadly in this. I think it's time you took a vacation, Mary Beth. A little sabbatical, like the one you took when Jade was born. Except that you won't go home this time. Your authors will miss you, of course. That is, if there are any left alive. I hear some of them have had a bit of bad luck.''

He stopped a few feet in front of me, and I shrank back against the fireplace. ''What do you know about that?''

''Well, there was that one unfortunate fellow who was writing an exposé about what we do at Courtland. I understand he talked a little too much about that in a bar one day.'' Roger smiled. ''I guess he can't get that book published now that he's dead. Fortunate for me, wouldn't you say?''

''Not really. Books are published posthumously all the time. In fact, I've had a seven-figure offer for Craig Dinsmore's book, and the contract will be signed by his estate. You can bet it'll be published, and it'll be the hit of the year. After all, the American public can't wait to nail pharmaceutical companies these days, the way they overcharge for drugs.''

He smiled. ''Contracts have a way of being canceled, Mary Beth. I would imagine that even publishers are open to a little bit of a nest egg these days.''

''If you're so sure of that, why did you kill Craig Dinsmore to stop him from publishing his book?''

Roger laughed. ''You give me too much credit, Mary Beth. I didn't kill the fellow.''

''Then who did? Some lackey you hired?''

''Tsk, tsk. You should have been a writer yourself. What an imagination.''

''The point is, you're finished, Roger. I have Craig

Dinsmore's manuscript, and it tells everything about the defective drugs you've been selling to the Middle East. The police already have a copy of it, and between that and Lindy's murder, you'll be getting the death penalty."

"Well, then. It seems I have nothing more to lose." Again he smiled. "Unless, of course, I manage to get Jade and me out of the country before the police arrive."

He lunged at me with the syringe, and I reached for the poker, but the stand wobbled, and it fell through my hand. Hanging from the fireplace mantel, though, was a large, decorative brass shovel. I grabbed it and, holding it with both hands, swung as hard as I could at Roger's arm. He cried out, but kept coming at me. My next hit was straight out, into his stomach area. This time the sharp edge of the shovel doubled him over in pain. I meant to go for his face next, but he grabbed the shovel as he was going down. Before he could stand up straight with it, I rabbit-punched him, both fists coming down hard on the back of his neck. I put all the power I could into it, and this time he crumpled to the floor.

I waited a moment to see if he was really out. I even kicked him—a lot harder than was necessary. He didn't move.

I ran to the dining room. "Jade! Jade, where are you?"

She was sitting quietly at a long, highly polished table, both hands over her ears as if to shut out our argument and sounds. She looked so little, so pitiful, I wanted to cry.

"Come here, honey. It's all right. Your mommy asked me to take care of you, remember?"

She didn't answer, but I picked her up and carried her quickly through a door that led into the hall and from there to the back door. She was so little for her age, like a tiny bird with fragile bones. Her arms came around my neck, and I patted her back as I ran. Passing the kitchen, I stopped dead in my tracks for a moment. Irene lay still on the floor by the sink, blood oozing from her head. I wanted to stop and see if she was all right, but I heard Roger groan, and knew it wouldn't be long before he'd be on us.

I ran with Jade out the back door and through the garden, then down the sidewalk to my car. I'd left it out of sight on a side street, but cursed myself for parking it closer to the front than the back. With every step I worried that Roger would come out the front door and cut us off.

Racing across the street, I stumbled now and then with my precious burden. At the car, I fumbled for the keys in my jeans pocket, my hand wet from fear. The keys kept slipping. Getting hold of them at last, I hit the button on the remote. The door locks opened, and I yanked on the back door, setting Jade as carefully as possible next to a blanket on the back seat. I locked her seat belt and said, "Put the blanket around you and duck down as much as you can, honey."

Every moment counted, and I couldn't take time to make sure she did it. Slamming the door shut, I climbed into the front and tried to start the car, my fingers trembling and missing the ignition several times. The engine finally started after what seemed an eternity.

"Jade, hang on!" I yelled.

I jammed my foot on the accelerator. In that same instant I saw a large black car peel out of the garage next to the garden. It came close enough that I could see Roger in the driver's seat. I tore down the steep hill and past stoplights, weaving my way through traffic, trying to put as much distance between us as possible. I could see Roger several cars behind us, though, and my hands were so wet now, the steering wheel kept slipping out of my grasp. I'd have to find a place to pull off and hide, and I couldn't take any streets that had heavy traffic. *Think, Mary Beth. You know this city. Think.*

Suddenly, I couldn't remember where the nearest police station was.

I was heading downhill toward the bay and the Golden Gate Bridge. I couldn't risk the bridge and getting caught up in slow traffic, so I turned right, off Division. Fisherman's Wharf was this way, but the congestion on the streets there was bad. I suddenly remembered the Exploratorium at the Palace of Fine Arts. A hands-on science center, it would be packed with kids out of school for the summer. In this gray car, we might be able to blend into the parking lot there, until I could catch my breath and decide what to do next.

I made some fast turns down side streets that put me near the Palace of Fine Arts. Finally I thought I'd lost Roger—he wasn't anywhere behind me now, that I could see. I pulled into the large north lot of the Exploratorium, but couldn't find an empty slot. I drove round and round, past hundreds of cars, and panic set in. Was Roger nearby, watching my lackluster attempt? Now and then I'd call back to Jade, "Are you all right, honey?" and she would give me a faint, "Yes," but I knew I needed to get her to a hospital as soon as possible. When I'd held her, I was sure she still had a fever.

I wasn't her legal guardian, though, and I couldn't authorize Jade's treatment or even explain what was wrong with her. My original plan had called for Lindy to be with us, to handle all that.

An alternative would be to take her to an emergency room and lie, telling them I was her mother but that I didn't have insurance, and I'd pay cash for her treatment. That would get her in there, but it wouldn't be long before they'd find out the truth. And what would I say to the doctors? That she'd ingested something toxic? They would see the needle marks on her arms and think I'd been abusing her. I'd have to tell them what her father had done to her, and they'd insist on talking to Roger, finding out if what I'd said was the truth.

To admit what he'd been doing, though, would

land him in jail. And not only would Roger deny everything, but he'd try to make me look crazy—just as he had with Lindy. He might even say I'd kidnapped his daughter and drugged her myself.

Which could end with my being locked up. And then who would take care of Jade?

The situation seemed hopeless. The best I could do was take her home with me, turn myself in, and hope that Roger would quickly be arrested for Craig's and Lindy's murders. It was possible I'd be released, and I could claim Jade as my daughter and get her help.

But where?

Then it came to me: Nia's father. Nia's father was a highly respected doctor in London. His specialty was neurology, as I recalled. But hadn't Nia said something about his working in biochemistry now, as well?

I didn't know if he could help Jade, but he might at least be able to recommend someone.

Thinking about all this was driving me wild. I focused on getting a parking slot, instead, and within minutes one became available. It was just ahead of us, and I slid into it with great relief. We were in a sea of hundreds of cars now, and even if Roger was still following us, this car was so nondescript that I didn't think he'd easily spot us.

Sitting there a moment, I tried to catch my breath and stop my hands from shaking.

"Mary Beth? I'm hungry," Jade said from the back seat.

I turned around, leaning over the seat and feeling a pang of guilt. "I'm so sorry, honey. Are you all right? I know this must be scary."

"I'm not afraid," she said, her chin going up. "I'd really like a hamburger, though. Daddy doesn't let me have hamburgers."

"Why not?" I asked, wondering if meat somehow interacted with the drugs he'd been giving her. "Do they make you sick?"

"No, he just doesn't think hamburger is good for me. He says I could get some coal-eye thing or whatever, and he wouldn't be able to treat me for a while."

I thought a minute. "You mean E. coli?" I asked.

"I guess so. He said a lot of kids got it once, from eating hamburgers."

"Well, that was a long time ago, honey. Most hamburgers are cooked better now. And we can ask to have them cooked really well."

I doubted that Roger was being a caring father when he kept Jade from ground beef. More likely, as Jade had implied, he didn't want her to get sick because that would interfere with his tests. How many other restrictions had he put on Jade throughout her short life so far?

I felt like crying. All those missed years. All the years when she might have been happy and well. If only—

But Jade was one tough kid. I had expected her to still be in shock, and here she was talking about hamburgers. "I may be able to get you a hamburger inside," I said. "I haven't been here in years, but they must have some sort of food."

Anything, rather than get trapped in a line at a fast-food place, with Roger on the lookout for us.

"If they don't have hamburgers, what would you like?" I asked. "How about candy or crackers from a machine?"

"Okay."

What a good little kid she was. Sitting there, good as gold, wrapped in the blanket, the sun making her auburn hair look even redder, the way it always had with mine.

Wiping my eyes dry, I looked around for Roger's car and still didn't see it anywhere.

"Okay, look," I said to Jade, "here's what we'll do."

Under ordinary circumstances, I would never had left a child her age alone in a car. But I couldn't take a six-year-old in a nightgown and bare feet inside with me; she would stand out too much.

"While I go in," I said, "I'd like you to lie down on the floor in back and cover up with your blanket so no one can see you. Can you do that? And will you promise not to move, even if someone tries to get in or bangs on the window?"

She nodded. "I always used to wait in the car when Nanny Irene went shopping, because I got too tired walking around the store. Afterward she'd take me out for ice cream, if I was good. Nanny told me never to unlock the door when I was alone in the car.''

"That's good," I said. "And honey, I don't mean to scare you, but it's especially important that we don't let your daddy find us right now. No matter what happens, just remember that your mommy asked me to take care of you. Okay?"

"Okay," she said in a small voice.

I reached over the seat, helping her to get settled on the floor. She lay in a fetal position, her legs drawn up to her chest, and I covered her over with the blanket. It wasn't till then that I realized I'd left the tote bag with her clothes and the toy rabbit behind.

"Make a tiny hole in the blanket to breathe through," I said. She did so immediately, and I could feel my heart breaking over and over for what she'd been through. The only thing that helped was that Lindy must have been a reasonably good mother, for Jade to have turned out this way.

It was a cool day, with a stiff breeze blowing off the bay. Even so, I rolled the front windows down an inch or so, to make sure the heat didn't rise too high in the car while I was gone. Then I reached inside the glove compartment for the knitted cap I'd brought with me from L.A., in case the nights grew cold as the fog rolled in. Tucking my hair up into it, I pulled the collar of my leather jacket up and hoped

I wouldn't be spotted immediately if Roger was anywhere nearby.

The parking slot I'd found was thankfully close to the Exploratorium building. I said a few last reassuring words to Jade, then locked the car doors and ran across to the building. On the way, I pulled money out of my jeans pocket. At the door I handed over the entrance fee, grabbed my change and half ran to where I remembered the café to be. I got turned around, though, and precious moments were lost. For every single one of them, my heart beat faster and faster.

I finally found the café and dashed in, looking for a menu and finding a blackboard instead. There were only deli sandwiches on it, no hamburgers. I picked out a turkey with lettuce, and then filled a tall paper cup with coffee. Grabbing a can of juice for Jade, I also picked up a small bag of chips. At the register I paid as quickly as possible, and walked with my bag of food back to the outer doors.

It was then that I saw him. He was on foot, walking along the aisles between cars. He was still toward the back of the lot, though, and two rows over from ours. Now and then he would bend over and look through the windows of a car, checking out the inside.

Could I risk his not seeing me if I made a run for my car?

No, don't run. If you run, you'll call attention to yourself.

Oddly, I felt as if Lindy were saying those words in my ear.

I waited until Roger had turned around to go down another aisle, and then I opened the Exploratorium door and walked as calmly as possible to the gray rental car. With every step my spine grew more rigid, as if I were trying to make myself invisible. *Don't run. Don't run.*

I was nearly there when I dared to look around. Roger was staring directly at me from one aisle away. When our eyes met he began to run toward me.

I nearly flew, getting to my car. I popped the front doors open with the remote, leaving the back ones locked. Yanking the driver door open, I jumped in, tossed the bag of food onto the seat, turned the key in the ignition and looked into the back. "Get up on the seat, Jade! Put your seat belt on!"

There was no sign of movement, and she didn't make a sound.

"Jade? Honey, it's me, Mary Beth. We have to get away. Sit up and put your seat belt on."

Still no sound. I looked back again and realized with horror that the back seat and floor were empty. Jade was gone.

I was so shocked to find Jade gone, I couldn't move for a moment or two. That was all the time Roger needed to get to my window and start banging his fist on it. "Open up, Mary Beth! Open the damn window!"

He's got Jade. He took her to his car, and now he's after me. He means to kill me.

I couldn't let him win. I would get Jade back somehow, but I'd have to live through this first.

"Why don't you call the police?" I yelled through the window. "Tell them how I took my daughter away from you, and why. Tell them her mother is lying dead on your living-room floor. It won't take them long to find out that you murdered her."

"Not me," he shouted. "You. I've made sure of that. Now give me back my daughter!"

I was confused. Give Jade back to him? But did that mean he didn't have her?

Where was she, then?

Had she followed me into the Exploratorium? *Dear God, let her be all right.*

I started the engine with one thing in mind: to get closer to the building, where people could see what Roger was doing. I'd make a scene, drive straight through the doors if I had to. *Just find Jade.*

But as the engine turned over, Roger pulled out a gun and aimed it at me through the window. I didn't give him a chance to do anything with it, jamming my foot on the accelerator and tearing off, heading for the Exploratorium doors.

The little rental car cleared the way of pedestrians like a tank, but I felt like a crazy woman. What was I thinking? I'd be arrested, and Jade would be taken away. If Roger didn't get her, the best I could hope for was that she'd be put in a foster home.

I was even more certain I was crazy when I imagined I heard her voice.

"Mary Beth? Help! Let me out!"

She's inside me, I thought frantically. *It's like when I held her and felt her heart becoming mine.*

But when she screamed again, the crazy feeling stopped and I knew exactly where she was—in the car's trunk.

I tapped the brake, refraining from slamming it on and possibly hurting Jade. When I climbed out of the car I saw that people stood in a circle around us, as people will do at the scene of an accident.

I realized then that I actually had reached the Exploratorium doors.

I punched the button that opened the trunk and ran to the back of the car. At the same time I scanned the crowd, looking for Roger. It took a moment, but I saw him standing outside his car in the parking lot, the door open as if he was about to get in.

At the trunk, I picked Jade up and breathed a prayer of gratitude. "Thank God you're safe."

"I saw him, and I thought I should hide," Jade said against my ear. "I pulled the latch and put the back seat down so I could get in the trunk."

I hugged her even harder. "You are so smart, and so brave."

"Nanny Irene taught me about the latch," she said

proudly. "She lets me put the seat down when she has groceries to put in the trunk."

I breathed another prayer, this time for Irene.

Turning with Jade, I realized that the crowd had no way of knowing what was going on, except that my child had somehow gotten stuck in the trunk of my car and now she was free. They began to applaud, and I smiled. Carrying Jade to the back seat I put her in, as before.

"Buckle up, honey. Good girl."

A security guard had joined the outer edges of the crowd, but I managed to get into the car and restart the engine before he could reach me. Backing away from the doors, I made a U-turn. Then I cleared the crowd and took off as fast as possible along the Marina Green.

There were only two reasonably close ways to get from San Francisco to San Jose. One was by Van Ness and Highway 101, but there was always heavy traffic that way, especially during the commuter rush.

The other way was via Nineteenth Avenue, which used to be fast, but could get bogged down when the lights weren't paced right. The upside was that Nineteenth did lead to 280, which sometimes wasn't too busy and would take us right to San Jose. From there I could take Route 17 to Santa Cruz, then head south to Carmel, where I had an old friend who would put us up for the night.

Provided that I managed to ditch Roger by then.

And I thought I could. He would most likely be expecting us to go to the airport, and when he didn't find us there, he'd head over to Interstate 5, since that was the fastest route to L.A.

I didn't think he'd ever expect me to take the slowest way home, along the coast.

So while Jade munched on her sandwich in the back, I headed out of San Francisco on 280, beginning to relax remembering trips with my own mom, who smoked constantly when she drove. Secondhand smoke never bothered me back then, and in fact I had fond memories of riding in the car with her at night along a lonely highway, the old Chevy's radio playing softly and the comforting scent of her cigarette filling the car. These days I'd be gasping for air after the first five minutes, but it was a nice memory and always would be, as long as I didn't end up with lung cancer someday.

I wondered if Jade and I would be able to take drives like that. Minus the smoke, of course.

When I got to Route 17, I took it over the hills to Santa Cruz. The traffic was thick but moving. In fact, it was moving dangerously fast, and I remembered that this route was sometimes called Blood Alley because of all the accidents along here. My hands tightened on the steering wheel, and my eyes never left the road. It was just about dark, and as I entered Santa Cruz it was impossible to tell if any of the headlights behind me might be Roger's.

The town, though, was alive with students sitting

out in courtyards and sidewalk restaurants. I felt safer here than I would on the dark highway that was ahead of us, so I decided to pull in to a gas station and fill up.

At the last minute, something told me to park alongside the station first, where the car couldn't be seen from the road. I sat there, waiting to see if Roger would pull in after me, or if his car passed us by. There was no sign of him, though, and after about five minutes I felt as if I'd really shaken him, and had just given in to nerves.

Driving around to the pumps, I got out and checked Jade first, to make sure she was covered. She had fallen asleep with the blanket, which I'd swiped from my hotel, pulled up to her ears. She looked like an angel, her cheeks pinker than ever and giving her a deceptively healthy appearance. Feeling her forehead, I thought her fever had gone up. That frightened me, as I didn't know what was causing it. I wished Lindy were here. Oh, God, did I wish Lindy were here.

Closing the door and setting the gas to pump, I realized that they might have a thermometer and children's Tylenol in the station's convenience store. I'd wake Jade, give her the Tylenol and a chance to use the bathroom. Then I'd get her to Carmel and a safe place to sleep for the night.

Fortunately, I knew just the place. It used to be a convent called The Prayer House, and now it was known as The Abby. Located in an isolated spot off

Carmel Valley Road, it was owned by a friend of mine, Abby Northrup. She'd bought it and turned it into a safe house for women who were in distress of any kind. Most of the surrounding population thought it was still a convent housing nuns, which in a way it was. But the nuns were women who'd left their original convents over disagreements with the Church, and who had "retired" at the Abby to follow their own beliefs.

By common agreement, no one ever talked about the battered women and children who came there from time to time—usually under the cover of darkness, and accompanied by one of Abby's "angels." The angels were nuns who worked on the streets and led battered women to her for overnight shelter. It wasn't an Underground Railroad, by any means, but absolute secrecy was a promise that Abby Northrup made personally to all who sought haven there.

The drive between Santa Cruz and Carmel would take only about an hour, so I felt even more relaxed as I pulled out of town with a full tank of gas and my purchases of a thermometer, children's Tylenol, juice and a bag of fish-shaped crackers for Jade. I'd also bought four large bottles of water, and had opened one to give Jade the Tylenol. The other bottles were to make sure she didn't dehydrate if anything unexpected happened, like the car breaking down, or a flat.

The thought of that as a possibility frightened me, but Jade was already asleep again when I pulled out of town on Highway 1. It helped that she'd accepted the situation we were in and seemed to be trusting me to take care of her.

I had remembered this stretch of Highway 1 as an easy drive, a two-lane road along the ocean most of the way. But I'd forgotten the fog, which at this time of year was often so thick it made the front of one's car impossible to see, especially at night. The only way to make time on this road under those conditions was to follow another car's taillights, and pray they didn't lead you straight into the sea.

I was relieved, therefore, when I saw a blur of red lights ahead. I sped up until I was just a few lengths behind, and then kept pace with them. I couldn't see the car though the heavy fog, just the faint red lights. But they kept a steady thirty-five miles per hour, and that was good enough for me. If for any reason they stopped suddenly, I'd have plenty of time to step on my own brakes. Pileups in this kind of fog in California were rampant, and that was the last thing I needed now.

As I drove, I talked to Jade, who'd woken up grouchy but was much better now after her fish crackers and juice. She hadn't mentioned Lindy even once, and I was grateful for that. But how could I ever explain Roger, her father? The psychological fallout from the years she had spent with him would probably be with her forever.

Forever. Would she be with me that long?

To have any claim on her, we'd both have to provide DNA for testing. That would prove I was her mother, but Roger could also prove he was her father. Could he wage a custody battle from prison? I doubted it, but if so, it might go on for years. And who would Jade live with those years?

The last thing in the world I wanted or would allow was for her to end up in a foster home until custody was decided. I would run with her, if I had to, and as far as I had to. If necessary, I'd keep running the rest of my life.

The drone of the car's engine, and the slow, steady pace of those two red taillights finally calmed me down. In fact, despite the sharp ocean air hitting my face through the open vents, I had to keep shaking my head to stay awake.

During one of those edge-of-sleep times, the car ahead stopped abruptly and I almost ran into it. Fortunately, it had one of those extra brake lights just under the rear window, easy to see.

Jamming on my own brakes, I said, "Sorry, Jade. Are you okay?"

"I'm fine," she said in that little voice I was beginning to realize she used when she was frightened but wouldn't admit it.

"There must be something in the road," I said as calmly as possible. "Don't worry. I'll just go and see what it is."

I was opening my door and had one leg out when the driver of the other car stepped out onto the road.

My breath caught. *Roger. Oh my God. I'd been following Roger all this time.*

I jerked my door shut, locked all the doors and looked frantically behind us. There wasn't another car on the road. It was pitch-dark, and we were totally alone.

I was frantic, but not too frantic to think. Roger was halfway to us when I stomped on the gas and drove straight at him. His eyes seemed to widen, like a deer's in headlights. But he didn't move aside.

If I'd been alone, I'd have hit him, and I wouldn't have cared. But Jade was with me. And he was still her father. She might be afraid of him, and with good reason, but it would be horrible for her to see him killed, especially after finding Lindy that way today.

At the last minute I swerved to miss him, but didn't let up on the gas. I kept driving as fast as possible, into the wall of fog, with only a faint blur of yellow line as a guide. Remembering this road as reasonably straight, I kept the wheels pointed ahead, even when I couldn't see. It was the most frightening thing I'd ever done. If I drove off the road, the car could get stuck in wet sand, and we'd be at Roger's mercy.

I didn't see him following at first, but then headlights appeared behind us. As they grew closer and closer, my hands tightened on the wheel and I tried to drive faster. I was so terrified of sliding off the road, though, my foot took on a life of its own and refused to press hard enough on the accelerator.

Roger drew nearer and I thought he was trying to pass us, hoping to block us off. But when he drew opposite my car he deliberately slammed into my left side, at the front wheel well.

The car swerved to the right. Jade screamed, and I did, too. Roger's child was in this car, and anything could happen. Jade could be killed.

My God, was that his intention?

I was sure of it when he ran into us again. This time I felt it more, and there was a screech of metal on metal that sounded like a thousand banshees.

"Jade!" I cried. "Do you have your seat belt on?"

"Yes," she whimpered. I could tell she was crying. "Why is Daddy doing that?"

So, there was no pretending it was a stranger out here in the middle of nowhere, trying to kill us.

"I don't know, honey. I think he's sick. You just stay buckled up. We'll be all right."

This time my foot didn't argue. I jammed the accelerator to the floor and took off like a bat out of hell, leaving Roger in the dust. He had the faster car, however, and I knew it wouldn't be long before he caught up to us.

I wondered if it would help to pull off on a side road. Most of them led to farms along here. But when people being chased pulled off the main highway and onto strange roads in the movies, I usually pounded on someone's arm and screamed, "No! Don't do that, you idiot! He'll catch you there!"

Funny thing is, he always did.

So I kept driving, my heart in my throat, and prayed for some kind stranger to appear on the seat beside me. Like in *Touched by an Angel,* or that old Michael Landon series.

Where were angels when you needed them?

Right here, I thought I heard a small voice say. I stole a quick look back at Jade, but amazingly, she was asleep again.

Then, suddenly, there were lights ahead of us. In the fog they looked strange, like an island lost at sea. But some of the patches of fog cleared and I saw what they were: Houses. Restaurants. Shops.

And a red gas station sign, riding above the mist like a ship's mast.

Oh, thank you, I said to whatever saints might still be listening. I had completely forgotten that Moss Landing was along here.

I didn't need gas, but with all the water she'd been drinking, I was sure Jade must need a bathroom again. The only question was, where could I take her that Roger wouldn't find us? He must still be close behind. If we stopped and just sat for a bit, where we couldn't be seen from the road, he might pass us by again, as he had out of Santa Cruz.

Only this time, I wouldn't continue on Highway 1. I knew another road, 156. It would take us over to 101, and from there I could get to the Carmel Valley.

I had called Abby Northrup from the gas station

in Santa Cruz, telling her what was going on and
that I needed help. She said she would wait up for
us, and she'd have food, milk and a warm bed waiting for Jade. For me, she'd have a bottle of wine and
lots of questions.

I couldn't wait.

But first I had to take care of Jade's needs and
make sure we were free of Roger.

With fear cramping my stomach and making me
feel ill, I cautiously drove up and down a few streets,
making sure Roger hadn't caught up and was trailing
right behind us. When I was satisfied about that, I
pulled into a grove of trees behind a gas station, and
turned the engine off. The fog would help us now. I
could no longer see the highway, so it wouldn't be
possible for Roger to see us, either.

Getting out of the car and opening Jade's door, I
said, "Honey, wake up. There's a bathroom here,
and you need to drink some more water."

She sat up obediently, and I wrapped the blanket
around her. She'd been sleeping with it in the warm
car, and she tried to shrug it off.

"I'm hot," she complained. "I don't want this."

"I know, honey, but that's just the fever. It's really cold out here tonight. I don't want you to get a
chill."

God, I was beginning to sound like my mother.

The rest room was near the back, and thankfully
it was open. I went in with Jade to hold the blanket
and make sure the toilet had been flushed by the

previous tenant, and that the floor and seat weren't too dirty.

They were passable. Jade sat down and seemed to drift off into contemplation. "I don't think I can go," she said finally.

"Just try," I said. "If you can't, it's all right."

Only moments later, all the water I'd been making her drink proved her wrong. She smiled at me, a huge, beautiful smile. "I did it!" she said.

"Yes, you did it."

I don't think I'd ever been so happy in my life as I was in that dank, not-too-clean bathroom that night.

My child. After all these years...my child. How could I have gotten so lucky?

I wrapped her gently in the blanket again, and carried her back to the car. Tucking her in with the seat belt around her, I planted a light kiss on her forehead. "I'm so glad you're here with me," I said. "I don't want you to worry about a thing, honey. We're going to be all right. Okay?"

"Okay," she said, smiling sleepily. I made her drink more water, and before I was back in the driver's seat, she had drifted off again.

Part of me was thankful for that, and part of me worried. Was this sleepiness from the fever? It had come down to 101.4 when I'd taken it in Santa Cruz. Fevers are good, I'd always heard. They're the body's sign that it's ridding itself of the illness. Until we got to Los Angeles, I could only hope that this was the case with Jade, and that nothing really bad was wrong with her. In L.A., I would call Nia's father and ask him for that referral. If he wasn't able to help, I'd take her to a doctor I'd heard about at UCLA, a specialist in the immune system. I didn't know how much he could do for her, but he would keep our visit confidential, and it was a place to start.

It was only a few miles south to Highway 156, the cutoff that would take us over to 101. As I drove, there was no sign of Roger, and I wondered if I'd actually managed to lose him. The other possibility was that it might have occurred to him that he'd better clean up the evidence of his crimes at home before the police—assuming I'd called them—arrived.

Whatever had happened, he was finally gone. I began to relax enough to eat some of the crackers and cheese I'd bought at the last gas station. The caffeine from a bottle of Pepsi was doing a nice job of waking me up, and I knew, suddenly, that things were going to be all right.

Don't get too comfortable, my mother used to say. *It's like spitting in the eye of God.*

Bless my mother, she was right about that. I just never remembered it until it was too late.

A few minutes later I turned off on 156. There was a full moon, and the fields and surrounding hills looked like the set of a movie. I heard Jade stir, and when she sat up and yawned I said, "Look at that moon, Jade. Isn't it beautiful?"

She leaned over to the window, and I tilted the rearview mirror so I could see her face. She looked sad.

"My mommy's up there," she said. "Isn't she?"

I wasn't sure how to answer.

"She told me if anything ever happened to her, like when Daddy was hitting her, I could look up at the moon and I'd know she was there."

My eyes filled with tears. "I'm sure she will be, honey. But you know what? Right now, I think she's still here with us, in our hearts. She's making sure you're safe."

"I don't even know who you are," Jade said softly. It wasn't said meanly, but as if she was trying hard to figure things out.

"I know you don't," I said. "But you will. And I'll always take care of you, Jade. I promise."

"Pinkie promise?"

I reached my hand back and stuck out my little finger. "Pinkie promise."

And God help me if I ever failed this precious little life.

It was then the car struck us from behind—hitting the back bumper, falling back, then hitting it again. I hadn't seen it because the rearview mirror was tilted, and the vehicle's headlights weren't on. It was nothing but a large black form on the road.

My heart in my throat, I grasped the wheel hard and tried to speed up. But just as before, Roger's car was faster. There was no getting away from him, and this road was as lonely, if not more so, than Highway 1.

I saw him coming at us again, and I knew this would be our last chance to survive whatever Roger had in store for us.

I called out to Jade as calmly as I could, "Jade, hold on tight. And keep your head down. Okay?"

"Okay."

I jammed on the brakes, pulling my car to a dead stop. Roger, who'd apparently been revving up to hit my bumper again, swerved at the last minute to avoid the inevitable crash. I watched as his car went off the road and rolled over and over in the field.

I'm ashamed to admit it, but I genuinely hoped he was dead.

The next instant, as if in answer to a prayer, Roger's car burst into flames. They rose higher and higher, lighting up the surrounding fields and hills with an eerie glow.

I stepped out of the car and stood there, feeling the heat of the flames on my face, even this far away.

"Is that Daddy?" Jade said in a shaky little voice from beside me. "Is he dead?"

"I think so," I said, picking her up and holding her close. "Are you okay?"

"Yes," she said in a voice that sounded older than

her years. "Mommy says it's going to be okay now."

"Your mommy?"

She nodded matter-of-factly. "A few minutes ago. She was here."

Irrationally, I looked into the back seat, as if expecting to see Lindy sitting there.

"Not there, silly," Jade said with a tiny smile. She patted her heart with her hand. "Here."

We pulled in to the driveway of The Abby before midnight, and true to her word, my friend was there to meet us at the door. She hadn't changed a bit, standing there in jeans, a white shirt and boots. Around her neck was a silver and turquoise necklace. The silver was exquisite, like fine lace.

Abby had been rich once. She wasn't doing too bad now, either, but most of her money went into her project here. I knew the jewelry had come from the days of her marriage, and that she probably hadn't bought anything new in years.

We hugged, and then she looked down at Jade and said, "She looks just like you, Mary Beth. No mistaking the genes. I can't wait till we talk."

"What's genes?" Jade asked.

Abby and I looked at each other, then smiled at Jade.

"They're the things that made you so beautiful," Abby said.

Jade smiled shyly, but she was nearly asleep on her feet. Abby took what seemed like a two-way radio from her shirt pocket. Pushing a button, she said, "Agatha, can you come down to the living room, please?"

She took us into a room that had a huge fireplace and was furnished in the Spanish style, to match the rest of the house. Although, the word *house* might be an understatement. Having been a convent once, The Abby was still very large.

A woman dressed in a brown nun's habit came in, her rosary beads clacking as she crossed the floor.

"Agatha, this is my friend, Mary Beth," Abby said. "And this beautiful person is Jade. Would you take Jade to the room we've fixed up for her, please? There's a warm nightie on the bed, and you can tell Sister Nella that our new visitor is ready for that warm milk and toast now."

She turned to Jade. "Is that all right, Jade? Do you like warm milk and toast?"

"Yes," she said, but her voice was soft and she clung to my arm so tightly, I wasn't sure if she'd go anywhere without me.

Sister Agatha had a nice way with kids, though. She talked to Jade gently, offering up little bribes for the morning. She told her that if she got a good night's sleep, and if her fever was down, she'd take her out to see the horses and chickens, and maybe the goats. She might even let her ride one of the horses.

Jade, who probably hadn't been out of the house for a long time until that day—and who almost certainly had never in her life been on a ranch—was thrilled. She went off hand in hand with her new best friend, and with hardly a glance back at me.

Abby placed a short crystal tumbler filled with wine in front of me. "Now, what else can I do for you?" she asked.

I sighed, picking the glass up and taking a sip. "Oh, this is so good," I said. The dark, rich wine tasted like blackberries. "Did you make it yourself?"

"That's one of the ones we make," she said. "The income helps to keep The Abby running. Now stop changing the subject. What can I do for you?"

"Just what you are doing," I said. "I am deeply grateful for a place to just sit quietly without being afraid. This past day—the last hour, in fact—has been horrendous. And I'm still shaking."

"Drink up," she said. "Wine is the Zoloft of the gods."

I followed her advice and took a couple of hefty swallows. Then I sat back and rested my head on the back of the soft, comfy sofa. It felt like heaven.

"Is it Jade's father?" Abby asked. "You told me something about it when you called from Santa Cruz, but there has to be more. Are you and Jade running from him?''

"We were. We aren't anymore.''

Her dark eyebrows lifted. "Something happen between Santa Cruz and here?''

I told her the whole story, starting with the way I'd become pregnant by Roger, and ending with him killing Lindy and probably Irene, the nanny, then trying to run us off the road a couple of hours before.

"He's dead,'' I said. "Unless, God forbid, he somehow escaped the fire.''

"Do you think he could have?''

"No. I don't know.''

"He must have been desperate to silence you,'' Abby said.

"Well, I told him the police had proof against him, a tell-all book about illegal dealings between his company and the Middle East. Roger already knew about the book and I think he killed one of my authors when he got caught trying to find it. He also ransacked my office for the manuscript, and even broke into my home.''

I told her about the ex-employees named in Craig's book, and the possibility that they would have testified against Roger.

"He didn't really admit to the break-ins or my author's murder, but once that book became public, it would have been over for him. He followed us,

I'm sure, just to get his hands on Jade. Then he would have disappeared with her.''

''What a monster,'' Abby said. ''If he hadn't died in that crash, I'd be inclined to kill him myself.''

Abby had a quiet, classic demeanor, but in her voice now was the angry tone of an avenger. And with good reason. She'd been horribly treated by her ex-husband, and it wasn't by coincidence that she'd set up this haven for abused women and children. Every time she helped a woman or child in trouble, she felt her mission was being fulfilled.

A short while later I checked on Jade, and saw that she was sleeping peacefully. I pulled her cover up over her shoulders and kissed her cheek.

My own dreams that night were not so peaceful, but by the time morning came, I'd forgotten them all.

I woke late and, after showering, I went into the kitchen, but didn't find anyone there. I poured myself a cup of coffee and went outside, where I found Jade out in the corral riding a horse, with Sister Agatha holding the reins and walking beside her. Jade was wearing jeans and a shirt that Sister Agatha said had been left behind by another child. Her complexion was healthy, rather than the feverish, mottled state it had been in since I'd first seen her the day before, and I was stunned to hear her laugh. Even more stunned when she called out, "Hi, Mary Beth! Look at me. I'm riding a horse!"

She went on to tell me the horse's name, Molly, and all about the colt Molly had delivered a month before. "Sister Agatha says if I come next summer I can ride her colt then, too!"

"Sister Nella gave Jade some tea with herbs," Sister Agatha said, smiling. "And her fever broke in the night. She ate a huge breakfast."

And how's that for an angel? that small voice inside me said. I smiled, admitting finally that—no doubt about it—the voice was Lindy's.

Thank you, I replied silently. *And thank you for raising such a beautiful child.*

We had lunch in the nuns' former refectory, which Abby had redecorated with bright, happy colors. Lunch was a hearty soup and homemade bread, slathered with fresh butter from a farm down the road. Dessert was old-fashioned rice pudding, with plump juicy raisins and lots of cinnamon and nutmeg. After the past couple of days, the meal tasted like a feast.

Jade asked to be excused so she could go out and see the horses again. She looked so much better, I didn't see any reason why not. Clearly, all this fresh air agreed with her. And Sister Agatha, Abby assured me, would be out there with her.

Jade slid off her chair with a happy smile, and I

watched as she trotted out through the kitchen to the back gardens, and then to the corral. Sister Agatha was there, waiting for her, just as Abby had said, and I saw her take Jade's hand and lead her around, pointing out things to her and talking. I was amazed at the change that had come over this little girl.

Abby and I sat across from each other at the table and talked. She sipped iced tea, and I toyed with leftover raisins in the pudding.

Abby and I had met when we were both working on a story years ago, in L.A. I was working at the television station, and Abby was a reporter with a small local newspaper. We were both following a story about a major crime. I hadn't seen Abby in three years, and I would have liked to stay longer than overnight, but I was anxious about whether I should get Jade to L.A. and good medical care.

"Tell me what you're thinking," Abby said, smiling. "Before you do in that raisin."

I shook my head. "I'm wondering if I should ask to leave Jade here, since she's doing so well. Not for long. A couple of days, at the most. It might be better than taking her to L.A. before I know what's waiting for me there."

"You know I'd say yes. She's a delightful child."

I shook my head. "I just don't see how I can leave her, though, Abby. I promised her I never would, and that I'd always take care of her."

"We'd take good care of her," Abby said. "She could stay as long as you like."

"Thanks. I really appreciate that. It's amazing how much she's improved in the few short hours we've been here. Her fever is gone, she seems happy...."

"But you just found her, and you don't want to be separated from her." Abby smiled.

"True," I admitted. "And regardless of how well she looks, she still has an immune system problem. I promised her mother I'd get her to a good doctor, and it's got to be my first priority."

"How will you do that if you're arrested?" she asked.

"I've been thinking about that. I'll go to a friend's house when I first get to Malibu, and in the morning I can make some phone calls to doctors before I go to my own house. I imagine there'll be a detective or two there to greet me."

"Now that you've found this book and the names of people at the pharmaceutical company who talked to your author, though, they won't have any cause to arrest you, will they? Roger should be their prime suspect, and since he's dead, the case could very well go away."

Abby was engaged to a Carmel police detective, Ben Schaeffer, and between being around him and her own legal problems with her ex in the past, she had picked up more than a casual knowledge of the law.

"Unfortunately," I said, "there are the other two murders I told you about. We haven't been able to link Roger to them. And until we do, that leaves me." I laughed shortly. "Though why on earth they'd think I killed Craig Dinsmore—my nearest thing to a cash cow right now—I don't know."

She reached for my hand. "You're not alone in this. Tell me what I can do. Anything. I can talk to Ben, too. I'm sure he'd be glad to help."

"Let me see how it goes first," I said. "I really think it's going to be all right. But thanks."

"Okay." Standing, Abby said, "Now, since you're not leaving until three, how about if we take Jade and go horseback riding in the hills."

"A splendid idea," I said, grateful to have something to take my mind off my impending arrest for a while.

Around three o'clock, Abby, Sister Agatha and I got Jade settled in the back seat of the rental car with extra clothes and a stuffed dog that she wouldn't let go of once Abby had given it to her. There was also a bag of healthy snacks, books, pens, crayons and other assorted toys to keep a six-year-old busy on a trip. On the seat next to the bag was a white jacket with pink rabbits on it, in case it was cold at the beach when we got home.

Jade seemed happy as a clam, sitting back there like a princess, surrounded by her little gifts.

I'd waited until three to leave as I wanted to get to L.A. after the sun went down. At this time of year that would be around eight, and it took five hours, more or less, to drive from Carmel to L.A.

Leaving the Carmel Valley, I crossed over to Interstate 5, the fastest route to L.A. The break at Abby's had been just what Jade and I both needed, and I even found myself singing old songs that reminded me of trips with my mother. Jade didn't join me, but when I'd sneak a look though the rearview mirror, I'd see her smiling. Once, she even hummed a bit, but when she caught me looking at her, she got shy and quit.

The trip was uneventful until we drove down out of the mountains into the L.A. basin. There the traffic was even thicker than the smog. I didn't think it wise to sit in a bumper-to-bumper parking lot, in case there was an APB out on me, so I cut over to surface roads that I knew would take me—eventually—to Malibu. I wasn't in a particular hurry, and as long as Jade was feeling well, I figured the later we got there, the better. We wouldn't be able to go to my house, but I knew where we could go, and that we'd be safe there.

It was long after dark when I turned onto PCH, and there was little traffic. I was careful not to break any traffic laws, and avoided passing my house. It was around a slight curve from Patrick's, and it was his driveway I pulled in to.

The driveway sloped downward alongside the house, and I drove down as far as possible so that the car wouldn't be visible from the road. Turning off the engine, I sighed, stretched and looked back at Jade, who was snacking on a granola bar that Abby's cook had made by hand for her.

"With good healthy herbs from our own garden," Nella had said. I had to admit that Jade was looking better and better.

Patrick's garage lights were out, which helped when we got out of the car. Since I didn't know who might be in the neighborhood—Detective Dan Rucker and the entire LAPD and ESPD, for instance—it seemed wisest to keep out of sight as much as possible.

The driveway was so dark I started to pick Jade up, but she wanted to walk. I took her by the hand, and since I remembered how bright Patrick's deck lights were, we walked away from the beach and up the driveway to the front of the house. I jumped when I heard a noise, sure that someone was in the bushes near the street. My hand tightened on Jade's, and every muscle went into battle mode.

Then I realized it was only bougainvillea, its dry petals rustling in a small breeze.

The porch light was out, which surprised me.

Again, I was grateful for the dark, and lifted the heavy knocker. Rapping three times, I waited.

Patrick didn't answer.

I rapped again, a couple of times. Still no answer. Knocking once more, I was about to turn around and leave when the door opened a crack.

"Who is it?" a woman's voice called out softly.

"Julia?"

I was only a little surprised to see Julia Dinsmore here. She didn't put the porch light on, but stood there a few moments, peering through the crack in the door.

"It's me," I said. "Mary Beth. Can we come in? It's urgent."

She opened the door a bit more and said, "Mary Beth! Hi. What's wrong?"

I held Jade close at my side. "It's a long story. This is Jade, and I'm taking care of her for her mother. We need a place to, uh, spend the night. I thought Patrick might—"

I was beginning to feel uncomfortable. What had I interrupted here? Patrick and Julia in a tryst?

She must have guessed what I was thinking, because she smiled reassuringly and waved us in. "Oh, sorry. Sure, c'mon in. We really aren't up to anything lewd. Just talking about old times."

"Are you sure?"

"Of course!"

I stepped over the threshold, saying to Jade when she hesitated, "It's okay, honey. Julia's a friend."

Following Julia into the living room, I said, "I really am sorry to intrude. I didn't expect to see you here."

"Just visiting with an old pal," she said, leading the way into the living room.

I looked around. "Where *is* Patrick?"

"He went out a few minutes ago for more wine. I guess there's something about talking over old times that gets the alcohol flowing."

I took Jade over to the sofa and helped her get her jacket off. She hadn't slept as much in the car today, and it was way past a six-year-old's bedtime.

I encouraged her to lie down on the sofa, and covered her over with the same throw Lindy had used the night we were here. Jade couldn't know this, of course, but I couldn't help wondering what this little girl must be thinking, having seen the only mother she ever knew dead, and then her father…

I didn't even want to think about that. Would Jade ever get over it?

I sat at the end of the sofa, my hand gently rubbing her feet through the blanket. Leaning my head back, I closed my eyes and sighed.

"Can I get you something?" Julia asked.

I opened my eyes and saw that she was standing over me, twisting her hands. She looked worried, as if she didn't know what to do with us.

"A glass of wine would be nice," I said. I looked at the sideboard and saw a bottle there. "I guess the wine is gone, though."

She followed my gaze. "What?"

"The wine must be gone, if Patrick's gone out for more."

"Oh. Oh, that? That's Cabernet. Patrick doesn't like red wine, so he went to get more Chardonnay. God knows how far he had to go to find an open liquor store at this hour, though."

"There's one a little ways down the highway," I said. "He probably went there."

"Oh. Well, he shouldn't be long, then."

She went over and poured me a glass of the Cab, which was warm and felt good going down. My nerves were a mess from everything that had happened since San Francisco, and my hand shook as I lifted the glass to my mouth.

Not as much as Julia's shook though. She had apparently spilled some wine on her dress when she carried it over to me.

She saw me looking at the stain, but didn't say anything.

"Some soda water might get that right out," I said.

"It's—it's okay. I was going to throw this dress out anyway."

She must be doing better than she'd let on, I thought. First, taxis all over L.A., and now simply ignoring a stain on a gold and white dress that looked like a designer item.

"Are you all right, Julia?" I asked. "You seem worried."

"No, it's just all that's happened, I guess. Getting the call about Craig, then the funeral…I think I'm just exhausted."

She sat in the chair across from me. "Do you mind if I ask you what's going on?" she said. "Who is this little girl, and why do you both look so drained?"

I glanced over at Jade and saw that she was asleep, her little chest moving up and down in tiny rises with each soft breath.

"It's a horribly long story, Julia. I should probably wait till Patrick gets back to tell it. But the short of it is, we've driven down from San Francisco, and it wasn't a good experience."

"Mmm. Fog along Moss Landing?"

"And then some. You've been caught in it?"

"Craig and I used to hike through the mountains in Santa Cruz and Carmel, and I remember some real scary drives up and down the coast between the two."

Her eyes welled and her mouth shook. She raised a hand as if to still them. "I never thought I'd miss him this much."

"I'm sorry. I guess Patrick's helped a lot, though?"

She nodded. Pulling herself together, she looked me straight in the eye and said, "Pardon me if this seems mean, Mary Beth, especially after you helped me the other day. But Patrick really doesn't need any trouble right now."

I felt a small jolt of surprise, like the kind when you're out on a date and you think you're going to get a ring, but get dumped instead.

"Trouble?" I asked.

"You must know the police are looking for you. They think you had something to do with Craig's murder. And maybe even Tony's and Arnold's. They've been around asking questions."

"Oh, God, I'm sorry. It never occurred to me that Patrick would be bothered like that. But Julia, surely you don't believe that I killed them!"

"Of course not. Not for a minute, Mary Beth. But since you and Patrick are close again—"

"Wait a minute. I'm going to represent him again. That doesn't mean we're 'close.' Not the way it sounds like you mean."

She looked flustered again. "No, not at all! I just meant that because of the connection, they seem to be focusing a lot on Patrick now. I think they may be looking at him as a possible accomplice."

"But that's crazy! Why would Patrick—"

I stood and walked over to the doors overlooking the deck. I was shaken by the implication that the police thought Patrick and I might be in some sort of conspiracy. If it had gone that far in just two days, I was in hotter water than I'd known.

Hadn't Dan shown his superiors and Lieutenant Davies Craig's CD, after all?

It was pitch-black outside, and I automatically reached for the switch that put the deck lights on. As Patrick had said, I do have a way of taking over. It was just too dark beyond the doors, and the thought that anyone could be standing there gave me the jitters.

I felt a bit silly when the lights flooded on, only to reveal that the deck was devoid of human life.

Julia came up behind me and said, "Mary Beth, I don't mean to be unkind. I just think it might be better for Patrick if you left. Now, I mean, before he gets back. If the police even get a hint that you're here, they'll probably come and arrest you *and* Patrick. I would hate to see that happen to him."

"I agree," I said. "I don't want to see that, either."

I walked over to the sofa and looked down at Jade. How much more could this child of mine take? How could I best protect her?

My plan had been to spend the night here, and in the morning call Nia's father in London, and the other doctor I knew of in L.A. Once I found out what could be done for Jade, and if she could be taken care of in L.A., I'd ask Nia to come home, and then turn myself in. Nia would take care of Jade, I knew, until I was able to.

Which I hoped wouldn't take long. I'd tell the police about Roger having killed Lindy and Irene, and about Craig's book and Roger's attempt to stop its publication by killing Craig.

But what if they still couldn't link Roger to the other two murders?

That's what it kept coming back to. If Roger had killed Craig, who had killed Tony and Arnold? And why?

I sat on the edge of the couch next to Jade, preparing to wake her up and leave with her, though I wasn't sure where I was going. Then I heard something: a small sound, nothing much, but at the same time so huge, it changed all our lives.

I looked at Julia, who seemed oblivious to it. I'd heard this sound before, though, when I was still Patrick's agent. We'd go out now and then to a restaurant or meetings and I'd wait here, tapping a foot impatiently, wondering if he'd ever finish checking his e-mail so we could leave.

It was the noise a computer makes when it's going online. One of those high-pitched squeals that's something like a fax machine. My own computer, and probably most people's don't go online by themselves. Someone has to hit the right keys.

I glanced at Julia again, my mind racing to assimilate this information but she was already heading for the front door, eager to show us out.

"I'll just take my glass to the kitchen," I said. Jade was still sleeping, and I hesitated, looking at her. But I had to take the chance that Julia wouldn't be after Jade.

She'd want me.

The minute I got to the kitchen I set my glass down, opened the basement door and ran down the steps, then over to Patrick's "cave"—the office he'd built for himself without any windows or view to distract him while he wrote.

The door was solid mahogany and heavy. Yanking it open with both hands, I found Patrick tied to his office chair with what seemed to be clothesline. There was adhesive tape over his mouth, but the look in his eyes was one of sheer relief.

I ran over to him and pulled the tape off.

"Ow!" he said. And then, "Thank God!" His voice was so hoarse he didn't sound like himself at all. "I heard you up there, and I managed to log online with my nose, but I wasn't sure you'd hear it."

"Your nose?" I said, half laughing. "My poor Patrick, I never wanted to mention it, but you do have an awesome nose. Are you okay?"

I glanced at his desk, looking for something to cut the rope.

"I will be," he said. "They're in that drawer. Scissors."

I pulled them out. "She'll be here in any minute. Let me call the police first," I said, picking up his desk phone to dial 911.

"Not a smart move, Mary Beth," Julia said from the doorway. "You should have taken that little brat and gotten out of here when you could."

"Mary Beth, go!" Patrick yelled. *"Run!"*

"Too late," Julia said. "Too late."

She was pointing a small pistol in my direction, the kind of weapon a woman carries in her purse. I backed off, raising both my hands palm out.

"You don't have to do this, Julia. You'll go to prison for life. Why would you want that?"

"Shut up," she said.

"It doesn't matter to her," Patrick said. "Don't you get it? She's already murdered three times."

His voice sounded angry, but there were tears in his eyes. "She killed them, Mary Beth. Tony, Craig and Arnold. She'll kill us now, too. She doesn't have anything left to lose."

"My dear Patrick," Julia said, "you are so right. I've got nothing to lose now. And with no one left to talk, who would ever suspect me? I'll just collect Craig's money and be on my way."

"If you mean his advance from the book, there isn't one," I said. "I haven't made a deal yet."

"Not to worry," Julia said. "Paul Whitmore told

me he offered you a seven-figure deal. As Craig's widow, I was going to instruct you to take the offer. Now I'll just have to make that deal myself. And even better, I won't have to pay you a commission."

I shook my head. "Sorry, but like you said, Julia, too late. Whitmore withdrew the offer late yesterday. I guess he didn't tell you that."

She paled. "You're lying. He told me at the funeral—"

"And yesterday he changed his mind. The fact that Craig is dead makes it a tough sell now. He won't be around to talk about the book on tour, and when it's nonfiction, that makes a big difference. I doubt anyone will touch it now."

"That's not possible. Craig told me this book was a sure best-seller. He said there would be more than enough money for both of us soon."

"Oh, God, Julia. All writers say that. They always think the next one's *the one*. And you told me yourself that Craig was a gambler. They lie all the time about money."

"No! No, it was different this time. He swore to me that this book would be a runaway best-seller. For God's sake, that's the only reason I stayed married to him this time! You can't imagine I'd really want him back. I hated the man. Hated his lazy habits, his addictions, the other women—"

She came closer with the gun, as if by threatening me she could somehow make me produce a pot of gold. "I need that money, Mary Beth! I'm on the verge of bankruptcy, and I'm losing my business!"

"Oh, well, not to worry, then," I said. "I'll tell Nia to forward Craig's checks to you. There won't be much, of course, just dribs and drabs of royalties from his old books now and then. Enough to pay the light bill—for a month or two."

She shook her head. "This isn't possible. I know you're lying. You have to be lying," she said numbly. The hand with the gun hung limply at her side.

"Keep telling yourself that, if it makes you feel better," I said. "But even if the book sold, don't you think that grabbing a ton of Craig's money so soon after his murder might just give the police reason to wonder about you? The Black Widow aspect of it, I mean."

She straightened and seemed to gain back her strength. And her anger.

"Not when they've got you to wonder about. I'm so glad you showed up, Mary Beth. Now I can make it look like you killed Patrick. This will be your fourth murder, of course, and the media will say you went nuts from too much pressure at work and began killing off your clients. You even used these handy-dandy little toys, and they'll be talking about that for years."

She reached into a pocket of her silk jacket and

pulled out an ornamental Chinese dildo, much like the ones all three men had been killed with.

''It would have been much nicer for you, of course, if you hadn't shown up when you did, Mary Beth. I was just about to shoot my old friend here and make it look like a suicide—complete with a letter saying he was wracked with guilt over the murder of his friends—when you knocked...and *knocked* and *knocked*...on that damn door.''

She held a hand to her head. ''You give me a headache, Mary Beth. I thought sure you'd wake up all the neighbors and they'd call the cops.''

''So you came up and let us in, knowing you were going to kill us?''

''Not at all. You might have been smart enough to leave when I told you to. You just weren't.''

''I *was* smart enough, though, to suspect there was something wrong when Patrick wasn't around and his deck lights, which he puts on every single night, without fail, were out. Didn't have time to think of that, huh, Julia?''

She smiled, but there was no humor in it. ''You might say I've been busy.''

''Too busy to think to turn the computer off, too, I guess. So it wouldn't squeal when it went online? Or how about the fact that Patrick *only* drinks Cabernet, and would never go out in the middle of the night for white wine? I didn't think of that until I heard the computer. Then I put the two together, and—how stupid of you, Julia.''

She looked disturbed by that, as if surprised that she hadn't worked out everything. ''I guess you were smarter than me after all, Mary Beth. Well, I have good and bad news for you. The good news is that you won't be a suspect anymore. The bad news is, you'll be dead. And so will that sweet little girl upstairs.''

I'd been willing to let her talk for a while. But that was the wrong thing to say.

Looking behind Julia to the door, I said, ''Jade! Don't come in here. Run!''

It was an old trick, but it worked. Julia turned to look and I lunged at her, taking her down before she could think to do anything but drop the gun. She was taller than I, but I knew the moves and she didn't. I had her pinned to the floor within seconds.

''Patrick, see if you can dial 911 with that magnificent nose,'' I said. ''Tell them we have the murderer of Craig Dinsmore, Tony Price and Arnold Westcott here.''

Julia tried to kick. She even spit at me. But she wasn't going anywhere.

''So tell me why she killed Tony and Arnold,'' I said to Patrick after we'd watched Julia being taken away. We were sitting on his deck with blankets around us, getting some much-needed fresh air.

Amazingly, Jade never woke up through it all. She was still asleep on the couch.

"That's the hideous thing about it," Patrick said. "She did it so no one would suspect she killed Craig. She wanted to make it look like a hate crime, and she was ready to tell the police that Craig was gay, even though he wasn't. But when the police started suspecting me of being in cahoots with you, she decided it might be a nice idea to make it look as if I were guilty, and I'd been so wracked with a guilty conscience, I'd killed myself."

I had been so sure Roger had killed Craig. Now I knew why there was no connection between him and Tony and Arnold.

"I never would have believed it," Patrick said. "I've known Julia for years, and there she was pointing a gun at me."

"So she actually killed Tony and Arnold for no reason at all? They didn't do anything to cause it?"

"Not a thing."

"That's just...incredible," I said. "And what about the Chinese dildos? How did they come to be the murder weapons?"

"Tony had bought one at her antiques shop in New York City last year. He brought one back to Arnold, and me, too, as gag gifts."

"But they must have cost a fortune," I said. "Tony would never spend that much money on a gag."

"As it happens, they were fakes. They probably set him back less than twenty bucks for all three, but we believed they were real, and instead of just tossing them in the trash, we kept them."

"But how could Julia know that?"

"She didn't. She brought several more along with her on the plane, in a sales case."

"Like I said, incredible. Uh...did you guys ever use them?" I asked curiously.

In the glow of the deck lights, I saw Patrick blush. "I don't know about Tony and Arnold, but I never used mine. It seemed...inelegant, somehow. Besides, I couldn't imagine any woman liking all that ornamentation. It must hurt like hell."

"Are you telling me you were never even tempted?" I said, laughing and punching him on the arm. "C'mon, admit it!"

"Oh, okay, I tried it out. *Once*." He grinned. "She told me she never wanted to see me again."

Sobering, I said, "I just have one more question. Tell me the truth, okay? Were Tony and Arnold gay?"

"Gayer than springtime," he said. "They just liked pretending they weren't, and I promised not to say anything."

"You know, Patrick," I said thoughtfully, "a lot has happened since we met. For a long while, I thought I didn't really know you. I'm sorry about that. I'm sure, now, it was all my own stuff."

"Remember us in that little Hollywood duplex, though?" he said. "No murders, no mad Julia. Bills, of course. But nothing, really, to worry about."

"I remember," I said. "And wouldn't it be nice if life were like that again?"

"Now who's being a romantic?" he teased. "And by the way, I owe you for that dinner the other night. I completely forgot to pay."

He leaned over from his chair and kissed me, and I had to admit I liked it. The sky was clear and the stars were brighter than I'd seen them in a long, long while. In the end, it had turned into a perfect night.

"Let's go inside," Patrick whispered, stroking my arm.

I nodded and we got up, alone together in the misty void of arousal.

Or almost alone.

"Where are you guys going?" Jade said from the door.

Epilogue

Six months later

It was almost Christmas, but on the beach in front of my house it was hotter than July. I'd pulled my socks off to wade along the shore, but Dan opted out, saying he might get paged for an emergency.

We followed behind Jade, who was running in and out of the water as tiny waves lapped at her ankles. Her hair was a coppery red in the sunlight, the same way mine used to be. As she got older it would lighten a bit from the Southern California sun, like mine. That's what the DNA counselor had told me when she confirmed that Jade was my daughter.

It had taken me only two days to get her out of Child Services. I fought them like the proverbial tiger for her cub, and they finally let me have her while the DNA tests were still pending. It helped that I had so many good people to speak up for me: Dan, Nia, Abby and even her fiancé, Ben, from the Carmel PD.

In fact, everything went amazingly well. I felt sure Lindy was behind that, just as she had helped us when we were on the road that night. I knew without a doubt that she wanted Jade with me, and I still thank her every day for that. I just wish we'd had more time to talk before she died.

Little Lindy Lou, the "airhead" cheerleader—and the best mother in the world.

Jade was proof of that. Lindy had only failed, if that was the right word, on one front: she couldn't go against her husband until she was absolutely certain he really was hurting her child. And by then it was too late. Not for Jade, but for her and for Jade's nanny, who had died in one mad moment that hadn't anything to do with her at all.

Did Irene try to stop Roger from killing Lindy? Or had she seen it happen, and he couldn't leave her as a witness to his crime? We'd probably never know; as they say, the dead don't talk.

Nia, it turned out, had originally left for London to talk to her father about a book she was writing, just as she'd said. At LAX, though, she'd met someone and been attracted to him. They spent three nights together at the London Ritz, and now they were talking about marriage. He was a doctor, and he seemed like a nice guy. I hoped they'd live happily ever after.

"The doctor Nia's father hooked me up with at UCLA," I said to Dan, "thinks the drugs harmed Jade's immune system, rather than making it stronger. He says it can be built up again. She needs lots of fresh air, good food and time to play. I intend to give that to her."

"Great. What about the emotional aspect?"

"You mean, has she forgotten Lindy and Roger and everything that happened? No, but she does call me Mommy sometimes."

"That's a big step."

I smiled. "Yeah. Her psychologist says it's a good sign. Jade's doing good work with her."

"Speaking of work, Nia says you've cut back to three days a week."

"Well, there are doctor visits, tests...they all take time, and I want to do everything I possibly can for Jade. I manage to read manuscripts here at home, though."

"Craig Dinsmore's book is the talk of the town, it seems."

I smiled again. "It's getting raves before it even hits the shelves. That's something, for a book that isn't even about Hollywood."

"I think the popular cause this year is the high cost of pharmaceutical drugs for the uninsured," he said.

"Cool. Let Hollywood climb on that bandwagon. It's a good one."

"What about Julia? Will she get any of the proceeds from Craig's book, when and if she ever gets out of prison?"

"I understand they'll go into a trust. I'm not sure she can benefit by her crime, though, and get any of Craig's money. Her lawyer is working on that."

"Not to change the subject, but would you like to go to dinner sometime?" he asked, taking my hand.

"I thought you were still upset with me for bailing on you that day. I haven't seen you for months."

"Only a couple of months," he pointed out. "And I never was upset with you."

"Oh, right. Evading arrest, lying to you, all those things you flung at me when I got back?"

"That was just me ranting," he said. "I have to rant. It's part of the job."

"Well, you might have told me. I thought I'd blown it with you."

He stopped walking and turned to me. "Would that bother you, Mary Beth? I hear you've been seen around town with Patrick Llewellen."

I laughed. "*Seen around town?* How quaint. You almost sound like Patrick. Who, by the way, is a good friend."

"So you aren't...*with* him now?"

I almost laughed again. It was nice to see he was a little bit jealous. But I got distracted. Ahead in the surf was the most beautiful thing that had ever happened to me. She was up to her knees in the waves, totally fearless. Next summer we'd drive up to Carmel Valley and she'd ride Molly's colt. She'd eat the healthiest food in the world, and she'd be with people who made her smile.

Thank you, I said for the thousandth time.

No problem, Lindy answered. *You're doing great.*

I realized then that tears were running down my

face, huge gobs of tears that wouldn't quit. My heart felt as if it were opening wide, like a bud that had been tight for too long and was gasping for air.

"Jade!" I called.

She turned and ran to me. "What's wrong, Mommy?"

I knelt down and took her in my arms. "Nothing, honey. I just love you so much. Have I told you that lately?"

"Sure." She rolled her eyes. "All the time."

"Well, just don't forget," I said. I held her against my heart while the tears just flowed and flowed and flowed, and when we both fell down in the sand we laughed and laughed and laughed.

Just the way Lindy and I always had.

MIRABooks.com

**We've got the lowdown on
your favorite author!**

☆ Read an excerpt of your favorite author's
newest book

☆ Check out her bio

☆ Talk to her in our Discussion Forums

☆ Read interviews, diaries, and more

☆ Find her current bestseller, and even her
backlist titles

All this and more available at

www.MiraBooks.com

If you enjoyed what you just read,
then we've got an offer you can't resist!

Take 2
bestselling novels FREE!
Plus get a FREE surprise gift!

MEG O'BRIEN

66932	CRIMSON RAIN	___ $6.50 U.S.	___ $7.99 CAN.
66807	GATHERING LIES	___ $6.50 U.S.	___ $7.99 CAN.
66586	SACRED TRUST	___ $5.99 U.S.	___ $5.99 CAN.
66516	CRASHING DOWN	___ $5.99 U.S.	___ $6.99 CAN.

(limited quantities available)

TOTAL AMOUNT $_____
POSTAGE & HANDLING $_____
($1.00 for one book; 50¢ for each additional)
APPLICABLE TAXES* $_____
TOTAL PAYABLE $_____
(check or money order—please do not send cash)

To order, complete this form and send it, along with a check
or money order for the total above, payable to MIRA Books,
to: **In the U.S.:** 3010 Walden Avenue, P.O. Box 9077, Buffalo,
NY 14269-9077; **In Canada:** P.O. Box 636, Fort Erie, Ontario,
L2A 5X3.

Name:_____
Address:_____ City:_____
State/Prov.:_____ Zip/Postal Code:_____
Account Number (if applicable):_____
075 CSAS

  *New York residents remit applicable sales taxes.
   Canadian residents remit applicable GST and provincial taxes.

MIRA®

Visit us at www.mirabooks.com   MMO1203BL